Praise for Lars Kepler's

THE SANDMAN

"If Jurek Walter reminds you of Hannibal Lecter, with his ability to impel people to act against their own impulse, you'll be forgiven. . . . As with Jurek Walter's powers of persuasion, I felt impelled by Lars Kepler to finish *The Sandman*. The characters got into my head and I couldn't rest until the mystery was revealed." —Jonathan Elderfield, Associated Press

"Kepler—actually the husband-and-wife team of Alexandra and Alexander Ahndoril—is really good at this stuff. The chapters are short, the characters are deftly drawn, and the action churns along." —*The Washington Post*

"Thriller fans will find it hard to escape *The Sandman*'s spell, for the suspense is unrelenting and the bite-size chapters end on cliffhangers. But unlike the villain, who makes victims go to sleep, his namesake novel will keep readers up all night." —*Shelf Awareness*

"I had been hearing about Lars Kepler's Joona Linna series of crime novels for years and have finally gotten around to reading them. I had really been missing out. . . . Do you enjoy getting scared out of your wits? Then I suggest you read *The Sandman*." —Vick Mickunas, *Dayton Daily News*

"This is a book that will keep you up all night, unable to turn off the light, because the pages almost literally fly beneath your fingers. . . . *The Sandman* is an excellent crime novel. . . . You won't be able to resist the urge to read all six Joona Linna novels, and you'll fervently wish there were more."
—*New York Journal of Books*

"Kepler doesn't pull any punches, and his care in creating characters will make readers deeply invested in their fates."
—*Publishers Weekly* (starred review)

"If any Scandinavian crime series is poised to top the characterization and gripping action of Stieg Larsson's Millennium series, it's this one. Kepler has crafted a phenomenal hero in Linna, who wields intuition, strategic genius, and refreshing vulnerability against a foe as compelling and calculating as Hannibal Lecter." —*Booklist* (starred review)

Lars Kepler

THE SANDMAN

Lars Kepler is the pseudonym of the critically acclaimed husband-and-wife team Alexandra Coelho Ahndoril and Alexander Ahndoril. Their number one internationally best-selling Joona Linna series has sold more than twelve million copies in forty languages. The Ahndorils were both established writers before they adopted the pen name Lars Kepler and have each published several acclaimed novels. They live in Stockholm, Sweden.

www.larskepler.com

THE SANDMAN

THE SANDMAN

A Joona Linna Novel

LARS KEPLER

Translated from the Swedish by

NEIL SMITH

Vintage Crime/Black Lizard
Vintage Books
A Division of Penguin Random House LLC
New York

FIRST VINTAGE CRIME/BLACK LIZARD EDITION, JANUARY 2019

The Library of Congress has cataloged the Knopf edition as follows:
Names: Kepler, Lars, author. | Smith, Neil (Neil Andrew), translator.
Title: The sandman / Lars Kepler ; translated from the Swedish by
    Neil Smith.
Other titles: Sandmannen. English.
Description: New York : Knopf, 2018.
Identifiers: LCCN 2017021057 (print) | LCCN 2017021057 (ebook)
Subjects: LCSH: Criminal investigation—Sweden—Fiction. | Serial
    murders—Sweden—Fiction. | GSAFD: Suspense fiction.
Classification: LCC PT9877.21.E65 (print) | LCC PT9877.21.E65 S2613
    2018 (ebook) | DDC 833/.92—dc23
LC record available at https://lccn.loc.gov/2017021057

Vintage Crime/Black Lizard Trade Paperback ISBN: 978-0-525-43305-7
eBook ISBN: 978-1-5247-3225-7

www.blacklizardcrime.com

Printed in the United States of America
10 9 8 7 6 5 4 3 2 1

THE SANDMAN

IT'S THE MIDDLE OF THE NIGHT, and snow is blowing in from the sea. A young man is walking across a high railroad bridge, toward Stockholm. His face is as pale as misted glass. His jeans are stiff with frozen blood. He is walking between the rails, stepping from tie to tie. Fifty meters beneath him, the ice on the water is just visible, like a strip of cloth. A blanket of snow covers the trees. Snow is swirling in the glow from the container crane far below, and the oil tanks at the harbor are barely visible.

Blood trickles down the man's lower left arm and drips from his fingertips.

The rails sing as a night train approaches the two-kilometer-long bridge.

The young man sways and sits down on the rail, then gets to his feet again and carries on walking.

The air is turbulent in front of the train, and the view is obscured by the billowing snow. The locomotive has already reached the middle of the bridge when the engineer catches sight of the man on the track. He blows his horn, and the figure almost falls. The man takes a long step to the left, onto the other track, and grabs hold of the flimsy railing.

His clothes flap around his body. The bridge shakes violently under his feet. He stands still with his eyes wide-open, his hands on the railing.

Everything is swirling snow and enveloping darkness.

His name is Mikael Kohler-Frost. He went missing thirteen years ago and was officially declared dead six years later.

1

THE STEEL GATE closes behind the new doctor with a heavy clang. The sound echoes down the spiral staircase.

Everything suddenly goes quiet, and Anders Rönn feels a shiver run down his spine.

Today is his first day working in the Secure Criminal Psychology Unit at Löwenströmska Hospital.

For the past thirteen years, the strictly isolated bunker has been home to the aging Jurek Walter.

The young doctor doesn't know much about his patient, except the diagnoses: Schizophrenia, nonspecific. Chaotic thinking. Recurrent acute psychosis, with erratic and extremely violent episodes.

Anders shows his ID at the entrance, removes his cell phone, and hangs the key to the gate in his locker before the guard opens the first steel security door. He goes in and waits for the door to close before walking to the next door. When a signal sounds, the guard opens the second door. Anders walks along the corridor toward the isolation ward's staff room.

Chief Physician Roland Brolin is a thickset man in his fifties, with sloping shoulders and cropped hair. He is smoking under the exhaust fan in the kitchen, leafing through an article on the pay gap between men and women in the healthcare industry.

"Jurek Walter must never be alone with any member of staff," he says. "He must never meet other patients. He never has any visitors, and he's never allowed out into the exercise yard. Nor is he—"

"Never?" Anders asks. "Surely it's not policy to keep someone—"

"No, it isn't," Roland says sharply.

"So what's he actually done?"

"Nothing but nice things," Roland says, heading toward the corridor.

Even though Jurek Walter has committed the most heinous crimes of any serial killer in Swedish history, he is completely unknown to the public. The proceedings against him in the Central Courthouse and at the Court of Appeal were held behind closed doors, and all the files are strictly confidential.

Anders and Roland pass through another security door, and a young woman with tattooed arms and pierced cheeks winks at them.

"Come back in one piece," she says cheerily.

"There's no need to worry," Roland says to Anders in a low voice. "Jurek Walter is a quiet elderly man. He doesn't fight, and he doesn't raise his voice. Our cardinal rule is that we never go into his cell. But Leffe, who was on the night shift last night, noticed that he had made some sort of knife and hidden it under his mattress, so, obviously, we have to confiscate it."

"How do we do that?" Anders asks.

"We break the rules."

"We're going into Jurek's cell?"

"You're going in. To ask nicely for the knife."

"I'm going in?"

Roland laughs loudly and explains that they're going to

pretend to give the patient his normal injection of risperidone but will actually be giving him an overdose of Zypadhera.

The chief runs his card through yet another reader and taps in a code. There's a bleep, and the lock of the security door whirrs.

"Wait," Roland says, holding out a little box of yellow earplugs.

"What are these for?"

Roland looks at his new colleague with weary eyes and sighs.

"Jurek Walter will talk to you, quite calmly, probably perfectly reasonably," he says in a grave voice. "He will convince you to do some things you'll regret. His words will play in your mind over and over again, and later this evening, when you're driving home, you'll swerve into oncoming traffic and smash into a semi, or you'll stop off at the hardware store to buy an ax before you pick up the kids from preschool."

"Should I be scared now?" Anders smiles and puts a pair of the earplugs in his pocket.

"No, but hopefully you'll be careful" Roland says.

Anders doesn't think of himself as lucky, but when he saw the advertisement in a medical journal for a full-time, long-term position at Löwenströmska Hospital, he had a good feeling. It's only a twenty-minute drive from home, and it could well lead to a permanent appointment. Since working as an intern at Skaraborg Hospital and in a health center in Huddinge, he has had to get by on temporary positions at the regional clinic of Sankt Sigfrids Hospital. The long drives to Växjö and the irregular hours proved difficult to manage with Petra's job in the Parks Department and Agnes's autism.

Only two weeks ago, Anders and Petra had been sitting at the kitchen table trying to work out what on earth they were going to do.

"We can't go on like this," Anders had said.

"But what alternative do we have?" she whispered.

"I don't know," Anders replied, wiping the tears from her cheeks.

Agnes's teaching assistant at her preschool had told them that Agnes had had a difficult day. She had refused to let go of her milk glass, and the other children had laughed. She hadn't been able to accept that break time was over, because Anders hadn't come to pick her up as he usually did. He had driven straight back from Växjö but hadn't reached the preschool until six o'clock. Agnes was still sitting in the dining room with her hands around the glass when he arrived.

When they got home, Agnes had stood in her room, staring at the wall beside the dollhouse, clapping her hands in that introverted way she had. They don't know what she can see there, but she says that gray sticks keep appearing, and she has to count them and stop them. She does that when she's feeling particularly anxious. Sometimes ten minutes is enough, but that evening she stood there for more than four hours before they could get her into bed.

2

THE LAST SECURITY DOOR CLOSES, and they head down
the corridor to the isolation cells. The fluorescent light in the
ceiling reflects off the linoleum floor. The textured wallpaper
has a groove worn into it from the rail on the food cart.

Roland puts away his pass card and lets Anders walk ahead
of him toward the heavy metal door.

Through the reinforced glass, Anders can see a thin man sitting on a plastic chair. He is dressed in blue jeans and a denim
shirt. The man is clean-shaven, and his eyes seem remarkably
calm. The many wrinkles covering his pale face look like the
cracked clay at the bottom of a dried-up riverbed.

Jurek Walter was found guilty of only two murders and
one attempted murder, but there's compelling evidence link-
ing him to nineteen others.

Thirteen years ago, he was caught red-handed in Lill-Jan's
Forest, on Djurgården, in Stockholm, forcing a fifty-year-old
woman back into a coffin in the ground. She had been kept in
the coffin for almost two years but was still alive. The woman
had sustained terrible injuries, she was malnourished, her
muscles had withered away, she had appalling pressure sores
and frostbite, and she had suffered severe brain damage. If
the police hadn't followed and arrested Jurek Walter beside
the coffin, he might never have been stopped.

Now Roland takes out three small glass bottles containing yellow powder, puts some saline into each of the bottles, shakes them carefully, then draws the contents into a syringe.

He puts in his earplugs and opens the small hatch in the door. There's a clatter of metal, and a heavy smell of concrete and dust hits them.

In a dispassionate voice, Roland tells Jurek that it's time for his injection.

The man lifts his chin and gets up slowly from the chair, turns to look at the hatch in the door, and unbuttons his shirt as he approaches.

"Stop and take off your shirt," Roland says.

Jurek steps slowly forward, and Roland quickly closes the hatch. Jurek stops, undoes the last buttons, and lets his shirt fall to the floor.

His body looks as if it had once been in good shape, but now his muscles are loose and his wrinkled skin is sagging.

Roland opens the hatch again. Jurek approaches and holds out his sinewy arm.

Anders washes his upper arm with rubbing alcohol. Roland pushes the syringe into the soft muscle and injects the liquid too quickly. Jurek's hand jerks in surprise, but he doesn't pull back his arm until he's been given permission. Roland hurriedly bolts the hatch, removes his earplugs, smiles nervously to himself, and then looks inside.

Jurek is stumbling toward the bed, where he stops and sits down.

Suddenly he twists to look at the door, and Roland drops the syringe.

He tries to catch it, but it rolls away across the floor.

Anders steps forward and picks up the syringe, and when

they both stand and turn back toward the cell, they see that the inside of the reinforced glass is misted. Jurek Walter has breathed on the glass and written "Joona" with his finger.

"What does it say?" Anders asks weakly.

"He's written 'Joona.'"

"What the hell does that mean?"

When the condensation clears, they see that Jurek Walter is sitting as if he hasn't moved. He looks at the arm where he got the injection, massages the muscle, then looks at them through the glass.

"It didn't say anything else?" Anders asks.

"No."

There's a bestial roar from the other side of the heavy door. Jurek has slid off the bed and is on his knees, screaming. The sinews in his neck are taut, his veins swollen.

"How much did you actually give him?" Anders asks.

Jurek's eyes roll back to the whites. He reaches out a hand to support himself and stretches one leg but topples over backward. He hits his head on the bedside table. Then he screams, and his body jerks spasmodically.

"Jesus Christ," Anders whispers.

Jurek falls to his back, his legs kicking uncontrollably. He bites his tongue, and blood sprays out over his chest. He lies there on his back, gasping.

"What do we do if he dies?"

"Cremate him," Roland says.

Jurek is cramping again, his whole body shaking, and his hands flail in every direction, until they suddenly stop.

Roland looks at his watch. Sweat is running down his cheeks.

Jurek Walter whimpers, rolls onto his side, and tries to get up, but fails.

"You can go inside in a couple of minutes," Roland says.

"Am I really going in there?"

"He'll soon be completely harmless."

Jurek is crawling on all fours, bloody slime drooling from his mouth. He sways and slows down until he finally slumps to the floor and lies still.

3

ANDERS LOOKS through the thick reinforced-glass window in the door. Jurek Walter has been lying motionless on the floor for the last ten minutes. His body goes limp as the cramps subside.

Roland pulls out a key and puts it in the lock, then pauses and peers in through the window before unlocking the door.

"Have fun," he says.

"What do we do if he wakes up?" Anders asks.

"He mustn't wake up."

Roland opens the door, and Anders goes inside. The door closes behind him, and the lock rattles. The cell smells of sweat, and something else as well. A sharp smell of vinegar. Jurek Walter lies completely still, breathing slowly.

Anders keeps his distance from him, even though he knows he's unconscious.

The acoustics in there are odd, claustrophobic, as if sounds follow movements too quickly.

His doctor's coat rustles softly with each step.

Jurek is breathing faster.

The tap is dripping in the sink.

Anders reaches the bed, then turns toward Jurek and kneels down.

He catches a glimpse of Roland watching him anxiously

through the reinforced glass as he leans over and tries to look under the fixed bed.

Nothing on the floor.

He moves closer, looking carefully at Jurek before lying flat on the floor.

He can't watch Jurek any longer. He has to turn his back on him to look for the knife.

Not much light reaches under the bed. Dust balls line the wall.

He can't help imagining that Jurek Walter has opened his eyes.

He sees something tucked between the wooden slats and the mattress. It's hard to tell what it is.

Anders stretches out his hand but can't reach it. He'll have to slide beneath the bed on his back. The space is so tight he can't turn his head. He slips farther in. Feels the unyielding bulk of the bed frame against his rib cage with each breath. His fingers fumble. He needs to get a bit closer. His knee hits one of the wooden slats. He blows a dust ball away from his face and carries on.

Suddenly he hears a dull thud behind him in the cell. He can't turn around and look. He just lies there, still, listening. His own breathing is so rapid he has trouble discerning any other sound.

Cautiously, he reaches out his hand and touches the object with his fingertips, squeezing in a bit farther in order to pull it free.

Jurek has fashioned a short knife with a very sharp blade from a piece of steel skirting.

"Hurry up," Roland calls through the hatch.

Anders tries to get out, pushing hard, and scratches his cheek.

Suddenly he can't move. He's stuck. His coat is caught, and there's no way he can wriggle out of it.

He imagines he can hear the sound of shuffling from Jurek. Perhaps it was nothing.

Anders pulls as hard as he can. The seams strain but don't tear. He realizes that he's going to have to slide back under the bed to free his coat.

"What are you doing?" Roland calls in a brittle voice.

The little hatch in the door clatters as it is bolted shut again.

Anders sees that one pocket of his coat has caught on a loose strut. He quickly pulls it free, holds his breath, and pushes himself out again. He is filled with a rising sense of panic. He scrapes his stomach and knee but grabs the edge of the bed with one hand and pulls himself out.

Panting, he turns around and gets unsteadily to his feet with the knife in his hand.

Jurek is lying on his side, one eye half open in sleep, staring blindly.

Anders hurries over to the door. He meets the chief's anxious gaze through the reinforced glass and tries to smile, but stress cuts through his voice.

"Open the door."

Roland Brolin opens the hatch instead.

"Pass me the knife first."

Anders gives him a quizzical look, then hands over the knife.

"You found something else as well," Roland Brolin says.

"No," Anders replies, glancing at Jurek.

"A letter."

"There wasn't anything else."

Jurek is starting to writhe on the floor, gasping weakly.

"Check his pockets," the chief says.

"What for?"

"Because this is a search."

Anders turns and walks cautiously to Jurek Walter. His eyes are completely shut again, but beads of sweat are starting to appear on his furrowed face.

Reluctantly, Anders leans over and feels inside one of his pockets. The denim shirt pulls tighter across Jurek's shoulders, and he lets out a low groan.

There's a plastic comb in the back pocket of his jeans. With trembling hands, Anders checks the rest of his pockets.

Sweat is dripping from the tip of his nose. He has to keep blinking hard.

One of Jurek's big hands opens and closes several times.

There's nothing else in his pockets.

Anders hears a distant alarm and turns back toward the reinforced glass. It's impossible to see if Roland is standing outside the door. The reflection of the lamp in the ceiling is shining like a gray sun in the glass.

He has to get out now.

It's taken too long.

Anders gets to his feet and hurries over to the door. Roland isn't there.

Jurek Walter is breathing fast, like a child having a nightmare.

Anders bangs on the door. His hands thud almost soundlessly against the thick metal. He bangs again. There's no sound. Nothing is happening. He taps on the glass with his wedding ring, then sees a shadow growing across the wall.

Anders feels a shiver run up his back and down his arms. With his heart pounding and his adrenaline rising, he turns around. He sees Jurek Walter slowly sitting up. His face is slack, and his pale eyes are staring straight ahead. His mouth is still bleeding, and his lips look strangely red.

4

JUREK WALTER is sitting on the floor and blinks at Anders a few times before he starts to get up.

"It's a lie," Jurek says, dribbling blood down his chin. "They say I'm a monster, but I'm just a human being."

He doesn't have the energy to stand and slumps back, panting, onto the floor.

"A human being," he repeats.

He puts one trembling hand inside his shirt, pulls out a folded piece of paper, and tosses it over toward Anders.

"The letter he was asking for," he says. "For the past seven years, I've been asking to see a lawyer. Not because I have any hope of getting out. I am who I am, but I'm still a human being."

Anders crouches down and reaches for the piece of paper without taking his eyes off Jurek. The crumpled man tries to get up again, leaning on his hands, and although he sways slightly, he manages to put one foot down on the floor.

Anders picks up the paper from the floor and finally hears a rattling sound as a key is inserted into the lock of the door. He turns and stares out through the reinforced glass, feeling his legs shake beneath him.

"You shouldn't have given me an overdose," Jurek mutters.

Open, open, Anders thinks. He hears breathing behind his back.

The door slides open, and Anders stumbles out of the cell, straight into the concrete wall of the corridor. He hears a heavy clang as the door shuts, then a rattle as the powerful lock responds to the turn of the key.

"The alarm sounded, and the door to the cell automatically locked, so I had to go override it," Roland says.

"This is insane."

"Did you find anything more?" Roland asks.

"Just the knife," Anders says.

"So he didn't give you anything?"

"No."

"It would be better if you gave it to me."

5

ANDERS RÖNN spends the rest of the day familiarizing himself with the new routines—doctor's rounds up on Ward 30, individual treatment plans, and discharge examinations—but his mind keeps going back to the letter in his pocket and what Jurek said.

At ten past five, Anders leaves the criminal-psychology ward and emerges into the cool air. Beyond the illuminated hospital precinct, the winter darkness has settled.

Anders keeps his hands in his jacket pockets and hurries across the pavement toward the large parking lot in front of the main entrance to the hospital.

It was full of cars when he arrived, but now it's almost empty.

He screws up his eyes and realizes that there's someone standing behind his car.

"Hello?" Anders calls, walking faster.

The man turns around and rubs his hand over his mouth. Roland Brolin.

Anders slows down as he approaches and pulls his key from his pocket.

Roland holds out his left hand, palm up.

"Give me the letter," he says. "You don't know what you're getting yourself into."

"What letter?"

"The letter Jurek gave you," he replies. "A note, a sheet of newspaper, a piece of cardboard."

"I found the knife that was supposed to be there."

"That was the bait," Roland says. "You don't think he'd put himself through all that pain for nothing?"

Anders looks at the chief as he wipes sweat from his upper lip with one hand.

"What do we do if the patient wants to see a lawyer?" he asks.

"Nothing," Roland whispers.

"Has he ever asked you that?"

"I don't know. I wouldn't have heard—I always wear ear-plugs." Roland smiles.

"But I don't understand why—"

"You need this job," Roland interrupts. "Your grades were poor, you're in debt, you've got no experience and no references."

"Are you finished?"

"You should give me the letter," Roland replies, clenching his jaw.

"I don't have a letter."

Roland looks him in the eye for a moment.

"If you ever find a letter," he says, "you're to give it to me without reading it."

"I understand," Anders says, unlocking the car door.

It seems to him that the chief looks slightly more relaxed as Anders gets in the car, shuts the door, and starts the engine. When Roland taps on the window, Anders ignores him, puts the car in gear, and pulls away. In the rearview mirror, Roland is standing and watching the car.

6

When Anders gets home, he quickly shuts the front door behind him, locks it, and puts the safety chain on.

From Agnes's room, he can hear Petra's soothing voice. Anders smiles to himself. She's already reading *Seacrow Island* by Astrid Lindgren to their daughter. It's usually much later before the bedtime rituals have reached story time. It must have been a good day again today. Anders's new job has meant that Petra has been able to cut down her own hours and spend more time with Agnes.

There's a damp patch on the hall rug around Agnes's muddy winter boots. Her wool hat is on the floor in front of the bureau. Anders goes in and puts the bottle of champagne that he picked up on the way home on the kitchen table, then stands and stares out at the garden.

He's thinking about Jurek Walter's letter and no longer knows what to do.

The branches of the big lilac bush are scratching at the window. He looks at the dark glass and sees his own kitchen reflected back at him. As he listens to the creaking branches, it occurs to him that he should go and get the shears from the storeroom.

"Just wait a minute," he hears Petra say. "I'll read to the end first."

Anders creeps into Agnes's room. The princess lamp in the
ceiling is on. Petra looks up from the book and meets his gaze.
She's got her light-brown hair pulled up into a ponytail and
is wearing her usual heart-shaped earrings. Agnes is sitting in
her lap and saying repeatedly that it's gone wrong and they
have to start the part about the dog again.

Anders approaches and crouches down in front of them.

"Hello, darling," he says.

Agnes glances at him quickly, then looks away. He pats her
on the head, tucks a lock of hair behind her ear, then gets up.

"There's food in the fridge, if you want to heat it up," Petra
says. "I just have to reread this chapter before I can come and
see you."

"It all went wrong with the dog," Agnes repeats, staring
at the floor.

Anders goes into the kitchen, gets the plate of food from
the fridge, and puts it down on the counter, next to the
microwave.

He pulls the letter out of the back pocket of his jeans and
thinks of how Jurek repeated that he was a human being.

In tiny, cursive handwriting, Jurek Walter had written a
few faint sentences on the thin paper. In the top right corner, the letter is addressed to a legal firm in Tensta. Jurek asks
for assistance in understanding why he has been sentenced
to secure psychiatric care. He would like to know whether he
can get the verdict reconsidered.

Anders can't put a finger on why he suddenly feels unsettled, but there's something strange about the tone of the letter
and the precise choice of wording, combined with the almost
dyslexic spelling mistakes.

Jurek's words echo in his mind as he walks into his study
and takes out an envelope. He copies the address from the
letter, puts the letter in the envelope, and sticks a stamp on it.

He leaves the house and heads off into the chill darkness, across the grass, toward the mailbox by the rotary. Once he's dropped the letter in the box, he stands and watches the cars passing on Sanda Road before walking home.

The wind is making the frosted grass around the house ripple like water. A rabbit bounds around the side of the house and into the back garden.

He opens the gate and looks up into the kitchen window. The whole structure resembles a dollhouse. Everything is lit up and open to view. He can see straight into the corridor, to the blue painting that has always hung there.

The door to their bedroom is open. The vacuum cleaner is in the middle of the floor. The cable is still plugged into the socket in the wall.

Suddenly Anders sees a movement. He gasps with surprise. There's someone in the bedroom—standing next to their bed.

Anders is about to rush inside when he realizes that the person is actually standing in the garden in back of the house. He's simply visible through the bedroom window.

Anders runs down the paved path, past the sundial, and around the corner.

The man must have heard him coming, because he's already running away. Anders can hear him forcing his way through the lilac hedge. He runs after him, holding the branches back, trying to catch a glimpse of him, but it's far too dark.

7

MIKAEL STANDS UP in the darkness when the Sandman blows his terrible dust into the room. He's learned that there's no point holding your breath: when the Sandman wants the children to sleep, they fall asleep.

He knows full well that his eyes will soon feel tired, so tired that he won't be able to keep them open. He knows he'll have to lie down on the mattress and become part of the darkness.

Mom used to talk about the Sandman's daughter, the mechanical girl, Olimpia. She creeps into children's rooms once they're asleep and pulls the covers up over their shoulders so they don't freeze.

Mikael leans against the wall, feels the furrows in the concrete.

The thin sand floats like fog. It's hard to breathe.

He coughs and licks his lips. They're dry and already feel numb.

His eyelids are getting heavy.

Now the whole family is swinging in the hammock. The summer light shines through the leaves of the lilac bower. The rusty screws creak.

Mikael is smiling broadly.

They're swinging high, and Mom's trying to slow them

down, but Dad keeps them going. They bump the table in front of them, and the glasses of strawberry juice tremble.

The hammock swings backward, and Dad laughs and holds up his hands like he's on a roller coaster.

Mikael's head nods, and he opens his eyes in the darkness, stumbles sideways, and leans his hand against the cool wall. He has turned toward the mattress, thinking that he should lie down before he passes out, when his knees suddenly give way.

He falls and hits the floor, trapping his arm beneath him, feeling the pain from his wrist and shoulder.

He rolls heavily onto his stomach and tries to crawl but doesn't have the energy. He lies there panting, with his cheek against the concrete floor. He tries to say something but has no voice left.

As he slips into oblivion, he hears the Sandman pad into the room, creeping on his dusty feet straight up the walls to the ceiling. He stops and reaches down with his arms, trying to catch Mikael with his porcelain fingertips.

Everything is black.

WHEN MIKAEL WAKES UP, his mouth is dry and his head aches. His eyes are grimy with sleep. He's so tired that he closes his eyes, but a sliver of his consciousness registers that something is different.

Adrenaline hits him like a gust of hot air.

He's wide awake now.

He sits up in the darkness and can hear from the acoustics that he's in a different room, a larger room.

He's no longer in the capsule.

He's completely alone.

He crawls cautiously across the floor and reaches a wall. His mind is racing. He can't remember how long it's been since he last thought of escape.

His body is still heavy from its long sleep. He gets up on shaky legs and follows the wall to a corner, then walks along the other wall and reaches a sheet of metal. He feels along its edges and realizes that it's a door, then runs his hands over its surface and finds a handle.

His hands are shaking.

Carefully, he pushes the handle down, and he is so prepared to meet resistance that he almost falls over when the door opens.

He takes a step into a bright room and has to shut his eyes.

It feels like a dream.

Just let me get out, he thinks.

His head is throbbing.

He squints and sees that he is in a corridor and moves forward on weak legs. His heart is beating so fast he can hardly breathe.

He's trying to be quiet but is still whimpering to himself with fear.

The Sandman will soon be back—he never forgets his children.

Mikael can't open his eyes properly but heads toward the fuzzy glow in front of him.

Maybe it's a trap, he thinks. Maybe he's being lured like an insect toward a bright light.

But he keeps on walking, running his hand along the wall for support.

He knocks into some big rolls of insulation, lurches sideways, and hits the other wall with his shoulder, but he manages to keep his balance.

He stops and coughs as quietly as he can.

The glow in front of him is coming from a pane of glass in a door.

He stumbles toward it and pushes the handle down, but the door is locked.

No, no, no . . .

He tugs at the handle, shoves the door, tries again. He feels like slumping to the floor in despair. Suddenly he hears soft footsteps behind him, but he doesn't dare turn around.

8

REIDAR FROST drains his wineglass, puts it down on the dining table, and closes his eyes. One of the guests is clapping. Veronica is standing in her blue dress, facing the corner with her hands over her eyes, and she starts to count.

The guests take off in different directions, and the sounds of footsteps and laughter spread through the many rooms of the manor house.

The rule is that they have to stick to the ground floor, but Reidar gets slowly to his feet, goes over to the hidden door, and creeps into the service passageway. Carefully, he climbs the narrow back stairs, opens the secret door in the wall, and emerges into the private part of the house.

He knows it's dangerous when he's alone, but he walks through the rooms anyway.

At every stage he closes the doors behind him, until he reaches the gallery at the far end.

Along one wall stand the boxes containing the children's clothes and toys. One box is open, revealing a pale-green space gun.

He hears Veronica call out, muffled by the floor and walls: "One hundred! Ready or not, here I come!"

Through the windows, he looks out over the fields and

paddocks. In the distance, he can see the birch-lined avenue that leads from his estate, Råcksta Manor, to the road.

Reidar pulls an armchair across the floor and hangs his jacket on it. He can feel how drunk he is as he bends down to pick up a rope that he brought in from an old tire swing.

Dust drifts through the air.

He sits down and looks up at the beam along the ceiling.

Muted laughter and cries can be heard from the party below, and for a few moments Reidar closes his eyes and thinks of the children, their little faces, wonderful faces, their shoulders and thin arms.

He can hear their high-pitched voices and quick feet running across the floor whenever he listens; the memory is like a summer breeze in his soul, but when it's gone, it leaves him cold and desolate again.

Happy birthday, Mikael, he thinks.

His hands are shaking so much that he can't tie a noose. He sits still, tries to breathe more calmly, then starts again, just as there's a knock on one of the doors.

He waits a few seconds, then lets go of the rope, rises from the chair, and picks up his jacket.

"Reidar?" a woman's voice calls softly.

It's Veronica. She must have been peeking while she was counting and saw him disappear into the passageway. She's opening the doors to the various rooms, and her voice gets clearer the closer she comes.

Reidar turns off the lights and leaves the nursery, opening the door to the next room and stopping there.

Veronica comes toward him with a glass of champagne in her hand. There is a warm glow in her dark, intoxicated eyes.

She's tall and thin, and her black hair is cut in a boyish style that suits her.

Veronica Klimt is Reidar's literary agent. He may not have written a word in the past thirteen years, but the three books he wrote before that are still generating a sizable income for them both.

Now they can hear music from the dining room below. Reidar stops at the sofa and runs his hand through his silvery hair.

"You're saving some champagne for me, I hope?" he asks, sitting down on the sofa.

"No," Veronica says, passing him her half-full glass.

"Your husband called me," Reidar says. "He thinks it's time for you to go home."

"I don't want to. I want to divorce him and—"

"You can't," he interrupts.

"Why do you say things like that?"

"Because I don't want you to think we have a future," he replies.

"I don't."

He empties the glass, closes his eyes, and feels the giddiness of being drunk.

"You looked sad, and I got worried."

"I've never felt better."

There's laughter now, and the music has been turned up so high it can be felt through the floor.

"Your guests are probably starting to wonder where you are."

"Then let's go and turn the place upside down," he says with a weary smile.

For the past seven years, Reidar has made sure to have people around him almost twenty-four hours a day. He has a vast circle of acquaintances. Sometimes he holds big parties at the house, sometimes more intimate dinners. It's especially difficult on certain days, like the children's birthdays. He knows that, without people around him, he could easily succumb to the grief.

9

REIDAR AND VERONICA open the doors to the dining room, and the throbbing music hits them. There's a crowd of people dancing around the table in the darkness. Some of them are still eating the dinner laid out on the table—venison and roasted vegetables.

The actor Wille Strandberg has unbuttoned his shirt. It's impossible to hear what he's saying as he dances his way through the crowd toward Reidar and Veronica.

"Take it off!" Veronica cries.

Wille laughs and pulls off his shirt, throws it at her, and dances in front of her with his hands behind his neck. His bulging, middle-aged stomach bounces in time with his quick movements.

Reidar empties another glass of wine, then dances up to Wille with his hips rolling.

The music goes into a quieter, gentler phase, and Reidar's old publisher, David Sylwan, takes hold of his arm and gasps something, his face sweaty and happy.

"What?"

"There's been no contest today," David repeats.

"Shooting?" Reidar asks. "Wrestling?"

"Shooting!" several people cry.

"Get the pistol and a few bottles of champagne," Reidar says with a smile.

The thudding beat returns, drowning out any further conversation. Reidar gets an oil painting down from the wall and carries it out through the door. It's a portrait of him, painted by Peter Dahl.

"I like that picture," Veronica says, trying to stop him.

Reidar shakes her hand from his arm. Almost all the guests follow him outside, into the ice-cold park. Fresh snow has settled into a smooth expanse on the ground. There are still flakes swirling beneath the dark sky.

Reidar strides through the snow and hangs the portrait on an apple tree, its branches laden with snow. Wille Strandberg follows, carrying a flare he found in a box in the mudroom. He tears off the plastic cover and pulls the string. There's a pop, and the flare starts to burn, giving off an intense light. Laughing, he stumbles over and puts the flare in the snow beneath the tree. The white light makes the trunk and naked branches glow.

Now they can all see the painting of Reidar holding a silvery pen in his hand.

Berzelius, a translator, has brought out three bottles of champagne, and David Sylwan holds up Reidar's old Colt with a grin.

"This isn't funny," Veronica says in a serious voice.

David stands next to Reidar, the Colt in his hand. He feeds five bullets into the chamber and spins the cylinder.

Wille Strandberg is still shirtless, but he's so drunk he doesn't feel the cold.

"If you win, you can choose a horse from the stables," Reidar mumbles, taking the revolver from David.

"Please, be careful," Veronica says.

Reidar moves aside, raises his arm, and fires but hits nothing, the blast echoing between the buildings.

A few guests applaud politely, as if he were playing golf.

"My turn," David says with a laugh.

Veronica stands in the snow, shivering. Her feet are burning with cold in her thin sandals.

"I like that portrait," she says again

"Me, too," Reidar says, firing another shot.

The bullet hits the top corner of the canvas. There's a puff of dust as the gold frame gets dislodged and hangs askew.

David pulls the revolver from his hand with a chuckle, stumbles and falls, and fires a shot up at the sky, then another as he tries to stand.

A couple of guests clap, and others laugh and raise their glasses in a toast.

Reidar takes the revolver back and brushes the snow off it. "It's all down to the last shot," he says.

Veronica goes over and kisses him on the lips. "How are you doing?"

"Fine," he says.

Veronica looks at him and brushes the hair from his forehead. The group on the stone steps whistle and laugh.

"I found a better target," cries a red-haired woman whose name he can't remember.

She's dragging a huge Spider-Man doll through the snow. Suddenly she loses her grip on the doll and falls to her knees, then gets back on her feet. Her leopard-print dress is flecked with damp.

"I saw it yesterday; it was under a dirty tarp in the garage," she exclaims jubilantly.

Berzelius hurries over to help her carry it. The doll is solid plastic and has been painted to look like Spider-Man. It's as tall as Berzelius.

"Well done, Marie!" David cries.

"Shoot Spider-Man," one of the women behind them calls.

Reidar looks up, sees the big doll, and lets the gun fall to the snow.

"I need to sleep," he says abruptly.

He pushes aside the glass of champagne Wille is holding out to him and walks back to the house on unsteady legs.

10

Veronica follows Marie as she searches the house for Reidar. They walk through rooms and halls. His jacket is lying on the stairs to the second floor, and they go up. It's dark, but they can see flickering firelight farther off. In a large room, they find Reidar sitting on a sofa in front of the fireplace. His cuff links are gone, and his sleeves are dangling over his hands. On the low bookcase beside him are four bottles of Château Cheval Blanc.

"I just wanted to say sorry," Marie says, leaning against the door.

"Oh, don't mind me," Reidar mutters, still gazing into the fire.

"It was stupid of me to drag the doll out without asking first," Marie continues.

"As far as I'm concerned, you can burn all the old shit," he replies.

Veronica goes over to him, kneels down, and looks up at his face with a smile.

"Have you been introduced to Marie?" she asks. "She's David's friend. I think."

Reidar raises his glass toward the red-haired woman, then takes a big gulp. Veronica takes the glass from him, tastes the wine, and sits down on the other end of the sofa.

She pushes off her shoes, leans back, and rests her bare feet in his lap.

Gently, he caresses her calf, the bruise from the new stirrup on her leather saddle, then up the inside of her thigh toward her groin. She lets it happen, not bothered by the fact that Marie is still in the room.

The flames are rising high in the huge fireplace. The heat is pulsating, and her face feels so hot it's almost burning.

Marie comes cautiously closer. Reidar looks at her. Her red hair has started to curl in the heat of the room. Her leopard-print dress is creased and stained.

"An admirer," Veronica says, holding the glass away from Reidar when he tries to reach it.

"I love your books," Marie says.

"Which books?" he asks brusquely.

He gets up and fetches a fresh glass from the dresser and pours some wine. Marie misunderstands the gesture and holds out her hand to take it.

"I presume you go to the bathroom by yourself," Reidar says, drinking the wine.

"There's no need—"

"If you want wine, then have some fucking wine," he interrupts.

Marie blushes and takes a deep breath. With her hand trembling, she takes the bottle and pours herself a glass. Reidar sighs deeply, then apologizes and says, in a gentler tone of voice, "I think this vintage is one of the better years."

Taking the bottle with him, he goes back to his seat.

Smiling, he watches as Marie sits down between him and Veronica on the sofa, swirls the wine in her glass, and tastes it.

Reidar refills her glass, looks her in the eye, then turns serious and kisses her on the lips.

"What are you doing?" she asks.

Reidar kisses Marie softly again. She moves her head away but can't help smiling. She drinks some wine, then leans over and kisses him.

He strokes the nape of her neck, under her hair, and moves his hand over her right shoulder; he can feel how the narrow strap of her dress has sunk into her skin.

She puts down her glass, kisses him again, and thinks that she must be mad as she lets him caress one of her breasts.

Reidar's throat hurts as he suppresses the urge to burst into tears. He strokes her thigh under her dress, feeling her nicotine patch, and moves his hand around to her backside.

Marie pats his hand away when he tries to pull down her underwear, then stands up and wipes her mouth.

"Maybe we should go back down and join the party again," she says, trying to sound neutral.

"Yes," he says.

Veronica is sitting motionless on the sofa and doesn't meet her inquiring gaze.

"Are you both coming?"

Reidar shakes his head.

"Okay," Marie whispers, and walks toward the door.

Her dress shimmers as she leaves the room. Reidar stares through the open doorway. The darkness looks like dirty velvet.

Veronica gets up, takes her glass from the table, and drinks. She has sweat patches under the arms of her dress.

"You're a bastard," she says.

"If it's any consolation, I hate myself, too," he says quietly.

He catches her hand and presses it to his cheek, looking into her sad eyes as he holds it there.

11

THE FIRE has gone out and the room is freezing cold when Reidar wakes up on the sofa. His eyes are stinging, and he thinks of his wife's story about the Sandman. The man who throws sand in children's eyes so that they fall asleep and stay asleep through the night.

"Shit," Reidar mutters, and sits up.

He's naked and has spilled wine over the leather upholstery. In the distance is the sound of an airplane. The morning light hits the dusty windows.

Reidar gets to his feet and sees Veronica curled up on the floor in front of the fireplace. She's wrapped herself in the tablecloth. The party downstairs is still going on but is more subdued now. Reidar grabs the half-full bottle of wine and leaves the room. He has a throbbing headache as he starts to climb the creaking oak stairs to his bedroom. He stops on the landing, sighs, and goes back down. He carefully picks up Veronica and lays her on the sofa, covers her, then retrieves her glasses from the floor and puts them on the table.

Reidar Frost is sixty-two years old and the author of three international best-sellers, the so-called Sanctum series.

Thirteen years ago, Reidar Frost ended up alone. Something happened to him that should never happen to anyone. His son and daughter vanished without a trace one night after they sneaked out to meet a friend. Mikael's and Felicia's bicycles were found on a footpath near Badholmen. Apart from one detective with a Finnish accent, everyone thought the children had been playing too close to the water and had drowned in Erstaviken fjard.

The police stopped looking, even though no bodies were found. Reidar's wife, Roseanna, couldn't deal with their loss. She moved in temporarily with her sister, asked for a divorce, and used the money from the settlement to move abroad. A couple of months later, she was found in her bath in a Paris hotel. She'd committed suicide. On the floor was a drawing Felicia had given her on Mother's Day.

The children have been declared dead. Their names are engraved on a headstone that Reidar rarely visits. The day they were declared dead, he invited his friends to a party, and he has kept it going ever since.

Reidar Frost is convinced he's going to drink himself to death, but at the same time, he knows he'd probably kill himself if he was left alone.

12

A TRAIN is thundering through the nocturnal winter landscape. The locomotive is pulling almost three hundred meters of boxcars behind it.

In the cab sits the train engineer with his hand resting on the controls. The noise from the engine and the rails is rhythmic and monotonous.

The snow rushes out of a bright tunnel formed by the two headlights. The rest is darkness.

As the train emerges from the broad curve around Vårsta, the engineer increases speed.

He's thinking that the snow is so bad that he's going to have to stop at Hallsberg, if not before, to check the braking distance.

Far off in the haze, two deer scamper off the rails and away across the white fields. They move through the snow with magical ease and disappear into the night.

He brakes gently as the train heads out across the high bridge. It feels like flying. The snow is swirling and twisting in the headlights.

The train is already in the middle of the bridge, high above the ice of Hallsfjärden, when he sees a flickering shadow through the haze. There's someone on the track. The engineer sounds the horn and sees the figure take a long step to the right, onto the other track.

The train is approaching very fast. For half a second, the man is caught in the glare of the headlights. He blinks. A young man with a dead face. His clothes are trembling on his skinny frame, and then he's gone.

The engineer isn't conscious that he's applied the brakes and that the whole train is slowing down. There's a rumbling sound and the screech of metal, and he isn't sure if he ran over the young man.

He's shaking and can feel adrenaline coursing through his body as he calls the emergency number.

"I'm a train engineer. I've just passed someone on the Igelsta Bridge. He was in the middle of the tracks, but I don't think I hit him."

"Is anyone injured?" the operator asks.

"I don't think I hit him. I only saw him for a few seconds."

"Where exactly did you see him?"

"In the middle of the Igelsta Bridge."

"On the tracks?"

"There's nothing but tracks up here—it's a fucking railroad bridge."

"Was he standing still, or was he walking in a particular direction?"

"I don't know."

"My colleague is alerting the police and ambulance in Södertälje. We'll stop all rail traffic over the bridge."

13

THE EMERGENCY CONTROL ROOM immediately dispatches police cars to both ends of the long bridge. Nine minutes later, the first car pulls off the road from Södertälje with its lights flashing and makes its way up the narrow gravel road alongside the train tracks. The road leads steeply upward and hasn't been plowed. Loose snow swirls up over the windshield.

The policemen leave the car at the end of the bridge and set out along the tracks with their flashlights on. It isn't easy going. Cars are passing far below them on the highway. The four railroad tracks narrow to two and stretch out over the industrial complexes of Björkudden and the frozen inlet.

The first officer stops and points. Someone has clearly been walking along the right-hand track ahead of them. The shaky beams of their flashlights illuminate footprints and traces of blood.

They shine their flashlights into the distance, but there's no one on the bridge as far as they can see. The lights at the harbor below make the snow between the tracks look like smoke.

Now the second police car reaches the other end of the deep ravine, more than a kilometer and a half away.

The tires crunch on the gravel as Police Constable Jasim Muhammed pulls up along the railroad line. His partner,

Fredrik Mosskin, has just contacted their colleagues on the bridge over the radio. The wind is making so much noise in the microphone that it's difficult to hear, but they pick up that someone was walking across the railroad bridge very recently.

The headlights illuminate a steep rock face. Fredrik ends the call and stares blankly ahead of him.

"What's happening?" Jasim asks.

"Looks like he's heading this way."

"What did they say about blood? Was there much blood?"

"I didn't hear."

"Let's go and look," Jasim says, opening his door.

The blue emergency lights play upon the snow-covered branches of the pine trees.

"The ambulance is on its way," Fredrik says.

There's no crust on the snow, and Jasim sinks in up to his knees. He pulls out his flashlight and shines it toward the tracks. Fredrik is slipping on the track bed but keeps climbing.

"What sort of animal has an extra asshole in the middle of its back?" Jasim asks.

"I don't know," Fredrik mutters.

"A police horse," Jasim says.

"What the . . . ?"

"That's what my mother-in-law told the kids." Jasim grins and heads up onto the bridge.

There are no footprints in the snow. Either the man is still on the bridge, or he's jumped. The cables above them whistle eerily.

The lights of Hall Prison are glowing through the haze below.

Fredrik tries to contact their colleagues, but the radio just crackles.

They head farther out across the bridge. Fredrik walks

behind Jasim with a flashlight in his hand. Jasim can see his own shadow moving across the ground, swaying oddly from side to side.

It's strange that their colleagues from the other side of the bridge aren't visible.

Out on the exposed bridge, the wind from the sea is bitter. Snow is blowing into their eyes. Their cheeks turn numb with cold.

Jasim screws up his eyes to look across the bridge. It disappears into swirling darkness. Suddenly he sees something at the edge of the light. A tall stick figure with no head.

Jasim stumbles and reaches his hand out toward the low railing; he sees the snow fall fifty meters onto the ice.

His flashlight hits something and goes out.

His heart is beating hard, and he peers forward again but can no longer see the figure.

Fredrik calls Jasim back, and he turns around. His partner is pointing at him, but it's impossible to hear what he's saying. Fredrik looks scared and starts to fumble with the holster of his pistol, and Jasim realizes that Fredrik's trying to warn him, that he was pointing at someone behind his back.

Jasim turns around and gasps for breath.

Someone is crawling along the track straight toward him. Jasim backs away and tries to draw his pistol. The figure gets to its feet and sways. It's a young man. He's staring at the policemen with empty eyes. His bearded face is thin; his cheekbones are sharp. He's swaying and seems to be having trouble breathing.

"Are you injured?"

The young man tries to speak but coughs and falls to his knees again.

"What's he saying?" Fredrik asks, with one hand on his gun.

"Are you injured?" Jasim asks again.

"I don't know, I can't feel anything, I—"

"Please, come with me."

Jasim helps him up and sees that his right hand is covered with red ice.

"I can't. . . . The Sandman took us. . . . I can't wake up. . . ."

14

THE DOORS of the emergency entrance at Södermalm Hospital close. A red-cheeked nurse helps the paramedics remove the stretcher and wheel it toward the ER.

"We can't find any identification. Nothing."

The patient is handed over to the triage nurse and taken into one of the treatment rooms. After checking his vital signs, the nurse realizes the patient is in critical condition.

Four minutes later, Dr. Irma Goodwin comes into the ER, and the nurse gives her a quick briefing: "Airways free, no acute trauma, but he's got poor saturation, fever, signs of concussion and weak circulation."

The doctor looks at the charts and goes over to the skinny man. His clothes have been cut open. His bony rib cage rises and falls with his rapid breathing.

"Still no name?"

"No."

"Give him oxygen."

The young man lies with his eyelids closed, trembling, as the nurse puts an oxygen mask on him.

He looks strangely malnourished, but there are no visible needle marks on his body. Dr. Goodwin has never seen anyone so white. The nurse checks his temperature from his ear again.

"Forty degrees Celsius. A high-grade fever."

Dr. Goodwin ticks the tests she wants to run on the patient, then looks at him again. His chest rattles as he coughs and briefly opens his eyes.

"I don't want to, I don't want to," he whispers. "I've got to go home, I've got to, I've got to—"

"Where do you live? Can you tell me where you live?"

"Live?" he asks, and gulps hard.

"He's delirious," the nurse says quietly.

"Are you in pain?"

"Yes," he replies with a confused smile.

"Can you tell me—"

"No, no, no, no, she's screaming inside me, I can't take it, I can't, I . . ."

His eyes roll back. He coughs and mutters something about porcelain fingers, then lies there gasping for breath.

Irma Goodwin decides to give the patient a vitamin B shot, antipyretics, and an intravenous antibiotic, benzylpenicillin, until the test results come back.

Through the door ahead of her, she can hear the staff nurse talking on the phone. Another ambulance is on its way in—a case of kidney failure. The staff nurse is putting together an emergency team and calling a surgeon.

Irma Goodwin stops and goes back to the unidentified patient's treatment room. The red-cheeked nurse is helping the other nurse clean a bleeding wound on the man's thigh. It looks like the young man ran straight into a sharp branch.

She stops in the doorway.

"Add a macrolide to the antibiotics," she says decisively. "One gram of erythromycin, intravenous."

The nurse looks up.

"You think he's got Legionnaires' disease?" she asks in surprise.

"Let's see what the test—"

Irma Goodwin falls silent as the patient's body starts to jerk. She looks at his white face and sees him slowly open his eyes.

"I've got to get home," he whispers. "My name is Mikael Kohler-Frost, and I've got to get home. . . ."

"Mikael Kohler-Frost," Irma says. "You're in Södermalm Hospital, and—"

"She's screaming, all the time!"

Irma leaves the treatment room and half runs to her office. She closes the door behind her, puts on her reading glasses, sits down at her computer, and logs in. She can't find him in the Health Service Database and tries the National Population Register instead.

She finds him there.

Irma Goodwin rereads the information about the patient in the emergency room.

Mikael Kohler-Frost has been dead for seven years and is buried in Malsta Cemetery.

15

DETECTIVE INSPECTOR JOONA LINNA is in a small room
whose walls and floor are made of bare concrete. He is on his
knees while a man in camouflage aims a pistol at his head,
a black Sig Sauer. The door is being guarded by a man who
keeps his Belgian assault rifle trained on Joona the whole time.

On the floor next to the wall is a bottle of Coca-Cola. The
light is coming from a ceiling lamp with a buckled aluminum
shade.

A cell phone buzzes. Before the man with the pistol
answers, he yells at Joona to lower his head.

The other man puts his finger on the rifle's trigger and
moves a step closer.

The man with the pistol talks into the cell phone, then listens, without taking his eyes off Joona. Grit crunches under
his boots. He nods, says something else, then listens again.

After a while, the man with the assault rifle sighs and sits
down on the chair just inside the door.

Joona kneels there completely still. He is wearing jogging
pants and a white sweat-soaked T-shirt. The sleeves are tight
across the muscles of his upper arms. He raises his head
slightly. His eyes are gray, like polished granite.

The man with the pistol talks excitedly into the phone,
then ends the call and seems to think for a few seconds before

taking four quick steps forward and pressing the barrel of the pistol to Joona's forehead.

"I'm about to overpower you," Joona says amiably.

"What?"

"I had to wait," he explains. "Until I had an opportunity for direct physical contact."

"I've just received orders to execute you."

"Yes, the situation's fairly acute, seeing as I have to get the pistol away from my face and ideally use it within five seconds."

"How?" the man by the door asks.

"In order to catch him by surprise, I can't react to any of his movements," Joona explains. "That's why I've let him walk up, stop, and take precisely two breaths. So I wait until he breathes out the second time before I—"

"Why?" the man with the pistol asks.

"I gain a few hundredths of a second, because it's practically impossible to do anything without first breathing in."

"But why the second breath in particular?"

"Because it's unexpectedly early and right in the middle of the most common countdown in the world: three, two, one. . . ."

"Got it." The man smiles, revealing a brown front tooth.

"The first thing that's going to move is my left hand," Joona explains to the surveillance camera up by the ceiling. "It'll move up toward the barrel of the pistol and away from my face in one fluid movement. I need to grasp the pistol, twist upward, and get to my feet, using his body as a shield. In a single movement. My hands need to prioritize the gun, but at the same time I need to observe the man with the assault rifle. Because, as soon as I've got control of the pistol, he's the primary threat. I use my elbow against his chin and neck as many times as it takes to get control of the pistol, then I fire three shots and spin around and fire another three shots."

The men in the room start again. The situation repeats. The man with the pistol gets his orders over the phone, hesitates, then walks up to Joona and pushes the barrel to his forehead. The man breathes out and is just about to breathe in to say something when Joona grabs the barrel of the pistol with his left hand.

The whole thing is remarkably surprising and quick, even though it was expected.

Joona knocks the gun aside, twisting it toward the ceiling in the same movement and getting to his feet. He jabs his elbow into the man's neck four times, takes the pistol, and shoots the other man in the torso.

The three blank shots echo off the walls.

The first opponent is still staggering backward when Joona spins around and shoots him in the chest.

He falls against the wall.

Joona walks over to the door, grabs the assault rifle and extra cartridge, and leaves the room.

16

THE DOOR hits the concrete wall hard and bounces back. Joona is changing the cartridge as he marches in. The eight people in the next room all take their eyes off the large screen and look at him.

"Six and a half seconds to the first shot," one of them says.

"That's far too slow," Joona says.

"But Markus would have let go of the pistol sooner if your elbow had actually hit him," a tall man with a shaved head says.

"Yes, you won some time there," a female officer agrees.

The scene is already repeating on the screen. Joona's taut shoulder, the fluid movement forward, his eye lining up with the sights as the trigger is pulled.

"Pretty damn impressive," the group commander says, setting his palms down on the table.

"For a cop," Joona concludes.

They laugh, leaning back, and the group commander scratches the tip of his nose as he blushes.

Joona accepts a glass of water.

Joona Linna is at Karlsborg Fortress to instruct the Special Operations Group in close combat. Not because he's a trained instructor but because he has more practical experience of the techniques they need to learn than just about anyone else in Sweden. When Joona was eighteen, he did his military service at Karlsborg as a paratrooper and was immediately recruited after basic training to a Special Operations unit.

Although a long time has passed since he left the military to study at the Police Academy, he still has dreams about his time as a paratrooper. He's back on the transport plane, listening to the deafening roar and staring out through the hydraulic hatch in the rear of the aircraft. The shadow of the plane moves over the pale water far below like a gray cross. In his dream, he runs down the ramp and jumps out into the cold air, hears the whine of the cords, feels his harness jerk as the parachute opens. The water approaches at great speed. The black inflatable boat is foaming against the waves far below.

Joona was trained in the Netherlands for effective close combat with bayonets, knives, and pistols. He was taught to exploit changing situations and to use innovative Krav Maga techniques.

"Okay, we'll take this situation as our starting point and make it progressively harder as the day goes on," Joona says.

"Like hitting two people with one bullet?" The tall man with the shaved head grins.

"Impossible," Joona says.

"We heard that you did it," the woman says with curiosity.

"Oh, no." Joona smiles, running his hand through his untidy blond hair.

His phone rings in his inside pocket. He sees on the screen that it's Nathan Pollock from the National Criminal Investigation Department. Nathan knows where Joona is and would call only if it was important.

"Excuse me," Joona says, then takes the call.

He drinks from the glass of water and listens with a smile that slowly fades. Suddenly all the color drains from his face.

"Is Jurek Walter still locked up?" he asks.

His hand is shaking so much that he has to put down the glass.

17

Snow swirls through the air as Joona runs out to his car
and gets in. He drives straight across the large exercise yard
where he trained as a young recruit. The tires screech as he
takes the corner and leaves the garrison.

Beads of sweat have appeared on his forehead, and his
hands won't stop shaking.

He overtakes a convoy of semis on the E20 highway just
before Arboga. He has to hold the wheel with both hands,
because the drag from the trucks makes his car shake.

He can't stop thinking about the phone call.

Nathan Pollock's voice was calm as he explained that
Mikael Kohler-Frost was still alive.

Joona had been convinced that the boy and his younger
sister were two of Jurek Walter's many victims. Now Nathan
was telling him that Mikael has been found by the police on a
railroad bridge and taken to Södermalm Hospital.

Pollock said that Mikael's condition was serious but not
life-threatening. He hadn't yet been questioned.

"Is Jurek Walter still locked up?" was Joona's first question.

"Yes, he's still in solitary confinement," Pollock replied.

"You're sure?"

"Yes."

"What about the boy? How do you know it's Mikael Kohler-Frost?" Joona asked.

"Apparently, he's said his name several times. That's as much as we know. And he's the right age," Pollock said. "Naturally, we've sent a saliva sample to the National Forensics Lab—"

"But you haven't informed his father?"

"We have to try to get a DNA match before we do that. I mean, we can't get this wrong."

"I'm on my way."

18

THE CAR moves along the black, slushy road, and Joona Linna forces himself not to speed up.

Mikael Kohler-Frost, he thinks.

Mikael Kohler-Frost has been found alive after all these years.

The name Frost alone is enough to make Joona relive the whole thing.

He overtakes a dirty white car and barely notices the child waving a stuffed toy at him through the window. He is immersed in his memories.

Thirteen years ago, Joona embarked on a preliminary investigation that would change his life entirely. Together with his colleague Samuel Mendel, he began to investigate the case of two people who had been reported missing in Sollentuna.

The first case was a fifty-five-year-old woman who went missing when she was out walking one evening. Her dog had been found in a passageway behind a supermarket, dragging its leash behind it. Two days later, the woman's mother-in-law vanished as she was walking the short distance between her retirement home and the bingo hall.

It turned out that the woman's brother had gone missing in Bangkok five years before. Interpol and the Foreign Ministry had been called in, but he had never been found.

There are no comprehensive figures for the number of people who go missing around the world each year, but everyone knows the total is disturbingly large. In the United States, almost one hundred thousand go missing each year; in Sweden, around seven thousand. Most of them show up, but there's still an alarming number who disappear. Only a very small proportion of the ones who are never found have been kidnapped or murdered.

Joona and Samuel were both relatively new at the National Crime Unit when they started to look into the case of the two missing women. Certain aspects were reminiscent of the disappearance of two people in Örebro four years earlier.

On that occasion, it had been a forty-year-old man and his son. They had been on their way to a soccer game in Glanshammar. They never arrived. Their car was found abandoned on a small forest road that was nowhere near the soccer field.

At first it was just an idea, a random suggestion: What if there were a direct link between the cases, in spite of the differences in time and location? In which case, it wasn't impossible that more missing people could be connected to these four.

The preliminary investigation consisted of the most common sort of police work, the sort that happens at a desk, in front of the computer. Joona and Samuel gathered and organized information about every unsolved missing-persons case in Sweden over the previous ten years. The idea was to see if there were any similarities in these other cases that could not be chalked up to coincidence. They layered the various cases on top of each other, as if they were on transparent paper—and slowly something resembling a constellation began to appear out of the vague motif of connected points. The unexpected pattern that emerged was that, in many of the cases, more than one member of the same family had disappeared.

Joona could remember the silence that had descended upon the room when they stepped back and looked at the results. Forty-five missing people matched that particular criterion. Many of those could probably be dismissed over the following days, but forty-five was still many more than could reasonably be explained by chance.

19

ONE WALL of Samuel's office in the National Crime Unit was covered by a large map of Sweden, dotted with pins to indicate the missing persons.

Obviously, they couldn't assume that all forty-five had been murdered, but for the time being they couldn't rule out any of them.

Because no known perpetrator could be linked to the timing of the disappearances, they started looking for motives and a modus operandi. There were no similarities to cases that had been solved. The murderer they were dealing with left no trace, and he hid his victims' bodies very well.

The choice of victim usually divides serial killers into two groups. One is organized killers, who always seek out an ideal victim who matches their fantasies as closely as possible. These killers focus on a particular type of person, exclusively seeking out prepubescent blond boys, for example. The other group consists of the disorganized killers; here it is the availability of the victims that counts. The victims primarily fill a role in the murderer's fantasies, and it doesn't particularly matter who they are or what they look like.

But the serial killer that Joona and Samuel were starting to envisage didn't seem to fit either of these categories. On the one hand, he was disorganized, because the victims were so varied, but, on the other hand, none of them was especially easy to get hold of.

They were looking for a serial killer who was practically invisible. He left no evidence, no intentional signature.

Days went by, and the women from Sollentuna were still missing.

Joona and Samuel had no concrete proof of a serial killer. They simply thought that there couldn't be any other explanation for all these missing people. Two days later, the preliminary investigation was downgraded and the resources reallocated.

But Joona and Samuel couldn't let it go, and they started to devote their free time during the evenings and weekends to the search.

They concentrated on the pattern that suggested that if two people had gone missing from the same family, there was an increased risk that more family members would go missing in the near future.

While they kept an eye on the family of the women who had vanished from Sollentuna, two children were reported missing from Tyresö. Mikael and Felicia Kohler-Frost. The children of the well-known author Reidar Frost.

20

HE REMEMBERS talking to Reidar Frost and his wife, Roseanna Kohler, three days after their two children went missing. He didn't mention his suspicions to the parents—that they had been murdered by a serial killer whom the police had stopped looking for, a murderer whose existence they could posit only in theory. Joona just asked his questions and let the parents cling to the idea that the children had drowned.

The family lived on Varvs Drive, in a beautiful house facing a sandy beach. There had been several mild weeks, and a lot of the snow had thawed. The streets and footpaths were dark and wet. There was barely any ice along the shoreline, and what remained was gray slush.

Joona remembers walking through the house, passing a large kitchen, and sitting down at a huge white table next to a window. But Roseanna had closed all the curtains, and although her voice was calm, her head was shaking the whole time.

The search for the children was fruitless. There had been countless helicopter searches, divers had been called in, and the water had been dragged for bodies. The surroundings had been searched by chain gangs of both volunteers and specialist dog units.

But no one had seen or heard anything.

Reidar Frost looked like a captured animal. He just wanted to keep on searching.

Joona had sat facing the two parents, asking routine questions about whether they had received any threats, if anyone had behaved oddly or differently, if they had felt they were being followed.

"Everyone thinks they fell in the water," the wife said, her head starting to shake again.

"You mentioned that they sometimes climb out of the window after their bedtime prayers," Joona went on.

"Obviously, they're not supposed to," Reidar said.

"But you did know that they sometimes take their bikes out to see a friend?"

"Rikard."

"Rikard van Horn, number seven Björnbärs Drive," Joona said.

"We've tried talking to Micke and Felicia about it, but . . . well, they're children, and I suppose we didn't think it was dangerous," Reidar replied, gently laying his hand over his wife's.

"What do they do at Rikard's?"

"They never stay for long, just play some Diablo."

"They all do," Roseanna whispered, pulling her hand away.

"On Saturday, they didn't bike to Rikard's, but went to Badholmen instead," Joona went on. "Do they often go there in the evening?"

"We don't think so," Roseanna said, getting up restlessly from the table, as if she could no longer keep her internal trembling in check.

Joona nodded. He knew that the boy, Mikael, had answered the phone just before he and his younger sister had left the house, but the number had proved impossible to trace.

It had been unbearable, sitting there across from the children's parents. Joona said nothing but felt more and more convinced that the children were victims of the serial killer. He listened and asked his questions, but he couldn't tell them what he suspected.

21

IF THE TWO CHILDREN were victims of this serial killer, and if they were correct in thinking that he would soon try to kill one of the parents as well, they had to make a choice.

Joona and Samuel decided to concentrate their efforts on Roseanna Kohler.

She had moved out to live with her sister in Gärdet, in northeastern Stockholm. The sister lived with her four-year-old daughter in a white apartment complex at 25 Lanfors Lane, close to Lill-Jan's Forest.

Joona and Samuel took turns keeping watch on the building at night. For a week, one of them would park nearby and sit in his car until dawn.

On the eighth day, Joona was leaning back in his seat, watching the building's inhabitants get ready for bed as usual. The lights went off in a pattern that he was starting to recognize. A woman in a silver-colored padded jacket went for her usual walk with her golden retriever; then the last windows went dark.

Joona's car was parked in the shadows on Porjus Road, between a dirty white pickup and a red Toyota. In the rearview mirror, he could see snow-covered bushes and a tall fence surrounding a power station. The residential area in front of him was completely quiet. Through the windshield, he watched the static glow of the streetlights.

He smiled to himself when he thought of dinner that night with his wife and little daughter. Lumi had been in a hurry to finish so she could continue examining Joona.

"I'd like to finish eating first," he had suggested.

But Lumi had adopted her serious expression and talked to her mother over his head, asking if he was brushing his teeth by himself yet.

"He's very good," Summa replied.

She explained with a smile that all of Joona's teeth had come in. Lumi put a piece of paper towel under his chin and tried to stick a finger into his mouth, telling him to open wide.

His thoughts of Lumi vanished as a light suddenly went on in the sister's flat. Joona saw Roseanna standing there in a flannel nightdress, talking on the phone.

The light went out again.

An hour passed, but the area remained deserted.

It was starting to get cold inside the car when Joona caught sight of a figure in the rearview mirror. Someone hunched over, approaching along the empty street.

22

Joona slumped down slightly in his seat and followed the figure's progress in the rearview mirror, trying to catch a glimpse of the face.

The branches of a rowan tree swayed as he passed.

In the gray lights from the power station, Joona saw that it was Samuel.

His colleague was almost half an hour early.

Samuel opened the car door and sat down in the passenger seat, which he pushed back so he could stretch out his legs; he sighed.

"Okay, so you're tall and blond, Joona, and it's really lovely being in the car and everything. But I still think I'd rather spend the night with Rebecka. I want to help the boys with their homework."

"You can help me with my homework," Joona said.

"Thanks." Samuel laughed.

Joona looked out at the road, at the building with its closed doors, the rusting balconies, the black windows.

"We'll give it three more days," he said.

Samuel pulled out a silver-colored thermos of chicken soup, which he called *yoich*.

"I don't know, I've been doing a lot of thinking," he said

seriously. "Nothing about this case makes sense. We're trying to find a serial killer who may not actually exist."

"He exists," Joona replied stubbornly.

"But he doesn't fit with what we've found out, he doesn't fit with any aspect of the investigation, and—"

"That's why—that's why no one has seen him," Joona said. "He's only visible because he casts a shadow over the statistics."

They sat next to each other in silence. Samuel blew on his soup, and beads of sweat broke out on his forehead. Joona hummed a tango and let his eyes wander from Roseanna's bedroom window to the icicles hanging from the gutters, then up at the snow-covered chimneys and vents.

"There's someone behind the building," Samuel suddenly whispered. "I'm sure I saw movement."

Samuel pointed, but everything was in a state of dreamlike peace.

A moment later, Joona saw snow fall from a bush close to the house. Someone had just brushed past it.

Carefully, they opened the car doors and crept out.

The sleepy residential area was quiet. All they could hear were their own footsteps and the electric hum from the power station.

There had been a thaw for a couple of weeks; then it had started to snow again.

They approached the windowless end of the building, walking quietly along the strip of grass, past a wallpaper shop on the ground floor.

The glow from the nearest streetlight reached out across the smooth snow to the open space behind the houses. They stopped at the corner and hunched over, checking for movement in the dense cluster of trees toward the Royal Tennis Club and Lill-Jan's Forest.

At first, Joona couldn't see anything in the darkness between the crooked old trees. He was about to give Samuel the signal to proceed when he saw the figure.

There was a man standing among the trees, as still as the snow-covered branches.

Joona's heart raced.

The slim man was staring like a ghost up at the window where Roseanna Kohler was sleeping.

The man showed no sign of urgency, had no obvious purpose.

Joona was filled with an icy conviction that the man in the garden was the serial killer whose existence they had speculated about.

The shadowy face was thin and wrinkled. The man just stood there, as if the sight of the house gave him a sense of calm satisfaction, as if he already had his victim in a cage.

They drew their weapons but were unsure of what to do. They hadn't discussed this in advance. Even though they had been keeping watch on Roseanna for days, they had never talked about what they would do if it transpired that they were right. They couldn't just rush over and arrest a man who was simply gazing at a dark window. They might find out who he was, but they would probably be forced to release him.

23

JOONA STARED at the motionless figure. He could feel the weight of his semiautomatic pistol and the chill of the night air on his fingers. He could hear Samuel's breathing beside him.

The situation was beginning to seem slightly absurd when, without warning, the man took a step forward. They could see he was holding a bag in one hand.

Afterward, it was hard to pinpoint what it was that had convinced them both that they had found the man they were looking for.

The man just looked up at the window of Roseanna's bedroom, then vanished into the bushes. The snow covering the grass crunched beneath their feet as they crept after him. They followed the fresh footprints through the forest until they reached an old railroad line.

Far off to the right, they could see the figure on the track. He passed below an electrical tower, crossing the tangle of shadows thrown by its frame. It was a railroad line that was still used, running from Värta Harbor through Lill-Jan's Forest.

Joona and Samuel followed, sticking to the deep snow beside the tracks to avoid being seen. The railroad continued beneath a viaduct and into the expanse of forest. Suddenly everything became much quieter and darker.

The black trees stood close together.

Joona and Samuel silently sped up, so as not to lose sight of him.

When they emerged from the curve around Uggleviken Marsh, the railroad stretching ahead of them was empty. The skinny man had left the track somewhere and gone into the forest.

They climbed up onto the rails and looked out over the white landscape, then started to walk back. The recent snow was largely untouched. They found a set of footprints they had missed earlier. Ten minutes before, they had been white and impossible to see in the weak light, but the ground beneath the snow was wet, and the prints left by his shoes were now as dark as lead.

They followed the tracks into the forest, toward the large reservoir. It was almost pitch-black among the trees. The murderer's footprints were crossed three times by the lighter tracks of a rabbit. At one point, it was so dark that they lost his trail again. They stopped, then spotted the tracks and hurried on.

Suddenly they began to hear high-pitched whimpering sounds, like an animal crying, but like nothing Joona or Samuel had ever heard before. They followed the footprints and drew closer to the source of the sounds.

What they saw between the tree trunks was something out of a grotesque medieval story. The man they had followed was standing in front of a shallow grave. The ground around him was covered with freshly dug earth. An emaciated, filthy woman was trying to get out of the coffin, crying and struggling to clamber up over the edge. But each time she was on her way up, the man pushed her down again.

For a couple of seconds, Joona and Samuel could only stand there, staring; then they took the safety catches off their weapons and rushed in.

The man wasn't armed, and Joona knew he should aim at his legs, but he couldn't help aiming at his heart. They ran over the dirty snow, forced the man onto his stomach, and cuffed both his wrists and feet.

Samuel stood panting, pointing his pistol at the man as he called Emergency Control. Joona could hear the sob in his voice.

They had caught a previously unknown serial killer. His name was Jurek Walter.

Joona carefully helped the woman out of the coffin and tried to calm her down. She lay on the ground, gasping. When Joona explained that help was on the way, he caught a glimpse of movement through the trees. Something large was running away. A branch snapped, fir trees swayed, and snow fell softly like cloth.

Perhaps it was a deer.

Joona realized later that it must have been Jurek Walter's accomplice, but right then all they could think about was saving the woman and getting the man into custody in Krono-berg Prison.

It turned out that the woman had been in the coffin for almost two years. Jurek Walter had regularly supplied her with food and water, then covered the grave over again. The woman had gone blind and was severely undernourished. Her muscles had atrophied, and compression sores had left her deformed. Her hands and feet were frostbitten.

At first, they assumed that she was merely traumatized, but as time passed, it became clear that she had suffered severe brain damage because of the cold and malnutrition.

24

JOONA LOCKED the door when he returned home at half past four that morning. His heart thudding with trepidation, he moved Lumi's warm, sweaty body closer to the middle of the bed before putting his arm around both her and Summa. He realized he wasn't going to be able to sleep but just needed to lie down with his family.

He was back in Lill-Jan's Forest by seven o'clock. The area had been cordoned off and was under guard, but the snow around the grave was already so churned up by the police, dogs, and paramedics that there was no point trying to find the tracks of a potential accomplice.

By ten o'clock, a police-dog unit had identified a location close to the Uggleviken Marsh, just two hundred meters from the woman's grave. A team of forensics experts and crime-scene analysts was called in, and a couple of hours later, the remains of a middle-aged man and a boy of about fifteen had been exhumed. They had both been squashed into a blue plastic barrel, and forensic examination indicated that they'd been buried almost four years before. They hadn't survived many hours in the barrel, even though there was a tube supplying them with air.

Jurek Walter was registered as a resident of Björnö Road, part of a large housing project built in the early 1970s, in the

Hovsjö district of Södertälje. It was the only address in his name. According to the records, he hadn't lived anywhere else since he arrived in Sweden from Poland in 1994 and was granted a work permit. He had taken a job as a mechanic for a small company, Menge's Engineering Workshop, where he repaired train gearboxes and renovated diesel engines. All the evidence suggested that he lived a solitary, peaceful life.

Joona and Samuel and the other officers didn't know what they might find in Jurek Walter's apartment: a torture chamber or trophy cabinet, jars of formaldehyde, freezers containing body parts, shelves bulging with photographic documentation?

The police had cordoned off the immediate vicinity of the apartment complex and the whole of the second floor. They put on protective clothing, opened the door, and started to set out boards to walk on so that they wouldn't ruin any evidence.

Jurek Walter lived in a two-room apartment measuring thirty-three square meters.

There was a pile of junk mail below the mail slot. The hall was completely empty. There were no shoes or clothes in the closet beside the front door.

They moved farther in.

Joona was prepared for someone to be hiding inside, but everything was perfectly still, as if time had abandoned the place.

The blinds were drawn. The apartment smelled of sunshine and dust.

There was no furniture in the kitchen. The fridge was open and switched off. Nothing to suggest it had ever been used. The pans on the stove had rusted slightly. Inside the oven, the operating instructions were still taped to the side. The only food they found in the cupboards were two cans of sliced pineapple.

In the bedroom was a narrow bed with no sheets, and inside the closet, one clean shirt hung from a metal hanger.

That was all.

Joona tried to work out what the empty apartment signified. It was obvious that Jurek Walter didn't live there. Perhaps he used it only as a postal address. There was nothing in the flat to lead them anywhere else. The only fingerprints belonged to Jurek himself.

He had no criminal record and had never been suspected of a crime. Jurek Walter had no private insurance and had never taken out a loan. His tax was deducted directly from his wages, and he had never claimed any tax credits.

There were many different registries—more than three hundred of them, all covered by the Personal Records Act. Jurek Walter was listed only in the ones that no citizen could avoid.

Otherwise, he was invisible.

He had never taken a sick day, had never sought help from a doctor or dentist.

He wasn't in the firearms registry or the vehicle registry. There were no school records, no registered political or religious affiliations.

It was as if he had lived his life with the express intention of being as invisible as possible. The few people he had been in contact with at his workplace knew nothing about him. They could only report that he never said much but was a very good mechanic.

When National Crime received a response from the Policja, their Polish counterparts, it turned out that Jurek Walter had been dead for many years. Because this Jurek Walter had been found murdered in a public restroom at the central train station, Kraków Główny, they were able to supply photographs and fingerprints.

Neither pictures nor prints matched the Swedish serial killer. Presumably, he had stolen the identity of the real Jurek Walter.

The man they had captured in Lill-Jan's Forest was becoming more and more of an enigma. They combed the forest for another three months, but after the man and boy in the barrel, no more of Jurek Walter's victims were found.

Not until Mikael Kohler-Frost turned up, walking across a bridge, heading for Stockholm.

25

A PROSECUTOR took over the responsibility for the preliminary investigation, but Joona and Samuel led the interviews, from the custody proceedings to the principal interrogation. Jurek Walter didn't confess to anything, but he didn't deny any crimes, either. Instead, he philosophized about death and the human condition. Because of the lack of supporting evidence, it was the circumstances surrounding his arrest, his failure to offer an explanation, and the forensic psychiatrist's evaluation that led to his conviction in the Stockholm Courthouse. His lawyer appealed the conviction, and while they were waiting for the case to be heard in the Court of Appeal, more interviews were held in Kronoberg Prison.

The staff at the prison were unfazed by most circumstances, but Jurek Walter's presence troubled them. He made them feel uneasy. Wherever he was, conflicts would suddenly flare up; on one occasion, two guards started fighting, and one of them ended up in the hospital. A crisis meeting was held, and new security procedures were agreed upon. Jurek Walter would no longer be allowed to come into contact with other inmates or use the exercise yard.

Samuel had called in sick, so Joona found himself walking alone down the corridor, past the row of white thermos flasks, one outside each of the green doors. The shiny linoleum floor had long black tears in it.

The door to Jurek Walter's cell was open. The walls were bare, and the window was barred. The morning light reflected off the worn plastic-covered mattress on the fixed bunk and the stainless-steel sink.

Farther along the corridor, a policeman in a dark-blue sweater was talking to a Syriac Orthodox priest.

"They've taken him to Interview Room Two," the officer called to Joona.

A guard was waiting outside the interview room, and through the window Joona could see Jurek Walter sitting on a chair, looking down at the floor. In front of him stood his legal representative and two guards.

"I'm here to listen," Joona said when he went in.

There was a short silence; then Jurek Walter exchanged a few words with his lawyer. He spoke in a low voice and didn't look up as he asked the lawyer to leave.

"You can wait in the corridor," Joona told the guards.

When he was on his own with Jurek Walter in the interview room, he moved a chair and pulled it so close that he could smell the man's sweat.

Jurek Walter sat still on his chair, his head drooping forward.

"Your defense lawyer claims that you were in Lill-Jan's Forest to free the woman," Joona said in a neutral voice.

Jurek stared at the floor for another couple of minutes, then, without the slightest movement, said, "I talk too much."

"The truth will do," Joona said.

"But it really doesn't matter to me if I'm found guilty of something I didn't do," Jurek said.

"You'll be locked up."

Jurek looked up at Joona and said thoughtfully: "I lost my

life a long time ago. I'm not scared of anything. Not pain. Not loneliness or boredom."

"But I'm looking for the truth," Joona said, intentionally naïve.

"You don't have to look for it. It's the same with justice or gods. You choose what serves your purposes."

"But you don't choose the lies," Joona said.

Jurek's pupils contracted. "In the Court of Appeal, the prosecutor's description of my actions will be regarded as proved beyond all reasonable doubt," he said without the slightest hint of a plea in his voice.

"You're saying that's wrong?"

"I'm not going to get hung up on technicalities, because there isn't really any difference between digging a grave and refilling it."

When Joona left the interview room that day, he was more convinced than ever that Jurek Walter was an extremely dangerous man. At the same time, he couldn't help considering the idea that Jurek had been trying to say that he was being punished for someone else's crimes. Of course he understood that it had been Jurek Walter's intention to sow a seed of doubt, but he couldn't ignore the possibility that there was actually a flaw in the prosecution's case.

26

THE DAY BEFORE the appeal, Joona, Summa, and Lumi went to dinner with Samuel and his family. The sun had been shining through the linen curtains when they started eating, but it was now evening. Rebecka lit a candle on the table and blew out the match. The light quivered over her luminous eyes and her one strange pupil. She had once explained that it was a condition called dyscoria and that it wasn't a problem: she could see just as well with that eye as with the other.

The relaxed meal concluded with a dark honey cake. Joona borrowed a kippah for the prayer, Birkat Hamazon.

That was the last time he saw Samuel's family.

The boys played quietly for a while with little Lumi before Joshua immersed himself in a video game and Reuben disappeared into his room to practice his clarinet.

Rebecka went outside for a cigarette, and Summa kept her company with her glass of wine.

Joona and Samuel cleared the table. As soon as they were alone they started talking about work and the following day's appeal.

"I'm not going to be there," Samuel said seriously. "I don't know, it's not that I'm frightened, but it feels like my soul gets dirty—that it gets dirtier every second I spend in his vicinity."

"I'm sure he's guilty," Joona said.

"But?"

"I think he has an accomplice."

Samuel sighed and put the dishes in the sink.

"We've stopped a serial killer," he said. "A lone lunatic who—"

"He wasn't alone at the grave when we got there," Joona interrupted.

"Yes, he was." Samuel started to rinse the dishes.

"It's not unusual for serial killers to work with other people," Joona objected.

"No, but there's nothing that suggests that Jurek Walter belongs to that category," Samuel said. "We've done our job. We're finished."

27

THE SUN was shining through the mottled glass in the windows of the Wrangelska Palace. Jurek Walter's lawyer explained that his client had been so badly affected by the trial that he couldn't bear to explain why he had been at the crime scene when he was arrested.

Joona was called as a witness, and he described their surveillance work and the arrest. Then the defense lawyer asked if Joona could see any reason at all to suspect that the prosecutor's account of events was based on a false assumption: "Could my client have been found guilty of a crime that someone else committed?"

Joona met the lawyer's anxious gaze, and in his mind's eye he saw Jurek Walter calmly pushing the woman back into the coffin every time she tried to get out.

"I'm asking you, because you were there," the defense lawyer went on. "Could Jurek Walter actually have been trying to rescue the woman in the grave?"

"No," Joona replied.

After deliberating for two hours, the Chair of the Court declared that the verdict of the Stockholm Courthouse was upheld. Jurek Walter's face didn't move a muscle as the more rigorous sentence was announced. He was to be held in a secure psychiatric clinic with extraordinary conditions applied to any eventual parole proceedings. Seeing as he was closely connected to numerous ongoing investigations, he was also subject to unusually extensive restrictions.

When the Chair of the Court had finished, Jurek Walter turned toward Joona. His face was covered with fine wrinkles, and his pale eyes looked straight into Joona's.

"Now Samuel Mendel's two sons are going to disappear," Jurek said in a measured voice. "And Samuel's wife, Rebecka, will disappear. But . . . No, listen to me, Joona Linna. The police will look for them, and when the police give up, Samuel will go on looking, but when he eventually realizes that he'll never see his family again, he'll kill himself."

Joona stood up to leave the courtroom.

"And your little daughter," Jurek Walter went on, looking down at his fingernails.

"Careful now," Joona said.

"Lumi will disappear," Jurek whispered. "And Summa will disappear. And when you realize that you're never going to find them . . . you're going to hang yourself."

He looked up and stared directly into Joona's eyes. His face was calm, as if things had already been settled the way he wanted.

Ordinarily, convicts are taken back to a holding cell until their destination and transportation to their permanent facility have been organized. But the staff at Kronoberg were so keen to be rid of Jurek Walter that they had arranged transport directly from the Wrangelska Palace to the Secure Criminal Psychology Unit, twenty kilometers north of Stockholm.

Jurek Walter was to be held in strict isolation in Sweden's most secure facility for an indeterminate amount of time. Samuel Mendel had regarded Jurek's threat as empty words from a defeated man, but Joona had been unable to escape the sense that the threat had been presented as a truth, a fact.

The investigation was downgraded when no other bodies were found. Although it wasn't dropped altogether, it went cold.

Joona refused to give up, but there were too few pieces of the puzzle, and the scant lines of inquiry they had turned out to be dead ends. Even though Jurek Walter had been stopped and convicted, they didn't really know any more about him than before.

He was still a mystery.

ONE FRIDAY AFTERNOON, two months after the appeal, Joona was sitting with Samuel at Il Caffè, close to police headquarters, drinking a double espresso. They were busy with other cases by then but still met up regularly to discuss Jurek Walter. Though they had been through all the material about him many times, they had found nothing to suggest that he had an accomplice. The whole thing was on the verge of becoming an in-joke, with the two of them weighing up innocent passersby as possible suspects. And then something terrible happened.

28

SAMUEL'S PHONE BUZZED on the café table, next to his espresso cup. The screen showed a picture of his wife, Rebecka. Joona listened idly to the conversation as he picked the crystallized sugar from his cinnamon bun. Evidently, Rebecka and the boys were heading out to Dalarö earlier than planned, and Samuel agreed to pick up some food on the way. He told her to drive carefully and ended the call with lots of kisses.

"The carpenter who's been repairing our veranda wants us to take a look at his work as soon as possible," Samuel explained. "The painter can start this weekend if it's ready."

Joona and Samuel returned to their offices in the National Crime Unit and didn't see each other again for the rest of the day.

Five hours later, Joona was eating dinner with his family when Samuel called. He was panting and talking so fast that it was difficult to make out what he was saying, but apparently Rebecka and the boys weren't at the house in Dalarö. They hadn't been there and weren't answering the phone.

"There's bound to be an explanation," Joona said.

"I've called the police, and all the hospitals, and—"

"Where are you now?" Joona asked.

"I'm out on the Dalarö road. I'm heading back to the house."

"What can I do?" Joona asked.

He had already thought the thought, but the hairs on the back of his neck still stood up when Samuel said: "Make sure Jurek Walter hasn't escaped."

Joona checked with the Secure Criminal Psychology Unit of the Löwenströmska Hospital at once and spoke to Chief Physician Roland Brolin. He was told that nothing unusual had occurred in the secure unit. Jurek Walter was in his cell and had been in total isolation all day.

When Joona called Samuel back, his friend's voice sounded different, shrill and hunted.

"I'm out in the forest." Samuel was nearly shouting. "I've found Rebecka's car. It's in the middle of the little road leading to the headland, but there's no one here. There's no one here!"

"I'm on my way," Joona said at once.

The police searched intensively for Samuel's family. All traces of Rebecka and the boys had vanished on the gravel road five meters from the abandoned car. The dogs didn't pick up any scent, just walked up and down, sniffing and circling without finding anything. The forests, roads, houses, and waterways were searched for two months. After the police had withdrawn, Samuel and Joona kept looking on their own. They searched with determination and with a fear that grew until it was on the brink of being unbearable. Not once did they discuss what this was all about. Both refused to voice their fears about what had happened to Joshua, Reuben, and Rebecka. They had witnessed Jurek Walter's cruelty.

29

THROUGHOUT THIS PERIOD, Joona suffered such terrible anxiety that he couldn't sleep. He watched over his family, following them everywhere, picking them up and dropping them off, and making special arrangements with Lumi's preschool, but he was forced to accept that this wouldn't be enough in the long term.

Joona had to confront his worst horror.

He couldn't talk to Samuel, but he could no longer deny the truth to himself.

Jurek Walter hadn't committed his crimes alone. Everything about Jurek Walter's understated grandiosity suggested that he was the leader. But after Samuel's family was abducted, there could be no doubt that Jurek Walter had an accomplice.

This accomplice had been ordered to take Samuel's family, and he had done so without leaving a single piece of evidence.

Joona realized that his family was next. It was only good fortune that had spared him so far.

Jurek Walter showed no mercy to anyone.

Joona brought this up with Summa on numerous occasions, but she refused to take the threat as seriously as he did. Though she humored him, accepting his concern and precautionary measures, she assumed that his fears would subside over time.

He had hoped that the police investigation that followed the disappearance of Samuel's family would lead to the capture of the accomplice. When the search first began, Joona saw himself as the hunter, but as the weeks went by, the dynamic changed. He knew that he and his family were the prey, and the calm he tried to demonstrate to Summa and Lumi was just a façade.

IT WAS HALF PAST TEN in the evening, and he and Summa were lying in bed reading when a noise from the ground floor made Joona's heart skip. The washing machine hadn't finished its cycle yet, and he could hear a zipper rattling against the drum. He couldn't help getting up and checking that all the windows downstairs were in one piece, the outside doors locked.

When he returned, Summa had switched off her lamp and was lying there watching him.

"What did you do?" she asked gently.

He forced himself to smile and was about to say something when they heard little footsteps. Joona turned and saw his daughter come into the bedroom. Her hair was sticking up, and her pajama pants had twisted around her waist.

"Lumi, you're supposed to be asleep," he sighed.

"We forgot to say good night to the cat," she said.

Every evening, Joona would read Lumi a story, and before he tucked her in for the night, they always had to look out the window and wave to the gray cat that slept in their neighbors' kitchen window.

"Go back to bed now," Summa said.

"I'll come and see you," Joona promised.

Lumi mumbled something and shook her head.

"Do you want me to carry you?" he asked, and picked her up.

She clung to him, and he suddenly noticed her heart pounding.

"What is it? Did you have a dream?"

"I only wanted to wave to the cat," she whispered. "But there was a skeleton out there."

"In the window?"

"No, he was standing on the ground," she replied. "Right where we found the dead hedgehog. He was looking at me."

Joona put her in bed with Summa.

"Stay here," he said.

He ran downstairs, not bothering to get his pistol from the gun cabinet, not bothering to put on shoes, just opened the kitchen door and rushed outside into the cold night air.

No one was there.

He ran behind the house, climbed over the neighbors' fence, and moved into the next garden. The whole area was quiet and still. He returned to the tree in the garden where he and Lumi had found a dead hedgehog the previous summer.

The tall grass just inside their fence had been disturbed. Somebody had definitely been standing there. From that spot you could see very clearly through Lumi's window.

Joona went inside, locked the door behind him, picked up his pistol, and searched the whole house before going back to bed. Lumi fell asleep almost instantly between him and Summa, and a little while later, his wife was asleep as well.

30

Joona had already tried to talk to Summa about going into hiding and starting a new life, but she had never encountered Jurek Walter. She didn't know the extent of what he had done, and she had doubts that he was behind Rebecka's, Joshua's, and Reuben's disappearance.

With fevered concentration, Joona began to confront the inevitable. A chill focus consumed him as he examined every detail, every aspect, and drew up a plan. A plan that would save all three of them.

The National Crime Unit knew almost nothing about Jurek Walter. The disappearance of Samuel Mendel's family after Jurek's arrest provided strong support for the theory that he had an accomplice. But this accomplice hadn't left a single shred of evidence. He was a shadow of a shadow.

Joona's colleagues said it was hopeless, but he wouldn't give up. Naturally, he understood it wouldn't be easy to find this invisible accomplice. It might take several years, and Joona was only one person. He couldn't search and protect Summa and Lumi at the same time, not every second. If he hired two bodyguards to accompany them everywhere, the family's savings would be exhausted in six months.

Jurek's accomplice had waited months before seizing Samuel's family. This man was in no hurry, patiently biding his time until he was ready to strike.

Joona tried to find a way for them to stay together. They could move, get new jobs and change identities, and live quietly somewhere. Nothing mattered more than being with Summa and Lumi.

But, as a police officer, he knew that protected identities aren't safe; they just give you breathing space. The farther away you got, the more breaths you managed to take, but in the file of Jurek Walter's suspected victims was a man who went missing in Bangkok, disappearing without a trace from the elevator in the Sukhothai Hotel.

There was no escape.

Eventually, Joona was forced to accept that there was something more important to him than being with Summa and Lumi. Their lives mattered more.

If he ran away or disappeared with them, it would be a direct challenge to Jurek to track them down. And Joona knew that, once you start looking, sooner or later you are going to find your quarry, no matter how hard they might try to hide.

Jurek Walter mustn't look, he thought. That's the only way not to be found.

There was only one solution. Jurek and his shadow had to believe that Summa and Lumi were dead.

31

By THE TIME Joona reaches the outskirts of Stockholm, the traffic has built up. Snowflakes are swirling around before vanishing on the damp asphalt of the highway.

He can't stand to remember how he arranged Summa's and Lumi's deaths in order to give them a different life. Nils Åhlén helped him but didn't like it. He understood that they were doing the right thing, assuming the accomplice really did exist. But if Joona was wrong, this would be a mistake of incomprehensible proportions.

Over the years, this doubt has settled over the pathologist's slender figure as a great sorrow.

The railings of the Northern Cemetery flicker past the car, and Joona remembers the day Summa's and Lumi's urns were lowered into the ground. The rain fell on the silk ribbons of their wreaths and pattered on the black umbrellas.

Both Joona and Samuel continued looking, but not together. They were no longer in touch with each other. Their different fates had made them strangers. Eleven months after his family disappeared, Samuel gave up searching and returned to duty. He lasted three weeks after abandoning hope. Early in the morning of a glorious March day, Samuel went to his summerhouse. He walked down to the beautiful beach where his boys used to swim, took out his service pistol, fed a bullet into the chamber, and shot himself in the head.

When Joona got the call from his boss telling him that Samuel was dead, he felt a deep, unsettling numbness.

JOONA HAD NEVER THOUGHT that he would be losing his family forever. He knew he had to refrain from meeting them, seeing them, touching them for a while. He realized that it might take years. Still, he had always been convinced that he would find Jurek Walter's accomplice and arrest him. But after ten years he had progressed no further than he had in the first ten days. The only evidence that the accomplice existed was that Jurek's prophecy for Samuel had come true.

Officially, there was no connection between the disappearance of Samuel's family and Jurek Walter; it was regarded as an accident. Joona was the only person who believed that Jurek's partner had taken them. He was convinced that he was right, even though he had started to accept that he wasn't going to find the accomplice.

But the important thing was that his family was still alive.

He stopped talking about the case, because it was impossible to ignore the likelihood that he was being watched. He felt condemned to a solitary life.

The years passed, and the fabricated deaths came to seem more and more real.

He had truly lost his wife and daughter.

JOONA PULLS UP BEHIND a taxi outside the main entrance of Södermalm Hospital, gets out, and walks through the falling snow toward the revolving glass door.

32

MIKAEL KOHLER-FROST has been moved from the emergency room of Södermalm Hospital to Ward 66, which specializes in acute and chronic cases of infection.

Dr. Irma Goodwin is now walking across the shiny vinyl floor with Joona. A light flickers above a framed print.

"His general condition is very poor," she explains as they walk. "He's malnourished, and he has pneumonia. The lab found the antigens for Legionnaires' in his urine."

"Legionnaires' disease?"

Joona stops in the corridor and runs his hand through his tousled hair. The doctor notices that his eyes have turned an intense gray, almost like burnished silver, and she hurriedly assures him that the disease isn't contagious.

"It's linked to specific locations with—"

"I know," Joona replies, and continues walking.

He remembers that the man who was found dead in the plastic barrel had been suffering from Legionnaires' disease. To contract the disease, you have to be somewhere with infected water. Cases of infection in Sweden are extremely rare. The Legionella bacteria grow in warm pools, water tanks, and pipes, but cannot survive if the temperature is too low.

"Is he going to be okay?" Joona asks.

"I think so. I gave him a macrolide immediately," she replies, trying to keep up with the tall detective.

"And that's helping?"

"It'll take a few days—he still has a high fever, and there's a risk of septic embolisms," she says, opening a door and ushering him through before following him into the patient's room.

Daylight is passing through the bag on the drip stand, making it glow. A thin, very pale man is lying on the bed with his eyes closed, muttering: "No, no, no. No, no, no, no."

His chin is trembling, and the beads of sweat on his brow merge and trickle down his face. A nurse is sitting beside him, holding his left hand and carefully cleaning the lacerations on it.

"Has he said anything?" Joona asks.

"He's been delirious, and it's hard to understand what he's saying," the nurse replies, taping a compress over the wound on his hand.

She leaves the room, and Joona carefully approaches the patient. When he looks at his emaciated features, he has no difficulty discerning the child's face he has studied in photographs: the neat mouth, the long, dark eyelashes. Joona thinks back to the most recent picture of Mikael. He was ten years old, sitting in front of a computer with a fringe of hair over his eyes, an amused smile on his lips.

The young man in the hospital bed coughs tiredly, takes a few irregular breaths with his eyes closed, then whispers to himself, "No, no, no . . ."

There's no doubt that the man lying in bed in front of him is Mikael Kohler-Frost.

"You're safe now, Mikael," Joona says.

Dr. Goodwin is standing behind him silently, looking at the emaciated patient.

He shakes his head and jerks, tensing every muscle in his body. The liquid in the drip bag turns the color of blood. He's trembling and starts to whimper quietly to himself.

"My name is Joona Linna. I'm a detective inspector, and I was one of the people who looked for you when you didn't come home."

Mikael opens his eyes a little but doesn't seem to see anything at first. Then he blinks a few times and squints at Joona.

"You think I'm alive. . . ."

He coughs, then lies back, panting, and looks at Joona.

"Where have you been, Mikael?"

"I don't know. I don't know anything. I don't know where I am."

"You're in Södermalm Hospital in Stockholm," Joona says.

"Is the door locked? Is it?"

"Mikael, I need to find out where you've been."

"I don't understand," he whispers.

"I need to find out—"

"What the hell are you doing with me?" he asks in a despairing voice, and starts to cry.

"I'm going to give him a sedative," the doctor says, and leaves the room.

"You're safe now," Joona explains. "Everyone here is trying to help you, and—"

"I don't want to. I don't want to."

He shakes his head and tries to pull the drip from his arm with tired fingers.

"Where have you been all this time, Mikael? Where have you been living? Were you hiding? Were you locked up, or—"

"I don't know. I don't understand."

"You're tired, and you have a fever," Joona says gently. "But you have to try to think."

33

MIKAEL KOHLER-FROST talks to himself in a low voice, moistening his mouth and looking up at Joona with big, questioning eyes. "I don't know. It's so hard to think," the young man whispers. "There's nothing to remember. It's just dark, I get mixed up. I mix up what was before and how it was in the beginning. I can't think, there's too much sand, I can't wake up."

He leans his head back and closes his eyes.

"You said something about how it was in the beginning," Joona says. "Can you try—"

"Don't touch me. I don't want you to touch me," he interrupts.

"I'm not going to."

"I don't want to—I don't want to—"

His eyes roll back, and he tilts his head in an odd, crooked way; then he shuts his eyes and his body trembles.

"There's no danger," Joona repeats. "There's no danger."

After a while, Mikael's body relaxes again, and he coughs and looks up.

"Can you tell me anything about how it was in the beginning?" Joona repeats gently.

"When I was little, we were huddled together on the floor," he says, almost soundlessly.

"So there were several of you at the start?" Joona asks, a shiver running up his spine.

"Everyone was frightened. I was calling for Mom and Dad, and there was a grown-up woman and an old man on the floor. They were sitting on the floor behind the sofa. She tried to calm me down, but . . . but I could hear her crying the whole time."

"What did she say?" Joona asks.

"I don't remember. I don't remember anything. Maybe I dreamed the whole thing. . . ."

"Do you remember any names?"

He coughs and shakes his head.

"Everyone was just crying and screaming, and the woman with the eye kept asking about two boys," he says, his eyes focused inwardly.

"Do you remember any names?"

"What?"

"Do you remember the names of—"

"I don't want to. I don't . . ."

"I'm not trying to upset you, but—"

"They all disappeared. They just disappeared," Mikael says, his voice getting louder. "They all disappeared. . . ." Mikael's voice cracks, and it's no longer possible to make out what he's saying.

Joona repeats that everything is going to be all right. Mikael looks him in the eye, but he's shaking so much he can't speak.

"You're safe here," Joona says. "I'm a police officer, and I'll make sure that nothing happens to you."

Dr. Goodwin comes into the room with a nurse. They walk over to the patient and gently put his oxygen tube back in his nose. The nurse injects the sedative solution into the drip while calmly explaining what she's doing.

"He needs to rest now," the doctor says to Joona.

"I have to know what he saw."

She tilts her head. "Is it very urgent?"

"No," Joona concedes. "Not really."

"Come back tomorrow, then," Dr. Goodwin says. "Because I think—"

Her cell phone rings, and she has a short conversation, then hurries out of the room. Joona is left standing by the bed as he hears her walk down the corridor.

"Mikael, what did you mean about the eye? You mentioned the woman with the eye—what did you mean?" he asks slowly.

"It was like . . . like a black teardrop."

"Her pupil?"

"Yes," Mikael whispers.

Joona looks at the young man in the bed, feeling his pulse roar in his temples, and his voice is brittle and metallic as he asks:

"Was her name Rebecka?"

34

MIKAEL IS CRYING as the sedative enters his bloodstream. His body relaxes, and his sobbing grows more weary, then subsides completely, seconds before he drifts off to sleep.

Joona feels oddly empty inside as he leaves the patient's room and pulls out his phone. He stops, pauses for breath, then calls his friend, Professor Nils "The Needle" Åhlén, who performed the autopsies on the bodies found in Lill-Jan's Forest.

"Nils Åhlén," he says as he takes the call.

"Are you sitting at your computer?"

"Joona Linna, how nice to hear from you," The Needle says in his nasal voice. "I was just sitting here in front of the screen with my eyes closed, enjoying its warmth. I was fantasizing that I'd bought a facial solarium."

"Elaborate daydream."

"Well, if you look after the pennies . . ."

"Would you like to look up some old files?"

"Talk to Frippe; he'll help you."

"No can do."

"He knows as much as—"

"It's about Jurek Walter," Joona interrupts.

A long silence follows.

"I've told you, I don't want to talk about that again," The Needle says.

"One of his victims has turned up alive."

"Don't say that."

"Mikael Kohler-Frost. He's got Legionnaires' disease, but it looks as though he's going to pull through."

"What files are you interested in?" The Needle asks with nervous intensity in his voice.

"The man in the barrel had Legionnaires' disease," Joona goes on. "But did the boy who was found with him show any signs of the disease?"

"Why are you wondering that?"

"If there's a connection, it ought to be possible to put together a list of places where the bacteria might be present. And then—"

"We're talking about millions of places," The Needle says.

"Okay."

"Joona. You have to realize, even if Legionella was mentioned in the other reports, that doesn't mean that Mikael was one of Jurek Walter's victims."

"So there were Legionella bacteria?"

"Yes, I found antibodies against the bacteria in the boy's blood, so he probably had Pontiac fever, a mild form of Legionnaires'," The Needle says with a sigh. "I know you want to be right, Joona, but nothing you've said is enough to—"

"Mikael Kohler-Frost says he met Rebecka," Joona interrupts.

"Rebecka Mendel?" The Needle asks.

"They were held captive together," Joona confirms.

There is a long silence. Then: "So . . . so you were right about everything, Joona," The Needle says. "You have no idea how relieved I am to hear that." He gulps hard down the line and whispers that they did the right thing after all.

"Yes," Joona says.

He and The Needle had arranged a fake car crash for Joona's wife and daughter.

Two dead bodies were cremated and buried in place of Lumi and Summa. Using fake dental records, The Needle had identified the bodies. He believed Joona, and trusted him, but it had been such a big decision, so momentous, that he has never stopped worrying about it.

JOONA DOESN'T DARE leave the hospital until two uniformed officers arrive to guard Mikael's room. On his way out, along the corridor, he calls Nathan Pollock and says they need to send someone to pick up the man's father.

"I'm sure it's Mikael," he says. "And I'm sure he's been held captive by Jurek Walter all these years."

Joona gets in the car and slowly drives away from the hospital as the windshield wipers clear the snow from his view.

Mikael Kohler-Frost was ten years old when he disappeared and has become a free man again at twenty-three.

Sometimes prisoners manage to escape, like Elisabeth Fritzl in Austria, who got away after twenty-four years as a sex slave in her father's cellar. Or Natascha Kampusch, who fled from her kidnapper after eight years.

Joona hopes that, like Elisabeth Fritzl and Natascha Kampusch, Mikael saw the man holding him captive. Suddenly a conclusion to all this seems possible. In just a few days, as soon as he is well enough, Mikael should be able to show the way to the place where he was held captive.

The car's tires rumble as Joona crosses the ridge of snow in the middle of the road to overtake a bus. As he drives past the House of Nobility, the city opens up in front of him once more, with heavy snow falling between the dark sky and the swirling black water below the bridge.

The accomplice must know that Mikael has escaped and can identify him, Joona thinks. Presumably, he has already tried to cover his tracks and switch to a new hiding place, but if Mikael can lead them to where he was held captive, Forensics would be able to find some sort of evidence, and the hunt would be on again.

There's a long way to go, but Joona's heart is already beating faster in anticipation.

The thought is so overwhelming that he has to pull over to the side of the Vasa Bridge and stop the car. Another driver blows his horn irritably. Joona gets out and steps up onto the pavement, breathing the cold air deep into his lungs.

A sudden migraine makes him stumble, and he grabs the railing for support. He closes his eyes for a moment, waits, and feels the pain ebb away before he opens his eyes again.

It's too early to think the thought, but he is well aware of what this means. His body feels weighted down by the realization. If he manages to catch the accomplice, there will no longer be any threat to Summa and Lumi.

35

It's too hot to talk in the sauna. Gold light is shining on their naked bodies and the pale sandalwood. It's scorching now, and the air burns Reidar Frost's lungs when he breathes in. Drops of sweat are falling from his nose onto the white hair on his chest.

The Japanese journalist Mizuho is sitting on the bench next to Veronica. Their bodies are both flushed and shiny. Sweat is running between their breasts, over their stomachs, and down into their pubic hair.

Mizuho is looking seriously at Reidar. She has come all the way from Tokyo to interview him. He told her good-naturedly that he never gives interviews but that she was very welcome to attend the party. She was probably hoping he would say something about the Sanctum series being turned into a manga film. She has been here for four days now.

Veronica sighs and closes her eyes.

Mizuho hadn't taken off her gold necklace before entering the sauna, and Reidar can see that it's starting to burn. Marie lasted only five minutes before she went off to the shower, and now the Japanese journalist leaves the sauna as well.

Veronica leans forward and rests her elbows on her knees, breathing through her half-open mouth as sweat drips from her nipples.

Reidar feels a sort of brittle tenderness toward her. But he doesn't know how to explain how desolate he feels. He doesn't know how to explain that everything he does now, everything he throws himself into, is just random fumbling for something to help him survive the next minute.

"Marie's very beautiful," Veronica says.

"Yes."

"Big breasts."

"Stop it," Reidar mutters.

She looks at him with a serious expression as she goes on: "Why can't I just get a divorce?"

"Because that would be the end for us," Reidar says.

Veronica's eyes fill with tears, and she is about to say something else when Marie comes back in and sits down next to Reidar with a little giggle.

"God, it's hot," she gasps. "How can you sit here?"

Veronica throws a scoop of water onto the stones. There's a loud hiss, and hot clouds of steam rise up and surround them for a few seconds. Then the heat becomes dry and static again.

Reidar is hanging forward over his knees. The hair on his head is so hot he almost scalds himself when he runs his hand through it.

"That's enough," he exhales, and climbs down.

The two women follow him outside into the soft snow. Dusk is spreading its darkness across the snow, which glows pale blue.

Heavy snowflakes drift as the three of them, naked, sink down to their calves in the deep snow.

David, Wille, and Berzelius are eating dinner with the other members of the Sanctum scholarship committee, and the drinking songs can be heard all the way out in the back of the garden.

Reidar turns and looks at Veronica and Marie. Steam rises from their flushed bodies. They're enveloped in veils of mist as the snow falls around them. He is about to say something when Veronica bends over and throws an armful of snow up at him. He backs away, laughing, and falls, vanishing into the loose snow.

He lies there on his back, listening to their laughter.

The snow feels liberating. His body is still burning hot. Reidar looks straight up at the sky, at the hypnotic snow falling from the center of creation, an eternity of drifting white.

A memory takes him by surprise. He is peeling off the children's snowsuits. Taking off hats with snow caught in the wool. He can remember their cold cheeks, their sweaty hair, and the smell of their wet boots.

He misses the children so intensely that his longing feels purely physical.

He wishes he were alone so he could lie in the snow until he loses consciousness, surrounded by his memories of Felicia and Mikael.

He gets to his feet with effort and gazes out across the white fields. Marie and Veronica are laughing, making angels in the snow, and rolling around a short distance away.

"How long have these parties been going on?" Marie calls to him.

"I don't want to talk about it," Reidar mumbles.

He is about to walk off and get drunk, but Marie is standing in front of him, legs apart. "You never want to talk. I don't know anything," she says with a laugh.

"Just leave me the fuck alone!" Reidar shouts, and pushes past. "What is it you want?"

"Sorry, I . . ."

"Leave me the fuck alone," he snaps, and disappears into the house.

The two women walk, shivering, back into the sauna. The steam on their bodies runs off as the heat closes around them again, as if it had never left.

"What's his problem?" Marie asks.

"There's a lot you don't know," Veronica replies simply.

36

REIDAR FROST is wearing a new pair of striped pants and an open shirt. The back of his hair is damp. He clutches a bottle of Château Mouton Rothschild in each hand.

That morning, he awoke with an ache of longing. He forced himself to go downstairs and wake his friends. They poured spiced schnapps into crystal glasses and rustled up some boiled eggs with Russian caviar.

Reidar is walking barefoot along a corridor lined with dark portraits. The snow outside casts an indirect light. In the reading room, with its shiny leather furniture, he stops and looks out the huge window. The view is like a fairy tale, as if the king of winter himself had blown snow across the fields.

Suddenly he sees flickering lights on the long avenue leading from the gates to the front of the house. The branches of the trees look like embroidered lace in the glow. A car approaching. The snow swirling into the air behind it is colored red by its taillights.

Reidar can't recall inviting anyone else to join them.

He is thinking that Veronica will have to take care of the new arrivals when he sees that it's a police car. Reidar stops and puts the bottles down on a chest, then goes back downstairs and pulls on the felt-lined winter boots beside the door.

He heads out into the cold air to meet the car as it arrives in the broad turning circle.

"Reidar Frost?" a woman in plainclothes says as she gets out of the car.

"Yes," he replies.

"May we go inside?"

"Here will do," he says.

"Would you like to sit in the car?"

"Does it look like it?"

The woman pauses. "We've found your son," she says, taking a couple of steps toward him.

"I see." He holds up a hand to silence the police officer.

He breathes and composes himself, then slowly lowers his hand.

"So where did you find Mikael?" he says in a voice that has become strangely calm.

"He was walking over a bridge—"

"What?! What the hell are you saying?" Reidar roars.

The woman flinches. She's tall and has a long ponytail down her back. "I'm trying to tell you that he's alive," she says.

"What is this?" Reidar asks, uncomprehendingly.

"He's been taken to Södermalm Hospital for observation."

"Not my son. He died many years—"

"There's no doubt that it's him."

Reidar is staring at her.

"Mikael's alive?"

"He came back."

"My son?"

"I know it's a shock, but—"

"I thought . . ."

Reidar's chin trembles as the policewoman explains that Mikael's DNA is a 100 percent match. The ground beneath him rolls like a wave, and he fumbles in the air for support.

"God," he whispers. "Dear God, thank you."

He seems completely broken. He looks up as his legs give way beneath him. The policewoman tries to catch him, but one of his knees hits the ground and he falls sideways.

The police officer helps him to his feet, and he is holding her arm when he sees Veronica run down the steps barefoot, wrapped in his thick winter coat.

"You're sure it's him?" he says, staring into the policewoman's eyes.

She nods.

"It's a one hundred percent match," she repeats. "It's Mikael Kohler-Frost, and he's alive."

He takes Veronica's arm as he follows the policewoman back to her car.

"What's going on, Reidar?" Veronica asks, sounding worried.

He looks at her. His face is confused, and he instantly appears much older.

"My little boy," he says.

37

FROM A DISTANCE, the white blocks of Södermalm Hospital look like tombstones looming out of the thick snow.

Moving like a sleepwalker, Reidar Frost buttons his shirt on the way to Stockholm and tucks it into his pants. He hears the police say that the patient who has been identified as Mikael Kohler-Frost has been moved from intensive care to a private room. It doesn't seem real.

Reidar's son was declared dead seven years ago.

Now Reidar is following the plainclothes officer down a long corridor and staring at the interwoven tracks left on the floor by the wheels of countless beds. He tries to tell himself not to hope too much, that the police might have made a mistake.

Thirteen years ago, his children disappeared when they were out playing one evening. The police thought that one of the siblings had fallen into the cold March water, and the other had been dragged in while trying to help the first one out.

Reidar had secretly hired a private-detective agency to investigate other possible leads, primarily everyone in the children's vicinity: all their teachers, soccer coaches, neighbors, the mailmen, bus drivers, gardeners, shop assistants, café staff, and anyone the children had interacted with on the phone or the Internet. Their classmates' parents were checked, and even Reidar's own relatives.

Long after the police had stopped looking, and when everyone with even the faintest connection to the children had been investigated, Reidar began to understand that it was over. But for several years after that, he walked along the coastline every day, expecting his children to be washed ashore.

REIDAR AND THE PLAINCLOTHES OFFICER wait while an old woman is wheeled into the elevator. They head over to the doors of the ward and pull on pale-blue shoe covers.

Reidar staggers and leans against the wall. He has wondered several times if he's dreaming and tries not to let his thoughts get carried away.

They pass nurses in white uniforms.

He can hear the noise of the hospital, but inside him there is nothing but an immense silence.

At the far end of the corridor, on the right, is Room 4. He bumps into a food trolley, sending a pile of cups to the floor.

It's as if he's become detached from reality as he enters the room and sees the young man lying in bed, with a drip attached to the crook of his arm and oxygen being fed into his nose. An IV bag hangs from the drip stand next to a white heart monitor attached to his left index finger.

Reidar stops and feels himself lose control of his face. Reality returns like a deafening torrent of emotions.

"Mikael," Reidar says gently.

The young man opens his eyes, and Reidar can see how much he resembles his mother. He puts his hand against Mikael's cheek. His own mouth is trembling so much that he can hardly speak.

"Where have you been?" Reidar asks, crying.

"Dad," Mikael whispers.

His face is frighteningly pale, and his eyes are tired. Thirteen years have passed, and the child's face that Reidar has buried in his memory has become a man's face, but so skinny.

"Now I can be happy again," Reidar breathes, stroking his son's head.

38

DISA IS FINALLY back in Stockholm from an archaeological expedition to the north of Sweden. She's waiting in his apartment, on the top floor of 31 Wallin Street. Joona is on his way home from buying some turbot that he's planning to fry and serve with rémoulade sauce.

All the lights of the city look like misty lanterns. As he passes Kammakar Street, he hears agitated voices up ahead. This is a dark part of the city. Rows of parked cars throw shadows. Dull buildings, streaked with snowmelt.

"I want my money," a gruff voice is shouting.

There are two figures in the distance, moving slowly along the railings toward the Dala steps. Joona walks toward them.

The two men are panting, staring at each other, hunched, drunk, and angry. One is wearing a checkered jacket and a fur hat. In his hand is a small, shiny knife.

"Fucking bastard," he rasps. "Fucking little—"

The other one has a full beard and a black overcoat with a tear on one shoulder and is waving an empty wine bottle in front of him.

"I want my money back, with interest," the bearded man repeats.

"Get away from me," the other man says, spitting blood on the snow.

A thickset woman in her sixties is leaning against a blue box of rock salt for the steps. The tip of her cigarette glows, lighting up her puffy face.

The man with the bottle backs under the snow-covered branches of a big tree. The other man stumbles after him. The knife blade flashes as he stabs the air. The bearded man moves backward, waving the bottle and hitting the other man in the head. The bottle breaks, and green glass flies around the fur hat. Joona has an impulse to reach for his pistol, even though he knows it's locked away in the gun cabinet.

The man with the knife stumbles but manages to stay on his feet. The other is holding the jagged remains of the bottle.

There's a scream. Joona jumps over the piled-up snow at the curb.

The bearded man slips on something and falls flat on his back. He's fumbling with his hand on the railing at the top of the steps.

"My money," he repeats with a cough.

Joona sweeps some snow off a parked car and presses it to make a snowball.

The man in the checkered jacket with the knife in his hand sways as he approaches the prone man.

"I'll cut you open and stuff you with your money—"

Joona throws the snowball and hits the man holding the knife in the back of the neck. There's a dull thud as the snow breaks up and flies in all directions.

"Shit," the man says, confused, as he turns around.

"Snowball fight, gentlemen!" Joona shouts, forming a new ball.

The man with the knife looks at him with a spark in his eye.

Joona throws again and hits the man on the ground in the middle of the chest, spraying snow in his face.

The man with the knife looks down at him, then laughs unkindly: "The snowman."

The man on the ground throws some loose snow up at him. The man with the knife backs off and puts the knife away. He is forming a snowball. The bearded man rises unsteadily, clinging to the railing.

"I'll get you," says the man packing the snowball.

He takes aim at the bearded man but abruptly turns around and throws it at Joona instead, hitting him on the shoulder.

For several minutes, snowballs fly in all directions. Joona slips and falls. The bearded man loses his hat, and the other man rushes over and fills it with snow.

The woman claps her hands, and is rewarded with a snowball to her forehead that sticks there like a white bump. The bearded man bursts out laughing and falls backward into a pile of old Christmas trees. The man in the checkered jacket kicks some snow over him but gives up. He's panting as he turns to look at Joona.

"Where the hell did you come from?" he asks.

"National Crime," Joona replies, brushing the snow from his clothes.

"The police?"

"You took my child," the woman mutters.

Joona picks up the fur hat and shakes the snow off before handing it to the man in the jacket.

"Thanks."

"I saw the shooting star," the drunken woman goes on, looking Joona in the eye. "I saw it when I was seven. And I wish you'd burn in the fires of hell and scream like—"

"You shut your mouth," the man in the checkered jacket shouts. "I'm glad I didn't stab my little brother, and—"

"I want my money," the other man calls with a smile.

39

THERE'S A LIGHT on in the bathroom when Joona gets home. He opens the door slightly and sees Disa lying in the bath with her eyes closed. She's surrounded by bubbles and is humming to herself. Her muddy clothes are in a big heap on the bathroom floor.

"I thought they'd locked you up in prison," Disa says. "I was ready to take over your apartment."

Over the winter, Joona has been under investigation by the Prosecution Authority's national unit for internal investigations, accused of wrecking a long-term surveillance operation and exposing the Security Police's rapid-response unit to danger.

"Apparently, I'm guilty," he replies, picking up her clothes and putting them in the washing machine.

"I said that right from the start."

"Yes, well . . ."

Joona's eyes have turned as gray as a rainy sky.

"Is it something else?"

"A long day," he replies, and goes out into the kitchen.

"Don't go."

When he doesn't come back, she climbs out of the bath, dries herself, and puts on a thin robe. The beige silk clings to her warm body.

Joona is standing in the kitchen, frying some baby potatoes golden brown, when she comes in.

"What happened?"

Joona glances at her. "One of Jurek Walter's victims has been found alive. He's been held captive all this time."

She takes a moment to process what he's said. "So you were right—there was an accomplice."

"Yes," he sighs.

Disa steps toward him, then gently rests her palm flat against the small of his back.

"Can you catch him?"

"I hope so," Joona says seriously. "I haven't had the chance to question the boy properly. He's not in a good state. But he should be able to lead us there."

Joona takes the frying pan off the heat, then turns and looks at her.

"What is it?" she asks, alarmed.

"Disa, you have to say yes to the archaeological research project in Brazil."

"I told you, I don't want to go," she says, then realizes what he means. "You can't think like that. I don't give a damn about Jurek Walter. I'm not scared. I won't be governed by fear."

He gently brushes aside the wet hair that has fallen over her face.

"Only for a little while," he says. "Until I get this sorted out."

She leans against his chest and hears the muffled double beat of his heart.

"There's never been anyone but you," she says. "When you stayed with me after your family's accident, well, that was . . . you know, that was when I . . . fell for you, as they say. But it's true."

"I'm worried about you."

She strokes his arm and whispers that she doesn't want

to go. When her voice breaks, he pulls her to him and kisses her.

"But we've seen each other through." Disa says, looking into his face. "I mean, if there's an accomplice who's a threat to us, why hasn't anything happened? It doesn't make sense."

"I know. I agree, but . . . I have to do this. I'm going after him, and it's happening now."

Disa can feel a sob rising in her throat. She fights it back down and turns her face away. Once she had been Summa's friend. That was how they met. And when his life fell apart, she was there.

He moved in and stayed with her for a while when things were at their very worst for him. At night, he would sleep on her sofa, and she would hear him moving around and knew that he knew she was lying awake in the next room. That he was looking at the door to her bedroom and thinking about her lying in there, more and more confused and hurt by how distant he was being, how cold. Until, one night, he got up, got dressed, and left her apartment.

"I'm staying." Disa wipes the tears from her face.

"You have to go."

"Why?"

"Because I love you," he says. "You must know that."

"Do you really think I'd go now?" she asks with a smile.

40

Jurek Walter is visible on one of the nine squares of the huge monitor. He paces the dayroom, walking around the sofa, then turning left past the television. He goes around the treadmill, turns left again, and walks back into his room.

Anders Rönn watches him from above on the screen.

Jurek washes his face and sits down on the plastic chair without drying himself. He stares at the door to the corridor as the water drips onto his shirt and dries.

My, the nurse, is sitting in the operator's chair. She checks the time, waits another thirty seconds, looks at Jurek, makes a note of his location on the computer, and locks the door from Jurek's room to the dayroom.

"He's getting cigarettes this evening. He likes that," she says.

"He does?"

Anders Rönn already thinks that the routines surrounding this one patient are so repetitive and static that it would be hard to tell the days apart if it weren't for the daily meeting up on Ward 30. The other doctors talk about their patients and care plans. He doesn't need to say anything. No one even expects him to repeat that the situation in the secure unit is unchanged.

"Have you ever tried talking to the patient?" Anders asks.

"With Jurek? We're not allowed to," she replies, and scratches her tattooed arm. "It's because . . . well, he says things you can't forget."

Anders hasn't spoken to Jurek Walter since that first day. He just makes sure that the patient gets his regular injection of neuroleptic drugs.

"Do you know if the computer system is working?" Anders asks. "I couldn't sign out of the medical records."

"In that case, you're not allowed to go home," she says.

"But I—"

"I'm joking," she says, laughing. "The computers down here are always crashing."

She gets up, grabs her bottle of Fanta from the desk, and goes out into the corridor. Anders sees that Jurek is still sitting completely motionless with his eyes open.

He follows My. When she reaches the brightly lit office he notices that her red underwear is visible through the white fabric of her scrubs.

"Now, let's see," she mutters, sitting in his chair and rousing the computer from standby mode. With a grin, she forces the program to close and logs in again.

Anders thanks her and asks her to restock the medication trolley if she has time.

"Don't forget to sign the requisition orders afterward," he says, then leaves.

He walks around the corner into the changing room. The ward is completely silent. He doesn't know what drives him to do it, but he opens My's locker and starts to rummage through her gym bag with trembling hands. He unfolds a damp T-shirt and a pair of pale-gray jogging pants, and finds a pair of sweaty underpants. He takes them out, lifts them to his face, and breathes in her scent. Suddenly it dawns on him that My could see him on the monitor the moment she returned to the control room.

41

WHEN ANDERS GETS HOME, the house is quiet and the light is off in Agnes's room. He locks the door behind him and goes into the kitchen. Petra is standing at the sink, rinsing the blender.

She's wearing baggy stay-at-home clothes: a Chicago White Sox T-shirt that's too big for her and yellow leggings that she's pulled up to her knees. Anders walks up behind her and puts his arms around her, smelling her hair and fresh deodorant. She's about to pull away when he moves his hands up to cup her heavy breasts.

"How's Agnes?" he asks, letting go of her.

"She has a new best friend at preschool," Petra says. "A little boy who started last week. Apparently, he's in love with her. I don't know if it's reciprocated, but she let him give her some LEGOs."

"Sounds like love," he says, sitting down.

"Tired?"

"I wouldn't mind a glass of wine—do you want one?" he asks.

"Want one?"

She smiles more broadly than she has for a long time.

"What do you mean by that?" he asks.

"Does what I want matter?" she whispers.

He shakes his head, and she looks at him with twinkling

eyes. They leave the kitchen and go silently into the bedroom. Anders locks the door to the hallway and watches as Petra opens the mirrored wardrobe door and pulls out a drawer. She removes a bundle of underwear and takes out a bag.

"So that's where you hide everything?"

"You're not supposed to make me feel embarrassed, now," she says.

He pulls the duvet aside, and Petra empties the contents of the bag, all the things they bought after she'd read *Fifty Shades of Grey*. He picks up the soft rope and ties her hands, loops it through the slatted headboard, then tightens it, making her fall onto her back with her hands above her head. He ties the rope to the bottom of the bed with two half-hitch knots. She parts her legs and squirms as he pulls off her leggings and underwear.

He loosens the rope again, loops it around her left ankle and ties it to the bedpost, then pulls it around the other post and ties her right ankle.

He pulls the rope, making her legs slowly spread open.

She's looking at him, her cheeks flushed.

He pulls harder and forces her thighs apart as far as they'll go.

"Careful," she says quickly.

"Keep quiet," he tells her, and sees her smile to herself.

He fastens the rope, then moves up the bed and pulls her T-shirt over her face so she can't see him. Her breasts sway as she tries to get the fabric off her face.

There's no way she can get loose—she's entirely helpless in this position, with her arms over her head and her legs pulled so far apart that her inner thighs must be aching.

Anders just stands there, watching her shake her head, and feels his heart beat faster, harder. Slowly he undoes his trousers as he sees her crotch start to glisten.

42

Joona enters the patient's room and sees an older man sitting by the boy's bed. It takes him a few seconds to recognize Reidar Frost. Though it's been years since he last saw him, Reidar has aged considerably more than that. The young man is asleep, but Reidar is sitting there holding his left hand in both of his.

"You never believed my children had drowned," the father says in a muted voice.

"No," Joona replies.

Reidar's gaze rests on Mikael's sleeping face. He turns to Joona and says, "Thank you for not telling me about the murderer."

Joona's suspicion that Mikael and Felicia Kohler-Frost had been among Jurek Walter's victims had been strengthened by the fact that it was due to the children's disappearance that he had been tracked down and arrested: he had first been spotted below their mother's window.

Joona looks at the young man's thin face, his straggly beard, his sunken cheeks, and the beads of sweat on his forehead.

When Mikael spoke about the way things were at the start, when Rebecka Mendel was there, he had been talking about the period shortly after his disappearance. This would have coincided with the first few weeks of Jurek Walter's incarceration, Joona thinks.

Since then, more than a decade of imprisonment has gone by. But Mikael managed to escape—it must be possible to find out where he was held.

"I never stopped looking," Joona says quietly to Reidar.

Reidar looks at his son, and his face cracks into an uncontrollable smile. He has been sitting like that for hours and still can't get enough of just gazing at his child.

"They're saying he's going to be fine. They've promised—they've promised there's nothing wrong with him," he says in a rough voice.

"Have you talked to him?" Joona asks.

"He's on a lot of painkillers, so he's mostly been asleep, but they say that's good; it's what he needs."

"I'm sure it is," Joona agrees.

"He's going to be fine. Mentally, I mean. It will just take a bit of time."

"Has he said anything at all?"

"Nothing I can understand," Reidar says. "He just sounds confused. But he recognized me."

Joona knows it's important to get him talking right from the outset. Remembering is a crucial part of the healing process. Mikael needs time, but he can't be left to himself. As time goes by, the questions can gradually probe deeper, but there's always the risk that a traumatized person will shut off entirely.

It could take months to map out everything that's happened, but he does need to ask the most important question today. If he can just get a name or a decent description of the accomplice, this nightmare could be over.

"I have to talk to him as soon as he wakes up," Joona says. "I need to ask him a few very specific questions, but he might find it a little difficult."

"As long as it doesn't frighten him," Reidar says. "I can't let that happen."

A nurse comes in and says hello, then checks Mikael's pulse and oxygen levels.

"His hands have gone cold," Reidar tells her.

"I'm going to give him something for the fever soon," the nurse assures him.

"He is getting antibiotics, isn't he?"

"Yes, but it can be a couple of days before those start to work," the nurse says as she hangs a new bag on the drip stand.

Reidar helps her, standing up and holding the tube out of the way to make it easier for her, then walks to the door with her.

"I want to talk to the doctor," he says.

Mikael sighs and whispers something to himself. Reidar stops and turns around. Joona leans forward and tries to hear what he's saying.

43

MIKAEL'S BREATHING has sped up, and he's tossing his head, his mouth moving. He opens his eyes and stares at Joona with a haunted expression.

"You have to help me. I can't lie here," he says. "I can't take it, I can't take it, my sister's waiting for me, I can feel her, I can feel . . ."

Reidar hurries over and takes his hand, holds it to his own cheek.

"Mikael, I know," he whispers, then gulps hard.

"Dad—"

"I know, Mikael. I think about her all the time."

"Dad," Mikael cries with anguish. "I can't, I can't, I . . ."

"Calm down," Reidar murmurs.

"She's alive, Felicia's alive," he cries. "I can't lie here, I've got to . . ."

He lets out a long, rattling cough. Reidar holds up his head and tries to help him. He keeps saying soothing things to his son, but Mikael's eyes are burning with boundless panic.

He sinks back into the pillow as tears run down his cheeks.

"What were you saying about Felicia?" Reidar asks quietly.

"I don't want to," Mikael gasps. "I can't just lie here—"

"Mikael," Reidar interrupts. "You need to be clearer."

"I can't take it—"

"You said that Felicia is alive," Reidar says carefully. "Why did you say that?"

"I left her. I left her behind," Mikael sobs. "I ran, and I left her behind."

"Are you saying that Felicia is still alive?" Reidar asks, for the third time.

"Yes, Dad," Mikael mumbles.

"Dear God," his father whispers, stroking his son's head. "Dear God."

Mikael coughs violently. A cloud of blood billows into the tube, and he gasps for air, then coughs again, and lies there panting.

"We were together the whole time, Dad. In the darkness, on the floor. But I left her."

Mikael falls silent, as though every last drop of strength has been exhausted. His eyes are unreadable.

"You have to tell us. . . ."

Reidar's voice cracks. He takes a deep breath and then goes on: "Mikael, you know you have to tell us where she is, so I can go and get her."

"She's still there. Felicia's still there," Mikael says weakly. "She's still there. I can feel her. She's scared."

"Mikael," Reidar pleads.

"She's scared, because she's on her own. She always wakes up at night crying until she realizes that I'm there."

Reidar feels his chest tighten. Big patches of sweat have formed under the arms of his shirt.

44

As Reidar listens to Mikael, one thought consumes his mind: He has to find Felicia. She must not be left on her own.

He walks over to the window and stares into the middle distance. Far below, some sparrows are sitting in the bare rosebushes. Dogs have pissed in the snow under a lamppost. Over at the bus stop, a glove is lying beneath the bench.

Somewhere behind him, he hears Joona Linna posing questions to Mikael. Joona's deep voice merges with the heavy thud of Reidar's heartbeat.

You only see your mistakes in hindsight, and some of them are so painful that you can hardly live with yourself. Reidar knows that he was an unfair father. That was never his intention; it just turned out that way. People always say that they love their children equally, he thinks. Yet we still treat them differently.

Mikael was his favorite.

Felicia always irritated him, and sometimes she made him so angry that he frightened her. Now it seems incomprehensible. After all, he was an adult and she was just a child.

I shouldn't have shouted at her, he thinks, staring out the overcast sky. His left armpit is really starting to hurt

"I can feel her," Mikael is telling Joona. "She's just lying there on the floor. She's so terrified."

Reidar lets out a groan as he feels a burst of pain in his chest. Sweat is running down his neck. Joona rushes over to him, grabs the top of his arm, and says something.

"It's nothing," Reidar says.

"Does your chest hurt?" Joona asks.

"I'm just tired," he replies quickly.

"You seem—"

"I have to find Felicia," he says.

A burning pain shoots through his jaw, and he feels another stab in his chest. He falls, hitting his cheek against the radiator, but all he can think about is how, the day she disappeared, he shouted at Felicia and told her she didn't deserve to be in a nice home.

He gets to his knees and is trying to crawl when he hears Joona rush back into the room with a doctor.

45

JOONA TALKS to Reidar's doctor, then returns to Mikael's room, hangs his jacket on the hook behind the door, pulls up the only chair, and sits down.

He has to get Mikael to talk about his memories.

An hour later, Mikael wakes up. He opens his eyes slowly, squinting against the light. As Joona repeats that his father's not in any danger, he shuts his eyes again.

"I need to ask you a question," Joona says seriously.

"My sister," he says.

Joona puts his cell phone on the bedside table and starts to record.

"Mikael, I have to ask you: do you know who was holding you captive?"

"It wasn't like that."

"Like what?"

"He just wanted us to sleep, that was all. We had to sleep."

"Who?"

"The Sandman," Mikael whispers.

"What did you say?"

"Nothing . . . I can't go on. . . ."

Joona looks down at his phone and checks that it's recording the conversation.

"I thought you mentioned the Sandman?" he presses. "You mean like Wee Willie Winkie, putting the children to sleep?"

Mikael looks him in the eye.

"He's real," he says. "He smells like sand. . . . He sells barometers during the day."

"What does he look like?"

"It's always dark when he comes."

"You must have seen something, surely?"

Mikael shakes his head, sobbing silently, his tears running onto the pillow.

"Does the Sandman have another name?" Joona asks.

"I don't know. He never says a word. He never spoke to us."

"Can you describe him?"

"I've only heard him in the darkness. His fingertips are made of porcelain, and when he takes the sand out of the bag they tinkle against each other, and . . ."

Mikael's mouth is moving, but no sound comes out.

"I can't hear what you're saying," Joona says.

"He throws sand in children's faces, and a moment later you're asleep."

"How do you know it's a man?" Joona asks.

"I've heard him cough," Mikael replies.

"But you never saw him?"

"No."

46

A VERY BEAUTIFUL WOMAN with Indian features is standing looking down at Reidar when he comes around. She explains that he's had a coronary spasm.

"I thought I was having a heart attack," he mutters.

"Naturally, we're considering X-raying the coronary arteries, and—"

"Yes," he sighs, sitting up.

"You need to rest."

"I found out . . . that my . . ." he says. but his mouth starts to tremble so much that he can't finish the sentence.

She touches his cheek and smiles as if he were an unhappy child.

"I have to see my son," he explains in a slightly steadier voice.

"You understand that you can't leave the hospital before we've investigated your symptoms," she says.

She gives him a small pink bottle of nitroglycerin for him to spray under his tongue at the first sign of pain in his chest.

Reidar walks to Ward 66, but before he reaches Mikael's room, he stops in the corridor and leans against the wall.

When he enters the room, Joona stands up and offers him the chair. His phone is still next to the bed.

"Mikael, you have to help me find her," he says as he sits down.

"Dad, what happened?" his son asks.

"It's nothing," Reidar replies, trying to smile. "The doctor says there's a bit of an issue with my arteries, but I don't believe that. Anyway, it doesn't matter. We have to find Felicia."

"She was convinced you wouldn't care. I said that that wasn't true, but she was sure you'd only be looking for me."

Reidar sits motionless. He knows what Mikael means, because he's never forgotten what happened on that last day. His son puts his bony hand on Reidar's, and their eyes meet once more.

"You were walking from Södertälje—is that where I should start looking?" Reidar asks. "Is that where she might be?"

"I don't know," Mikael says.

"But you must remember something," Reidar goes on.

"I don't. I'm sorry," his son says. "There's nothing to remember."

Joona is leaning on the end of the bed. Mikael's eyes are half open, and he's clutching his father's hand tightly.

"You said before that you and Felicia were together, on the floor, in the darkness," Joona begins.

"Yes," Mikael whispers.

"How long was it just the two of you? When did the others disappear?"

"I don't know," he replies. "I can't say. Time doesn't work the way you think."

"Describe the room."

Mikael looks into Joona's gray eyes with a tortured expression.

"I never saw the room," he says. "Apart from, at the start, when I was little . . . there was a bright light that was sometimes switched on, when we could look at each other. But I don't remember what the room looked like. I was just scared."

"But you do remember something?"

"The darkness. There was almost nothing but darkness."

"There must have been a floor," Joona says.

"Yes," Mikael whispers.

"Go on," Reidar says softly.

Mikael looks away from the two men. He stares into space as he starts to talk about the room he was trapped in for so long.

"The floor . . . It was hard and cold. Maybe five meters one way, three meters the other. And the walls were made of solid concrete. There was no echo when you hit them."

47

REIDAR SQUEEZES HIS HAND. Mikael closes his eyes and lets the images and memories guide his words.

"There's a sofa, and a mattress that we pull away from the drain when we need to use the tap," he says, gulping hard.

"The tap," Joona repeats.

"And the door . . . It's made of iron or steel. It's never open. I've never seen it open. There's no lock on the inside, no handle . . . and next to the door there's a hole in the wall. That's where the bucket of food appears. It's only a little hole, but if you stick your arm in and reach up, you can feel a metal hatch with your fingertips."

Reidar sobs as he listens to Mikael.

"We try to save the food," he says, "but sometimes it runs out. Sometimes it would take so long that we'd just lie there listening for the hatch, and when we did get something we'd end up being sick . . . and sometimes there was no water in the tap. . . . We got thirsty, and the drain started to smell."

"What sort of food was it?" Joona asks.

"Just scraps, mainly. Bits of sausage, potato, carrot, onions. Macaroni."

"The person who gave you the food—he never said anything?"

"In the beginning, we would scream for help whenever the hatch opened, but then it would slam shut and we would go without food. After that, we tried talking to whoever opened it, but we never got an answer. We always listened. . . . We could hear breathing, shoes on a concrete floor—the same shoes every time."

Joona checks that the recording is still working. He can hardly fathom the extreme isolation that the siblings have endured.

"You heard him moving around," Joona says. "Did you ever hear anything else from outside?"

"What do you mean?"

"Birds, dogs barking, cars, trains, voices, airplanes, TV, laughter, shouting, sirens? Anything at all?"

"Just the smell of sand."

The sky outside the hospital window is dark now, and hailstones are falling against the glass.

"What did you do when you were awake?"

"Nothing. Well, when we were still little, I managed to pull a loose screw out of the bottom of the sofa. We used it to scratch a hole in the wall. The screw got so hot it almost burned our fingers. We kept going for ages. There was nothing but cement at first, but then, after five centimeters or so, we hit some metal mesh. We kept going through one of the gaps, and a short distance further on we hit more mesh. It was impossible. . . . It's impossible to escape from the capsule."

"Why do you call the room 'the capsule'?"

Mikael smiles in a way that makes him look incredibly lonely.

"It was Felicia who started that. She imagined we were out in space, that we were on a mission. . . . That was back in the beginning, but I went on thinking of the room as the capsule."

Reidar raises a trembling hand to his mouth. His face struggles with emotion.

"You say it's impossible to escape, yet that's precisely what you did," Joona says.

48

Carlos Eliasson, head of the National Crime Unit, is walking through a light snow shower from a meeting in Rådhuset and talking to his wife on the phone. Right now, police headquarters looks like a summer palace in a wintry park. The hand holding the phone is so cold that his fingers ache.

"I'm going to be deploying a lot of resources."

"Are you sure Mikael's going to get better?"

"Physically, absolutely."

Carlos stamps the snow from his shoes when he reaches the pavement.

"That's fantastic," she murmurs.

He hears her sigh as she sits down on a chair.

"I can't tell them about my last conversation with Mikael's mother," he says after a brief pause. "I just can't, can I?"

"No," she replies.

"What if it turns out to be crucial to the investigation?" he asks.

"You can't," she says gravely.

Carlos continues up Kungsholms Street and glances at his watch; he hears his wife tell him that she's got to go. "See you tonight," she says quietly.

Over the years, police headquarters has been extended,

one piece at a time. The various sections reflect changes in fashion. The most recent part is up by Kronoberg Park. That's where the National Crime Unit is based.

Carlos goes through two different security doors, walks past the covered inner courtyard, and takes the elevator up to the eighth floor. There's a worried expression on his face as he removes his coat and walks past the row of closed doors. A newspaper clipping on a noticeboard flutters in his wake. It's been there since the evening the police choir was voted off *Sweden's Got Talent*.

There are already five other officers in the meeting room. On the pine table are glasses and bottles of water. The yellow curtains have been drawn back, and snow-covered treetops are visible through the low windows. The officers are all doing their best to appear upbeat, but beneath the surface their thoughts have taken a darker turn. The meeting that Joona has called is due to start in two minutes. Benny Rubin has taken off his shoes and is telling Magdalena Ronander what he thinks of the new security evaluations.

Carlos shakes hands with Nathan Pollock from National Homicide Commission. As usual, Nathan is wearing a dark-gray jacket, and his gray ponytail hangs down his back. Beside him sits Anja Larsson in a silver blouse and pale-blue skirt.

"Anja's been trying to modernize us. We're supposed to learn how to use the Analyst's Notebook program." Nathan smiles. "But we're too old for that."

"Speak for yourself," Tommy Kofoed, the forensic technician, mutters sullenly.

"You smell a bit like mothballs," Anja jokes. "You do all look like you've been around the block a few times."

Carlos stands at the end of the table, and the somber look on his face makes even Benny shut up.

"Welcome, all of you," Carlos says, without his usual smile.

"As you may have heard, some new information has come to light concerning Jurek Walter, and, well, the preliminary investigation can no longer be regarded as concluded."

"What did I tell you?" a quiet voice with a Finnish accent says.

49

CARLOS TURNS AROUND and sees Joona Linna standing in the doorway. The tall detective's black coat is sparkling with snow.

"Joona isn't always right, of course," Carlos says. "But I have to admit, this time ..."

"So Joona was the only person who thought Jurek Walter had an accomplice?" Nathan Pollock asks.

"Well, yes."

"And a lot of people got very upset when he said Samuel Mendel's family were among the victims," Anja says quietly.

"True." Carlos nods. "Joona did some excellent work, no question. I'd only recently been appointed back then, and perhaps I didn't listen to the right people, but now we know. And now we can go on to ..."

He falls silent and looks at Joona, who steps into the room.

"I've just come from Södermalm Hospital," he says curtly.

"Have I said something wrong?" Carlos asks.

"No."

"Perhaps you think there's something else I should say?" Carlos asks, looking embarrassed as he glances at the others. "Joona, it was thirteen years ago. It's water under the bridge now, isn't it?"

"Yes."

"And you were absolutely right back then, as I just said."

"What was I right about?" Joona asks, looking at his boss.

"What were you right about?" Carlos repeats forcefully. "You were right that Jurek had an accomplice. You were right about everything, Joona. Is that enough now? I think that's probably enough."

Anja turns away to hide her smile. Joona nods, and Carlos sits down with a sigh.

"Mikael Kohler-Frost's general condition is already much better, and I've questioned him a couple of times. Naturally, I was hoping that Mikael would be able to identify the accomplice."

"Maybe it's too soon," Nathan says.

"No. Mikael can't give us a name or a description. He can't even give us a voice, but—"

"Is he traumatized?" Magdalena Ronander asks.

"Yes, he's traumatized, but he's simply never seen him," Joona says, meeting her gaze.

"So we've got nothing at all to go on?" Carlos whispers.

Joona steps forward. His shadow falls across the table.

"Mikael calls his kidnapper the Sandman. I asked Reidar Frost about it, and he explained that the name comes from a bedtime story the children's mother used to tell them. The Sandman is some sort of personification of sleep. He throws sand in children's eyes to make them fall asleep."

"That's right," Magdalena says with a smile. "And the proof that the Sandman has been there are the little gritty deposits at the corners of your eyes when you wake up."

"The Sandman," Pollock says thoughtfully, and jots something down in his black notebook.

"Anja, can you play this recording for me?" Joona asks.

She takes Joona's phone and connects it to the wireless sound system.

"Mikael and Felicia Kohler-Frost are half German. Rose-anna Kohler moved to Sweden from Schwabach when she was eight years old," Joona explains.

"That's south of Nuremburg," Carlos adds.

"The Sandman is their version of Wee Willie Winkie," Joona goes on. "And every evening, before the children said their prayers, she would tell them a little more about him. Over the years, she mixed up the story from her own child-hood with a lot of things she made up herself, and with frag-ments from E. T. A. Hoffmann's original short story about the barometer salesman and the mechanical girls. Mikael and Felicia were only ten and eight years old, and they thought it was the Sandman who had taken them."

The men and women sitting around the table watch Anja prepare the recording of Mikael's account. Their faces are sol-emn. For the first time, they're about to hear a surviving vic-tim of Jurek Walter talk about what happened.

"In other words, we can't identify the accomplice," Joona says. "Which leaves the location. If Mikael can lead us back there, then . . ."

50

As they listen, Nathan Pollock takes notes and Magdalena Ronander types nonstop on her laptop.

There's a hiss from the loudspeakers, and certain sounds, like the rustle of paper, are emphasized, while others are barely audible. At times, Reidar's sobbing can be heard.

"You say it's impossible to escape," they hear Joona say. "Yet that's precisely what you did."

"It *is* impossible. It wasn't like that," Mikael Kohler-Frost replies.

"How was it, then?"

"The Sandman blew his dust over us, and when I woke up I realized I wasn't in the capsule anymore," Mikael says. "It was completely dark, but I could hear that the room was different and could tell that Felicia wasn't there. I felt my way forward until I came to a door with a handle, and I opened it and found myself in a corridor. I don't think I was aware that I was escaping, I just knew I had to keep moving. I came to a locked door and thought I'd ended up in a trap, because the Sandman might have come back any second. . . . I panicked and broke the glass with my hand and reached through to unlock it. I ran across a storeroom full of boxes and bags of cement, and then I saw that the wall to the right was nothing more than a plastic sheet stapled in place. I was having trouble breathing, and I could feel my fingers bleeding as I tried to pull down the plastic. I knew I'd hurt myself on the glass, but I didn't care; I just kept going across a big concrete floor. The room wasn't finished, and I kept going until I found myself walking on snow. The sky wasn't completely dark yet. I saw that the world actually existed. You know, before, the thought of it was like a dream, but now it just felt natural—the air, the landscape. I ran past a backhoe with a blue star on it and went into the forest and started to realize that I was free. I ran through trees and undergrowth and got covered in snow. I never looked back, just kept on going, across a field and up into a clump of trees, and suddenly I couldn't go any further. A broken branch had jabbed straight into my thigh. I was completely stuck, I couldn't move. Blood was running down into the snow, and it hurt badly. I tried to pull free, but I was stuck. . . . I thought I might be able to break the branch, but I was too weak; I just couldn't do it. So I stood there. I was sure I could hear the Sandman's porcelain fingers clicking. When I turned to look behind me, I slipped and the branch came out. I don't know if I passed out. . . . I was much slower after that, but I got to my feet and walked up a slope. I was stumbling and kept thinking I couldn't go any further. Then I was crawling, and I found myself on a railroad track. I have no idea how long I walked. I was freezing, but I kept going. Occasionally, I could see houses in the distance, but I was so exhausted that I stuck to the tracks. . . . It was snowing more and more, but it was like I was walking in a trance; it never occurred to me to stop. I just wanted to get away."

51

WHEN MIKAEL has stopped talking and the hissing noise from the speakers has ceased, there's total silence in the meeting room. Carlos stands up. He's biting one of his thumbnails as he stares blankly into space.

"We abandoned two children," he eventually says. "They were missing, but we said that they were dead and just went on with our lives."

"We were actually convinced that that was true, though," Benny says gently.

"Joona wanted to carry on," murmurs Anja.

"But in the end, even I didn't believe they were still alive," says Joona.

"And there was nothing left to go on," Pollock points out. "No evidence, no witnesses."

Carlos's cheeks are pale as he puts a hand to his neck and tries to undo the top button of his shirt.

"But they were alive," he says, almost in a whisper.

"Yes," Joona replies.

"I've seen a lot, but this . . ." Carlos says, tugging at his collar again. "I just can't understand why. I mean, why the hell? I don't get it, I just . . ."

"There's nothing to get," Anja says kindly.

"Why would anyone keep two children locked up for all

those years?" he goes on, his voice raised. "Making sure that they survived, but nothing more, no blackmail, no violence, no abuse. . . ."

Anja tries to lead him from the room, but he resists and grabs Nathan Pollock's arm.

"Find the girl," he says. "Whatever you do, find her today."

"I'm not sure—"

"Find her!" Carlos cuts in, then lets Anja guide him from the meeting room.

Anja returns shortly afterward. The members of the group mutter and look through their papers. Benny is sitting with his mouth open, absentmindedly poking at Magdalena's gym bag with his toes.

"What's wrong with you all?" Anja asks sharply. "Didn't you hear what the boss said?"

The group quickly agrees that Magdalena should put together a response team and a forensics unit while Joona tries to identify a preliminary search area to the south of Södertälje Station.

Joona studies a printout of the last picture that was taken of Felicia. He doesn't know how many times he's looked at it. Her eyes are big and dark, and her long black hair is draped over her shoulder in a loose braid. She's holding a riding hat and smiling shrewdly at the camera.

"Mikael Kohler-Frost says he started walking just before it got dark," Joona begins, gazing at the large-scale map on the wall. "When exactly did the train engineer raise the alarm?"

Benny checks his laptop.

"At three-twenty-two," he replies.

"They found Mikael here," Joona says, drawing a circle around the northern end of the Igelsta Bridge. "It's hard to imagine he could have been walking any faster than five kilometers an hour, if he was wounded and suffering from Legionnaires' disease."

Anja uses a ruler to measure the farthest distance Mikael could have walked from the south, at that speed and on a map of that scale, then draws a circle using a large compass. Twenty minutes later, they've managed to identify five current construction projects that could match Mikael's description.

A six-foot plasma screen is now showing a hybrid of a map and a satellite picture. Benny is still meticulously adding information to the computer connected to the plasma screen. Beside him, Anja is sitting with two telephones, gathering supplementary information, while Nathan and Joona discuss the various building sites.

Five red circles on the map mark the ongoing construction projects within the preliminary search area. Three of them are in residential areas.

Joona is standing in front of the map, his eyes following the railroad line. He points at one of the two other circles, in the forest close to Älgberget.

"This is the one," he says.

Benny clicks the circle and brings up the coordinates, and Anja reads out a short description of the building works. They are building a new server farm for Facebook, but work has been at a standstill for the past month because of environmental objections.

"Do you want me to get hold of the plans?" Anja asks.

"We'll set out immediately," Joona says.

52

THE SNOW is lying undisturbed on the bumpy track through the forest. A large area has been cleared. Pipes and wires are in place, and the drains have been installed. Ten acres of concrete foundations have been laid, and several ancillary buildings are more or less complete, though others are just shells. There's a thick layer of snow on the bulldozers and dump trucks.

During the drive to Älgberget, Joona received detailed plans on his cell phone. Anja had acquired them from the local planning department.

Magdalena Ronander examines the map with the rapid-response unit before they leave their vehicles and approach the site from three directions.

They're creeping through the edge of the forest. It's dark among the tree trunks. They swiftly take up their positions, approaching cautiously as they observe the open area.

A strange, somnolent atmosphere hangs over the place. A large backhoe is parked in front of a gaping shaft.

Marita Jakobsson, a middle-aged police superintendent with years of experience, runs over and crouches down beside a pile of blasting mats. She carefully scans the buildings through her binoculars before waving the rest of the group forward.

Joona draws his pistol and heads toward a low building

with the others. Snow is blowing off the roof and drifting through the air.

They're all wearing bulletproof vests and helmets, and two of them are carrying Heckler & Koch assault rifles.

They pass an unfinished wall and head up onto the bare concrete foundations.

Joona points toward a sheet of protective plastic that's flapping in the wind. It's hanging loose between two struts.

The group follows Marita through a storeroom and over to a door whose window has been smashed. There are black bloodstains on the floor and sill of the door.

There's no doubt that this is the place Mikael escaped from.

The glass crunches beneath their boots. They creep into the corridor, opening door after door and securing each room in turn.

They're vacant.

In one room is a crate of empty bottles, but otherwise there's nothing.

So far, it's impossible to tell which room Mikael was in when he woke up, but everything suggests that it was one of the rooms along this corridor.

The rapid-response unit members sweep efficiently through each room before withdrawing to their vehicles.

Now Forensics can get to work.

The forest is also searched with dog patrols.

Joona is standing with his helmet in his hand, looking at the snow as it sparkles on the ground. I knew we weren't going to find Felicia here, he thinks. The room that Mikael called the capsule had thick, reinforced walls, a water tap, and a hatch for food. It was constructed to hold people captive.

Joona has read Mikael's medical records and knows that the doctors found traces of the anesthetic drug sevoflurane in his soft tissues. Now he's thinking that Mikael must have been drugged and moved here while he was unconscious. That matches his description of just waking up to find himself in a different room. He fell asleep in the capsule and woke up here.

For some reason, Mikael was moved here, after all these years. Had it finally been time for him to end up in a coffin when he managed to escape?

The temperature is dropping as Joona watches the police officers return to their vehicles.

If Mikael was drugged, then there's no way he can lead them to the capsule. He never saw anything.

Nathan Pollock waves to Joona to let him know it's time to leave. Joona starts to raise his hand but gives up.

It can't end like this. It can't be over, he thinks, running his hand through his hair.

What's left to be done?

As Joona walks back toward the car, he already knows the terrifying answer to his own question.

53

Joona turns in to the garage, takes a ticket, then drives down the ramp and parks. He remains seated as a man from the carpet warehouse above gathers up shopping carts.

When he can't see anyone else in the parking lot, Joona gets out of the car and goes over to a shiny black van with tinted windows, opens the side door, and climbs in.

The door closes silently behind him, and Joona says a muted hello to Carlos Eliasson, chief of the National Crime Unit, and the head of the Security Police, Verner Zandén.

"Felicia Kohler-Frost is being held in a dark room," Carlos begins. "She's been there for more than ten years, together with her older brother. Now she's entirely alone. Are we going to abandon her? Say she's dead and leave her there?"

"Carlos," Verner says in a soothing voice.

"I know, I've lost all detachment." He smiles, raising his hands apologetically. "But I really do want us to do absolutely everything we can this time."

"I need a large team," Joona says. "If I can have fifty people, we can try to pick up all the old threads, every missing-persons case. It might not lead to anything, but it's our only chance. Mikael never saw the accomplice, and he was drugged before he was moved. He can't tell us where the capsule is.

We're going to keep talking to him, but I don't believe he knows where he's been kept for the past thirteen years."

"But if Felicia is alive, then she's probably still in the capsule," Verner says in his deep voice.

"Yes," Joona agrees.

"How the hell are we going to find her? It's impossible," Carlos says. "No one knows where the capsule is."

"No one apart from Jurek Walter," Joona says.

"Who can't be questioned," Verner says.

"No," Joona replies.

"Because he's utterly psychotic, and—"

"No, he was never that," Joona interrupts.

"All I know is what it says in the forensic medical report," Verner says. "They wrote that he was schizophrenic, psychotic, prone to chaotic thinking, and extremely violent."

"Only because that's what Jurek wanted it to say," Joona replies.

"So you think he's healthy? Is that what you mean, that there's nothing wrong with him?" Verner asks. "What the hell is this? Why wasn't he interrogated, then?"

"There are strict restrictions. He must be kept in total isolation," Carlos says. "In the verdict of the Supreme Court—"

"It must be possible to get around the terms of the sentence." Verner sighs, stretching out his long legs.

"Maybe," Carlos says.

"And I've got some very skilled people who've interrogated people suspected of terrorist—"

"Joona's the best," Carlos interrupts.

"No, I'm not," Joona responds.

"It was you who tracked down and apprehended Jurek, and you're about the only person he spoke to before his trial."

Joona shakes his head and looks out at the deserted garage through the tinted window.

"I've tried," he says slowly. "But it's impossible to fool Jurek. He isn't like other people. He isn't unhappy. He doesn't need sympathy. He won't say anything."

"Do you want to try?" Verner asks.

"I can't," says Joona.

"Why not?"

"Because I'm frightened," he replies simply.

Carlos looks at him.

"I know you're only joking," he says nervously.

Joona turns to face him. His eyes are hard and as gray as wet slate.

"Surely we have no reason to be scared of an old man who's already locked up," Verner says, scratching his head. "He should be scared of us. For God's sake, we could rush in, pin him down on the floor, and scare the shit out of him. I mean, be seriously fucking tough."

"It won't work," Joona says.

"There are methods that always work," Verner goes on. "I have a secret group who were involved in Guantánamo."

"Obviously, this meeting has never taken place," Carlos says in a hurry.

"I very rarely have meetings that have," Verner says, then leans forward. "My group knows all about waterboarding and electric shocks."

Joona shakes his head. "Jurek isn't scared of pain."

"So we just give up?"

"No," Joona says. His seat creaks as he leans back.

"What do you think we should do?" Verner asks.

"If we go in and talk to Jurek, the only thing we can be sure of is that he'll be lying. He'll steer the conversation, and once he finds out what we want with him, he'll get us to start bargaining, and we'll end up giving him something we'll only regret."

Carlos looks down and scratches his knee irritably.

"What does that leave us with?" Verner asks.

"I don't know if it's even possible," Joona says, "but if you could place an agent as a patient in the same secure psychiatric unit as—"

"I don't want to hear any more," Carlos interrupts.

"To get Jurek's attention in the first place, it would have to be someone completely convincing, an agent with true inner rage," Joona goes on.

"Christ," Verner mutters.

"A patient," Carlos whispers.

"Someone who might be useful to him. Someone he could exploit," Joona continues.

"What are you saying?"

"We need to find an agent who's so exceptional that Jurek Walter becomes curious."

"Do you have anyone in mind?" Carlos asks.

"There is only one," Joona says.

54

THE PUNCHING BAG lets out a sigh, and the chain rattles. Saga Bauer moves nimbly to one side, follows the movement of the bag with her body, and strikes again. Two blows, causing a sound that rumbles off the walls of the empty boxing gym.

She's practicing a combination of two quick left jabs—one high, one low—followed by a hard right hook.

The black punching bag sways and the hook creaks. Its shadow crosses Saga's face, and she punches again. Three rapid blows. She rolls her shoulders, moves backward, glides around the punching bag, and strikes once more.

Her long blond hair flies out with the rapid movement of her hips, flicking across her face.

Saga loses track of time when she's training, and all thoughts vanish from her head. She's been on her own in the gym for the past two hours. The last of the others left while she was doing her skipping. The lamps above the boxing ring are switched off, but the bright glow from the vending machine is shining through the doorway. There's snow swirling outside the windows, around a sign for a dry cleaner's and along the pavement.

From the corner of her eye, Saga sees a car stop in the street outside the boxing club, but she continues with the same combination of blows, trying to increase their power. Drops of sweat hit the floor next to a smaller punching bag that has been removed from its cable.

Stefan walks in. He stamps the snow from his feet, then stands quietly for a moment. His coat is undone, showing the pale suit and white shirt underneath.

She goes on punching as she sees him take off his shoes and come closer.

The only sounds are the thump of the bag and the rattle of the chain.

Saga wants to keep training. She's not ready to break her concentration yet. She lowers her brow and attacks the bag with a rapid series of punches, even though Stefan is standing right behind it.

"Harder," he says, holding the bag in place.

She throws a straight right, so hard that he has to take a step back. She can't help laughing, but before he's managed to regain his balance, she punches again.

"Give me some resistance," she says, with a hint of impatience in her voice.

"Come on, Saga. Let's go."

She fires off another salvo of punches, allowing herself to succumb to a deep well of rage. This rage makes her feel weak, but it's also what makes her keep fighting, long after others have given up.

The heavy blows rattle the chain of the punching bag. She slows herself down, even though she could go on for ages.

Panting, she takes a couple of easy steps backward. The bag continues to swing. A light shower of concrete dust falls from the catch in the ceiling.

"Okay, I'm happy now." She smiles at him, pulling off her boxing gloves with her teeth.

He follows her into the women's changing room and helps her remove the strapping from her hands.

"You hurt yourself," he murmurs.

"It's nothing," she says, looking at her hand.

Her gym clothes are wet with sweat. Her nipples are showing through her damp bra, and her muscles are swollen and pumped with blood.

Saga Bauer is an inspector with the Security Police, and she's worked with Joona Linna on two big cases. She's not just an elite-level boxer but a very good sniper, and she has been specially trained in advanced interrogation techniques.

She's twenty-seven years old, her eyes are as blue as a summer sky, she has colorful ribbons braided into her long blond hair, and she is improbably beautiful. Most people who see her are filled with a strange, helpless sense of longing.

The hot shower mists up the mirrors. Saga stands solidly with her legs apart and her arms hanging by her sides as the water washes over her. A large bruise is forming on one thigh, and the knuckles of her right hand are bleeding.

She looks up, wipes the water from her face, and sees Stefan watching her intensely.

"What are you thinking?" Saga asks.

"That it was raining the first time we had sex," he says quietly.

She remembers that afternoon well. They had been to a matinee at the movies, and when they emerged onto the street it was pouring with rain. Though they ran to his studio, they got drenched anyway. Stefan has talked about how unembarrassed she was as she undressed and hung her clothes over the radiator, then stood there picking out notes on his piano. He said that he knew he shouldn't stare but that she lit up the room like molten glass, like a princess from a fairy tale.

"Get in the shower," Saga says.

"We don't have time. We're already late for our reservation."

She looks at him with a little wrinkle between her eyebrows.

"Is that what matters to you?" she asks.

He smiles uncertainly. "What do you mean?"

"I want to know what matters to you."

Stefan holds out a towel and says, "Now's not the time for this."

55

IT'S SNOWING as they get out of the taxi at the jazz club Fasching. Saga turns her face toward the sky and feels the snow fall on her warm skin.

The cramped nightclub is already packed. Candles flicker in frosted lanterns, and snow slides down the windows facing Kungs Street.

Stefan hangs his coat on the back of a chair and goes over to the bar to order.

Saga's hair is still wet, and she shivers as she takes off her green parka, its back dark with dampness.

Stefan puts two vodka martinis and a bowl of pistachios on the table. They sit across from each other and drink a silent toast. Saga is about to say how hungry she is when a thin man in glasses comes over.

"Jacky," Stefan says, surprised.

"I thought I could smell cat piss." Jacky grins.

"This is my girl," Stefan says.

Jacky glances at Saga and nods, then whispers something to Stefan, who laughs.

"No, seriously, you've got to play with us," Jacky says. "I'm sure your little princess can take care of herself for a few minutes."

He points to the corner, where an almost black double bass and a half-acoustic Gibson guitar stand ready.

Saga can't quite hear what they're saying over the chatter of the crowd. They're talking about some legendary gig, a contract that's the best they've had so far, and a cleverly put-together quartet. She lets her eyes roam around the bar as she waits. Stefan says something to her as Jacky pulls him to his feet.

"Are you going to play?" Saga asks.

"Just one song," Stefan calls with a smile.

She waves him off. The noise in the bar subsides as Jacky takes the microphone. "Ladies and gentlemen, Stefan Johansson," he introduces.

Stefan sits down at the piano. "April in Paris," he says, and starts to play.

56

SAGA WATCHES STEFAN half close his eyes. Her skin breaks out in goose bumps as the music takes over and seems to shrink the room. The lighting is soft and shimmering.

Jacky starts to play gently ornate harmonies, and then the bass joins in.

Saga knows that Stefan loves this. But she can't let go of the fact that they'd promised just to sit and talk, for once. She'd been looking forward to this all week.

Slowly she eats the pistachios, gathering a heap of empty shells and waiting. She feels a peculiar angst because of how he walked away from her. She knows that she's being irrational and keeps telling herself not to be childish. When her drink is finished, she moves on to Stefan's. It's no longer cold, but she drinks it anyway.

She looks over at the door just as a red-cheeked man takes a picture of her with his phone. She's tired and is considering going home to sleep, but she'd really like to talk to Stefan first.

Saga has lost track of how many numbers they've played. John Scofield, Mike Stern, Charles Mingus, Dave Holland, Lars Gullin, and a long version of a song she doesn't know the name of, from that record with Bill Evans and Monica Zetterlund.

Saga looks at the heap of pale nutshells, the toothpicks in

the martini glasses, and the empty chair facing her. She goes over to the bar and gets a bottle of Grolsch, and when she's done with it she heads to the bathroom.

Some women are adjusting their makeup in front of the mirror. The stalls are all occupied, and she has to wait in line. When one of the stalls is finally free, she goes in, locks the door, sits down, and just stares at the white door.

An old memory comes to her: Her mother lying in bed, her face marked by sickness. Saga was only seven years old and was trying to comfort her, telling her everything would soon be all right, but her mother didn't want to hold her hand.

"Stop it," Saga whispers to herself, but the memory won't let go.

Her mother got worse, and Saga had to find her medication, help her take her tablets, and hold the glass of water.

Saga sat on the floor beside her mother's bed, looking up at her, fetching a blanket when she was cold, trying to call her dad each time her mom asked her to.

When her mom finally fell asleep, Saga can remember switching off the little lamp, curling up on top of the bed, and wrapping her mother's arms around her.

She doesn't usually think about this—she manages to keep her distance from the memory—but this time it's just there, and her heart is beating hard in her chest as she leaves the bathroom.

Their table is still empty; the glasses are still there, and Stefan is still playing. He's maintaining eye contact with Jacky, and they're responding playfully to each other's improvisations.

She forces her way through to the musicians. Stefan is in the middle of a long, meandering solo when she puts a hand on his shoulder.

He startles, looks at her, then shakes his head irritably. She grabs his arm.

"Let's go," she says.

"I'm playing," Stefan says through gritted teeth.

"But we agreed—" she begins.

"For God's sake," he whispers sharply.

Saga backs away and knocks over a glass of beer on top of one of the amplifiers. It falls to the floor and shatters.

Beer splashes up onto Stefan's clothes.

She stands still, but his eyes are focused solely on the keys of the piano.

She waits a moment, then returns to their table. A few men have sat down in their chairs. Her green parka is lying on the floor. She snatches it up and hurries out into the snow.

57

SAGA BAUER spends the whole of the following morning in one of the Security Police's generously proportioned meeting rooms with four other agents, three analysts, and two people from Admin. Most of them have laptops or tablets in front of them, showing a gray screen with a diagram illustrating the extent of nonwireless communication traffic across the country's borders over the past week.

Under discussion are the analytical database of the signals-intelligence unit, new search methods, and the seemingly rapid radicalization of thirty or so Islamic extremists.

"Even if Al-Shabaab have made extensive use of the Al-Qimmah network," Saga is saying, "I don't think it will give us much. Obviously, we need to continue what we're doing, but I still say we should try to infiltrate the group of women on their periphery, as I mentioned before, and—"

The door opens and the head of the Security Police, Verner Zandén, comes in, raising his hand apologetically.

"I'm sorry to interrupt," he says in his rumbling voice as he catches Saga's eye. "But I was just thinking of going for a little stroll and would very much appreciate your company."

She nods and logs out but leaves her laptop on the table to exit the meeting room with Verner.

It's extremely cold as they step out into the street, and the tiny crystals in the air are lit up by the hazy sunlight. Verner walks with long strides, and Saga hurries along beside him.

They pass Fleming Street in silence, walk through the gate to the health center, across the circular park surrounding the chapel, and down the steps toward the ice of Barnhusviken.

The situation is feeling more and more odd, but Saga refrains from asking any questions.

Verner gestures with his hands and turns left onto a bicycle path. Some small rabbits scamper for cover under the bushes as they approach. The snow-covered park benches are soft shapes in the white landscape. They turn in between two of the tall buildings lining Kungsholms Street and go up to a door. Verner taps in a code, opens the door, and leads her into the elevator.

In the scratched mirror, Saga can see snowflakes covering her hair. They're melting, forming glistening drops of water. When the creaking elevator stops, Verner takes out a key with a plastic card attached and unlocks a door that bears the telltale signs of attempted burglaries. He nods to her to follow him inside.

They walk into an entirely empty flat. Someone has recently moved out. The walls are full of holes where pictures and shelves have been removed. There are large dust balls on the floor and a forgotten IKEA Allen wrench.

The toilet flushes, and Carlos Eliasson, chief of the National Crime Unit, comes out. He wipes his hands on his trousers and shakes hands with Saga Bauer.

"Can I offer you something to drink?" Carlos asks.

He fills a couple of plastic cups with tap water and holds them out.

"Perhaps you were expecting lunch?" Carlos says as he sees the mystified look on her face.

"No, but—"

"I have some cough drops," he says, pulling out a little box.

Saga shakes her head, but Verner takes the box from Carlos, taps out a couple, and pops them into his mouth.

"Quite a party," Verner says.

Carlos clears his throat. "Saga, as you've no doubt realized, this is an extremely unofficial meeting."

"What happened?" Saga asks.

"Have you heard of Jurek Walter?"

"No."

"Not many people have, and that's just as well," Verner says.

58

A RAY OF SUNLIGHT is twinkling on the dirty kitchen window as Carlos Eliasson hands Saga Bauer a dossier. She opens the folder and finds herself staring directly into Jurek Walter's pale eyes. She moves the photograph and starts to read the thirteen-year-old report. Her face turns white, and she sits down on the floor with her back against the radiator, still reading, looking at the pictures, glancing through postmortem reports and reading the details of his unique sentence.

When she closes the file, Carlos tells her how Mikael Kohler-Frost was found wandering across the Igelsta Bridge after being missing for thirteen years.

Verner gets out his phone and plays the recording of the young man describing his captivity and escape. Saga listens to his anguished voice, and when she hears him talk about his sister, her cheeks turn red. She looks at the photograph in the folder. The little girl is standing with her loose braid and riding hat, smiling as if she were planning something mischievous.

When Mikael's voice falls silent, she stands up and paces the empty kitchen, then stops in front of the window.

"We have nothing more to go on now than they had thirteen years ago," Verner says. "We don't know anything. But Jurek Walter knows. He knows where Felicia is, and he knows who his accomplice is."

Verner explains that it's impossible to get the truth out of Jurek Walter in a conventional interrogation.

"Not even torture would work," Carlos says, leaning back against the windowsill.

"What the hell? Why don't we do what we usually do, then?" Saga asks. "Surely all we have to do is recruit just one damn informant. One of the nurses, or a psychiatrist who can—"

"Joona says—sorry to interrupt," Verner cuts in. "But Joona says that Jurek may already have influence over members of the staff. That's the way Jurek functions. It's just too risky to take a chance, since we don't know who he may have gotten to."

"So what the hell do we do?"

"Our only option is to install a trained agent as a patient in the same institution," he replies.

"Why would he talk to a patient?" Saga asks skeptically.

"Joona thinks we need to find an agent who's so exceptional that Jurek Walter ends up curious enough to want to know more."

"Curious how?"

"Curious about them as a person, and not just because they represent the possibility of getting out," Carlos replies.

"Did Joona mention me?" she asks in a serious voice.

"You're our first choice," Verner says firmly.

"Who's your second choice?"

"There isn't one," Carlos replies.

"How would this be arranged, in purely practical terms?" she asks.

"The bureaucratic machinery is already hard at work," Verner says. "One decision leads to another, and if you accept the mission, you just have to climb on board."

"Tempting," she mutters.

"We'll arrange for you to be sentenced to secure psychiatric care in the Court of Appeal and transferred at once to Karsudden Hospital."

Verner goes over to the tap and refills his plastic cup. "We spotted something that might work to our advantage, a formulation in the original County Council permit—the one that was granted when the psychiatric unit at Löwenströmska Hospital was first set up."

"It states very clearly that the ward is designed to offer treatment to three patients," Carlos adds. "But for the past thirteen years, they've had just one patient, Jurek Walter."

Verner drinks noisily, then crumples up his cup and tosses it in the sink.

"The hospital administrators have always tried to fend off other patients," Carlos goes on. "But they're perfectly aware that they have to accept more if they receive a direct request."

"Which is precisely what's happening now. The Prison Service Committee has called an extraordinary meeting, where the decision will be made to transfer one patient from the secure psychiatric unit at Säter to Löwenströmska, and another from Karsudden Hospital."

"In other words, you would be the patient from Karsudden," Carlos says.

"So, if I agree to this, I'd be admitted as a dangerous patient?" she asks.

"Yes."

"Are you going to give me a criminal record?"

"A decision from the National Judiciary Administration will probably be sufficient," Verner replies. "But we need to create an entire identity, with guilty court verdicts and psychiatric evaluations."

59

SAGA STANDS in the empty apartment with the two police chiefs. Every fiber of her being is screaming at her to say no.

"Is this illegal?" she asks. Her mouth has gone dry.

"Yes, of course. And it's extremely confidential," Carlos replies.

"Extremely?" she replies, the corner of her mouth curling.

"At National Crime, we'll be declaring it confidential, so that the Security Police can't see the file."

"And I'll make sure that it's declared confidential by the Security Police, so National Crime can't see it," Verner goes on.

"No one will know about this unless there's a direct request from the government," Carlos says.

Saga looks out of the window at the paneled façade of the neighboring building. A chimney vent glints at her, and she turns back toward the two men.

"Why are you doing this?" she asks.

"To save the girl," Carlos says, with a smile that doesn't reach his eyes.

"And I'm supposed to believe that the heads of National Crime and the Security Police are working together to—"

"I knew Roseanna Kohler," Carlos interrupts.

"The mother?"

"We were in the same class at Adolf Fredrik's Music School. We were pretty close. We—it's been very tough, very . . ."

"So this is personal?" Saga asks, taking a step back.

"No, it's . . . it's the only right thing to do. You can see that for yourself," he replies, gesturing toward the folder.

When Saga's expression doesn't change, he goes on: "But if you want me to be honest . . . I'm not sure we would have had a meeting quite like this if it wasn't personal."

He starts fiddling with the sink tap. Saga watches him and senses that he's not telling her the whole truth. "In what way is it personal?" she asks.

"It's not important," he replies hastily.

"You're sure?"

"What's important is that we actually do this. It's the right thing to do, the only right thing, because we believe the girl can still be saved."

"But we have to hurry. It's possible that she has Legionnaires' disease, like her brother," Verner says. "So the plan is to send in an agent as quickly as we possibly can—that's all, no large-scale operation."

"Obviously, we don't know if Jurek Walter's going to say anything, but there's a chance. And everything suggests that it's our only chance."

Saga stands perfectly still with her eyes closed for a long while.

"What happens if I say no?" she asks. "Will you let the girl die in that damn place?"

"We'll find another agent," Verner says.

"Go ahead, then," Saga says, and begins to walk toward the hall.

"Do you want to think about it?" Carlos calls.

She stops with her back to the two police chiefs and shakes her head. Light filters through her thick hair with the interwoven ribbons.

"No," she replies, and walks out of the apartment.

60

Saga takes the subway to Slussen, then walks the short distance to Stefan's studio on Sankt Pauls Street. She'd called him a few times, but he hadn't picked up.

She feels relieved to have declined the difficult task of infiltrating Löwenströmska and getting involved in the Jurek Walter case.

She strides up the steps and unlocks the door with the key that Stefan gave her. She can hear the sound of the piano. She goes in, sees Stefan sitting at the piano, and stops. His blue shirt is unbuttoned. He has a bottle of beer next to him, and the room smells of cigarette smoke.

"I'm sorry for walking out on you yesterday," she says after a brief pause.

He goes on playing, softly, radiantly.

"Can we talk?" she tries again.

Stefan's face is turned away, but she has no trouble hearing what he says: "I don't want to have this conversation right now."

"Look, I'm sorry," she repeats. "But you—"

"I'm playing," he interrupts.

"But we need to talk about what happened."

"Just go," he says, standing up to face her.

Saga pushes him in the chest, so forcefully that he takes a

step back and knocks over the piano stool. He stands there with his hands by his sides, looking her straight in the eye.

"This isn't working," he says simply.

He picks up the piano stool and rearranges his sheet music.

"You're overreacting," she says.

"I don't want you to be upset," he says with an emptiness in his voice that transforms her anger into dread.

"What is it?" she asks.

"This isn't working. We're always fighting. We can't be together, we . . ."

He goes quiet. She's starting to feel sick.

"Because I wanted to spend time with you last night?" she manages to say.

Stefan glances up at her.

"You're the most beautiful woman I've ever seen, and you're smart and funny, and I ought to be the happiest man alive. I'm probably going to regret this for the rest of my life, but I don't think we can be together."

"I don't understand," she whispers. "Because I got mad? Because I disturbed you when you were playing?"

"No, it's . . ."

He sits down again and shakes his head.

"I can change," she says, and looks at him for a moment before going on. "It's already too late, isn't it?"

When he nods, she turns and leaves the room. She goes out into the hallway, picks up an old stool, and throws it at the mirror. The splinters fall to the floor, shattering again as they hit the hard tiles. She shoves the front door open and runs down the stairs, straight out into the radiant blue winter light.

61

SAGA RUNS along the pavement, between the buildings and the bank of snow lining the road. She breathes in the icy air so deeply that it hurts her lungs. She crosses the road, runs across Maria Square, then stops on the other side of Horns Street. She gathers some snow from a car roof and presses it to her hot, stinging eyes, then runs the rest of the way home.

Her hands are shaking as she unlocks the door. She lets out a whimper as she steps into the hall and closes the door behind her. She lets the keys fall to the floor, kicks off her shoes, and walks straight through the apartment to her bedroom.

Saga picks up the phone and dials the number, then stands while she waits. After six rings, she is put through to Stefan's voice mail. She doesn't listen to his message, just throws the phone at the wall as hard as she can.

Still fully dressed, she lies down on the double bed and curls up. In the back of her mind, she can understand why she feels like this. When she was little, she woke up in her dead mother's arms.

Saga Bauer can no longer remember how old she was when her mother got sick. But when she was five, she learned that her mom had a serious brain tumor. The illness changed her mom in terrible ways. The poisoned cells made her distant and increasingly irritable.

Her dad was hardly ever home. She hates remembering how he let them down. As an adult, she's tried to tell herself that he was only human; he couldn't help being weak. She repeats it like a mantra, but her fury at him won't subside. It's incomprehensible that he left and handed the burden to his young daughter. She doesn't want to think about it and never talks about it. It just makes her angry.

The night the illness finally claimed her mother, she was so tired she needed help taking her medication. Saga gave her pill after pill and ran to get more water.

"I can't take any more," her mom whispered.

"You have to."

"Just call Daddy and tell him I need him."

Saga did as her mom asked and told her dad that he had to come home now.

"Mommy knows I can't," he replied.

Later that evening, her mom was very weak. She didn't eat anything other than her medication and shouted at Saga when she knocked over the bottle of pills on the rug. Her mom was in terrible pain, and Saga tried to comfort her.

Her mom just asked Saga to call her dad and tell him she'd be dead before morning.

Saga cried and said her mom couldn't die, that she didn't want to live if her mom died. Her tears were trickling into her mouth. She sat on the floor, listening to the sound of her own crying and her dad's answering machine.

When her mom finally fell asleep, Saga turned off the little lamp and stood by the bed. Her mom's lips were shiny, and she was breathing heavily. Saga curled up in her warm embrace and fell asleep, exhausted. She slept beside her mom until she woke up early the next morning, frozen.

———

SAGA GETS OUT OF BED, takes off her coat, and lets it fall to the floor. She gets a pair of scissors from the kitchen and studies herself in the bathroom mirror. She can't see the fairy-tale princess everybody says she reminds them of.

Maybe I'm the only person who can save Felicia, she thinks, looking sternly at her own reflection.

62

A MEETING was held just two hours after Saga Bauer told her boss that she'd changed her mind and was going to accept the job.

Now Carlos Eliasson, Verner Zandén, Nathan Pollock, and Joona Linna are waiting in an apartment on the top floor of 71 Tanto Street, with a view of the rainbow arch of the railroad bridge.

The apartment is furnished in a modern style, with white furniture and recessed lighting. On the large dining table in the living room are plates of sandwiches from a nearby restaurant.

"I'm responsible for Saga. I want to bring at least one more agent into the ward, as a member of the staff, one who sits in the control room and keeps watch over every moment," Verner says.

"Jurek will know," Joona says. "Never underestimate him. He will know, and he will see the connection with the new patient, and—"

"I'll take the risk," Verner interrupts.

"Then both Saga and Felicia are going to die."

Carlos is about to say something when Saga walks in. Verner stares at her and looks almost frightened, and Nathan Pollock slumps down at the table with a sad look on his face.

Saga has shaved off her long hair. She has several grazes on her scalp. Her pale, beautiful head is graceful, with its small ears and her long, narrow neck. Her eyes are swollen from crying.

Joona Linna walks over and gives her a hug. She holds him hard for a while, pressing her cheek to his chest and listening to the beat of his heart.

"You don't have to do this," he says against her head.

"I want to save the girl," she replies quietly.

She holds on for a few more seconds, then goes into the kitchen.

"You know everyone here," Verner says, pulling out a chair for her.

"Yes." Saga nods.

She drops her dark-green parka on the floor and sits down. She's wearing her usual clothes: a pair of black jeans and a zip-up hoodie from the boxing club.

"If you really are prepared to go undercover in the same unit as Jurek Walter, we need to act at once," Carlos says, unable to hide his enthusiasm.

"I looked through your contract with us, and there are a few things that could be improved," Verner adds quickly.

"Good," she mutters.

"We may have room to increase your salary, and—"

"I don't really give a shit about that right now," she interrupts.

"You're aware that there are certain risks associated with this mission?" Carlos asks.

"I want to do this," she says firmly.

Verner pulls a gray phone from his bag, puts it on the table next to his usual cell phone, taps out a short text message, and looks up at her.

"Shall we begin, then?" he asks.

When she nods, he sends the message, which vanishes with a faint whoosh.

"We have a few hours now to prepare you for what you'll be faced with," Joona says.

"Let's get started," she says calmly.

The men take out folders, open laptops, spread out their papers. The table is covered by big maps of the area around Löwenströmska Hospital, the drains, and a detailed plan of the psychiatric unit. Saga feels a shiver run through her arms when she sees how extensive the preparations are.

"You're going to get a conviction from the Uppsala District Court, and you'll be sent to the women's section of Kronoberg Prison first thing tomorrow morning," Verner explains. "In the afternoon, you'll be driven to Karsudden Hospital outside Katrineholm. That'll take an hour or so. By then, the Prison Service Committee will be evaluating the proposal to transfer you to Löwenströmska."

"I've started sketching out a diagnosis that you'll need to look at," Nathan Pollock says, giving Saga a tentative smile. "You'll be given a medical history, with a juvenile psychiatric record, emergency treatments, diagnoses, and all sorts of medication, leading up to the present."

"I understand," she says.

"Do you have any allergies or illnesses we should know about?"

"No."

"No problems with your liver or heart?"

"No," Saga says.

63

ON THE PALE WOODEN BOOKSHELF of the borrowed apartment, there's a framed photograph of a family in a pool. The dad's nose is red with sunburn, and the two children are laughing as they hold up inflatable crocodiles.

"We have very little time," Nathan Pollock says.

"The worst-case scenario is that Felicia has already been abandoned," Joona says, unable to conceal the anxiety in his voice.

"What do you mean?" Saga asks.

"One possible explanation for why Mikael was able to escape is that Jurek's accomplice is ill, or—"

"He could have died, or he might just have taken off," Carlos interjects.

"We aren't going to make it in time," Saga whispers.

"We have to," Carlos says.

"If Felicia doesn't have access to water, there's nothing we can do—she'll die today or tomorrow," Pollock says. "If she's as ill as Mikael, she probably won't survive more than another week, but at least that gives us a chance. Even if the odds are very low."

"If she's only having to go without food, we may have three or four weeks," Verner says.

"We have so little to go on," Joona says. "We don't know if

the accomplice is continuing as if nothing's happened, or if he's buried Felicia alive. All we know is that she was still there when Mikael escaped."

"I can't take this," Carlos says, getting to his feet. "I just want to cry when I think—"

"We don't have time for tears at the moment," Verner interrupts.

"All I'm trying to say is—"

"I know, I feel the same," Verner says, raising his voice. "But in just over an hour, the Prison Service Committee will hold an extraordinary meeting to make the official decision to move patients to the secure unit at Löwenströmska, so—"

"I don't even know what I'm supposed to be doing," Saga says.

"By then, we need to have your new identity settled," Verner goes on. "We need to have your medical history completed and the forensic psychology report. The District Court judgment will have to be added to the National Judiciary Administration database, and your temporary transfer to Karsudden needs to be organized."

"We'd better get a move on," Pollock says.

"But Saga wants to know what the mission is," Joona says.

"It's just that it's difficult for me to ... I mean, how can I have an opinion about what you're discussing if I don't even know what's expected of me?" Saga says.

"We can still cancel the operation," says Verner.

"No. It's not that. I understand that I have to take care of myself," Saga answers.

"On your first day, you'll need to place a tiny microphone in the dayroom, with a receiver and transmitter," Verner says.

"That sounds risky."

"There's no way for us to do it for you. No matter how we arrange it, with a fake repair of the ventilation system or something like that, it would still be suspicious in combination with the arrival of the new patient," explains Joona.

"And then it would all be over," Saga says.

"All security cameras in the bunker are connected to a separate control room, which is absolutely impossible for us to hack," says Pollock.

"Do you mean that our people can't—"

"Listen, it's not a wireless network. It's a closed system of cables in the concrete walls. There's no way to get access in the time frame we have."

"I see," Saga says quietly.

"You have to make him talk," says Pollock, and hands her a plastic folder containing the microphone.

"Smuggled in up my backside?" she asks.

"No, they're bound to conduct a full body-cavity search," Verner replies.

"You need to swallow it, then vomit it back up before it reaches your duodenum, and if necessary swallow it again," Pollock explains.

"Never leave it in longer than four hours," Verner says.

"And I continue to do this until I have a chance to plant it in the common room," Saga says.

"We're going to have people positioned in a van who'll be listening to everything in real time," Pollock says.

"Okay, I get that part," Saga says. "But giving me a District Court conviction, a whole bunch of psychiatric evaluations, and all that—"

"We need that because—"

"Let me finish," she interrupts. "I'll have a coherent back-

ground, I'll be in the right place and I'll plant the microphone, but . . ."

The look in her eyes is hard and her lips are pale as she
looks at each of them in turn.

"But why the hell would Jurex Walter tell me anything?"

64

NATHAN IS STANDING UP, Carlos has both hands over his face, and Verner is fiddling with his cell phone.

"I don't understand why Jurek Walter would talk to me," Saga repeats.

"Obviously, we're taking a chance," Joona says.

"In the unit, there are three separate secure rooms. That's why the facility can be coed. The secure rooms open out into a shared dayroom containing a treadmill and a television concealed behind reinforced glass," Verner explains. "Jurek has been held in isolation for thirteen years, so I don't know how much the dayroom has been used."

Nathan Pollock pushes the floor plan of the secure unit over and points out Jurek's room and the dayroom next to it.

"If we're really unlucky, the staff won't allow the patients to see each other, and then there would be nothing we can do," Carlos admits.

"As we said, it's too dangerous to involve the hospital personnel," Joona says.

"I understand," Saga says. "But I'm thinking more about the fact that I have no idea, not a fucking clue, how I might approach Jurek if I actually do meet him."

"You're going to ask to see a representative from the administrative court and demand a fresh risk assessment," Carlos says.

"Why?"

"Jurek is looking for any way to reach outside the isolation," Joona answers.

"He himself is hemmed in by restrictions," Pollock says. "So he'll be watching you closely and will probably ask questions, seeing as your visit will be a sort of window on the world."

"What should I expect from him? What does he want?" Saga says.

"He wants to escape," Joona responds firmly.

"Escape?" Carlos repeats incredulously, tapping a pile of reports. "He hasn't made a single attempt to escape in all the time he's—"

"He won't try if he knows he won't succeed," Joona says.

"And you think he'll say something under these circumstances that could lead you to the capsule?" Saga asks, with no effort to hide her skepticism.

"We now know that Jurek has an accomplice, which means that he at least has the capacity to trust other people," Joona says.

"So he's not paranoid," Pollock adds.

Saga smiles. "That does make things easier."

"None of us imagines that Jurek's going to confess just like that," Joona says. "But if you can persuade him to talk, sooner or later he might say something that can get us closer to Felicia."

"You've spoken to him," Saga says to Joona.

"Yes, he talked to me because he was hoping I'd change my testimony, but he never got close to anything personal."

"So why would he with me?"

"Because you're exceptional," Joona replies, looking her straight in the eye.

65

SAGA GETS UP and wraps her arms around herself, looking at the sleet through the window.

"Our most difficult task right now is justifying the transfer to the secure unit at Löwenströmska, while simultaneously selecting a crime and a diagnosis that won't lead to heavy medication," Verner says.

"The whole mission will probably fail if you're put in a straitjacket or given electroconvulsive therapy," Pollock says bluntly.

"Shit," she whispers, and turns to face them again.

"Jurek's an intelligent man," Joona says. "It's not easy to manipulate him, and it will be very dangerous to lie to him. But he doesn't have a lust for murder. He does not kill for pleasure."

"We need to create a perfect identity," Verner says, his eyes fixed on Saga.

"I've been giving this some thought, and I think it makes sense to give you a schizophrenic personality disorder," Pollock says, peering at her with his narrow black eyes.

"Will that be enough?" Carlos asks.

"If we throw in recurrent psychotic attacks with violent outbursts . . ."

"Okay." Saga nods, but her cheeks start to blush red.

"You're kept calm with eight milligrams of Trilafon three times a day," he says.

"Just how dangerous is this mission?" Verner eventually asks, seeing as Saga hasn't posed the question.

"Jurek is extremely dangerous, the other patient who'll be arriving at the same time as Saga is also dangerous, and we'll have no control over her treatment once she's there," Pollock says.

"So you can't guarantee the safety of my agent?" Verner says.

"No," Carlos replies.

"You're aware of this, Saga?" Verner asks.

"Yes."

"Only a very select group will know about this mission, and we won't have any visuals of what's going on inside the secure unit," Pollock says. "So, if for some reason we don't hear you over the microphone, we'll break off the mission after twenty-four hours—but until then you'll have to take care of yourself."

Joona puts the detailed plan of the secure unit in front of Saga and points at the dayroom with his pen.

"As you can see, there are security locks here and three automated doors there," Joona says. "It won't be easy, but in an emergency you could try to barricade yourself in here, or possibly also here or here. And if you're outside the security lock, the operations room and this storeroom are clearly the best options."

"Is it possible to get past this passageway?" she asks, pointing.

"Yes, but not here," he says, crossing off the doors that can't be forced without cards and codes. "Lock yourself in and wait for help."

Carlos starts to leaf through the papers on the table.

"But if something goes wrong at a later point, I want to show you—"

"Hang on a minute," Joona interrupts. "Have you memorized the plan?"

"Yes," Saga says.

Carlos pulls out the large map of the area surrounding the hospital.

"If the situation requires, we'll be sending emergency vehicles from here," he says, indicating the road behind the hospital. "We'll stop here, next to the big exercise yard. But if you can't make it there, go up into the forest till you get to this point."

"Good," she says.

"The response units will probably go in here and through the drains, depending on the nature of the alarm."

"As long as you don't blow your cover, we can get you out and everything will be back to normal," Verner says. "Nothing will have happened. We'll change the National Judiciary Administration records back to the way they were before. You'll have no criminal conviction and will never have received treatment anywhere."

A silence fills the room. It had suddenly become apparent how minuscule their chance of success was. "How many of you think my mission is actually going to succeed?" Saga asks quietly.

Carlos nods uncertainly and mutters something.

Joona just shakes his head.

"Maybe," Pollock says. "But it will be difficult—and dangerous."

"Do your best," Verner says, putting his hand on her shoulder for a moment.

66

SAGA TAKES NATHAN POLLOCK'S comprehensive character profile into a pink bedroom with pictures of teen pop stars on the walls. Fifteen minutes later, she returns to the kitchen. She walks slowly and stops in the middle of the floor. The shadows of her long eyelashes dance on her cheeks. The men fall silent and turn to look at the slender figure with the shaved head.

"My name is Natalie Andersson and I have schizophrenic personality disorder, which makes me a bit of an introvert," she says, sitting down on a chair. "But I've also had recurrent psychotic episodes, with some extremely violent outbursts. That's why I've been prescribed Trilafon. I'm okay at the moment with eight milligrams, three times a day. The pills are small and white, and they make my breasts so sore I can't sleep on my front. I also take Cipramil, thirty milligrams, or Seroxat, twenty milligrams."

While speaking, she has secretly pulled the tiny microphone out of the lining of her pants.

"When I was really bad I used to get injections of Risperdal, and Oxascand for the side effects."

Under cover of the tabletop, she removes the protective plastic from the glue and sticks the microphone under the table.

"Before Karsudden and the verdict from the Uppsala District Court, I escaped from a nonsecure ward at the Bålsta psychiatric unit and killed a man in the playground behind Gredelby School in Knivsta, then, ten minutes later, another man, in the driveway of his house on Dagg Lane."

The little microphone comes loose from the table and falls to the floor.

"After I was arrested, I was transferred to the acute psychiatric unit at the University Hospital in Uppsala. I was given twenty milligrams of Stesolid and one hundred milligrams of Cisordinol injected into my backside. They kept me strapped up for eleven hours, and then I was given a solution of Heminevrin. It was really cold, and I got all congested and had a really bad headache."

Nathan Pollock claps his hands. Joona bends down and picks the microphone up off the floor.

He smiles as he holds it out to her. "The glue needs four seconds to firm up."

Saga takes the microphone and turns it over in her hand.

"Are we all in agreement about this identity?" Verner asks. "In seven minutes, I have to enter it into the National Judiciary Administration database."

"I think it sounds good," Pollock says. "But, Saga, this evening you'll need to memorize the rules at Bålsta and learn the names and physical features of the staff and the other patients."

Verner nods. "You have to become one with your new identity, so you don't even have to think before reeling off phone numbers and imaginary family members, birthdays, past addresses, dead pets, ID numbers, schools, teachers, workplaces, colleagues, their personal habits, and—"

"I'm not sure that's the right approach," Joona interrupts.

Verner stops mid-sentence and looks at Joona. Carlos

nervously sweeps some crumbs off the table with his hand. Nathan Pollock leans back expectantly.

"I can learn all that," Saga says.

Joona's eyes are as dark as lead now.

"Now that Samuel Mendel is no longer with us," Joona says, "I can reveal that he had remarkable knowledge of long-term infiltration techniques for high-risk undercover work."

"Samuel?" Carlos says skeptically.

"I can't explain how, but he knew what he was talking about," Joona says.

"Was he Mossad?" Verner asks.

"I can only say that when he told me about his method I realized that he was right, and that's why I've never forgotten what he said," Joona continues.

"We've already determined the best method," Verner says, a note of strain in his voice.

"When you're working undercover, you speak as little as possible, and only in short sentences," Joona says.

"Why short sentences?" Carlos asks.

"To sound authentic," Joona goes on, addressing Saga directly. "Never pretend to feel things, never pretend to be angry or happy, and always mean what you say."

"Okay," Saga says warily.

"And the most important thing," Joona continues, "is to never say anything but the truth."

"The truth," Saga repeats.

"We'll make sure that you get your diagnoses," Joona explains. "But you need to claim that you're healthy."

"Because it's true," Verner murmurs.

"You don't even need to know about the crimes you committed—you need to claim that it's all lies."

"Because that wouldn't be a lie," Saga says.

"Holy shit," Verner says.

Saga's face flushes as she realizes what Joona is saying. She gulps, then says slowly, "So, if Jurek asks me where I live, I just tell him that I live on Tavast Street in Södermalm?"

"That way, you'll remember your answer if he asks more than once."

"And if he asks about my ex-boyfriend, I tell the truth?"

"That's the only way you're going to sound genuine and remember what you've said."

"What if he asks what my job is?" she says, laughing. "Shall I say I'm an inspector with the Security Police?"

"In a secure psychiatric unit, that would probably work." Joona grins. "But otherwise, if you're asked a question that really would give you away, you can always ignore it. That would be a perfectly honest reaction—you don't want to answer."

Verner smiles as he scratches his head. The atmosphere in the room is suddenly buoyant.

"I'm starting to believe in this now," Pollock says to Saga. "We'll give you your psychological evaluations and criminal record, but you just answer any questions honestly."

Saga gets up from the table, and her face is calm as she says:

"My name is Saga Bauer, and I'm perfectly healthy and completely innocent."

67

POLLOCK IS SITTING next to Verner as he logs into the National Judiciary Administration database and types in the twelve-digit code. Together they add the dates when charges were brought, when the application to go to trial was filed, and when the main hearing was held. They classify the crimes, formulate the forensic psychiatric report, and input the fact that the Uppsala District Court found the accused guilty of two unusually violent cases of premeditated manslaughter. At the same time, Carlos adds Saga Bauer's crimes, sentence, and sanctions to the criminal records register of the National Police Authority.

Verner moves on to the National Board of Forensic Medicine's database and uploads a copy of the forensic psychiatric report.

"How are we doing in terms of time?" Saga asks.

"Fairly well, I think," Verner says, glancing at his watch. "In precisely two minutes, the Prison Service Committee will be gathering for a special meeting. They'll check the National Judiciary Administration database and make the decision to transfer two patients to the secure psychiatric unit at Löwenströmska."

"You never explained why there have to be two new patients," Saga says.

"So that you'll be less exposed," Pollock replies.

"We imagine Jurek would become suspicious if a new patient suddenly appeared after so many years," Carlos explains. "But if a patient from the secure unit at Säter shows up first, followed a day or so later by one from Karsudden, with a bit of luck you won't attract quite as much scrutiny."

"You're being moved because you're dangerous and an escape risk, and the other patient has requested a transfer himself," Pollock says.

"Time to let Saga go now," Verner says.

"Tomorrow night you'll be sleeping in Karsudden Hospital," Pollock says.

"You'll have to tell your family you're on a secret mission abroad," Verner begins. "You'll need someone to look after bills, pets, houseplants—"

"I'll figure it out," she interrupts.

Joona picks up her parka from where she dropped it on the floor and holds it up for her to put on.

"Do you remember the rules?" he asks quietly.

"Say little, talk in short sentences, mean what you say, and stick to the truth."

"I have one more rule," Joona says. "It probably varies from person to person, but Samuel said you should avoid talking about your parents."

She shrugs. "Okay."

"I don't know why he thought that was so important."

"I think it would be wise to listen to Samuel's advice," Verner agrees.

"Yes, I'd say so."

Carlos puts two sandwiches in a bag and gives them to Saga.

"I should remind you that, in there, you'll be a patient, nothing more. You won't have access to police information or rights," he says gravely.

Saga looks him in the eye. "I know."

"It's important that you understand this," Verner says.

"I'm going to go home and get some rest," Saga says, and walks toward the hall.

As she's sitting on a stool, tying her boots, Joona comes out to her. He squats down beside her.

"It'll soon be too late to change your mind," he whispers.

"I want to do this, Joona." She smiles, meeting his gaze.

"I know," Joona says. "It'll be fine, as long as you don't forget how dangerous Jurek is. He affects people, changes them, rips their souls out like—"

"I'm not going to let Jurek get to me," she says. She stands up and begins to fasten her coat.

"He's like—"

"I'm a big girl," she interrupts.

"I know."

Joona holds the door open for her and accompanies her out onto the landing. He hesitates, and she leans against the wall.

"What is it you want to say?" she asks gently.

A few seconds of silence follow. The elevator is waiting motionless on their floor. A police car races past outside, sirens blaring.

"Jurek will do anything he can to escape," Joona says in a somber voice. "You cannot let that happen. You're like a sister to me, Saga, but it would be better if you died than if he got out."

68

Anders Rönn is sitting at the big conference table, waiting. It's already half past five. The pale, impersonal room is full of the usual members of the hospital committee, two representatives from General Psychiatry, Chief Physician Roland Brolin, and the head of security, Sven Hoffman.

The hospital manager, Rikard Nagler, is still talking on the phone as his secretary hands him a glass of iced tea.

Snow is falling slowly outside the window.

All conversation in the room ceases when the hospital manager puts his empty glass on the table, wipes his mouth, and begins the meeting.

"It's good that you all could make it," he says. "I received a call from the Prison Service Committee an hour ago."

He pauses. People shift in their seats and look up at him.

"They've decided that the secure unit is going to admit two new patients at short notice," he continues. "We've been very spoiled with just one patient, and an old, quiet one at that."

"Because he's biding his time," Roland says gravely.

"I called this meeting to hear your thoughts about what this means in terms of security and our current procedures," the manager says, ignoring Roland's comment.

"What sort of patients are they sending?" Anders asks.

"Naturally, they're both high-risk," the manager replies.

"One is in the secure unit at Säter, and the other is in the psychiatric unit at Karsudden after—"

"It's not going to work," Roland says.

"Our secure unit was built to house three patients," the hospital manager responds. "Times have changed. We all have to do what we can to cut costs, and we can't—"

"Yes, but Jurek is . . ."

Roland falls silent.

"What were you going to say?"

"It's impossible for us to handle any more patients," Roland says.

"Even though we have a direct obligation to accept them."

"Find some excuse."

The manager laughs wearily and shakes his head.

"You've always seen him as a monster, but he—"

"I'm not scared of monsters," Roland interrupts. "But I'm smart enough to be scared of Jurek Walter."

The manager smiles at Roland and then whispers something to his secretary.

"I'm still fairly new," Anders says. "Has Jurek Walter ever caused any problems here?"

"He made Susanne Hjälm disappear," Roland replies.

Silence descends on the room. One of the doctors from General Psychiatry takes off his glasses, then puts them back on.

"I was told that she was on a leave of absence—for a research project, I think it was?" Anders says.

"We're calling it a leave of absence," Roland says.

"I'd very much like to hear what happened," Anders says, a vague anxiety growing inside him.

"Susanne smuggled out a letter from Jurek Walter but regretted it," Roland explains. "She called me and told me everything. She was completely . . . I don't know . . . she was crying and promising that she'd burned the letter. She was frightened and kept saying she wasn't going to go in to see Jurek again."

"She's taken a leave of absence," the hospital manager says forcefully.

A few people laugh, while others look troubled. Sven Hoffman projects an image of the secure unit onto the white screen.

"In terms of security, we have no problem managing more patients," he says. "But we'll need to maintain a higher level of alert to start with."

"Jurek Walter cannot be allowed to interact with other people," Roland persists.

"Well, he's going to have to now. You'll just need to ensure that security isn't compromised," the manager says, looking at the others.

"It won't work. And I want it in the minutes that I'm abdicating responsibility for the secure unit. It will have to come under the umbrella of General Psychiatry, or become a separate—"

"Don't you think you're overreacting?"

"This is exactly what Jurek Walter has been waiting for all these years," Roland says, his voice breathless with agitation.

He gets up and leaves the room without another word.

"I'm sure I can take care of three patients, regardless of their diagnoses," Anders offers, leaning back in his chair.

The others look at him in surprise. The hospital manager puts down his pen.

"I don't actually understand the problem," Anders continues, glancing at the door through which Roland disappeared.

"Go on," the manager says, nodding.

"It's merely a matter of medication," Anders says.

"We can't just keep them sedated." Hoffman laughs.

"Of course we can, if it's absolutely necessary," Anders says with a boyish smile. "Take Sankt Sigfrids, for instance. We were stretched so thin that we didn't have the capacity to deal with a lot of incidents."

The hospital manager regards him intently. Anders raises his eyebrows and shrugs. "We know that heavy medication is perhaps . . . uncomfortable for the patient," he says. "But if I were responsible for the secure unit, I wouldn't want to take any risks."

69

AGNES IS SITTING on the floor in a pair of pajamas, blue with bees on them. She's clutching her little white hairbrush and feeling the bristles with her fingertip, one by one, as if she were counting them. Anders sits in front of her, holding her Barbie doll and waiting.

"Brush the doll's hair," he says.

Agnes doesn't look up at him. She goes on picking at each individual bristle, one row after another, slowly and with the utmost concentration.

He knows she doesn't play spontaneously like other children, but she does play in her own way. She has trouble understanding what other people see and think. And she's never given her Barbie dolls names. She just tests their mechanics, bending their arms and legs and twisting their heads around.

But he has learned from courses organized by the Autism and Asperger Association that she can be trained to play if the various parts of the game are divided up sequentially.

"Agnes? Brush the doll's hair," he repeats.

She stops fiddling with the brush, holds it out, and pulls it through the doll's blond hair, then repeats the movement twice more.

"She looks lovely now," Anders says.

Agnes starts picking at the brush again.

"Have you seen how lovely she looks?" he asks.

"Yes," she says, without looking.

Anders gets out a Sindy doll, and before he even has time to say anything, Agnes reaches forward and brushes its hair, smiling.

Three hours later, when Agnes is asleep, Anders settles down on the couch in front of the television and watches *Sex and the City*. In front of the house, heavy snowflakes are falling through the yellow glow of the streetlights. Petra's at a staff party. Her coworker Victoria picked her up at five o'clock. She said she wasn't going to be late, but it's almost eleven now.

Anders drinks a sip of cold tea and sends Petra a text to tell her that Agnes brushed her dolls' hair.

He's tired, but he'd like to tell her about the meeting at the hospital, and how he's assumed responsibility for the secure unit and has a guarantee of permanent employment.

During the commercial break, Anders goes to turn out the light in Agnes's room. The nightlight is shaped like a life-size rabbit. It gives off a lovely pink light, casting a soft glow on the sheets and on Agnes's relaxed face

The floor is littered with LEGO pieces, dolls, doll furniture, plastic food, pens, princess tiaras, and a whole porcelain tea set.

Anders can't understand how the room became such a mess.

He has to shuffle forward to keep from stepping on anything. The toys rattle slightly as they slide around the wooden floor. As he's reaching for the light switch, he imagines he can see a knife on the floor beside the bed.

The big Barbie house is in the way, but he can make out a glint of steel through the little doorway.

Anders tiptoes closer and leans over. His heart starts to pound when he sees that the knife looks like the one he found in the secure cell.

He doesn't understand. He gave the knife to Roland Brolin.

Agnes begins to whimper anxiously in her sleep.

Anders crawls over the floor and sticks his hand through the ground floor of the dollhouse, opens the little door wide, and reaches for the knife.

The floor creaks, and Agnes coughs slightly as she exhales.

Something is glinting in the darkness under the bed. It could be the shiny eyes of a teddy bear. It's difficult to tell through the tiny colored windows of the dollhouse.

"Ow," Agnes whispers in her sleep. "Ow, ow."

Anders has just managed to touch the knife with his fingertips when he sees the twinkling eyes of a wrinkled face under the bed.

It's Jurek Walter—and he moves fast as lightning, grabbing Anders's hand and pulling.

Anders wakes up when he snatches his hand back. He's gasping as he realizes that he fell asleep on the couch in front of the television. He switches it off and sits there, his heart racing.

Car headlights shine in through the window. A taxi turns around and disappears. Then the front door opens softly.

It's Petra.

He hears her go to the bathroom and pee. He walks slowly closer, toward the light of the bathroom spilling into the corridor.

70

ANDERS STANDS IN THE DARK, watching Petra in the mirror above the sink. She brushes her teeth, spits, cups her hand to lift some water to her mouth, then spits again.

When she sees him, she startles.

"You're awake."

"I was waiting for you," Anders says.

"That's sweet of you."

She turns out the light, and he follows her into the bedroom. She sits down on the edge of the bed and rubs cream into her hands and elbows.

"Did you have a good time?"

"It was okay. It was a goodbye party for Lena."

Anders grabs her left hand and holds her tightly by the wrist. She looks into his eyes.

"You know we have to be up early tomorrow."

"Shut up," he says.

She tries to pull free, but he grabs her other hand and pushes her down onto the bed.

"Ow—"

"Just shut up!"

He forces one knee between her thighs, and she tries to twist aside, then lies still.

"I mean it—red light. I have to get some sleep," she says gently.

"I've been waiting for you."

She regards him for a moment, then nods.

"Lock the door."

He gets off the bed and listens for sounds from the corridor, but the house is quiet, so he locks the door. Petra has taken off her nightgown and is opening the box. With a smile, she gets out the soft rope and the bag with the whip, the vibrator, and the big dildo, but he pushes her onto the bed.

She tells him to stop. He roughly pulls off her underwear, leaving red marks on her hips.

"Anders, I—"

"Don't look at me," he interrupts.

"Sorry."

She doesn't resist as he ties her more tightly than usual. It's possible that drinking has made her less sensitive. He ties the rope around one of the bedposts and forces her thighs apart.

"Ow," she whimpers.

He grabs the blindfold, and she shakes her head as he yanks it down over her face. She tries to pull loose, tugging at the ropes so hard that her heavy breasts swing.

"You're so beautiful," he whispers.

It's four o'clock by the time they finish and he unknots the ropes. Petra takes out the ripped underwear he stuffed in her mouth when she asked him to stop. She is silent, her body trembling as she massages her sore wrists. Her hair is sweaty, her cheeks are streaked with tears, and the blindfold has slipped down around her neck.

71

SAGA ABANDONS any attempt to sleep at five o'clock. Ninety minutes left. Then they're coming to get her. Her body feels heavy as she pulls on her running pants and leaves the apartment.

She jogs a couple of blocks, then speeds up toward Söder Mälarstrand. There's no traffic this early. She runs along the silent streets. The fresh snow is so airy, she can barely feel it under her feet.

She knows she can still change her mind, but today's the day she's going to give up her freedom.

Södermalm is asleep. The sky is black above the glow of the streetlights.

Saga considers the fact that she hasn't been given an alias, that she's being admitted under her name and doesn't have to remember anything but her medication, past and present. Intramuscular injections of Risperdal, she repeats silently. Oxascand for the side effects. Stesolid and Heminevrin.

Pollock had explained that it didn't matter what her diagnosis was. "You still have to know exactly what medication you're on," he said. "It's a matter of life or death. The medication is what helps you survive."

An empty bus swings into the deserted but well-lit terminal for the Finland ferries.

"Trilafon, eight milligrams, three times a day," she whispers as she runs. "Cipramil, thirty milligrams. Seroxat, twenty milligrams."

Just before she reaches the Photography Museum, Saga turns onto the steep steps leading away from Stadsgårdsleden. She reaches the top step and looks out across Stockholm as she goes over Joona's rules once more.

I have to keep to myself, say little, and speak only in short sentences. I have to mean what I say and tell only the truth.

That's all, she thinks.

She tries to sprint the final stretch along Tavast Street to her building.

Saga runs up the stairs, kicks off her shoes onto the hall mat, and goes straight into the bathroom for a shower.

It feels strange to be able to dry herself so quickly afterward, without all that long hair. All she has to do is rub a towel over her head.

She pulls on the most basic underwear she owns: a white sports bra and a pair of panties she wears only when she has her period. A pair of jeans, a black T-shirt, and a faded sweatshirt.

All of a sudden she has butterflies in her stomach.

It's almost twenty past six. They're picking her up in eleven minutes. She puts her watch back on the bedside table, next to her glass of water. Where she's going, time is dead.

First she'll be going to Kronoberg Prison, but she'll only be there for a couple of hours before she's transported to Katrineholm. Then she'll spend a day or so at Karsudden Hospital before they transfer her to the secure psychiatric unit at Löwenströmska.

She walks slowly through the apartment, switching off lights and pulling plugs, before going into the hall and putting on her green parka.

It's not such a difficult mission, she tells herself again.

Jurek Walter is an elderly man. He's probably heavily medicated and not really with it.

She knows he's guilty of terrible things, but all she has to do is stay calm, wait for him to approach her, and wait for him to say something that could be useful.

Either it'll work, or it won't.

It's time to leave now.

Saga turns off the lamp in the hall and goes out into the stairwell.

She's thrown out all the perishable goods from the fridge, but she doesn't bother to have someone look after the apartment, water the flowers, or pick up the mail.

72

SAGA DOUBLE-LOCKS the door and goes downstairs to the main entrance. She feels a flutter of anxiety as she sees the Prison Service van waiting in the dark street. She opens the door and gets in beside Nathan Pollock.

"It's dangerous to pick up hitchhikers," she says, trying to smile.

"Did you get any sleep?"

"A bit," she replies, and fastens her seat belt.

"I know you already know this," Pollock says, glancing at her, "but I'm still going to remind you not to try to manipulate him into revealing any information."

He puts the van in gear and pulls out into the silent street.

"That's the hardest thing," Saga says. "What if he only wants to talk about soccer? What if he doesn't talk at all?"

"That will just be how it is. There'll be nothing you can do about it."

"But Felicia might only survive a few more days."

"That's not your responsibility," Pollock replies. "This infiltration is a gamble. We all know that. We've agreed on that. We can't second-guess the results. What you're doing is entirely separate from the ongoing preliminary investigation. We're going to keep talking to Mikael Kohler-Frost, follow up on all the old lines of inquiry, and—"

"But no one believes we'll be able to save Felicia unless Jurek starts talking to me."

"You can't think like that," Pollock says.

"Okay. I'll stop now." She tries to smile.

"Good."

She starts tapping her feet. Her pale-blue eyes are glassy, as if she's lost in thought.

Dark buildings flit past the van.

Saga puts her keys, wallet, and other loose possessions in a Prison Service bag for personal belongings.

Before they reach Kronoberg Prison, Pollock hands her the microphone inside a silicon capsule and a small portion of butter.

"Digestion of fatty foods takes longer," he says. "But I don't think you should ever wait more than four hours."

She opens the pack of butter, swallows the contents, then examines the microphone in the soft capsule. It looks like an insect in amber. She straightens up, pops the capsule in her mouth, tips her head back, and swallows. It hurts her throat, and she can feel herself breaking out into a sweat as it slowly slips down.

73

THE MORNING is still as black as midnight, and all the lights are on in the women's section of Kronoberg Prison.

Saga takes two steps forward and stops when they tell her to. She tries to shut herself off from the world around her and not look at anyone.

The radiators are ticking.

Nathan Pollock puts her bag of personal belongings on the counter and hands over Saga's papers. He is given a written receipt and then disappears.

From now on, she will have to cope on her own, no matter what happens.

The automated gates whirr, then fall silent.

No one looks at her, but she can't help noticing the way the atmosphere tenses when the guards realize that she has the highest security classification. She is to be kept in strict isolation until her transfer.

Saga keeps her eyes fixed on the yellow vinyl floor, not answering any questions.

She is patted down before being led along a corridor for the full-body search.

Two thickset women are discussing a new television series as they guide her through a door with no window in it. The room looks like a small medical examination room, with a narrow bunk covered with a roll of paper, and locked cabinets along one wall.

"Remove all your clothes," one of the women says in a blank voice as she pulls on a pair of latex gloves.

Saga does as she is told and drops her clothes in a heap on the floor. When she is naked, she stands under the bare fluorescent light with her arms hanging by her sides.

Her body is girlishly slender, toned, and athletic.

The guard with the gloves breaks off mid-sentence and stares at Saga.

"Okay," one of them sighs after a few seconds.

"What?"

"Let's just do what we have to do."

Carefully, they begin examining Saga, shining a light in her mouth, nose, and ears. They tick boxes off a list, then instruct her to lie on the bunk.

"Get on your side and pull one knee up as far as you can," the woman with the gloves says.

Saga obeys, unhurriedly, and the woman moves between the bunk and the wall behind her back. She shivers and feels her skin break out in goose bumps.

The dry paper rustles against her cheek as she turns her head. She shuts her eyes tight as lubricant is squeezed from a bottle.

"This is going to feel a little cold now," the woman says, sticking two fingers as far up Saga's vagina as she can.

It doesn't hurt, but it's extremely unpleasant. Saga tries to breathe evenly but can't help gasping as the woman sticks a finger in her anus.

The examination is over in a matter of seconds, and the woman quickly pulls off the gloves and throws them away. She hands Saga a piece of paper to wipe herself with and explains that she'll be given new clothes while she's there.

Dressed in a baggy green outfit and a pair of white sneakers, she is taken to her cell in Ward 8:4. Before they close and lock the door behind her, they ask amiably if she'd like a cheese sandwich and a cup of coffee. Saga shakes her head.

Once the women are gone, Saga stands completely still in her cell for a moment.

It's hard to know what time it is, but before it's too late she goes over to the sink. She fills her hands with water, drinks some, and sticks her fingers down her throat. She coughs, and her stomach clenches. After a couple of hard, painful cramps, the microphone comes back up.

Her eyes water as she washes the capsule and then rinses her face.

She lies on the bunk and waits, hiding the microphone in her grasp.

The corridor outside is silent.

Saga can smell the toilet and drain in the floor as she stares at the ceiling and reads the messages and names that have been carved into the walls over the years.

Rectangles of sunlight have moved left, toward the floor, by the time Saga hears footsteps outside. She pops the capsule in her mouth, stands up, and swallows as the lock clicks and the door opens.

It's time for her to be taken to Karsudden Hospital.

The uniformed guard signs her out, along with her possessions and transfer documents. Saga allows them to cuff her hands and ankles.

74

THE POLICE TEAM consists of thirty-two people in total, mostly civilian staff and officers from the surveillance and detection units of the National Crime Unit.

In one of the big conference rooms on the fifth floor, the walls are covered with maps marking the locations associated with the Jurek Walter case. Color photographs of the missing people are surrounded by constellations of their families, colleagues, and friends.

Old interviews with relatives of the victims are examined again, and new interviews are conducted. Medical and forensic reports are checked, and anyone who knew any of the victims is spoken to, no matter how peripheral the relationship.

Joona Linna and his team are standing in the winter light by the window, reading a transcript of the latest interview with Mikael Kohler-Frost. As they read, a somber mood settles over the group. There's nothing in Mikael's account that can propel the investigation forward. The analysts have looked at the tangible evidence, and there's precious little of it.

"Nothing," Petter Näslund mutters, rolling up the transcript.

"He says he can feel his sister's movements, that she reaches for him every time she wakes up in the darkness," Benny

Rubin says with a pained expression on his face. "He can feel how much she hopes he will return."

"I don't believe any of that," Petter interrupts.

"We have to assume that Mikael is telling the truth, at least in some form," Joona says.

"But this business with the Sandman," Petter says. "I mean . . ."

"Even with the Sandman," Joona replies.

"He's talking about a character in a fairy tale," Petter retorts. "Are we going to question everyone who sells barometers, or—"

"As a matter of fact, I've already compiled a list of manufacturers and dealers," Joona says with a smile.

"What the hell?"

"I'm aware that there's a barometer salesman in E. T. A. Hoffmann's story about the Sandman," Joona goes on. "And I know Mikael's mother used to tell them a bedtime story about the Sandman. But none of that precludes the possibility that a version of him might actually exist in real life."

"We don't have a fucking thing, and we might as well admit it," Petter says, tossing the transcript onto the desk.

"Almost nothing," Joona gently corrects him.

"Mikael was sedated when he was moved to the capsule and sedated when he was taken away from it." Benny sighs, rubbing a hand over his bald head. "It's impossible even to start identifying a location. In all likelihood, Felicia is in Sweden—but even that isn't certain."

Magdalena Ronander goes over to the whiteboard and lists what little information they have about the capsule: concrete, electricity, water, Legionella bacteria.

Because Mikael has never seen the accomplice or heard him speak, they know nothing beyond the fact that it is a man. That's all. Mikael was sure that the coughs he heard came from a man.

Everything else in the description can be traced back to childhood fantasies about the Sandman.

Joona leaves the room, takes the elevator down, walks out of police headquarters, and continues up Fleming Street, across the Sankt Erik Bridge and into Birkastan.

The attic apartment of 19 Rörstrands Street is where Athena Promachos is based.

When the goddess Pallas Athena is depicted as a beautiful girl with a lance and a shield, she is known as Athena Promachos, the goddess of war.

Athena Promachos is also the name of a secret group put together to investigate the material that Saga Bauer is expected to provide while she is undercover. The group doesn't exist in any official records and has no budget from either the National Criminal Investigation Department or the Swedish Security Police.

Athena Promachos consists of Joona, Nathan, Corinne Meilleroux from the Security Police and Forensics Officer Johan Jönson.

As soon as Saga is transferred to the secure unit at Löwenströmska, they'll be working around the clock to receive, collate, and analyze the surveillance recordings.

Athena Promachos will be assisted by three other officers who are responsible for recording the transmissions from the microphone. They will work from a minibus belonging to the local council's Parks Department that has been parked on hospital grounds. All the material will be saved on hard disks, encrypted, and sent to Athena Promachos's computers with a delay of no more than a tenth of a second.

75

ANDERS LOOKS at the time again. The new patient from the secure unit at Säter Prison is on his way to the isolation unit. Prison Service transport has called to warn Anders that the man is anxious and aggressive. They've given him ten milligrams of Stesolid en route, and Anders has prepared a syringe with another ten milligrams. An older prison guard named Leif Rajama tosses away the packaging for the syringe and waits with his feet planted apart in a combative stance.

"I don't think he'll need more than that," Anders says, not quite managing to summon a smile.

"It usually depends on how much the search upsets them," Leif says. "I try to tell myself that my job is to help people who are having a hard time, even if they may not actually want help."

The guard on the other side of the reinforced glass is notified that the patient is on his way in. There's a metallic clang through the walls, then a muffled cry.

"This is only the second patient," Anders says. "We won't know how things will be until all three are in place."

"It'll be fine," Leif reassures him.

The security monitor shows a view of the staircase with two security guards holding up a patient who is unable to walk unaided. The patient is a thickset man with a blond mustache and glasses that have slid down his narrow nose. His eyes are closed, and sweat is running down his face.

Anders glances at Leif. They can hear the patient babbling nonsensically—something about dead slaves and the fact that he has wet himself.

"I'm standing in piss, right up to my knees, and—"

"Hold still," the guards order, and lay him down on the floor.

"Ow, it hurts," he whimpers.

The guard behind the glass accepts the transfer documents from the senior transport officer.

The patient is lying on the floor with his eyes shut, gasping. Anders tells Leif that they won't need to administer any more Stesolid, then pulls his pass card through the reader.

76

JUREK WALTER is walking at a moderate pace on the tread-mill. His face is turned away from the camera.

Anders Rönn and the head of security, Sven Hoffman, are in the surveillance room, watching him on the monitor.

"You know how to sound the alarm and how to switch it off," Hoffman says. "You know that someone with a pass card must accompany the guards when they interact with the patients."

"Yes," Anders says, with a hint of impatience in his voice. "And the security door behind you has to be locked before you open the next one."

Sven nods.

"If the alarm sounds, guards will show up within five minutes."

"We won't be sounding any alarms," Anders says. On the monitor, he sees the new patient come into the dayroom.

They study the patient as he sits down on the brown sofa, holding one hand over his mouth as if trying not to vomit. Anders thinks of the handwritten notes from Säter, detailing aggression, recurrent psychosis, narcissism, and an antisocial personality disorder.

"We'll have to conduct our own evaluation," Anders says. "And I'll increase his medication if there's the slightest reason to."

The main monitor in front of him is divided into nine squares, one for each of the nine cameras in the unit. Airlocks, security doors, corridors, the dayroom, and the patients' rooms are all filmed. There aren't enough staff to monitor the cameras at all hours, but there always has to be someone with operational knowledge of the security system on duty in the unit.

"You'll be spending a lot of time in the office, but you should still know how these things work," Sven says, gesturing toward the monitors.

"We'll all have to pitch in, now that we have more patients," Anders replies.

"The basic principle is that everyone on the staff should know where all the patients are at all times."

Sven clicks on one of the squares, and an image of the changing room immediately fills the second monitor alongside the main screen. Anders can see the nurse, My, taking off her wet coat.

The changing room is reflected on the screen with unexpected clarity. There are five yellow metal lockers, a shower, and doors to the bathroom and corridor.

The outline of My's breasts can be seen beneath a black T-shirt with an illustration of the angel of death on it. She gets out her uniform, lays it on the bench, then puts a pair of Birkenstock sandals on the floor.

Sven clicks away from the changing room and enlarges the image from the dayroom instead. Anders forces himself not to look at the smaller square as My starts to unbutton her black jeans.

He sits down and tries to sound nonchalant as he asks if the videos are stored.

"We don't have the right to do that—not even in exceptional circumstances." Sven winks at him.

"Shame," Anders says, running a hand over his short brown hair.

Sven starts to cycle through the various cameras, checking the corridors and security locks.

"We cover everything where—"

A door opens in the distance. They hear the hum of the coffee machine, and then My walks into the surveillance room.

"What are you doing huddled in here?" she asks with a grin.

"Sven's going through the security system with me," Anders replies.

"And here I was thinking you were watching me in the changing room," she jokes with a sigh.

77

They grow quiet and focus on the screen that shows the dayroom. Jurek Walter is still walking on the treadmill with long, even strides. Bernie Larsson gradually slips down off the sofa until he is slumped on the ground with his neck against the seat cushion. His shirt slides up, and his round stomach moves as he breathes. His face is sweaty. He bounces one of his legs nervously and seems to be talking to the ceiling.

"What's he doing?" My asks, glancing at the others. "What's he saying?"

Anders shrugs. "No idea."

The only sound audible in the surveillance room is the ticking of a golden Japanese cat waving its paw.

Anders thinks back to Bernie Larsson's medical notes from Säter. Twenty-one years ago, he was sentenced to secure psychiatric care and chemical castration for what was described as a series of bestial attacks.

Now he's back on the sofa, yelling up at the ceiling. Saliva is spraying from his mouth. He's making aggressive slicing gestures with his hands, and he throws the cushion beside him onto the floor.

Jurek Walter does what he has always done. When he has completed nine kilometers on the treadmill, he gets off and heads in the direction of his room.

Bernie shouts something at him as he leaves. Jurek stops in the doorway and turns back toward the dayroom.

"What's happening now?" Anders asks anxiously.

Sven picks up his radio, calls two colleagues, and hurries out. Anders leans forward and watches as Sven appears on one of the screens. He's walking along the corridor, talking to the other guards. He pauses outside the security lock, evaluating the situation.

Nothing happens.

Jurek is standing in the doorway, between the rooms, in a spot where his face is in shadow. He's not moving, but both Anders and My can see that he's talking. Bernie is sprawled on the sofa, his eyes closed as he listens. The whole scenario plays out in little more than a minute. Jurek turns and disappears into his room.

"Back to your lair," My mutters.

One of the other monitors shows Jurek from above. Slowly, he walks into his room, sits on the plastic chair directly beneath the camera, and stares at the wall.

After a while, Bernie Larsson gets up from the sofa. He wipes his mouth a few times before shuffling off to his room.

Another monitor shows Bernie Larsson going over to the sink, leaning forward, and running water over his face. Then he walks back to the dayroom door, presses his thumb against the inside of the frame, and slams the door shut as hard as he can. The door bounces back, and Bernie sinks to his knees, screaming.

78

PETTER NÄSLUND is standing in front of a large-scale map of the residential area from which the two Kohler-Frost children disappeared. He frowns as he pins up photographs from the old investigation. Magdalena walks in, greets him with a quick hello, and goes over to the whiteboard. She strikes through the lines of inquiry they managed to follow up on yesterday. Benny Rubin, Johnny Isaksson, and Fredrik Weyler are sitting around the conference table, jotting down notes.

"We need to take another look at everyone who was employed at Menge's Engineering Workshop at the same time as Jurek Walter," she says.

"I've compiled the interviews from yesterday with Rikard van Horn, the friend of the Kohler-Frost children," Johnny says.

"Who's calling Reidar Frost today?" Petter asks, twirling a pen between his fingers.

"I can take care of that," Magdalena volunteers.

"Wonder if they want us to keep looking for Wee Willie Winkie," Benny says.

"Joona wants us all to take the whole Sandman thing seriously," Petter reminds him.

"I found this great clip on YouTube," Benny says, searching his phone.

"Do we have to?" Magdalena sighs, picking up a heavy file from the table.

"But have you seen that clown who hides from stupid cops?" Benny asks, putting down his phone.

"No," Petter replies.

"No, because I'm probably the only person in the room who's actually managed to catch sight of him." Benny laughs.

Magdalena is smiling as she opens the file.

"Who's going to help me find the last people connected to Agneta Magnusson?" she asks.

Agneta was the woman who was found alive in the grave in Lill-Jan's Forest when Jurek was caught. The two bodies in the plastic barrel buried nearby were her brother and nephew.

"Her mother vanished years ago, and her dad disappeared just after she was found."

"Didn't they all disappear?" Fredrik Weyler asks.

"Not her husband," Magdalena says, glancing at the file.

"This whole thing's so sick," Fredrik says.

79

STANDING ON THE FRONT PORCH, Magdalena Ronander says hello to the large woman who's just opened the door. She has fine laugh lines at the corners of her eyes and the name SONJA tattooed on her shoulder.

Everyone with even the most tentative connection to Agneta Magnusson was questioned by the police thirteen years ago. All their homes were searched by forensics officers, as well as their storage facilities, cars, boats, and other property.

"I called earlier," Magdalena says, showing her police ID.

"Oh, yes." The woman nods. "Eror's waiting for you in the living room."

Magdalena follows the woman through the little 1950s-style house. There's a smell of fried steak and onions from the kitchen. A man in a wheelchair is sitting in a living room with dark curtains.

"Is that the police?" he asks in a dry voice.

"Yes, it's the police," Magdalena says, pulling over the piano stool and sitting down in front of the man.

"Haven't we talked enough?"

It's been thirteen years since anyone questioned Bror Engström about what happened in Lill-Jan's Forest, and in that time he's grown old, she thinks.

"I need to know more," Magdalena says gently.

Bror Engström shakes his head.

"There's nothing left to say. Everyone vanished. In just a few years, they were all gone. My Agneta, and . . . her brother and nephew . . . and then Jeremy, my father-in-law. He stopped talking when . . . when they went missing, his children and grandson."

"Jeremy Magnusson," Magdalena says.

"I liked him a lot. But he missed his children so terribly."

"Yes," Magdalena says quietly.

Bror Engström's clouded eyes close at the memory.

"One day he was just gone—him, too. Then I got my Agneta back. But she was never herself again."

"No," Magdalena says.

"No," he whispers.

She knows that Joona made countless visits to see the woman in the long-term-care ward. She never regained the power of speech and died four years ago. The brain damage was too severe for anyone ever to reach her again.

"I suppose I should sell off Jeremy's land," the man says, "but I can't do it. Those forests meant everything to him. He was always trying to get me to go up to the hunting cabin with him, but it never quite worked out. And now it's too late."

"Where's the cabin?" she asks, taking out her phone.

"Way up in Dalarna, beyond Tranuberget, not far from the Norwegian border. I still have the maps from the Land Registry somewhere, if Sonja can find them."

The hunting cabin isn't on the list of locations searched by Forensics. Although it's probably nothing, neglecting it seems like a significant oversight. Joona said that they must leave no stone unturned.

80

A POLICE OFFICER and a forensics expert are making their way on snowmobiles across the deep snow between the dark trunks of the pine trees. In some areas, they can move faster by using cleared boundary lines and foresters' tracks, leaving a cloud of smoke and snow behind them.

Stockholm wanted them to investigate a hunting cabin beyond Tranuberget. Apparently, it had been owned by a Jeremy Magnusson, who disappeared thirteen years ago. They have been asked to conduct a thorough forensic examination of the cabin and to take video footage and photographs. Any potential evidence or biological matter is to be secured.

The two men know that the Stockholm Police are hoping to find something at the cabin that might shed light on the disappearance of Magnusson and other members of his family. It should have been searched thirteen years ago, but at the time the police hadn't been aware of its existence.

Roger Hysén and Gunnar Ehn are driving snowmobiles side by side down a slope at the edge of the forest in blinding light. They emerge onto a sunlit plain where everything is glistening white, completely untouched, and continue swiftly across the ice before swinging north into denser forest once more.

The forest has grown so wild on the southern slope of

Tranuberget that they almost miss the building entirely. The low timber shack is engulfed in snow, which is piled up higher than the windows and a few feet thick on the roof, leaving only a few silver-gray timber planks visible.

They get off their snowmobiles and begin to dig the cabin out.

Faded curtains hang inside the small windows.

The sun nudges the treetops as it sinks toward the horizon.

When the door is finally uncovered, they're sweating. The forensics expert, Gunnar Ehn, can feel his scalp itching under his hat.

Tree branches rub together in the wind and fill the air with a desolate creaking sound.

In silence, the two men roll out a sheet of plastic in front of the door and unpack boards to walk on. They put on protective outfits and gloves.

The door is locked, and there's no key on the hook under the eaves.

"The daughter was found buried alive in Stockholm," Roger Hysén says, glancing briefly at his colleague.

"I've heard the talk," Gunnar says. "It doesn't bother me."

Roger inserts a crowbar into the crack next to the lock and pushes. The frame creaks. He pushes it farther in and shoves harder. The frame splinters, and Roger gives the door a tentative tug, then pulls as hard as he can. It swings open and bounces back.

"Shit," Roger whispers behind his mask.

The draft from the unexpected movement has made all the dust that had settled inside the house fly up into the air. Gunnar mutters that it doesn't matter. He reaches into the dark cabin and puts two boards on the floor.

Roger hands over the video camera. Gunnar stoops under the low lintel and enters the cabin.

It's so dark inside that he can't see anything. The dust in the air is suffocating.

Gunnar sets the camera to record, but its light won't switch on. He tries recording the room anyway, but all he manages to get are vague outlines.

The whole cabin resembles a murky aquarium. There's an odd-looking shadow in the middle of the room, like a large grandfather clock.

"What's happening?" Roger calls from outside.

"Give me the other camera."

Gunnar trades the video camera for the photo camera. He checks the viewfinder, but all he sees is black. He snaps a picture at random. The flash fills the room with a white glow.

Gunnar screams when he sees the long, thin figure in front of him. He takes a step back, loses his footing, and drops the camera. He puts out an arm to regain his balance and knocks over a coat stand.

"What the fuck was that?"

He backs out, hitting his head on the lintel and cutting himself on the loose splinters sticking out from the door frame.

"What's happening? What's going on?" Roger asks.

"Someone's in there," Gunnar says, gritting his teeth.

Roger manages to switch on the video camera light and slowly makes his way inside. The floor creaks. The light from the camera searches through the dust and over the furniture. A branch scratches against the window and sounds like someone knocking.

"Oh," he gasps.

In the dim light, he sees that a man has hanged himself from a beam in the roof. A very long time ago. The body is thin, and the skin has dried out and is stretched across the face. The mouth is wide-open and black. His leather boots are on the floor.

The door groans open as Gunnar comes back in.

The sun has vanished behind the treetops, and the windows are dark. Gingerly, they spread out a body bag beneath the corpse.

The branch hits the window again and scrapes over the glass.

Roger reaches over to hold the body while Gunnar cuts the rope, but just as he touches the swaying corpse, its head comes loose from the neck. The body collapses at their feet. The skull thuds on the wooden floor, dust swirls up around the room once more, and the old noose swings noiselessly.

81

SAGA IS GAZING out the window of the van. The chains attached to her handcuffs rattle with the motion of the vehicle. She didn't want to think about Jurek Walter. Since she accepted the mission, she's managed to keep him out of her mind. But that's no longer possible. After three days of monotony at Karsudden Hospital, she's on her way to the secure unit of Löwenströmska. Her encounter with Jurek is drawing closer.

In her mind's eye, she can clearly see the photograph that was at the front of his file: his wrinkled face and those clear, pale eyes.

Jurek worked as a mechanic and lived a solitary and withdrawn life until his arrest. There was nothing in his apartment that could be linked to his crimes, yet he was caught red-handed.

Saga had been drenched with sweat by the time she finished reading the reports and looking at the images of the crime scenes. One large color photograph showed the forensics team's bright numbered signs in the clearing next to a heap of damp soil, a grave, and an open coffin.

The Needle had produced a thorough report on the woman's injuries after she'd been buried alive for two years.

Saga feels carsick and looks out at the road and trees sliding past. She thinks about how malnourished the woman was and about her pressure sores, frostbite, and lost teeth. Joona had described how the emaciated woman had tried to climb out of the coffin time after time but Jurek kept pushing her down.

Saga knows she shouldn't be lingering over this.

A shudder of anxiety spreads out from her stomach.

She tells herself that under no circumstances can she allow herself to feel afraid. She's in control of the situation.

The van brakes, and the handcuffs rattle.

The plastic barrel and the coffin had both been equipped with air tubes leading aboveground.

Why didn't he just kill them?

It's incomprehensible.

Saga considers what Mikael Kohler-Frost had said about his captivity, and she thinks of Felicia alone in the capsule, the little girl with the loose braid and riding hat.

It has stopped snowing, but there's no sign of the sun. The sky remains overcast. The van leaves the old main road and eases right as it enters the hospital grounds. A woman in her forties is sitting in the bus shelter with two shopping bags in her hands, taking deep drags on a cigarette.

Government approval is required to establish a secure unit, but Saga knows that the legislation allows plenty of leeway for the institutions to conduct their own evaluations. Ordinary laws and rights cease to apply inside those locked doors. There's no real scrutiny or supervision. The staff are lords of their own Hades, as long as none of their patients escape.

82

SAGA'S HANDS AND ANKLES are still cuffed as she is led down an empty corridor by two armed guards. They're both walking fast and holding her upper arms tightly.

It's too late to change her mind now—she's on her way to meet Jurek Walter.

The textured wallpaper is scratched and the baseboards scuffed. The closed doors they pass on the way have small plastic signs with numbers on them.

Saga has a stomachache and tries to stop but is pushed onward.

"Keep moving," one of the guards says.

The isolation unit at Löwenströmska Hospital has a very high security level, far above the requirements for most psychiatric hospitals. The building itself is basically impossible to break into or out of. The rooms have fireproof steel doors, fixed inner ceilings, and walls that have been reinforced with an inch of metal plate.

A heavy gate clangs shut behind them as they head down the stairs.

The guard at the security door leading to the cells takes the bag of Saga's possessions, checks the documentation, and signs Saga in on the computer. An older man with a baton hanging from his belt is visible on the other side of the door.

He's wearing big glasses and has wavy hair. Saga looks at him through the scratched reinforced glass.

The man with the baton takes Saga's papers, leafs through them, peers at her for a moment, then continues reading them.

Saga's stomach is cramping. She needs to lie down. She tries to breathe steadily but feels a sudden jolt of pain and leans forward.

"Stand still," the guard says in a neutral voice.

A younger man in a doctor's coat appears beyond the door. He pulls a pass card through the reader, taps in a code, and walks out to meet her.

"My name is Anders Rönn. I'm acting chief here," he says.

After a superficial search, Saga follows the doctor and the guard with the wavy hair through the security locks. She can smell their body odor in the confined space before the second door opens.

Saga recognizes the layout of the ward from the plans she has memorized.

They walk around a corner and over to the unit's cramped surveillance room. A woman with pierced cheeks is sitting in front of the monitors. She blushes when she sees Saga but greets her with a friendly hello before looking down and writing something in her logbook.

"My, would you remove the cuffs from the patient's ankles?" the young doctor asks.

The woman nods, gets on her knees, and unlocks the cuffs. The hair on her head lifts slightly from the static in Saga's clothes.

The young doctor and the guard walk Saga out of the control room to one of the three doors in the corridor.

"Unlock the door," the doctor orders the man with the baton.

The guard takes out a key, opens the door, then tells her to go in and stand on the red cross on the floor with her back to the door.

She does as he asks and hears the lock click as the key is turned again.

In front of her is another metal door. She knows that this one is locked and leads straight out into the dayroom.

The room is furnished with no thought to anything but security and function. All it contains is a bed fixed to the wall, a plastic chair, a plastic table, and a toilet, with no seat or lid.

"Turn around, but stay on the cross."

She does as she's told and sees that the little hatch in the door is open.

"Come slowly over here and hold out your hands."

Saga walks over to the door, clasps her hands tightly together, and puts them through the narrow opening. The cuffs are removed, and she backs away from the door again.

She sits down on the bed while the guard informs her of the unit's rules and routines.

"You can watch television and socialize with the other patients in the dayroom between one o'clock and four o'clock," he concludes, then looks at her for a few moments before closing and bolting the hatch.

Saga remains seated. She knows that she is in position now, that her mission has started. The seriousness of the moment makes her stomach tingle, and the feeling spreads through her arms and legs. She's a closely guarded patient in the secure unit, and she knows that the serial killer Jurek Walter is very close.

She curls up on her side, then rolls onto her back and stares up at the CCTV camera in the ceiling. It's hemispherical in shape, as black and shiny as a cow's eye.

It's been a long time since she swallowed the microphone, and she doesn't dare leave it any longer. She can't let the microphone slip too far down her digestive tract. When she goes over to the tap and drinks some water her stomachache kicks in again.

Breathing slowly, Saga kneels down by the drain in the floor, turns away from the camera, and sticks two fingers down her throat. She vomits the water back up. She sticks her fingers in deeper and regurgitates the little capsule containing the microphone and quickly hides it in her hand.

83

THE SECRET INVESTIGATIVE TEAM, Athena Promachos, has been listening to the sounds of Saga Bauer's stomach for two hours since she arrived at Löwenströmska.

"If anyone walked in now, they'd think we were some sort of New Age sect," Corinne says with a smile.

"It's actually quite beautiful," Johan Jönson says.

"Relaxing." Pollock grins.

The whole team are sitting with their eyes half closed, listening to the gently bubbling, fizzing sounds.

Suddenly there's a roar that almost blows out the loudspeakers as Saga vomits up the microphone. Johan Jönson knocks over his can of Coca-Cola, and Nathan Pollock jumps out of his seat.

"Well, at least we're awake now." Corinne laughs, and her jade bracelets jangle pleasantly as she runs an index finger over one eyebrow.

"I'll call Joona," Nathan says.

"Good."

Corinne Meilleroux opens her laptop and notes the time in the logbook. Corinne is fifty-four years old, with a French-Caribbean background. She wears her gray-streaked black hair tied in an updo held with a clasp at the back of her neck.

JOONA IS STANDING in Mikael Kohler-Frost's hospital room. Reidar is sitting on a chair, holding his son's hand. The three of them have been talking for four hours, trying to identify any fresh details that could help pinpoint the place where Mikael was held captive with his sister. But the young man's memories are fractured and often incoherent. His thirteen years of confinement have left him deeply scarred.

Nothing new has emerged, and Mikael looks very tired.

"You need to get some sleep," Joona tells him.

"No," Mikael says.

"Just for a while." The detective smiles as he switches off the recording. He pulls a newspaper out of his coat pocket and sets it down in front of Reidar.

"I know you asked me not to," Reidar says, meeting his gaze without wavering. "But how could I live with myself if I don't do absolutely everything I can?"

"I understand," Joona says. "But it could cause problems, and you have to be prepared for that."

One whole page of the paper displays a digital image of how Felicia might look today. A young woman bearing a strong resemblance to Mikael, with high cheekbones and dark eyes. Her black hair is shown hanging loose around her pale, serious face. Large lettering announces that Reidar is offering a reward of twenty million kronor to anyone who can provide information that leads to Felicia's rescue.

"We've already been flooded with e-mails and calls," Joona explains. "We're trying to follow up with all of them, but . . . I'm sure most of them mean well. They believe they've seen something. But there are still plenty just hoping to get rich."

Reidar slowly folds the newspaper.

"Joona, I'm doing whatever I can. I . . . my daughter's been held captive for so long, and she might die without ever—"

His voice cracks, and he looks away for a moment.

"Do you have children?" he asks, his voice barely audible.

Before Joona has time to lie, his phone rings in his jacket. He apologizes, answers it, and hears Pollock's voice informing him that Athena Promachos's audio is live.

84

SAGA LIES DOWN on the bed with her back to the camera and carefully peels the silicon covering off the microphone. Barely moving at all, she slips the microphone into the cuff of her pants.

Suddenly there's an electronic buzz from the door to the dayroom. The lock clicks. It's open. Saga sits up, her heart beating hard.

The microphone needs to be installed in an advantageous position right away. She might get only one chance. She can't miss it. She'll be discovered if she gets searched.

She doesn't know what the dayroom looks like, if the other patients are in there, or if there are cameras or guards.

Maybe the room is nothing but a trap where Jurek Walter is waiting for her.

No, there's no way he could possibly know about her mission.

Saga throws the pieces of silicon in the toilet and flushes them away. She goes over to the door, opens it a crack, and hears a rhythmic throbbing sound, cheerful voices from the television.

She remembers Joona's advice and forces herself to go back to her bed and sit down.

Never show any urgency, she thinks. Never do anything unless you have a valid reason for doing it, a justification.

Through the crack in the door, she can hear music from the television, the drone of the treadmill, and heavy footsteps.

A man with a sharp, stressed voice speaks occasionally but never gets a response.

Both patients are out there.

Saga knows she has to go in and install the microphone.

She walks to the door again and stands there, trying to control her breath.

The smell of aftershave hits her.

She grasps the door handle, takes a deep breath, looks down at the floor, and throws open the door. She can hear the rhythmic thuds more clearly as she steps into the dayroom, her head still lowered. She doesn't know if she's being watched but decides to let them get used to the sight of her before looking up.

A man with a bandaged hand is sitting on the sofa in front of the television, and another is marching on the treadmill. The man on the treadmill is facing away from her, but she's sure it's Jurek.

The man on the sofa belches and swallows several times. He wipes the sweat from his cheeks and nervously bounces his leg. He's overweight and in his forties, with thin hair, a blond mustache, and glasses.

"Obrahiim," he mutters, staring at the television.

He suddenly points at the screen.

"There he is," he says loudly. "I'd turn him into my slave, my skeleton slave. Fucking hell . . . Look at those lips. . . . I'd—"

He falls silent abruptly as Saga walks across the room, stops in one corner, and turns toward the television. It's a repeat of the European Figure Skating Championships in Sheffield. The sound and image are degraded by the reinforced glass. Though she can feel the man on the sofa looking at her, she doesn't meet his gaze.

"I'd whip him first," he goes on, still facing Saga. "I'd make him really scared, like a whore. . . . I mean, fucking hell . . ."

He coughs, leans back, closes his eyes and grimaces as if waiting for pain to pass, gropes his neck with his hand, then lies there panting.

Jurek is still striding along on the treadmill. He looks bigger and stronger than she imagined. There's an artificial palm in a pot next to the machine. Its dusty leaves sway as he walks.

Saga looks around for somewhere to hide the microphone—preferably away from the television, to minimize background noise. The back of the sofa would make sense, but she can't really imagine Jurek as the sort to sit and watch television.

The man on the sofa tries to get up and looks as if he's about to throw up from the effort. He cups his hand over his mouth and swallows a few times before sinking back into his seat.

"Start with the legs," he says. "Cut everything off, peel the skin away, muscles, sinew. . . . He can keep his feet, so he can walk quietly. . . ."

85

Jurek turns off the treadmill and leaves the room without giving either of them so much as a glance. The other patient slowly gets up.

"Zyprexa makes you feel like shit . . . and Stemetil doesn't work on me. It just fucks my insides up."

Saga stays where she is, facing the television, watching as the figure skater accelerates, and listening to the sound of metal blades cutting across the ice. She can feel the other patient's eyes as he lumbers toward her.

"My name's Bernie Larsson," he says conspiratorially. "They don't think I can fuck, with all the bastard Suprefact in my system, but they don't know a fucking thing."

He jabs his finger in her face, but she stands her ground, her heart pounding.

"They don't know a fucking thing," he repeats. "They're so fucking brain-damaged."

He staggers aside and burps loudly. Saga is weighing the risks of placing the microphone on the artificial palm next to the treadmill.

"What's your name?" Bernie asks, breathing heavily.

She doesn't answer, just stands there with her eyes lowered, looking toward the television. Her time is running out. Bernie moves behind her, sticks his hand around, and pinches her hard on the nipple. She pushes his hand away. Anger starts to bubble up inside her.

"Little Snow White." His sweaty face is close to hers. "What's the matter with you? Can I feel your head? It looks so fucking soft. Like a shaved cunt."

From the little she's seen of Jurek, the treadmill is what he's most interested in inside the dayroom. He was on it for at least an hour and then went straight back into his room.

Saga walks over to the treadmill and steps onto it. Bernie follows her, biting a fingernail and pulling off a sharp fragment.

"Do you shave your cunt? You have to do that, yeah?"

Saga turns and stares at him intently. His eyelids are heavy, and his eyes have a drugged look about them. His blond mustache hides the scar left by a cleft palate.

"Never touch me again," she says.

"I can kill you," he says, scratching her neck with his sharpened nail.

She feels the wound sting as a voice is broadcast from the loudspeaker: "Bernie Larsson, step back."

He tries to touch her between the legs. The doors open, and a guard with a baton comes in. Bernie moves away from Saga and holds up his hands in a gesture of surrender.

"No touching," the guard says sternly.

"Okay, I know, fucking hell."

Bernie feels his way wearily over to the armrest of the sofa and sits down heavily. He shuts his eyes and belches.

Saga gets off the treadmill and turns to the guard.

"I want to see a legal ombudsman," she says.

"Stay where you are," the guard says, glancing at her.

"Can you pass on the message?"

Without replying, the guard goes over to the security door and is let out. It's as if she hadn't said anything, as if her words had stopped in midair before reaching him.

Saga turns away and walks toward the artificial palm. She sits down on the edge of the treadmill, right next to it, and looks at one of its lower leaves. The underside isn't too dirty, and the glue on the microphone should be able to firm up in four seconds.

Bernie is staring up at the ceiling, licking his lips. Saga watches him as she slides a finger into the cuff of her pants and retrieves the microphone. She pulls off one of her shoes and leans forward to adjust its tongue, shielding her palm from the camera. She shifts slightly and is just reaching out to the leaf to attach the microphone when the sofa creaks.

"I've got my eye on you, Snow White," Bernie says.

She calmly withdraws her hand, puts her foot back in her shoe, and sees Bernie watching her as she sticks the Velcro down.

86

SAGA GETS ON THE TREADMILL, thinking that she'll have to wait for him to return to his room before she plants the microphone. Bernie takes a couple of steps toward her and reaches out to steady himself against the wall.

"I come from Säter," he mumbles with a smile.

She doesn't look at him but is aware that he's coming closer.

"Where were you before you came here?" he asks.

He pauses, then punches the wall hard before looking at her again.

"Karsudden," he says in a squeaky voice. "I was at Karsudden, but I moved here because I wanted to be with Bernie. . . ."

Saga catches a shadow crossing the third doorway as someone pulls back from it. She realizes that Jurek Walter is standing there listening to them.

"You must have met Yekaterina Ståhl at Karsudden," Bernie says in his normal voice.

She shakes her head. She can't remember anyone with that name. She doesn't know if he's talking about a patient or a guard.

"No," she responds. It's an honest answer.

"Because she was at Sankt Sigfrids." He grins and spits on the floor. "So who did you meet?"

"No one."

He mutters something about skeleton slaves, then stands in front of the treadmill and watches her.

"All right, but I get to touch your cunt if you're lying," he says, scratching his mustache. "Deal?"

She stops the treadmill, stands there for a moment, and considers her strategy of sticking to the truth. She was actually at Karsudden.

"What about Micke Lund, then? You must have seen Micke Lund if you were there," he says, flashing a smile. "Tall fellow. Scar across his forehead."

She shakes her head, unsure what to say. She could leave it at that, but instead says, "No."

"Fucking weird."

"I sat in my room watching TV."

"There aren't any TVs in the rooms there, you're fucking lying, you're a—"

"There are in isolation," she interrupts.

She can't tell whether he knew that. He's breathing hard and staring at her. He licks his lips and comes closer.

"You're my slave," he spits out slowly. "Fucking hell, that's brilliant. You lie there, sucking my toes. . . ."

Saga gets off the treadmill and returns to her cell. She lies on her bunk and hears Bernie standing by her door for a while, calling for her.

"Shit," she whispers.

She'll have to be quick tomorrow. She'll sit down on the edge of the treadmill, adjust her shoes, and attach the microphone. She'll use the treadmill, she won't look at anyone, and when Jurek comes in she'll just get off the treadmill and leave the dayroom.

Saga visualizes the angle of the wall adjacent to the reinforced glass over the television. The camera's view must be partially obscured by the protruding section. She'll have to watch out for that blind spot. That's where she was standing when Bernie pinched her nipple. That was why the staff didn't react.

She's been at Löwenströmska for just over five hours, and already she's exhausted. The metal-encased room feels more claustrophobic now. She closes her eyes and reminds herself why she's here. In her mind's eye, she can see the girl in the photograph. All of this is for her sake, for Felicia.

87

THE ATHENA GROUP sit completely still and listen to the broadcast from the dayroom in real time. The sound quality is poor, muffled and distorted by loud scraping noises.

"Is it going to sound like this the whole time?" Pollock asks.

"She hasn't positioned the microphone yet. It's still on her," Johan Jönson replies.

"As long as she doesn't get searched . . ."

They listen to the recording again. They can hear the rasping of Saga's clothes, her shallow breathing, the percussive steps on the treadmill, and the noise of the television. The members of Athena Promachos are being guided through the closed world of the secure unit with the help of audio alone.

"Obrahiim," a slurred voice says

The entire group is suddenly very focused. Johan Jönson raises the volume slightly and applies a filter to reduce the hissing.

"There he is," the man continues. "I'd turn him into my slave, my skeleton slave."

"I thought that was Jurek," says Corinne.

"Fucking hell," the voice goes on. "Look at those lips . . . I'd . . ."

They listen in silence to this patient's aggressive torrent of words and hear a guard come in and break up the confrontation. After the intervention, there's a short period of silence. Then the patient starts to interrogate Saga about Karsudden with suspicion.

"She's handling it well," Pollock says through clenched teeth.

Eventually, they hear Saga leave the dayroom. She hasn't managed to position the microphone.

She swears quietly to herself.

There's silence until the electronic lock on the door clicks shut.

"Well, at least we know that the technology seems to work," Pollock says.

"Poor Saga," Corinne whispers.

"She should have positioned the microphone," Johan Jönson mutters.

"She didn't have a chance."

"But if she blows her cover, then—"

"She won't," Corinne says.

"Jurek's said nothing so far," Pollock says, glancing over at Joona.

"What if he stays silent? All this will have been in vain," Jönson sighs.

Joona says nothing, but he's thinking that something was conveyed in the brief section of the recording. For several minutes, it was as if he could feel the physical presence of Jurek, as if Jurek was in the dayroom, even though he hadn't said anything.

"Let's listen to it one more time," he says, checking the clock.

"Are you going somewhere?" Corinne asks, raising her neat black eyebrows.

"I'm meeting someone," Joona says, returning her smile.

"Finally, a bit of romance, huh?"

88

JOONA WALKS into a white-tiled room with a long sink against one wall. Water is running from an orange hose into a drain in the floor. The body from the hunting cabin in Dalarna is lying on a plastic-covered autopsy table. Its sunken brown chest has been sawed open, and yellow liquid is trickling into the stainless-steel trough.

"Tra-la-la-la-laa—we'd catch the rainbow," The Needle sings to himself. "Tra-la-la-la-laa—to the sun . . ."

He pulls out a pair of latex gloves and is blowing into them when he sees Joona standing in the doorway.

"You should record an album with everyone in Forensics." Joona smiles.

"Frippe's a very good guitar player," The Needle replies.

The light from the powerful lamps in the ceiling reflects off his aviator glasses. He's wearing a white polo under his doctor's coat.

They hear footsteps in the corridor; moments later, Carlos Eliasson strolls in, wearing pale-blue shoe covers on his feet. "Have you managed to identify the body?" he asks, stopping abruptly when he catches sight of the corpse on the table.

The raised edges make the autopsy table look like a draining rack where someone has left a piece of dried meat or some strange, blackened root. The corpse is desiccated and distorted, its severed head placed above the neck.

"There's no doubt that it's Jeremy Magnusson," The Needle replies. "Our forensic dentist compared the body's oral characteristics with Magnusson's dental records."

The Needle leans over, takes the head in his hands, and opens the wrinkled black hole that was Jeremy Magnusson's mouth.

"He had an impacted wisdom tooth, and—"

"Please," Carlos says, beads of sweat glinting on his forehead.

"The palate is gone," The Needle says, forcing the mouth open a bit farther. "But if you feel with your finger—"

"Fascinating," Carlos interrupts, then looks at his watch. "Do we have any idea how long he was hanging there?"

"The drying process would probably have been impeded slightly by the low temperatures," The Needle replies. "But if you look at the eyes, the conjunctiva dried out very quickly, as did the undersides of the eyelids. The parchmentlike texture of the skin is uniform, apart from around the neck, where it was in contact with the rope."

"Which means?" Carlos says.

"The postmortal process forms a sort of diary, an ongoing life after death, as the body changes. And I would estimate that Mr. Magnusson hanged himself—"

"Thirteen years, one month, and five days ago," Joona says.

"Good guess," The Needle says.

"I just got a scan of his goodbye note from Forensics," Joona says, taking out his phone.

"Suicide," Carlos says.

"Everything points to that, even if Jurek Walter could feasibly have been there at the time," The Needle replies.

"Jeremy Magnusson was on the list of Jurek's most likely

victims," Carlos says. "And if we can write off his death as suicide . . ."

A thought is flitting through Joona's mind. It's as if there's some sort of hidden association tucked away but resonating with this conversation—one he can't quite grasp.

"What did he say in the note?" Carlos asks.

"He hanged himself just three weeks before Samuel and I found his daughter, Agneta, in Lill-Jan's Forest," Joona says, bringing up the image of the note.

I don't know why I've lost everyone. My children, my grandson, and my wife.

I'm like Job, but with no restitution.

I have waited, and that waiting must end.

He took his life in the belief that everyone he loved had been taken from him. If he had only put up with loneliness for a little longer, he would have gotten his daughter back.

89

REIDAR FROST has ordered food from the noodle house to be delivered to the hospital. Steam is rising from beef-and-cilantro dumplings, spring rolls that smell strongly of ginger, rice noodles with chopped vegetables and chili, fried pork chops, and chicken soup. He's ordered eight different dishes, because he doesn't know what Mikael likes anymore.

Just as he emerges from the elevator and starts walking along the corridor, his phone rings.

Reidar puts the bags down by his feet, sees that the call is from a private number, and hurries to answer, "Reidar Frost."

The phone is silent apart from a crackling sound.

"Who is this?" he asks.

Someone groans in the background.

"Hello?"

He's on the point of ending the call when someone whispers, "Daddy?"

"Hello?" he repeats. "Who is this?"

"Daddy, it's me," a strange, high voice whispers. "It's Felicia."

The floor starts to spin under Reidar's feet.

"Felicia?"

It's almost impossible to hear her voice now.

"Daddy? I'm so scared, Daddy. . . ."

"Where are you? Please, darling?"

He hears giggling and feels a shiver run through his whole body.

"Darling Daddy, give me twenty million kronor."

It's obvious now that it's a man disguising his voice and trying to make it sound higher.

"Give me twenty million and I'll sit in your lap and—"

"Do you know anything about my daughter?" Reidar asks.

"You're such a bad writer it makes me sick."

"Yes, I am. But if you know anything about—"

The call ends, and Reidar's hands are shaking so much that he can't tap in the number for the police. He tries to pull himself together and tells himself that he's going to report the call, even though it won't lead anywhere, and the police are bound to think he has only himself to blame.

90

IT'S EVENING, but Anders Rönn is still at the hospital. Leif has gone home, and a muscular woman named Pia Madsen is working the evening guard shift. She doesn't say much, mostly sits there reading thrillers and yawning. Anders wants to check up on the third patient, the young woman.

She arrived directly from Karsudden Hospital and shows no sign of wanting to communicate with the staff. Her medication is extremely conservative, considering the results of the psychiatric evaluation. She is regarded as dangerous and an escape risk. The crimes she was convicted of in the District Court are deeply unpleasant.

As Anders watches her, he can't believe the reports are true, even though he knows they must be.

Anders finds himself staring at the new patient on the screen again.

She's as slim as a ballet dancer, and her shaved head makes her look fragile.

She's astonishingly beautiful.

Maybe she was only prescribed Trilafon and Stesolid at Karsudden Hospital because she's so beautiful.

After his meeting with hospital management, Anders has almost complete authority over the secure unit.

For the foreseeable future, he is making the decisions about the patients.

He has consulted with Dr. Maria Gomez in Ward 30. Usually, an initial period of observation would be advisable, but he could go in and give her an intramuscular injection of Haldol now. The thought makes him tingle, and he is filled with a heady, unfamiliar sense of anticipation.

Pia Madsen returns from the bathroom. A bit of toilet paper is stuck to one of her shoes and is trailing after her. She's approaching along the corridor with shuffling steps, her face lethargic. Her eyelids are half closed, until she looks up and meets his gaze. "I'm not that tired," she says with a laugh. She removes the toilet paper and throws it in the trash, then sits down at the control desk next to him and looks at the time. "Shall we sing a lullaby?" she sighs, before logging on to the computer and switching out the lights in the patients' rooms.

The image of the three patients stays on Anders's retina for a while. Just before everything went dark, Jurek was already lying on his back in bed, Bernie was sitting on the floor holding his bandaged hand to his chest and Saga was sitting on the edge of her bed, looking angry and vulnerable in equal measure.

"They're already part of the family," Pia says, then opens her book.

91

At nine o'clock, the staff turns out the ceiling light. Saga is sitting on the edge of her bed. The microphone is still tucked into the cuff of her pants. It seems safest to keep it close until she's able to position it. Without the microphone, the whole mission will be pointless. She waits, and a short while later, a gray rectangle becomes visible through the darkness. It's the thick glass window in the door. The shapes in the room glow in a foggy landscape. Saga gets up and goes over to the darkest corner, lies down on the cold floor, and starts doing sit-ups. After three hundred, she rolls over, gently stretches her abdominal muscles, and starts doing push-ups.

Suddenly she gets the feeling that she's being watched. Something's different. She stops and looks up. The glass window is darker, shaded. In a hurry, she sticks her fingers into the cuff of her pants and takes out the microphone but drops it on the floor.

She hears steps, then a metallic scraping sound against the door.

Saga sweeps her hands quickly over the floor, finds the microphone, and puts it in her mouth just as the lamp in the ceiling comes on.

"Stand on the cross," a woman says in a stern voice.

Saga is still on all fours with the microphone in her mouth. Slowly she gets to her feet as she tries to gather saliva.

"Hurry up."

She takes her time walking toward the cross, looking up at the ceiling, then down at the floor again. She stops on the cross, turns her back nonchalantly toward the door, raises her eyes to the ceiling, and swallows. Her throat hurts badly as the microphone slips down.

"We met earlier," a man says in a drawling voice. "I'm in charge here, and I'm responsible for your medication."

"I want to see a lawyer," Saga says.

"Take your top off and walk slowly over to the door," the first voice says.

She takes off her blouse, lets it fall to the floor, turns, and walks toward the door in her washed-out bra.

"Stop. Hold both your hands up, turn your arms around, and open your mouth wide."

The metal hatch opens, and she expects to receive the little cup with her pills.

"I've changed your medication, by the way," the man with the drawling voice says.

Saga sees the doctor fill a syringe with a milky-white emulsion and suddenly grasps the full significance of what it means to be under these people's power.

"Stick your left arm through the hatch," the woman says.

She realizes she can't refuse, but her pulse quickens as she obeys. A hand grabs her arm, and the doctor rubs his thumb over the muscle in her forearm. She suppresses the panicked instinct to fight her way free.

"I understand that you've been getting Trilafon," the doctor says, giving her a look she can't read. "Eight milligrams, three times a day. But I was thinking of trying—"

"I don't want to," she says.

She tries to pull her arm back, but the guard is holding it

tight, and Saga can tell that she's capable of breaking it. The guard forces her arm down, making her stand on tiptoe.

Saga wills herself to breathe evenly. What are they going to give her? A clouded drop is hanging from the point of the needle. She tries to pull her arm back again. A finger strokes the thin skin over the muscle. There's a prick, and the needle slides in. She can't move her arm. A chill spreads through her body. She looks at the doctor's hands as the needle is withdrawn and a small compress stops the bleeding. She pulls her arm free and retreats from the two figures behind the glass.

"Now go sit on the bed," the guard says in a hard voice.

Her arm stings where the needle went in, as if it had burned her. An immense weariness spreads through her body. She doesn't have the energy to pick up her shirt from the floor, just stumbles and takes a step toward the bed.

"I've given you Stesolid to help you relax," the doctor says.

The room lurches, and she fumbles for support but can't reach the wall with her hand.

"Shit," Saga gasps.

Tiredness sweeps over her. Just as she's thinking that she needs to lie down on the bed, her legs give way. She collapses and hits the floor, a jolt running through her body and jerking her neck.

"I'll be coming in shortly," the doctor continues. "I was thinking we might try a neuroleptic drug that sometimes works very well. It's called Haldol Depot."

"I don't want to," she says quietly, trying to roll onto her side.

She opens her eyes and blinks through the dizziness. One hip is throbbing from the fall. A tingling sensation rises from her feet, making her more and more drowsy. She doesn't have the energy to get up. Her thoughts are slowing. She tries again to raise her head but is completely impotent.

92

HER EYELIDS ARE HEAVY, but she forces herself to look. The light from the lamp in the ceiling is strangely clouded. The metal door opens, and a man in a white coat comes in. It's the young doctor. He's holding something in his slender hands. The lock on the door clicks behind him. She blinks her dry eyes and sees the doctor put two vials of yellow oil on the table. Carefully, he opens the plastic packaging of a syringe. Saga tries to crawl under the bed, but she's too slow. The doctor grabs hold of her ankle and starts to pull her out. She tries to cling on and rolls to her back. Her bra slides up, uncovering her breasts as he drags her out.

"You look like a princess," she hears him whisper.

"What?"

She looks up to see his moist gaze and tries to cover her breasts, but her hands are too weak.

She shuts her eyes again and just lies there waiting.

Suddenly the doctor rolls her over onto her stomach. He pulls down her pants and underwear. She fades out and is awoken by a sharp prick on the top of her right buttock, then another, lower down.

———

Saga wakes up in the darkness on the cold floor and realizes that she's been covered with a blanket. Her head hurts, and she has little feeling in her hands. She sits up, adjusts her bra, and remembers the microphone in her stomach.

There's very little time.

She could have been asleep for hours.

She crawls over to the drain in the floor, sticks two fingers down her throat and throws up some acrid liquid. She gulps hard and tries again. Her stomach cramps, but nothing comes up.

"Shit."

She has to have the microphone tomorrow so she can place it in the dayroom. She can't let it disappear. She gets up on wobbly legs and drinks some water from the tap, then kneels and tries again. The water comes back up, but she keeps her fingers in her throat. The meager contents of her stomach trickle down her forearm. Gasping for breath, she sticks her fingers in deeper, setting off the gag reflex. She throws up bile until her mouth is filled with the bitter taste. She coughs and sticks her fingers down once more. This time, she finally feels the microphone come up through her throat and into her mouth. She catches it in her hand and hides it, even though the room is dark, then stands up, washes it under the tap, and tucks it into the cuff of her pants again. She spits out a mixture of bile and slime, rinses her mouth and face, spits again, drinks some water, and lies down on the bed.

Her feet and fingertips are cold. She has a vague itch in her toes. As Saga adjusts her pants, she realizes that her underwear is inside out. She isn't sure if she put them on wrong herself or if something else happened. She curls up under the blanket and carefully slides one hand down to her crotch. It isn't sore, but it feels strangely numb.

93

Mikael Kohler-Frost is sitting at a table in the dining room of his hospital ward. One hand is wrapped around a cup of warm tea as he speaks to Magdalena Ronander of National Crime. Reidar is too agitated to sit, but he stands by the door and watches his son for a while before going down to the entrance to meet Veronica Klimt.

Magdalena smiles at Mikael, then gets out the bulky interview protocols and puts them on the table. They fill four spiral-bound folders. She leafs through to the bookmarked page, then asks if he's ready to continue.

"I only ever saw the inside of the capsule," Mikael explains, as he's done so many times before.

"Can you describe the door again?" she asks.

"It's made of metal, and it's completely smooth. In the beginning, you could pick little flakes of paint off with your fingernails. There's no keyhole and no handle."

"What color is it?"

"Gray, as I remember."

"And there was a hatch that—"

She breaks off when she sees him wipe the tears from his cheeks and turn his face away.

"I can't tell Dad," he says, his lips trembling. "But if Felicia doesn't come back . . ."

Magdalena pauses and goes around the table, hugs him, and says that everything is going to be okay.

"I know," he says. "I know I'd kill myself."

REIDAR FROST has barely left Södermalm Hospital since Mikael was admitted. He's been renting a room at the hospital, on the same floor as Mikael, so he can be with his son.

Even though Reidar knows it wouldn't do any good, it's all he can do to stop himself from running out to join the search for Felicia. He's paid for notices in the national newspapers every day, pleading for information and promising a reward. He's employed a team of the country's best private detectives to look for her. Her absence is tearing at him, preventing him from sleeping, and forcing him to roam the corridors hour after hour.

The only thing that calms him is watching Mikael get stronger with each passing day. Inspector Joona Linna said that it would be a huge help for the investigation if Reidar stayed with his son, letting him talk at his own pace, listening and writing down every memory, every detail.

When Reidar reaches the entrance, Veronica is already waiting for him inside the glass doors that lead to the snow-covered parking lot.

"Isn't it a bit early to be sending Micke home?" she asks, handing over the bags.

"They say it's fine." Reidar smiles.

"I bought a pair of jeans, and sweatpants, shirts, T-shirts, a thick sweater, and a few other—"

"How are things at home?" Reidar asks.

"Lots of snow," says Veronica, laughing. She tells him that the last few guests have finally left.

"Even my cavaliers?" Reidar asks.

"No, they're still there. . . . You'll see."

"What do you mean?"

Veronica just shakes her head and smiles. "I told Berzelius that they're not allowed to come here, but they're very keen to meet Mikael," she replies.

"Are you coming up?" Reidar asks, smiling and adjusting her collar.

"Another time," Veronica replies, looking him in the eye.

94

As REIDAR DRIVES, Mikael sits there in his new clothes, changing stations on the radio. Suddenly he stops. Satie's ballet music fills the car like warm summer rain.

"Dad, I can't remember this landscape," Mikael says.

"You've never been here. I had to move."

"But my room? And Felicia's?"

"I've kept all your stuff."

Reidar bought the run-down estate because he could no longer stand the nosy neighbors in Tyresö.

Snow-covered fields spread out before them. They turn into the long driveway, where Reidar's three friends have lit torches up to the house. When they stop and get out of the car, Wille Strandberg, Berzelius, and David Sylwan appear on the steps.

Berzelius takes a step forward and hesitates, as if he doesn't know whether to embrace or shake hands with the young man. Then he hugs Mikael hard.

Wille wipes tears away behind his glasses.

"You're all grown up, Micke," he says. "I've—"

"Let's go inside," Reidar interrupts, coming to his son's rescue. "We need to eat."

David blushes and shrugs apologetically: "We've organized a backward party."

"What's that?" Reidar asks.

"You start with dessert and conclude with the starter." Sylwan smiles, slightly embarrassed.

Mikael is the first one through the imposing doorway. He stops and leans one hand against the wall, as if he's about to faint. The broad oak tiles in the hallway smell as if they've recently been scrubbed.

There are balloons hanging from the ceiling of the dining room, and on the table is a large cake decorated with a figure of Spider-Man made out of colored marzipan.

"We know you're grown up, but you used to like Spider-Man and love cake, so we thought . . ."

"We got it wrong," Wille concludes.

"I'd love to try some," Mikael says, and lowers his eyes.

"That's the spirit!" David laughs.

"Then there's pizza, and alphabet soup to finish up with," Berzelius says.

They sit down at the huge oval table.

"I remember this one time when you said you would keep an eye on the cake in the kitchen until the guests arrived," Berzelius says, cutting Mikael a large slice. "It was completely hollow by the time we came to light the candles."

Reidar excuses himself and leaves the table. He tries to smile with the others, but his heart is pounding with angst. He misses his daughter so much it hurts, enough to make him want to scream. Seeing Mikael sitting there with that childish cake, pale and trembling as if resurrected from the dead. Reidar takes a few deep breaths and goes out into the hall, remembering the day he buried the children's empty caskets next to Roseanna's ashes. Then he went home. Invited everyone to a party and was never properly sober again.

He stands in the hall, looking back into the dining room, where Mikael forces himself to eat while Reidar's friends try to make conversation with the lost boy. Reidar knows he shouldn't keep doing this, but he gets out his phone and calls Joona.

"It's Reidar," he says. A faint pressure is building in his chest.

"I heard that Mikael was discharged," the detective says.

"But Felicia. I have to know. She's, she's so . . ."

"I know, Reidar," Joona says gently.

"You're doing what you can," Reidar whispers. He has to sit down.

He hears the detective ask something, but he ends the call in the middle of a sentence.

95

REIDAR LEANS against the wall and feels the texture of the wallpaper under his hand. He notices some dead flies on the dusty base of the lamp.

Mikael had said that Felicia didn't think he'd look for her, that she was sure he didn't care about her going missing.

The pressure in Reidar's chest rises. He glances toward the corridor, where he threw off his coat with the little nitroglycerin spray. He tries to breathe deeply, takes a few steps, and stops. He was an unfair father. He knows that.

Felicia had turned eight that January.

Mikael was always so sharp and aware. He would listen to you attentively and do whatever was expected of him.

Felicia was different.

Reidar was full of his own importance back then. He would write all day, answering letters from his readers, give interviews, sit for photo shoots, and travel internationally for book launches. He never felt he had enough time, and he hated it when people kept him waiting.

Felicia was always late.

That day—when the unimaginable happened, when Reidar was abandoned by whatever god might be out there—began with a perfectly ordinary morning. The sun was shining.

Felicia was always slow and unfocused. Roseanna had already put clothes out for her that morning, but it was Reidar's job to make sure that the children got to school on time. Roseanna had to leave early to drive into Stockholm before the rush-hour traffic made the commute interminable.

Mikael was ready to go by the time Felicia sat down at the kitchen table. Reidar buttered toast for her, poured her some cereal, and set out the chocolate powder, milk, and a glass. She sat and read the back of a cereal box, tore off the corner of her toast, and rolled it into a buttery lump.

"We're in a bit of a hurry," Reidar said in a measured tone.

She spooned some chocolate powder from the packet without moving it closer to the glass and managed to spill most of it on the table. Leaning forward on her elbows, she started to draw in the spilled powder with her fingers. Reidar told her to wipe the table, but she didn't answer, just licked the finger covered in chocolate powder.

"You know we have to be out the door by ten past eight if we're going to get there on time?"

"Yeah," she muttered, then got up from the table.

"Brush your teeth," Reidar said. "Mom's laid your clothes out in your room."

He decided against telling her off for not putting her glass away or wiping the table.

REIDAR'S CHEST FEELS TIGHT. Pain courses down his arm, and he struggles to breathe. Mikael and David Sylwan are suddenly there beside him. He tries to tell them that he's fine. Berzelius runs over with his coat, and they hunt through the pockets for his medication.

He takes the bottle, sprays under his tongue, and then drops it on the floor as the pressure in his chest eases. He hears them discussing whether they should call an ambulance. Reidar shakes his head and notices that the nitroglycerin spray has triggered a growing headache.

"Go and eat," he tells them. "I'm all right. I just—I need to be alone for a while."

96

REIDAR IS SITTING on the floor with his back against the wall. He wipes his mouth with a trembling hand and forces himself to confront the memory again. It was eight o'clock when he went into Felicia's room. She was sitting on the floor, reading. Her hair was a mess, and she had chocolate smeared around her mouth and across one cheek. She had crumpled up her freshly ironed blouse and skirt to form a cushion to sit on. She had one leg in her woolly tights and was still sucking her sticky fingers.

"You need to be on your bike in nine minutes," he told her. "Your teacher warned us that you can't be late any more this semester."

"I know," she said in a monotone, without looking up from her book.

"And wash your face. It's filthy."

"Leave me alone," she muttered.

"I don't want to nag," he tried to say. "I just don't want you to be late. Can't you understand that?"

"You're nagging so much it's making me sick," she said to the book.

He'd had enough. He grabbed her arm and dragged her into the bathroom. He turned on the tap and scrubbed her face roughly.

"What's wrong with you, Felicia? Why can't you ever do anything right?" he yelled. "Your brother's ready. He's waiting for you, and he's going to be late because of you. But you don't care. You're just a little brat. You don't deserve to be in a nice, tidy home like this."

She started to cry, which only made him angrier.

"What's wrong with you?" he went on.

He started tugging at her hair with a brush, his hands rough with rage. She screamed and swore at him, and he stopped.

"What did you say?"

"Nothing," she muttered.

"It sounded like something."

"Maybe there's something wrong with your ears," she whispered.

He dragged her out of the bathroom, opened the front door, and shoved her out so hard that she fell over.

Mikael was standing by the garage door, waiting with both bicycles. He had refused to ride off without his sister.

REIDAR HOLDS HIS HEAD in his hands. Felicia had been a child and had been acting like a child. Being late and having messy hair hadn't really mattered to her.

He remembers the way Felicia had stood in the driveway in her underwear. Her right knee was bleeding, her eyes were red, and she still had some chocolate powder on her neck. Reidar was shaking with anger. He went back inside and got her blouse, skirt, and jacket and threw them on the ground in front of her.

"What did I do?" she sobbed.

"You're ruining this family," he said.

"But I—"

"Say you're sorry. Say you're sorry this instant."

"Sorry," she said as she wept. "I'm sorry."

She looked at him with tears streaming down her cheeks.

"Get dressed," he replied.

He watched her get dressed, shoulders heaving as she cried. He watched as she wiped the tears from her cheeks and climbed onto her bicycle, blouse half tucked in and coat open. He stood there as his rage subsided and heard his little daughter cry as she rode her bicycle off to school.

He was able to put the argument behind him. He wrote all day and felt pleased with his progress. He hadn't bothered to get dressed, just sat in front of the computer in his robe. He hadn't brushed his teeth or shaved. He hadn't even made the beds or cleared the dining table. He thought he'd say all this to Felicia and explain that he was just like her, but he never got the chance.

He was out late, having dinner with his German publisher, and by the time he got home that evening, the children were already asleep. He and Roseanna discovered their empty beds the following morning. There's nothing in his life that he regrets more than the way he treated Felicia.

It's unbearable to think of her lying there alone in that terrible room.

97

SAGA WAKES UP the next morning when the light in the ceiling comes on. Her head feels heavy, and she can't focus. Under the blanket, she feels for the microphone with her numb fingertips.

The woman with the pierced cheeks is standing outside the door, shouting that it's time for breakfast. Saga gets up, takes the narrow tray through the hatch, and sits down on the bed. She forces herself to eat the sandwiches.

The situation is already becoming intolerable. She won't be able to handle this much longer.

She touches the microphone cautiously and wonders if she should ask to break off the mission.

She goes over to the sink on unsteady legs, brushes her teeth, and washes her face with ice-cold water.

I can't abandon Felicia, she thinks.

Saga sits on the bed and stares at the door until the lock to the dayroom clicks open. She counts to five, stands up, and drinks water from the tap. She can't look too eager. She wipes her mouth with the back of her hand, then walks out into the dayroom.

She's the first one there, but the television is on behind the reinforced glass as if it's never been switched off. She can hear angry shouting from Bernie Larsson's room. It sounds as if he's trying to destroy his table. She hears his breakfast tray hit the floor. He's screaming as he throws the plastic chair at the wall.

Saga gets on the treadmill, switches it on, takes a few steps, then pauses it and sits down on the edge, close to the palm. She pulls off one shoe, pretending there's something wrong with the inner sole. Her hands are still cold and slightly numb. She knows she has to hurry, but she must be careful not to move too quickly. She blocks the camera's view with her body and tugs the microphone from her pants with trembling fingers.

"Fucking whores!" Bernie shouts.

Saga removes the protective wrapping from the microphone. The little object slips from her hand, but she catches it against her thigh. She hears footsteps as she presses the microphone to the underside of the bottom leaf. She holds it for a few extra seconds before letting go.

Bernie pulls open his door and comes into the dayroom. The palm leaf is still swaying from her touch, but the microphone is finally in position.

"Obrahiim," he whispers, and stops in his tracks when he sees her.

Saga remains seated, tugs at her sock, smoothing out a crease, then puts her shoe back on.

"Fucking hell," he says, coughing.

She stands up and gets back on the treadmill. Her legs are weak beneath her, and her heart is racing.

"They took my pictures," Bernie says, panting as he sits down on the sofa. "I hate those fucking . . ."

Saga's whole body feels oddly exhausted. Sweat is trickling down her back, and her pulse is throbbing in her ears. It must be because of the medication. She slows the pace of the treadmill but still has trouble keeping up.

Bernie lies back with his eyes closed, bouncing his leg restlessly.

"Shit!" he exclaims.

He sways toward the treadmill and stands directly in front of Saga.

"I was top of the class," he says, spraying spit in Saga's face. "My teacher used to feed me raisins during breaks."

"Bernie Larsson, step back," a voice says over the loud-speaker.

He stumbles to the side and takes a step back, straight into the palm.

98

BERNIE ALMOST FALLS OVER the palm. Instead, he kicks it, walks around the treadmill, and approaches Saga again.

"They're so fucking terrified of me that they pump me full of Suprefact. Because I'm a real fucking machine, a big fucking stud."

Saga looks up at the camera. She was right. Its view is blocked by the glass case around the television. There's a narrow blind strip that the camera can't reach, no more than a meter at most.

Bernie is breathing close behind her, but she ignores him and continues walking.

"Snow White, you're sweating between your butt cheeks," he says. "Your cunt's probably pretty sweaty now. I can get you some tissues."

On the television, a man dressed as a chef is talking animatedly as he arranges crabs on a barbecue.

The far door opens, and Jurek comes into the dayroom. Saga catches a glimpse of his furrowed face and immediately lowers her eyes and stops the machine. She steps down, panting from the exertion, and walks toward the sofa. Jurek shows no sign of having noticed. He gets on the treadmill and switches it on. His heavy steps drown out the sound of the television.

Saga looks at the chef, who is frying red onion rings in a pan. Bernie comes closer, wiping sweat from his neck.

"You can keep your cunt when you're my skeleton slave," he says, moving behind her. "I'll cut off all the rest of your flesh and—"

"Quiet," Jurek says.

Bernie stops speaking and looks at her, forming the word "whore" with his mouth, then licking his fingers and grabbing her breast. She reacts instantly, seizing his hand and pulling him into the camera's blind spot. She punches him hard on the nose. The cartilage cracks and she can hear his nose break. She spins around, gaining momentum from the movement, and hits Bernie over the ear with a lightning-fast right hook. He's about to lurch into the range of the camera, but she stops him with her left hand. He stares at her through his crooked glasses. Blood pours through his mustache and over his mouth.

Still consumed by rage, Saga holds him in the blind spot and hits him with another right hook. His head is knocked aside, his cheeks flap, and his glasses fly off and hit the wall.

Bernie sinks to his knees, his head hanging, as blood drips onto the floor.

Saga pulls his head up, sees that he's about to black out, and punches him in the nose once more.

"I warned you," she growls, letting go of him.

Bernie falls forward and throws his arms out to stop himself. Blood drips from his face through his hands and onto the vinyl floor.

Saga steps away, breathing hard. Jurek Walter has gotten off the treadmill and is watching her with his pale eyes. His face is motionless, his body strangely relaxed.

As she walks past Jurek toward her own room, the thought that crosses Saga's mind is that she's ruined everything.

99

THE COMPUTER'S FAN WHIRRS as Anders logs in. The second hand moves jerkily on a clock with an image of Bart Simpson's face on the dial. Anders remembers that he has to leave early today because he's attending a class on Socratic conversations at the Autism Education Center.

A Post-it note next to the keyboard says that it's recycling week. He has no idea what that means.

Once the secure unit's medical-chart program opens up, he types in his username and password. He checks the log, then taps in Saga Bauer's ID number, to make a note about her medication.

Twenty-five milligrams of Haldol Depot, he writes. Two intramuscular injections in the outer top quadrant of the gluteal region.

It was the right decision, he thinks, and in his mind's eye he can see her writhing on the floor with her breasts exposed.

Her pale nipples had stiffened. Her mouth had been afraid.

If that doesn't help her, he can try Cisordinol, although that can sometimes have serious side effects. Possibly extrapyramidal symptoms, combined with problems with vision, balance, and orgasm.

Anders closes his eyes and remembers how he pulled down the patient's underwear.

"I don't want to," she had repeated several times.

But he didn't have to listen to her. He did what he had to do. Pia Madsen had supervised the intervention.

He gave her two injections in the buttock and stared between her legs at her blond pubic hair and pink, closed vagina.

Anders goes to the surveillance room. My is already sitting at the control desk. She shoots him a friendly glance as he walks in.

"They're in the dayroom," she says.

Anders leans over her and looks at the screen. Jurek is on the treadmill. Saga is standing and watching television. She seems fairly unaffected by the new medication. Bernie goes over to her, says something, and stands behind her.

"What's he doing now?" Anders asks.

"Bernie seems unsettled," My says, frowning.

"I would really have liked to increase his dosage yesterday. Maybe I should have."

"He keeps following the new patient, chattering manically—"

"Damnit," Anders says, a note of stress in his voice.

"Leif and I are ready to go in," My reassures him.

"But you shouldn't have to," he says. "That means the medication is wrong. I'm raising his dose this evening from two hundred to four hundred milligrams."

Anders watches as Bernie circles Saga. The other cameras show security doors, corridors, and empty cells. In one square, Sven Hoffman has a mug of coffee in his hand outside the security lock leading to the dayroom. He's talking to two of the guards.

"Shit," My suddenly yells, and pulls the emergency alarm.

100

A HARSH, pulsing sound echoes through the room. Anders is still staring at the dayroom on the monitor. The light in the ceiling reflects off the dusty glass of the screen. He leans forward. He can see only two patients. Jurek is standing next to the television, and Saga is on her way to her room.

My is on her feet, shouting something into the emergency radio unit. The desk lamp topples over, and her office chair rolls back into the filing cabinet. She's yelling that Bernie Larsson is injured and that the response team has to go in immediately.

Only now does Anders notice that Bernie is hidden behind the protruding section of the wall.

All he can see is a bloody hand on the floor. Bernie must be right in front of Jurek.

"You have to go in," My repeats into the radio unit several times, then rushes out.

Anders remains seated and watches as Jurek leans over and drags Bernie by his hair to the middle of the room.

A trail of blood shimmers on the floor.

He sees Leif giving instructions to two guards outside the security lock as My runs up to join them.

The alarm is still ringing.

Bernie's face is covered in blood. His eyes are twitching spasmodically, and his arms are flailing in the air.

Anders locks the door to Patient Room 3, then checks in with Sven over the radio. A group of guards is being sent down from Ward 30.

Someone switches off the alarm.

Anders's radio bleeps, and he can hear someone breathing hard.

"I'm opening the door now, repeat, opening the door," My calls.

Jurek's impassive face is visible on the screen. He's standing over Bernie as the injured patient coughs and sprays blood across the floor.

Guards and orderlies with batons are amassing outside the dayroom. Their expressions look tense.

The outer door locks, and there's a rumbling sound.

Jurek says something to Bernie, bends forward, and hits him hard across the mouth.

"Christ," Anders mutters.

The emergency team enters the dayroom and fans out. Jurek stands up and shakes the blood from his hand, then takes a step back and waits.

"Give him forty milligrams of Stesolid," Anders tells My.

"Four ampoules of Stesolid," My repeats over the radio.

Three guards approach from different directions with their batons raised. They shout at Jurek to move away and instruct him to kneel on the floor.

Jurek looks at them, slowly sinks to his knees, and closes his eyes. Leif takes a few quick steps forward and hits Jurek on the back of the neck with his baton. It's a hard blow. Jurek's head jerks forward, and his body follows. He falls to the floor and stays there.

The second guard holds a knee on Jurek's spine as he grabs his arms and twists them behind his back. My is unwrapping a syringe. On the screen, Anders can see her hands shaking.

Jurek is lying on his stomach. Two guards are holding him down now, and they cuff his wrists and pull down his pants so that My can inject straight into his muscle.

101

ANDERS LOOKS into the emergency doctor's brown eyes and quietly thanks her. Her white coat is flecked with Bernie's blood.

"His nasal bone has been reset. I've stitched up his eyebrow, but tape was fine everywhere else. He probably has a concussion, so you'll need to keep him under close supervision."

"We always do," Anders replies, glancing at Bernie on the monitor.

He's lying on his bed, his face covered in bandages. His mouth is half open, and his bulging stomach moves in time with his breathing.

"He said some really revolting things," the doctor says as she walks out.

Leif returns to the surveillance room and runs his hand through his wavy hair. "That was unexpected."

"I've reviewed the chart," Anders says. "This is the first time in thirteen years that Jurek has done anything violent."

"Maybe he doesn't like company," Leif suggests.

"Jurek's an old man, and he's used to having things his way, but he has to understand that that's not going to work from now on."

"How are we going to make him understand that?" Leif says, and smiles grimly.

Anders pulls his card through the reader and lets Leif in ahead of him. They go past Patient Rooms 3 and 2 and stop outside Jurek's cell.

Anders looks into the room. Jurek is lying on the bed, strapped down.

Leif takes a pair of earplugs out of his pocket and offers them to Anders, but he shakes his head.

"Lock the door once I'm inside, and be ready to sound the alarm."

"Just go in and do what you need to. Don't talk to him, and pretend you can't hear what he's saying," Leif says.

Anders goes in and hears Leif quickly lock the door behind him. Jurek's wrists and ankles are fastened to the edges of the bed. Thick fabric straps are stretched across his thighs, hips, and torso. He still looks tired after the emergency tranquilizer, and blood has dribbled out of one ear. The blood from his nose has congealed, and his nostrils appear oddly black.

"I've decided to change your medication in light of what happened in the dayroom," Anders says.

"Yes. I was expecting a punishment," Jurek says hoarsely.

"I'm sorry you choose to see it like that, but it's my responsibility to prevent violence in this ward."

102

ANDERS LINES UP the vials of yellow liquid for the injection on the table. The restraint belts fix Jurek's body to the bed, but his eyes follow the doctor's every move.

"I can't feel my fingers," Jurek says, trying to free his right hand.

"You know we have to take emergency measures sometimes," Anders says.

"The first time we met, you looked scared. Now you're looking for fear in my eyes," Jurek says.

"Why do you think that?" Anders asks.

Jurek takes several breaths, then moistens his mouth and looks Anders in the eye.

"I can see that you're preparing three hundred milligrams of Cisordinol, even though you know that's too much and that the combination with my normal medication is risky."

"I've reached a different conclusion," Anders says, feeling his cheeks blush.

"Yet you'll write in my notes that you've tried merely fifty milligrams."

Anders doesn't respond. He prepares the syringe and checks that the needle is completely dry.

"You know that an overdose could be fatal," Jurek continues. "But I'm strong, so I'll probably be okay. Still, I'll scream, I'll suffer terrible cramps, and I'll lose consciousness."

"There's always a risk of side effects," Anders says laconically.

"Pain doesn't bother me."

Anders squeezes a couple of drops from the needle. One drop runs down the syringe.

"The other patients seem to have unsettled you," Anders says, without looking at Jurek.

"You don't have to make excuses to me," Jurek says.

Anders presses the needle into Jurek's thigh, injects three hundred milligrams of Cisordinol, and waits.

Jurek gasps. His lips quiver, and his pupils contract to pinpricks. Saliva dribbles from his mouth, down his cheek and neck. His body twitches and jerks, then suddenly goes completely rigid, his head straining backward, his back bowed off the bed, the straps over his body straining.

He remains in that position, without breathing.

The frame of the bed creaks.

Anders stares at him. He's having a protracted seizure.

Suddenly the tonic state ends, and Jurek's body begins to spasm instead. He's jerking uncontrollably, biting his tongue and emitting guttural roars of pain.

Anders tries to tighten the straps across his body. Jurek's arms are pulling so hard that his wrists start to bleed.

He sinks back, whimpering, as the blood drains from his face.

Anders steps away and can't help feeling satisfied when he sees tears trickling down Jurek's cheeks.

"It'll feel better soon," he lies.

"Not for you," Jurek gasps.

"What did you say?"

"When I chop your head off and throw it in—"

Jurek is interrupted by a fresh wave of cramps. He screams as his head twists to one side. A fan of veins stands out on his throat as the bones in his neck crack. His whole body starts to shake again, making the bed rattle.

103

Saga lets ice-cold water run over her hands. Her swollen knuckles are sore, and she has three small cuts on them.

Everything's gone wrong.

She lost control and attacked Bernie, and Jurek was blamed.

Through the door she heard the guards shouting about four ampoules of Stesolid before they dragged him into his cell.

They thought he was the one who had attacked Bernie.

Saga turns off the tap, lets water drip from her hands onto the floor, and sits down on the bed. Adrenaline has been replaced with a quivering heaviness in her muscles.

An emergency doctor was called in to take care of Bernie. She heard him babbling feverishly until the door closed.

Saga is so frustrated she's almost in tears. Her complete inability to control her damn emotions. Her goddamn anger has ruined everything. She shudders. It's possible that Jurek will want revenge for getting the blame.

The security doors clatter, and she hears rapid steps in the corridor, but no one comes to her cell.

Silence.

Saga sits on the bed with her eyes closed as growls start to reverberate through the walls. Her heart beats faster. She listens as Jurek lets out a guttural howl and screams with pain. She thinks she can hear someone kicking his bare heels against the reinforced steel of the bed frame. It sounds a bit like a fist hitting a punching bag.

Saga stares at the door, thinking about electric shocks and lobotomies.

Jurek's voice cracks as he screams. She hears heavy thuds.

Then silence.

Now all she can hear is the gentle clicking of the water pipes in the wall. Saga gets up and stares through the thick glass of the window in the door. The young doctor walks past. He stops and looks at her with a blank expression.

Living here is much more difficult than she imagined. Instead of crying, she goes through her mission in her head, running through the rules for long-term infiltration and the purpose of the entire operation.

Felicia Kohler-Frost is completely alone in a locked room. She could be starving and may have Legionnaires' disease.

Time is running out.

Saga knows that Joona is looking for the girl, but without any clues from Jurek, the chances of making a breakthrough aren't good.

Saga has to stick it out for a while longer.

The life she left behind had left her first. Stefan is gone. She has no family.

As the light goes out, she shuts her eyes and feels them pricking.

104

Joona is in one of the large offices at headquarters, along with part of the investigative team. The walls are covered with maps, photographs, and printouts of the tip-offs that are currently being prioritized. On a map of Lill-Jan's Forest, the sites of the various discoveries are clearly marked.

With a yellow pen, Joona traces the railroad line from the harbor through the forest.

"Jurek used to work on railroad switches," he says. "It's possible that the victims were buried in Lill-Jan's Forest because of this railroad line."

"Like the Railroad Killer, Ángel Reséndiz," Benny Rubin says.

"So why the hell don't we just go in and interrogate Jurek?" Petter Näslund demands.

"It wouldn't work," Joona responds.

"Petter, I assume you've read the psychiatric report?" Magdalena Ronander says. "Is there really any point interrogating someone who's both schizophrenic and psychotic, and who—"

"We have eighteen thousand kilometers of railroad lines in Sweden," Petter interrupts. "We might as well get digging."

Joona can't help thinking that Petter Näslund has a point. Jurek is the only person who can lead them to Felicia before it's too late. They're checking every single line of inquiry from the old investigation, and they're looking into all the tip-offs that have come in, but they're not making any progress. Saga Bauer is their only real hope. Yesterday she beat up another patient and Jurek was blamed. But that isn't necessarily a bad thing, Joona thinks. It might even help bring them together.

IT'S GETTING DARK OUTSIDE, and pinpricks of snow land on Joona's face as he gets out of the car and hurries in to Södermalm Hospital. He spots Dr. Goodwin as soon as he walks in. The door to one of the examination rooms is open. A woman with a split lip and a bleeding wound on her chin is sitting quietly while Dr. Goodwin talks to her.

There's a smell of damp wool, and the floor is slippery with slush. A construction worker sits on one of the benches with one foot in a fogged-up plastic bag.

Joona waits until Dr. Goodwin emerges from the room, then walks with her down the corridor toward another examination room.

"This is the third time she's been here in as many months," Dr. Goodwin says.

"You should refer her to a women's shelter," Joona says.

"I already have. But what good will that do?"

"It helps," Joona insists.

"So what can I do for you?" she asks, stopping outside the door.

"I need to know about the progression of Legionnaires' disease—"

"He's going to be fine," she interrupts, opening the door.

"Yes, but what if he hadn't been treated?" Joona says.

"How do you mean?" she asks.

"We're trying to find his sister," Joona says. "And it seems likely that she would've been infected at the same time as Mikael."

"In that case, it would be serious," Dr. Goodwin says.

"How serious?"

"Without treatment—it depends on her general condition, but she probably has a high fever by now."

"And then what?"

"She'll be coughing already and having trouble breathing. It's impossible to say with any degree of accuracy, but I'd say that by the end of the week she'll be at risk of brain damage. And, well, you know that Legionnaires' disease can be fatal."

105

THE NEXT MORNING, Saga is even more worried about what happened in the dayroom. She has no appetite.

She can't let go of her failure. Instead of building trust, she has once again managed to unleash conflict.

Jurek must hate her now.

She isn't particularly scared for herself, because security in the ward is so high.

But she'll have to be very careful, while never showing any signs of fear.

When the lock clicks, she walks into the dayroom, clearing these thoughts from her head. The television is already on. Three people sit in a cozy studio and chat about winter gardens.

She's the first one into the dayroom and immediately gets on the treadmill.

Her legs feel clumsy, her fingertips are numb, and with every step the plastic leaves of the palm shake.

Bernie is shouting in his room.

Someone has cleaned up the blood from the floor.

Jurek's door opens. His entrance is preceded by a shadow. Saga forces herself not to look at him. With long strides, he heads straight for the treadmill.

Saga gets off the machine and steps aside to let him pass. He has black scabs on his lips, and his face is ashen and gray. He climbs onto the machine, then just stands there.

"You were blamed for what I did," she says.

"You think?"

Jurek's hands are shaking when he starts the treadmill. She can feel the vibrations through the floor. The palm trembles with each step.

"Why didn't you kill him?" he asks, glancing at her.

"Because I didn't want to," she says.

She meets his pale eyes for a moment and feels her blood pumping. The realization that she's in direct contact with Jurek Walter catches up with her.

"It would have been interesting to watch you do it," he says quietly.

He looks at her with unfeigned curiosity.

"You're here, which means you've probably killed people," he says.

"Yes, I have," she replies after a pause.

He nods. "It's inevitable."

"I don't want to talk about it," Saga mumbles.

"Killing is neither good nor bad," Jurek says calmly. "But it feels strange the first few times, like eating something you didn't think was edible."

Saga suddenly remembers the first time she killed another person. The man's blood had squirted up over the trunk of a birch tree. Even though there was no need, she had fired a second shot and watched through the telescopic sight as the bullet struck within a half-inch or so above the first.

"I did what I had to do," she whispers.

"Just like yesterday."

"Yes, but I didn't mean for you to be punished."

Jurek stops the machine.

"I've been waiting for this for quite a long time, I have to say," he explains.

"I could hear your screams through the walls," Saga says.

"Those screams," he replies, "they were the result of our new doctor's giving me an overdose of Cisordinol. They're nature's reaction to pain. Something hurts, and the body screams, even though there's no point. Plus, in this instance, it actually felt like an indulgence, because I knew that this opportunity would never come again otherwise."

"What opportunity?"

"They won't ever let me see a lawyer, but there are other opportunities, other ways out of here."

His eyes are strangely pale and remind her of metal.

"You think I can help you," she whispers. "That's why you took the blame."

"I can't let the doctor get scared of you," he says.

"Why?"

"Anyone who ends up here is violent," Jurek says. "The staff knows you're dangerous. Your medical notes say so, and the forensic psychiatrist's report says so. But that's not what any-one sees when they look at you."

"I'm not that dangerous."

Even though she hasn't said anything she regrets—she's told only the truth and hasn't revealed anything—she feels peculiarly exposed.

"Why are you here? What have you done?" he asks.

"Nothing," she replies curtly.

"What did they say you did in court?"

"Nothing."

A flash of a smile flickers on his face.

"You're a real siren, aren't you?"

106

THE MEMBERS OF ATHENA PROMACHOS are eavesdropping on the conversation as it happens.

Joona stands next to the large speaker, listening to Jurek's choice of words, his phrasing, the nuances in his voice, his breathing.

Johan Jönson monitors the audio quality on his laptop.

Corinne transcribes the conversation onto her laptop so they can see the words on the big screen. The sound her long fingernails make against the keyboard is strangely soothing.

Nathan Pollock's silver-streaked ponytail is hanging over his suit vest. He's taking notes.

The group is completely silent. Sun pours through the balcony doors, which look out onto glistening, snow-topped roofs.

They hear Jurek Walter tell Saga she's a real siren, then leave the room.

After a few seconds of silence, Nathan leans back in his chair and claps his hands. Corinne is shaking her head, impressed.

"Saga's brilliant," Pollock mutters.

"Even if we haven't heard anything that could lead us to Felicia," Joona says, turning to face the others, "contact has been established, which is seriously good work. And I think she's made him curious."

"I have to admit, I was worried when she let herself be provoked by the other patient," Corinne says, squeezing a lime wedge into a glass of water and passing it to Pollock.

"But Jurek deliberately assumed responsibility for the attack," Joona says slowly.

"Yes. Why did he do that? He must have heard her the day before yesterday, when she told the guard she wanted to see a lawyer," Pollock says. "That's why Jurek can't allow the doctor to become afraid of her, because then she wouldn't be allowed any visits from—"

"He's new," Joona interrupts. "Jurek says the doctor's new."

"So what?" Johan asks.

"When I spoke to Chief Physician Brolin on Monday, he said there hadn't been any changes in the secure unit."

"That's right," Pollock says.

"It might be nothing," Joona says. "But why would Brolin tell me that they had the same staff they'd always had?"

107

Joona Linna drives north up the E4. A Max Bruch violin concerto is playing on the radio. The shadows and falling snow in front of the cars merge with the music. Corinne calls.

She tells him that, of all the doctors who have been added to the payroll of Löwenströmska Hospital over the past two years, only one of them works in the field of psychiatry.

"His name's Anders Rönn. Prior to this job, he's only ever had temporary positions, at a psychiatric unit in Växjö."

"Anders Rönn," Joona repeats.

"Married to Petra Rönn, who works in recreational administration for the council. One daughter, mildly autistic. I'm not sure if that's at all useful, but you might as well know," she says.

"Thanks, Corinne," Joona says.

He turns off the highway at Upplands Väsby. The old road to Uppsala is lined on one side by black oaks. The fields beyond the trees slope down toward a lake.

He parks the car outside the main entrance to the hospital and hurries in, walking across the unmanned reception to the Department of General Psychiatry.

He passes the secretary and heads straight for the chief's closed door. He opens it and walks in. Roland Brolin looks up from his computer and takes off his bifocal glasses. Joona lowers his head slightly but still manages to nudge the low ceiling lamp. He holds his police ID up to Roland, then starts to ask the same questions as before.

"How is the patient?"

"I'm afraid I'm busy right now, but—"

"Has Jurek Walter done anything unusual recently?" Joona interrupts in a harsh tone.

"I've already answered that," Roland says, turning back toward his computer.

"And the security routines haven't changed?"

The thickset doctor sighs wearily. "What are you doing?"

"Is he still getting intramuscular Risperdal?" Joona asks.

"Yes," Brolin says.

"And the staffing in the secure unit remains unchanged?"

"Yes, like I told you—"

"Is the staff in the secure unit unchanged?" Joona repeats.

"Yes," Roland says with a hesitant smile.

"Is there a new doctor named Anders Rönn working in the secure unit?"

"Well, yes—"

"So why are you saying the staff is unchanged?"

A blush appears below the doctor's tired eyes.

"He's only a temp," Roland explains. "Surely you understand that we have to bring in temps sometimes?"

"Who is he standing in for?"

"Susanne Hjälm. She's on leave of absence."

"How long has she been gone?"

"Three months."

"What's she doing?"

"I don't actually know. Staff don't have to give reasons for leaves of absence."

"Is Anders Rönn working today?"

Roland looks at his watch and says coldly: "I'm afraid he's finished for the day."

Joona gets out his phone and leaves the room. Anja Larsson answers.

"I need addresses and phone numbers for both Anders Rönn and Susanne Hjälm," he says curtly.

108

Joona has just pulled out of the hospital grounds and is speeding up along the old main road when Anja calls back.

"Anders Rönn's address is number three Balders Drive, in Upplands Väsby," she tells him.

"I'll find it," he says, stepping on the brake as he turns south.

She says coolly that she'll check out Susanne Hjälm.

Joona heads back to the Upplands Väsby junction on the E4 and has just turned onto Sanda Road to look for Anders's house when Anja calls again.

"This is a little weird," she says in a serious tone. "Susanne Hjälm's phone is switched off. As is her husband's. He hasn't shown up at work for the past three months, and their two children haven't been at school, either. The girls are both out sick, with doctor's notes, but the school has been in touch with Social Services."

"Where do they live?"

"Number twenty-three Biskop Nils Drive, in Stäket, on the way to Kungsängen."

Joona pulls over to the side of the road and lets the truck behind him pass.

"Send a patrol to the address," Joona says, then does a U-turn.

The front right wheel bumps up on the curb, the car's suspension lurches, and the glove compartment pops open.

He's trying not to think too far ahead or make assumptions, but he keeps his foot on the gas pedal and ignores the red lights. By the time he reaches the on-ramp to the highway, he's already going 160 kilometers an hour.

109

JOONA PASSES an old Volvo on Route 267. The tires roll
softly over the ridge of snow between the lanes. He turns on
his high beams, and the deserted road becomes a tunnel of
light with a black roof over a white floor. He speeds past the
fields, where the snow takes on a blue tone in the deepening
darkness; then the road travels through thick forest until the
lights of Stäket are flickering ahead of him and the landscape
opens up toward Lake Mälaren.

What has happened to the psychiatrist's family?

Joona brakes and turns right, driving into a small residential
area with snow-covered fruit trees and rabbit hutches on the
lawns in front of the houses.

The weather is worsening. Thick snow is slanting in from
the lake.

Twenty-three Biskop Nils Drive is one of the last houses.
Beyond it there's nothing but forest and rough terrain.

Susanne Hjälm's home is a large white villa with pale-blue
shutters and a red-tiled roof.

There are no lights on in the house, and the driveway is
thick with untouched snow.

Joona stops just beyond the house and barely has time to
put the hand brake on before the patrol car from Upplands-
Bro Police pulls up a short distance away.

Joona gets out of the car, grabs his coat and scarf from the back seat, and walks over to his uniformed colleagues as he buttons his coat up.

"Joona Linna, National Crime," he says, holding out his hand.

"Eliot Sörenstam."

Eliot has a shaved head, brown eyes, and a little vertical strip of beard on his chin.

The other officer shakes Joona's hand firmly and introduces herself as Marie Franzén. She has a cheerful, freckled face, blond eyebrows, and a ponytail high up at the back of her head.

"Nice to see you in real life," she says, smiling.

"You came quickly," Joona says.

"I have to get home after this and braid my daughter Elsa's hair," she says in a friendly manner. "She's desperate to have curly hair for preschool tomorrow."

"We'd better hurry up, then," Joona says as they set off toward the house.

"Marie's been on her own with her daughter for five years, but she's never taken a sick day or left early," Eliot says. "She's the best partner I've ever had."

"That's a lovely thing to say—considering you're a Capricorn," she adds with real warmth in her voice.

There are lights in the windows of most of the houses on the road, but number 23 is ominously dark.

"There's probably a good explanation," Joona tells the two officers. "But neither of the parents has been at work for the past few months, and the children haven't been to school."

The low hedge facing the road is covered with snow, and the green plastic mailbox is bursting with envelopes and catalogues.

"Are Social Services involved?" Marie asks.

"They've been out here already, but they say the family is

away," Joona replies. "Let's try knocking. Then we're probably going to have to question the neighbors."

"Do we suspect a crime?" Eliot asks, looking at the virgin snow on the drive.

Joona can't help thinking of Samuel Mendel. His whole family vanished. The Sandman took them, just as Jurek had predicted. But this is different. Susanne Hjälm had told the school that the children were sick and had signed the doctor's notes herself.

110

THE TWO POLICE OFFICERS follow Joona up to the house. The snow crunches under their feet.

No one's been here for weeks.

A loop of garden hose is sticking out of the snow next to a children's sandbox.

They go up the steps to the porch and ring the bell, wait awhile, then ring again.

They listen for noise from the house. Clouds of breath rise from their mouths. The porch creaks beneath them.

Joona rings again.

He has a bad feeling that he can't shake but says nothing. There's no reason to worry his colleagues.

"What do we do now?" Eliot asks.

Leaning on the little bench, Joona bends over and peers through the narrow hall window. He can see a brown stone floor and striped wallpaper. The glass prisms hanging from the wall lamps are motionless. He looks back at the floor. The dust bunnies by the wall are still. He's just thinking that the air inside the house doesn't seem to be moving when one of the balls of dust rolls under the dresser. Joona leans closer to the glass, cupping his hands to the pane, and sees a shadowy figure in the hall.

Someone standing with hands raised.

It takes Joona a second to realize that he's seeing his own reflection in the hall mirror, but adrenaline is already coursing through his body. In the reflection, he sees umbrellas in a stand, the security chain on the inside of the front door, and the red hall rug. There don't seem to be any shoes or winter coats.

Joona knocks on the window, but nothing happens.

Everything is still.

"Let's go and have a word with the neighbors," he says.

But instead of heading back to the road, he starts to walk around the house. His colleagues stay on the driveway, watching him with curiosity.

Joona passes a snow-covered trampoline, then stops. There are tracks from some animal leading through the gardens. Light from a window in the house next door stretches out like a golden sheet across the snow.

Everything is completely silent.

Where the garden ends, the forest begins. Pinecones and needles are sprawled out on the thinner snow beneath the trees.

"Aren't we going to talk to the neighbors?" Eliot asks, bemused.

"I'm coming," Joona says.

"What?"

"What did he say?"

"One second."

Joona pads a bit farther through the snow, his feet and ankles getting cold. A bird feeder is swinging outside the dark kitchen window.

He rounds the corner of the house. Something isn't right.

Snow has drifted against the wall of the house, and shimmering icicles are hanging off the sill below the window closest to the forest.

But why only that one?

As he gets closer, he sees the neighbors' porch light reflected in the window.

There are four long icicles, and a series of smaller ones.

He's almost reached the window when he notices a dip in the snow, next to an air vent close to the ground. Which means that every now and then warm air comes out of the vent.

That's why there are icicles in that spot.

Joona leans forward and listens. All he can hear is the sound of wind moving through the treetops.

The silence is broken by voices from the house next door. Two children shouting angrily at each other. A door slams, and the voices get quieter.

A faint scraping sound makes Joona bend down toward the vent again. He's holding his breath and thinks he can hear a quick whisper from the vent that sounds like a command.

Instinctively, he draws back, uncertain whether he imagined the whisper. He has spun around and seen the other officers, standing in the driveway under the dark trees, when suddenly he realizes what he saw a moment ago.

When he looked through the narrow hall window and saw himself in the mirror, he was so startled that he missed the most important detail.

The door's security chain was latched, which can be done only from inside the house.

Joona runs back to the front of the house. Loose snow flies up around his legs. He digs out his lock picks from his inside pocket and goes up the steps to the porch.

"There's someone in there," he says quietly.

His colleagues look at him in astonishment as he picks the lock, opens the door carefully, closes it again, and then jerks the door forward hard to break the security chain.

Joona gestures to them to keep behind him.

"Police!" he calls into the house. "We're coming in!"

111

THE THREE POLICE OFFICERS walk into the hall and are struck at once by the acrid stench of old trash. The house is silent and as cold as it is outside.

"Is anyone home?" Joona calls.

All they can hear are their own movements. The sounds from the next house don't carry inside. Joona reaches out to switch on the light, but it doesn't work.

Marie turns on her flashlight behind him. She points it nervously in different directions as they move deeper into the house. Joona notices his own shadow grow and slide across the closed blinds.

"Police," he calls again. "We only want to talk."

They enter the kitchen and see a mound of empty packaging under the table: cornflakes, pasta, flour, and sugar.

"What the hell is this?" Eliot mutters.

The fridge and freezer are dark and empty. All the kitchen chairs are missing, and on the windowsills, next to the closed curtains, the houseplants have withered.

It's only from the outside that it looks as if the family has left.

They walk into a television room with a corner sofa. Joona steps over the cushions that have been pulled off it.

Marie whispers something that he can't make out.

The thick curtains covering the windows reach all the way to the floor.

Through the door to the hallway they can see a staircase leading down to the basement.

They stop when they see a dead dog with a plastic bag taped around its head. It's lying on the floor in front of the television stand.

Joona continues toward the hallway and staircase. He can hear his colleagues' footsteps behind him.

Marie's breathing has sped up.

The beam from her flashlight is shaking.

Joona moves to one side so he can see into the unlit corridor. Down the hall, the bathroom door is ajar.

Joona gestures to the others to stop, but Marie is already next to him, pointing the flashlight toward the stairs. She takes a step closer and tries to see farther down the corridor.

"What's that?" she whispers, unable to control the nervousness in her voice.

There's something lying on the floor by the bathroom. She points the flashlight in that direction. It's a doll with long blond hair.

The light hovers over its shiny plastic face.

Suddenly the doll is pulled in behind the door.

Marie smiles and takes a long stride forward, but at the same moment there's a stomach-churning bang.

The flash as the shotgun goes off fills the corridor like lightning.

Marie is hit hard in the back, and the hail of shot cuts right through her neck.

Her head flies back, and blood spurts out of the exit wound in her throat.

The flashlight hits the floor.

Marie is already dead when she takes one last step with

her head hanging loose. She collapses in a heap with one leg folded beneath her, her hips lifted at an odd angle.

Joona draws his pistol and releases the safety catch. The corridor leading to the stairs is empty. There's no one there. Whoever fired the shot must have disappeared into the cellar.

Blood is bubbling from Marie's neck, steaming in the chill air.

The flashlight is rolling slowly over the floor.

"Oh God, oh God," Eliot whispers.

Their ears are ringing from the blast.

A child suddenly appears with the doll in her arms. She slips on the blood, lands on her back, and vanishes into the darkness by the staircase. Footsteps thud down the stairs and disappear with a clatter.

112

Joona kneels and takes a quick look at Marie. There's nothing to be done.

Eliot is yelling and sobbing into his radio, calling for an ambulance and backup.

"Police," Joona shouts down the stairs. "Put the weapon down and—"

The shotgun goes off again, and the shot hits the wooden stairs, sending up a cascade of splinters.

Joona hears the metallic click as the gun snaps open. He rushes over. Just as he reaches the staircase, he hears the little sigh of the first empty cartridge being released.

Taking several steps at a time, Joona races down the dark stairs, pistol raised.

Eliot picks up the flashlight to give him some light, and the beam reaches the bottom of the stairs just in time for Joona to stop himself before he's impaled.

At the foot of the stairs, the kitchen chairs have been piled up to form a barricade. The protruding legs have been sharpened into spears, and kitchen knives have been fixed to them with duct tape.

Joona aims his Colt Combat over the barricade into a room containing a pool table.

There's no sign of anyone. Everything's quiet again.

The adrenaline in his body makes him strangely calm, as if he were in a new, sharper version of reality. He lifts his finger off the trigger and loosens the rope tied to the end of the banister to help him get around the barricade.

"What the hell are we supposed to do?" Eliot asks with panic in his voice as he comes down.

"Are you wearing a bulletproof vest?"

"Yes."

"Shine the flashlight further into the cellar," Joona says.

There are two empty shotgun cartridges on the floor, surrounded by broken glass and empty food cans. Eliot is breathing rapidly, holding the flashlight next to his pistol as he shines it into the corners. It's warmer down here, and there's a sharp smell of sweat and urine.

Wire is strung across the passageway at neck height, forcing them to duck down. Behind them, the wires tap against each other.

They hear whispering. Joona stops and signals to Eliot. A ticking sound, followed by footsteps.

"Run, run," someone urges.

Cold air rushes in, and Joona hurries forward while the shaky beam from Eliot's flashlight sweeps around the cellar. There is a boiler room to their left; in the other direction, concrete steps lead up to an open cellar door.

Snow blows in over the steps.

Joona has already caught sight of the concealed figure as the beam of light glints off the knife blade.

He takes another step forward and hears shallow breathing followed by a sudden whimper.

A tall woman with a dirty face rushes out with a knife in her hand, and Joona instinctively aims his pistol at her torso.

"Watch out!" Eliot cries.

In a split second, Joona decides not to shoot. Without

thinking, he moves toward her and then steps aside quickly as she lunges. He blocks her arm, grabs it, and lets his shoulders follow through on the movement, hitting the left side of her neck with his lower right arm. The blow is so firm and swift that it knocks her backward.

Joona grips the arm holding the knife. There's a cracking sound, like two stones knocking together underwater, as her elbow breaks. The woman falls to the floor, howling with pain.

The knife clatters to the ground. Joona kicks it away, then aims his pistol toward the boiler room.

113

A MIDDLE-AGED MAN is lying over the geo-energy pump. He's been tied up with rope and duct tape, and there's a rag in his mouth.

Eliot cuffs the woman to a water pipe as Joona cautiously approaches the man, explains that he's a police officer, and removes the gag.

"The girls," the man gasps. "They ran out. Please don't hurt the girls, they're—"

"Is there anyone else here?"

Eliot has already disappeared up the concrete steps.

"Only the girls."

"How many?"

"Two. Susanne gave them the shotgun. They're just scared. They've never used a gun. Please don't hurt them," the man begs desperately. "They're just scared."

Joona runs up the steps and into the back garden. Behind him, the man calls out over and over again, telling him not to hurt the girls.

Footsteps lead across the garden and straight into the forest. A beam of light is flickering among the trees.

"Eliot," Joona shouts. "There are only children out here!"

He follows the tracks into the forest and feels the sweat on his face cooling.

"They're armed!" Joona calls.

He runs toward the light between the trees. Twigs snap under his weight. Ahead of him, he can see Eliot running through the snow with his pistol and flashlight.

"Wait!" Joona shouts. Eliot doesn't seem to hear.

Loose snow falls from a tree with soft thumps.

In the weak light, he can make out the children's tracks among the trees, at different angles, and then the straight line of Eliot's steps following them.

"They're just kids!" Joona cries again, trying to gain on him by sliding down a steep slope.

He slips onto his hip, bringing down loose stones and pine-cones, and scrapes his back on something but gets to his feet again as he reaches the bottom.

Through the dense foliage, he can see the searching beam of the flashlight. Close by, a skinny girl is standing next to a tree, holding the shotgun in both hands.

Joona runs straight through the thicket of dry twigs. He tries to shield his face, but his cheeks get scratched. He sees Eliot's frame moving between the tree trunks; then the little girl behind the tree steps out and fires the gun at the policeman.

The cloud of shot hits the snow a meter in front of the barrel. The butt jerks back, and the girl's thin frame is thrown by the recoil. Eliot spins around and aims his pistol at her.

"Wait!" Joona shouts, trying to force his way through the branches.

He ends up with snow all over him and inside his coat, but the branches give way. He emerges on the other side and stops abruptly.

Eliot Sörenstam is sitting on the ground with his arms around the sobbing girl. A few steps away, her little sister is standing and staring at them.

114

Susanne Hjälm's arms are cuffed behind her back. Her broken elbow juts out at an odd angle. She's screaming hysterically and giving fierce resistance as two uniformed police officers drag her up the cellar steps. The blue lights from the emergency vehicles make the snowy landscape ripple like water. Neighbors are watching events from a distance, like silent ghosts.

Susanne stops screaming when she sees Joona and Eliot emerge from the forest. Joona is carrying the younger girl, and Eliot is holding the other one by the hand.

Susanne's eyes open wide, and she breathes hard in the ice-cold winter night. Joona puts the girl down so she and her sister can go over to their mother. They hug for a long time, and she tries to calm them.

"It's going to be all right now," she says. "Everything's going to be all right."

An older female officer starts talking to the girls, trying to explain that their mother needs to go with the police.

The father is led out of the cellar by the paramedics, but he's so weak that he has to be put on a stretcher.

Joona follows as the officers lead Susanne through the deep snow toward one of the police cars in the drive. They put her in the back seat while a senior officer talks to a prosecutor over the phone.

"She needs to go to the hospital," Joona says, stamping the snow from his shoes.

He walks over to Susanne. She's sitting quietly in the car, her face turned toward the house as she tries to catch a glimpse of her daughters.

"Why did you do this?" Joona asks.

"You'd never understand," she says. "No one can understand."

"Maybe I can," he says. "I was the person who arrested Jurek Walter thirteen—"

"You should have killed him," she interrupts, looking him in the eye for the first time.

"What happened?"

"I should never have spoken to him," she says through gritted teeth. "We're not supposed to, but I never imagined...."

She goes quiet and looks up at the house again.

"What did he say?"

"He ... demanded that I mail a letter," she whispers.

"A letter?"

"There are a ton of restrictions limiting what he's allowed to do, so I couldn't, but I, I .. "

"You couldn't send it? Where's the letter now?"

"Maybe I should talk to a lawyer," she says.

"Do you still have the letter?"

"I burned it," she says, then turns away again.

Tears start to trickle down her exhausted, dirt-smeared face.

"What did the letter say?"

"I want to see a lawyer before I answer any more questions," she says resolutely.

"This is important, Susanne," Joona persists. "You're going

to get medical treatment now, and you can see a lawyer, but first I need to know where the letter was supposed to be sent. Give me a name, an address."

"I don't remember. It was a PO box."

"Where?"

"I don't remember. There was a name," she says, shaking her head.

Joona watches as the older daughter is carried toward an ambulance on a stretcher. She looks scared and is trying to undo the straps holding her on.

"Do you remember the name?"

"It wasn't Russian," Susanne whispers. "It was—"

The daughter panics in the ambulance and starts screaming.

"Ellen!" Susanne cries. "I'm here, I'm here!"

Susanne tries to get out of the car, but Joona forces her to stay where she is.

"Leave me alone!"

She struggles to pull free and get out. The doors of the ambulance close and everything is quiet again.

"Ellen!" she calls.

The ambulance drives off, and Susanne turns her head away with her eyes closed.

115

WHEN ANDERS RÖNN gets home from the autism and Asperger's support group, Petra is sitting at the computer, paying bills. He goes over and kisses her on the back of the neck, but she shrugs him off. He tries to smile and pats her cheek.

"Stop it," she says.

"Can we try to be friends?"

"You went way too far," she tells him.

"I know. Sorry. I thought you wanted—"

She cuts him off. "Well, stop thinking that."

Anders nods and then goes to check on Agnes. She's sitting by her dollhouse with her back to him and a hairbrush in her hand. She has brushed all the dolls' hair and has piled them on top of one another in a dollhouse bed.

"Very nice job," Anders says.

Agnes turns, shows him the brush, and meets his gaze for a few seconds.

He sits down next to her and puts his arm around her thin shoulders. She pulls away.

"Now they're all asleep," Anders says cheerily.

"No," she says.

"What are they doing, then?"

"They're looking."

She points at the dolls' painted eyes, wide-open.

"You mean they can't sleep if they're looking? But you can pretend—"

"They're looking," she repeats, and starts to move her head anxiously.

"I can see that," he says in a soothing voice. "But they're lying in bed, just like they should be, and that's a really good—"

"Ow, ow, ow . . ."

Agnes moves her head jerkily, then claps her hands three times. Anders holds her in his arms, kisses her head, and whispers that she's done really well with the dolls. Her body relaxes, and she starts to line up LEGOs along the floor.

The doorbell rings, and Anders goes to answer it, glancing at Agnes again before leaving the room.

The outside light shows a tall man in a suit, with wet trousers and a torn pocket. The man's hair is curly and mussed. His cheeks are dimpled, and his eyes look serious.

"Anders Rönn?" he says with a Finnish accent.

"Can I help you?" Anders asks.

"I'm from the National Crime Unit," he says, showing his police ID. "Can I come in?"

116

ANDERS STARES AT THE MAN. For a fleeting moment, he feels a chill of fear. He opens the door to let the man in. A thousand thoughts race through his mind as he asks whether his guest would like coffee.

Petra's called a women's helpline and talked.

Roland Brolin has fabricated some sort of complaint against him.

They've figured out that he isn't really qualified for his job.

The tall detective says his name is Joona Linna and politely declines the coffee. He goes into the living room and sits down in an armchair. He gives Anders a friendly but appraising look that makes him feel like a guest in his own home.

"You're filling in for Susanne Hjälm in the secure unit," the detective inspector says.

"Yes," Anders replies.

"What are your thoughts on Jurek Walter?"

Jurek Walter, Anders thinks. Is this just about Jurek Walter? He relaxes. "I can't discuss individual patients," he says sternly.

"Have you spoken to him?" the man asks, with a sharp look in his gray eyes.

"We have no conversational therapy in the secure unit,"

Anders says, running a hand through his short hair. "But, obviously, the patients talk."

Joona Linna leans forward.

"You're aware that the Supreme Court applied specific restrictions to Jurek Walter because it deemed him to be extremely dangerous?"

"Yes," Anders says. "But everything becomes a matter of interpretation. It's my responsibility as a doctor to weigh restrictions and treatment against each other."

The detective nods. "He asked you to send a letter, didn't he?"

Anders loses his grip for a moment, then reminds himself that he's the one with the power, the one who makes decisions regarding the patients.

"Yes. I did mail a letter for him," he replies. "I considered it an important way of building trust between us."

"Did you read the letter before you sent it?"

"Yes, of course. He knew I would. It was nothing remarkable."

The detective's gray eyes darken as his pupils expand.

"What did it say?"

Anders doesn't know if Petra has come in, but it feels as if she's standing behind his back, watching them.

"I don't remember exactly," he says, uncomfortably aware that he's blushing. "It was a formal letter to a legal firm—something I consider to be a human right."

"Yes," the detective says, without taking his eyes off him.

"Jurek Walter wanted a lawyer to visit him in the unit, to help him assess the possibilities of getting a retrial. That was more or less what he wanted. And if there was to be a retrial, he wanted a private defense lawyer to represent him."

The living room is silent.

"What address?" the detective inspector asks.

"Rosenhane Legal Services—a PO box in Tensta."

"Would you be able to reconstruct the exact wording of the letter?"

"I only read it once. Like I said, it was very formal and polite, though there were a number of spelling mistakes."

"Spelling mistakes?"

"More like dyslexic errors," Anders explains.

"Did you discuss the letter with Chief Physician Brolin?"

"No," Anders replies. "Why would I do that?"

117

Joona goes back to his car and sets off toward Stockholm. He calls Anja and asks her to check out Rosenhane Legal Services.

"Do you have any idea what time it is?"

"The time," he repeats. It occurs to him that it's only been a few hours since Marie Franzén was shot and killed. "Sorry. Let's do this tomorrow."

He realizes that she's already ended the call. A couple of minutes pass before she calls him back.

"There's no Rosenhane," she says. "No law firm, and no lawyer, either."

"There was a PO box address," Joona insists.

"Yes, in Tensta, I found that," she replies. "But it's been closed down, and the lawyer who was renting it doesn't exist."

"I see."

"Rosenhane is the name of an extinct aristocratic family," she says.

"Sorry I called so late."

"You can call me whenever you like."

The address is a trail that doesn't lead anywhere, Joona is thinking. No PO box, no law firm, no name.

It suddenly occurs to him how strange it is for Anders Rönn to call Jurek Walter dyslexic.

I've seen his writing, Joona thinks.

What Anders interpreted as cyslexia could have been the result of long-term medication but is more likely a code to communicate with his accomplice.

His thoughts return to Marie. Now there's a child waiting for a parent who'll never come home.

She shouldn't have rushed forward, but he knows he could have made the same mistake if his operational training hadn't been so deeply ingrained. He would have been killed, just like his own father.

Maybe Marie's daughter has been told the news by now. Joona knows the world will never be the same for her. When Joona was eleven, his father, a police officer, was killed with a shotgun. He had been called to an apartment where there had been reports of a domestic disturbance. Joona remembers sitting in his classroom when the headmaster came in and got him later that day. The world was never the same again for him.

118

IT's MORNING, and Jurek is striding along on the treadmill. Saga can hear his ponderous breathing. On the television, a man is making his own rubber balls. Colorful spheres are floating in glasses of water.

Her instinct is telling her that she should avoid all contact with Jurek, but every conversation she has with him increases her colleagues' chances of finding Felicia.

The man on television is warning viewers against using too much glitter, because it can affect the ball's ability to bounce.

Saga walks over to Jurek. He steps off the treadmill and gestures to her to take over.

She thanks him, gets on, and starts walking. Jurek stands alongside, watching her. Her legs are still tired and her joints sore. She tries to speed up, but her breath is already labored.

"Have you had your injection of Haldol?" Jurek asks.

"Had it the first day," she replies.

"From the doctor?"

"Yes."

"Did he come in and pull your pants down?"

"I was given Stesolid first," she replies quietly.

"Was he inappropriate?"

She shrugs.

"Has he been in your room more times?"

Bernie comes into the dayroom and walks straight over to the treadmill. His broken nose has been covered with white fabric tape. One eye is swollen shut. He looks at her and coughs quietly.

"I'm your slave now. Fucking hell I'm here, and I shall follow you for all eternity, like the pope's butler, till death do us part."

He wipes the sweat from his top lip and seems unsteady.

"I shall obey every—"

"Sit down on the sofa," Saga interrupts without looking at him.

He burps and swallows several times.

"I shall lie on the floor and warm your feet. I am your dog," he says, and sinks to his knees with a sigh. "What do you want me to do?"

"Go and sit on the sofa," Saga repeats.

She's walking slowly on the machine. The palm leaves are swaying. Bernie crawls over, tilts his head, and looks up at her.

"Anything, I'll obey you," he says. "If your breasts are getting sweaty, I can wipe—"

"Go and sit on the sofa," Jurek says in a detached voice.

Bernie crawls away instantly and lies down on the floor in front of the sofa. Saga has to lower the speed of the machine slightly. She forces herself not to look at the swaying palm leaf and tries not to think about the microphone.

Jurek is watching her. He wipes his mouth, then rubs his hand through his short metal-gray hair.

"We can get out of the hospital together," he says calmly.

"I don't know if I want to," she says.

"Why not?"

"I don't really have anything left outside."

"Left?" he repeats quietly. "Going back is never an option. But there are better places than this."

"And probably some worse."

He looks genuinely surprised and turns away with a sigh.

"What did you say?" she asks.

"I just sighed, because it occurred to me that I can actually remember a worse place," he says, gazing at her with a distant look in his eye. "The air was filled with the hum of high-voltage electricity wires. The roads were wrecked by big bulldozers. And the tracks were full of water and red clay up to your waist. But at least I could still open my mouth and breathe."

"What do you mean?"

"That worse places might be preferable to better ones."

"You're thinking about your childhood?"

"I suppose so," he says.

Saga stops the treadmill and leans forward on the handles. Her cheeks are flushed, as if she'd run ten kilometers. She knows she should continue the conversation without seeming too eager and get him to reveal more.

"Do you have a hiding place? Or are you going to find a new one?" she asks, without looking at him.

At once she realizes that her question is far too direct. She forces herself to meet his gaze.

"I can give you an entire city if you like," he replies seriously.

"Where?"

"Take your pick."

Saga shakes her head with a smile. She suddenly remembers a place she hasn't thought of for many years.

"When I think about other places . . . I only ever think about my grandfather's house," she says. "I had a swing in a tree. . . . I don't know, but I still like swings."

"Can't you go there?"

"No," she responds, and gets off the treadmill.

119

THE MEMBERS of Athena Promachos are listening to the conversation between Jurek and Saga.

Nathan Pollock has written down the words "high-voltage electricity wires," "big bulldozers," "red clay."

Joona stands by the speaker. A cold shiver runs up his spine as Saga talks about her grandfather. She can't let Jurek inside her head, he thinks. The image of Susanne Hjälm flits through his memory. Her dirty face and the terrified look in her eyes down there in the cellar.

"Why can't you go there if you want to?" he hears Jurek ask.

"It's my dad's house now," Saga replies.

"And you haven't seen him for a while?"

"I haven't wanted to," she says.

"If he's alive, he's waiting for you to give him another chance," Jurek says.

"No," she says.

"Obviously, that depends on what happened, but—"

"I was little. I don't remember much," she explains. "But I know I used to call him all the time, promising I'd never pester him again if he would just come home. I'd sleep in my own bed and sit politely at the table and ... I don't want to talk about it."

"I understand," Jurek says. His words are almost drowned out by a rattling sound.

There's a whining noise, then the rhythmic thud of the treadmill.

120

Jurek is back on the treadmill. He looks stronger again. His strides are forceful, but his pale face is calm.

"You're disappointed in your father because he was absent," he says.

"I remember all those times I called him. I mean, I needed him."

"But your mother—where was she?"

Saga pauses. She's saying too much now, but at the same time she has to respond to his openness. It's an exchange, or else the conversation risks becoming superficial again. It's time for her to say something personal, but as long as she sticks to the truth, she'll be on safe territory.

"Mom was sick when I was little. I only really remember the end," Saga replies.

"She died?"

"Cancer. She had a malignant brain tumor."

"I'm sorry."

Saga remembers the tears trickling into her mouth, the plastic smell of the phone, her hot ear, the light coming through the grimy kitchen window.

Maybe it's because of the medication, her nerves, or Jurek's penetrating gaze. She hasn't talked about this for years. She doesn't know why she's doing so now.

"It was just that Dad—he couldn't deal with her illness. He couldn't stand being at home."

"That's why you're angry."

"I was too little to take care of my mom. I tried to help her with her medication, and I tried to comfort her. She would get headaches in the evenings and just lie in her bedroom, crying."

Bernie crawls over and tries to sniff between Saga's legs. She shoves him away, and he rolls straight into the artificial palm.

"I want to escape, too," he says. "I'll come with you. I can bite—"

"Shut up," she interrupts.

Jurek turns around and looks at Bernie, who's sitting there grinning and peering up at Saga.

"Am I going to have to put you down?" Jurek asks him.

"Sorry, sorry," Bernie whispers, and gets up from the floor.

Jurek starts walking again. Bernie sits on the sofa and watches television.

"I'm going to need your help," Jurek says.

Saga doesn't answer.

"I think human beings are more tied to their families than any other creature," Jurek goes on. "We do everything we can to stave off separation."

"Maybe."

"You were only a small child, but you took care of your mother."

"Yes."

"Could she even feed herself?"

"Most of the time. But toward the end she had no appetite," Saga says.

"Did she have an operation?"

"I think she only had chemotherapy."

"In tablet form?"

"Yes. I used to help her every day."

Bernie is sitting on the sofa but keeps glancing at them. Every now and then, he gingerly touches the bandage over his nose.

"What did the pills look like?" Jurek asks, and speeds up slightly.

"Like normal pills," she replies.

She suddenly feels uneasy. Why is he asking about the drugs? There's no reason for it. Maybe he's testing her? Her pulse increases as she tells herself that it isn't a problem, because she's only telling the truth.

"Can you describe them?" he asks.

Saga opens her mouth to say that it's been too long, but all of a sudden she remembers the white pills among the long brown strands of the shag rug. She had knocked the jar over and was crawling around next to the bed, picking up the pills.

The memory is vivid.

She had gathered the pills in her cupped hand and blown the fluff from the rug off them. In her hand she had been holding something like ten little round pills. On one side they were imprinted with two letters in a square.

"White, round," she says. "With letters on one side. 'KO.' I have no idea why I remember that."

121

Jurek turns off the treadmill, then stands there smiling to himself for a long while as he catches his breath.

"You say you gave your mother cytostatic medication— that is, chemotherapy. But you didn't."

"Yes, I did," she says.

"The medicine you describe is codeine phosphate," he says.

"Painkillers?" she asks.

"You don't prescribe codeine for cancer—only strong opiates, like morphine and Ketogan."

"But I can remember the pills exactly. There was a groove on one side."

"Precisely," he says.

"Mom said—"

She falls silent, and her heart is beating so hard she's scared he'll hear it. Her anxiety must be showing on her face. Joona warned me, she thinks. He told me not to talk about my parents.

She gulps and looks down at the worn floor.

It doesn't matter, she thinks, and walks off toward her room.

It happened. She said too much. But she stuck to the truth the whole time.

She hadn't had a choice. Not answering his questions would

have been far too evasive. It was a necessary exchange, but she isn't going to say any more now.

"Wait," Jurek says, very gently.

She stops, still facing away.

"I knew that the court decision would never be reviewed, and I realize that I'm never going to get parole. But now that you're here, I can finally leave this hospital."

Saga turns and studies his thin face.

"What could I possibly do?" she asks.

"It'll take a few days to prepare everything," he replies. "But if you can get hold of some sleeping pills—five Stesolid tablets . . ."

"How can I get them?"

"You stay awake, say you can't sleep, ask for ten milligrams of Stesolid, hide the pill, then go to bed."

"Why don't you do it yourself?"

A smile breaks out on Jurek's cracked lips. "They'd never give me anything. They're too frightened of me. But you're a siren. Everyone sees how beautiful you are, not how dangerous."

This could be what it takes to win Jurek's confidence. She decides to go along with his plan, as long as it doesn't get too risky.

"You took the punishment for what I did, so I'll help you," she replies.

"But you don't want to come?"

"I've got nowhere to go."

"You will."

"Tell me," she asks, venturing a smile.

"The dayroom's closing now," he says, and walks out.

She feels strangely off-kilter, as if he already knows everything about her, even before she tells him.

Of course it wasn't chemotherapy medication. She just assumed it was, without really thinking. You don't administer chemotherapy drugs like that. They have to be taken at strict intervals. The cancer was probably far too advanced. All that was left to do was pain relief.

When she returns to her cell, she feels as if she's been holding her breath all the way through her encounter with Jurek Walter.

She lies down on the bunk, completely exhausted.

She'll stay passive from now on and let Jurek reveal his plans to the police.

122

IT'S ONLY FIVE TO EIGHT in the morning, but all the members of the Athena group are assembled in the attic apartment. Pollock has washed the mugs and left them upside down on a checkered blue tea towel.

After the dayroom doors were locked yesterday, they sat there analyzing the wealth of material until seven o'clock in the evening. They listened to the conversation between Jurek Walter and Saga Bauer, organizing and evaluating the information they heard.

"I'm worried that Saga's being too personal," Corinne says as Pollock hands her a cup of coffee. "Of course, she's walking a tightrope, because without volunteering a part of herself she can't build trust."

"She's in control of the situation," Pollock says, opening his black notebook.

"Let's hope so," Joona mutters.

"Saga's brilliant," Johan Jönson says. "She's getting him to talk."

"But we still don't know anything about Jurek," Pollock says, tapping the table with a pen. "Apart from the fact that that's not his real name."

"And that he wants to escape," Corinne says, raising her eyebrows.

"Yes," Joona says.

"But what does he have in mind? What does he want five sleeping pills for? Who's he planning to give them to?" Corinne asks with a frown.

"He can't drug the staff, because they're not allowed to take anything from him," Pollock says.

"Let's allow Saga to continue doing what she's doing," Corinne says after a brief pause.

"I don't like it," Joona says.

He stands up and goes over to the window. It has started snowing again.

"Before we move on," Joona continues, turning to face the room, "I'd like to hear the recording one more time, in particular the bit where Saga says she might not want to leave the hospital."

"We've only listened to it thirty-five times so far," Corinne sighs.

"I know, but I get this feeling that we're missing something," he explains, in a voice sharpened with conviction. "To begin with, Jurek sounds the same as usual when he says there are better places than the hospital, but when Saga responds that there are probably worse places, too, she manages to throw him off-balance."

"Maybe," Corinne says, looking down.

"No 'maybe' about it," Joona insists. "I've spent hours talking to Jurek, and I can tell when his voice changes. It becomes reflective, but only for a few moments, when he's describing the place with the red clay."

"And the high-voltage electricity wires and big bulldozers," Pollock says.

"I know there's something there," Joona says. "Not only does Jurek seem to surprise himself when he starts describing what sounds like a genuine memory, but—"

"But it doesn't go anywhere," Corinne interrupts.

"I want to listen to the recording again," Joona says, turning toward Johan.

123

JOHAN LEANS FORWARD and moves the cursor on the screen across the sequence of sound waves. The speakers crackle and hiss. The rhythmic sound of footsteps on the treadmill becomes audible.

"We can get out of the hospital together."

There's a knocking, then a rustling noise that gets gradually louder.

"I don't know if I want to."

"Why not?"

"I don't really have anything left outside."

"Left? Going back is never an option. But there are better places than this."

"And probably some worse."

More knocking, then a sigh.

"What did you say?"

"I just sighed, because it occurred to me that I can actually remember a worse place."

His voice is oddly soft and hesitant as he continues: "The air was filled with the hum of high-voltage electricity wires. The roads were wrecked by big bulldozers. And the tracks were full of water and red clay up to your waist. But at least I could still open my mouth and breathe."

"What do you mean?" Saga says.

Applause and more laughter from the television.

"That worse places might be preferable to better ones," Jurek replies, almost inaudibly.

The sounds of breathing and heavy footsteps merge with the drone of the treadmill.

"You're thinking about your childhood?" Saga says.

"I suppose so," Jurek whispers.

They sit in silence as Johan stops the recording and frowns at Joona.

"We're not going to get any further with this," Pollock says.

"What if Jurek's saying something that we're not hearing?" Joona persists, pointing at the screen. "There's a gap in the recording, isn't there? Just after Saga says there are worse places outside the hospital."

"He sighs," Pollock says.

"That's what it sounds like, but are we sure that's what he does?" Joona asks.

Johan scratches his stomach, moves the cursor back, raises the volume, and plays the segment again.

"I need a cigarette," Corinne says, picking up her shiny handbag from the floor.

The speakers hiss, and there's a loud creaking sound followed by an exhalation.

"What did I say?" Pollock says.

"Try playing it slower," Joona insists.

Pollock is drumming nervously on the table. The clip plays again at half-speed, and now the sigh sounds like a storm sweeping ashore.

"He's sighing," Corinne says.

"Yes, but there's something about the pause and the tone of his voice afterward," Joona says.

"Tell me what I should be looking for," Johan says, frustrated.

"I don't know. I want you to imagine that he's actually saying something, even if it isn't audible." Joona can't help smiling
at his own cryptic answer.

"I can certainly try."

"Isn't it possible to isolate and amplify the sound until we
know for certain if there's anything in that silence or not?"

"If I increase the sound pressure and intensity a few hundred times, the footsteps on the treadmill would burst our
eardrums."

"So get rid of the footsteps."

Johan Jönson shrugs and makes a loop of that segment,
stretches it out, and then divides the sound into thirty different curves, ordered by hertz and decibels. He highlights some
of the curves and gets rid of them.

Each excised curve appears on a smaller screen.

Corinne and Pollock walk onto the balcony to get some
fresh air. They gaze out across the rooftops and the Philadel-
phia Church.

Joona remains seated and scrutinizes the painstaking work.

After thirty-five minutes, Johan leans back and listens to
the cleaned-up loop at various speeds, then removes another
three curves and plays the result.

What's left sounds like a heavy stone being dragged across
a concrete floor.

"Jurek Walter sighs," Johan declares, and stops the playback.

"Shouldn't those be lined up as well?" Joona says, pointing
to three of the deleted curves on the smaller screen.

"No, that's just an echo that I removed," Johan says, then
looks suddenly thoughtful. "But I could actually try to remove
everything except the echo."

"He could have been facing the wall," Joona says.

Johan Jönson highlights and moves the curves of the echo
back again, multiplies the sound pressure and intensity by

three hundred, and replays the loop. Now, as it's repeated at just under normal speed, the dragging sound resembles a shaky exhalation.

"Isn't there something there?" Joona asks with renewed concentration.

"There could be," Johan says.

"I can't hear it," Corinne says.

"Well, it doesn't sound as much like a sigh now," Johan admits. "But we can't do any more to it: after this point, the longitudinal sound waves start to blur with the transversal, and because they're running at different rates, they'll only cancel each other out."

"Try anyway," Joona says impatiently.

124

JOHAN JÖNSON purses his lips together as he surveys the fifteen different curves.

"You're really not supposed to do this," he mutters.

With surgical precision, he adjusts the timing of the curves and extends some of the peaks to longer plateaux.

He replays the loop, and the room is filled with strange underwater sounds. Corinne stands with her hand over her mouth as Jönson stops it, makes some more adjustments, pulls certain sections farther apart, then plays it again.

Sweat has broken out on Pollock's forehead.

There's a deep rumble from within the loudspeakers, followed by a long exhalation divided into indistinct syllables.

"Listen," Joona says.

What they can hear is a slow sigh that's been unconsciously formed out of a thought. Jurek Walter isn't using his larynx, just moving his lips and tongue as he breathes out.

Johan moves one of the curves slightly, then gets up from his chair with a grin as the loop of the whisper repeats over and over again.

"What's he saying?" Pollock says in a tense voice. "It sounds a bit like 'Lenin.'"

"Leninsk," Corinne says, wide-eyed.

"What?" Pollock says.

"There's a city called Leninsk-Kuznetsky," she says. "But because he mentioned red clay, I think he means the secret city."

"A secret city?" Pollock mutters.

"The cosmodrome at Baikonur is well-known," she explains, "but fifty years ago the town was called Leninsk, and it was top secret."

"Leninsk in Kazakhstan," Joona says. "Jurek has a childhood memory from Leninsk."

Corinne sits down at the table, tucks her hair behind her ear, and explains: "Kazakhstan was part of the Soviet Union in those days, and it was so sparsely populated that they could build an entire town without the rest of the world noticing. There was an arms race going on, and they needed research bases and launch sites for rockets."

"Kazakhstan is a member of Interpol," Pollock says.

"If they can give us Jurek's real name, we can start to uncover his background," Joona says. "Then the hunt would really be on."

"It shouldn't be impossible," Corinne says. "We now have a location and an approximate age. We know he arrived in Sweden in 1994. We have pictures of him, we've documented the scars on his body, and—"

"We have his DNA and blood type," Pollock says.

"So either Jurek's family was part of the local Kazakhstan population, or they were among the scientists, engineers, and military personnel who were sent there from Russia."

"I'll put everything together," Pollock says quickly.

"I'll try to get hold of the National Security Committee in Kazakhstan," Corinne says. "Joona? Do you want me to . . ."

She stops and gives him a quizzical look. Joona meets her gaze and nods. He picks up his coat from a chair and starts walking toward the hall.

"Where are you going?" Pollock calls after him.

"I need to talk to Susanne Hjälm," Joona mutters.

125

When Corinne was talking about the scientists who were sent to the test facility in Kazakhstan, Joona was reminded of his conversation with Susanne Hjälm in the police car. Just before her daughter started shouting from the ambulance, he had asked if Susanne could remember the address on Jurek's letter.

She had said it was a PO box address and was trying to remember the name when she said it wasn't Russian.

Why had she said the name wasn't Russian?

Joona shows his ID to the guard. They walk through the women's section of Kronoberg Prison together.

The guard stops outside a thick metal door. Joona looks in through the window. Susanne is sitting motionless, eyes closed. Her lips are moving, as if she is praying under her breath.

When the guard unlocks the door, she startles and opens her eyes. She begins rocking her upper body when she sees Joona come in. Her broken arm is in a cast, and the other is hugging her stomach.

"I need to talk to you about—"

"Who's going to protect my girls?" she asks desperately.

"They're with their father now," Joona tells her, looking into her anguished eyes.

"No. No. He doesn't understand—he doesn't know. No one knows. You have to do something. You can't just leave them."

"Did you read the letter Jurek gave you?" Joona asks.

"Yes," she whispers. "I did."

"Was it addressed to a lawyer?"

She looks at him and starts to breathe more calmly. "Yes."

Joona sits down next to her on the bunk.

"Why didn't you send it?" he asks quietly.

"Because I didn't want him to get out," she says, sounding distraught. "I didn't want to give him the slightest chance. You won't be able to understand. No one can."

"I'm the one who arrested him, but—"

"Everyone hates me," she continues, not listening. "I hate myself. I couldn't see anything. I didn't mean to hurt that police officer, but you shouldn't have been there. You shouldn't have been trying to find me, you should—"

"Do you remember the address on the letter?" Joona interrupts.

"I burned it. I thought it would end. I don't know what I thought."

"Did he want it sent to a law firm?"

Susanne's body is shaking violently.

"When can I see my children?" she wails. "I have to tell them I did everything for them, even if they never understand, even if they hate me—"

"Rosenhane Legal Services?"

She looks at him, wild-eyed, as if she'd already forgotten he was there.

"Yes, that was it," she says.

"When I asked you before, you said the name on the address wasn't Russian," Joona says. "Why would it have been Russian?"

"Because Jurek spoke Russian to me once."

"What did he say?"

"I can't take it anymore, I—"

"Are you sure he was speaking Russian?"

"He said such terrible things. . . ."

126

Susanne stands up on the bed. She's beside herself. She turns to face the wall as she sobs, trying to hide her face with her one good hand.

"Please, sit down," Joona says gently.

"He mustn't, he mustn't. . . ."

"You hid your family in your cellar because you were afraid of Jurek."

Susanne looks at him, then starts pacing back and forth on the bed.

"No one would listen to me, but I know he speaks the truth. I've felt his fire on my face."

"I would have done the same thing you did," Joona says seriously. "If I believed I could protect my family from Jurek that way, I would have done the same thing."

She stops with a curious look in her eye.

"I was supposed to give Jurek an injection of Zypadhera. He'd been given a sedative and was lying on his bed. He couldn't move. Sven Hoffman opened the door, I went in, and I gave Jurek the injection in his buttock. As I was putting a bandage on it, I explained that I didn't want anything to do with his letter. I wasn't going to send it. I didn't say I'd already burned it, I just said . . ."

She falls silent and tries to pull herself together before

continuing. She holds her hand to her mouth for a while, then lets it fall: "Jurek opened his eyes and looked straight at me and started to speak Russian. I don't know if he knew I could understand. I'd never told him I once lived in Saint Petersburg—"

She breaks off and lowers her head.

"What did he say?"

"He promised to cut Ellen and Anna open . . . and let me choose which one would bleed to death," she says, then smiles to stop herself from going to pieces. "Patients can say the most terrible things. You have to put up with all sorts of threats. But it was different with Jurek."

"Are you sure he was speaking Russian and not Kazakh?"

"He spoke an unusually refined Russian, as if he were a professor at Lomonosov."

"You told him you didn't want anything to do with his letter," Joona says. "Were there any other letters?"

"Only the one he was responding to."

"So he received a letter first?" Joona asks.

"It was addressed to me, from a lawyer who was offering to review his rights and options."

"And you gave it to Jurek?"

"I don't know why. I suppose I was thinking that it was a human right, but he isn't human."

She starts crying and takes a few steps back on the mattress.

"Try to remember what—"

"I want my children. I can't take it," she whimpers, pacing on the bed again. "He's going to hurt them."

"You know that Jurek is locked up in the secure—"

"Only when he wants to be," she interrupts, and stumbles. "He fools everyone. He can get in and out."

"That's not true, Susanne," Joona says gently. "Jurek hasn't left the secure unit once in thirteen years."

She looks at him, then says, through white, cracked lips: "You don't know anything."

For a moment it looks as if she's about to start laughing.

"Do you?" she says. "You really don't know anything."

She blinks her dry eyes, and her hand is shaking as she raises it to brush her hair from her face.

"I saw him in the parking lot in front of the hospital," she says quietly. "He was just standing there, looking at me."

The bed creaks under her feet, and she puts her hand out to steady herself against the wall. Joona tries to calm her down: "I appreciate that his threats were—"

"You're so stupid," she yells. "I've seen your name written on the glass—"

She takes a step forward, slips off the bed, hits her neck on the edge of the bed frame, and collapses in a heap on the floor.

127

CORINNE PUTS her phone down on the table and shakes her head, sending a waft of expensive perfume over to Pollock.

He's been waiting for her to conclude the call and has been thinking of asking if she'd like to have dinner with him one evening.

"Nobody seems to know anything about Jurek," she says. "I spoke to an Anton Takirov at Kazakhstan's National Security Committee. He told me that Jurek Walter isn't a Kazakh citizen faster than I can open my laptop. I was very polite and asked them to conduct a new search, but this Takirov just sounded insulted and said that they did actually have computers in Kazakhstan."

"Maybe he's not good at talking to women."

"When I tried to tell Mr. Takirov that DNA matching can take a bit of time, he said that they had the most modern system in the world. He just wanted to get rid of me."

"So they didn't even give it a try."

"But we have a good relationship with the Federal Security Service of the Russian Federation these days. Dmitry Urgov just called me back. Unfortunately, they don't have anything that matches what I sent them. He said he'd personally ask the national police to look through the pictures and check their DNA register."

Corinne closes her eyes and massages her neck. Pollock tries to suppress the urge to offer to help.

"My hands are warm," Pollock ventures, just as Joona Linna comes in.

"Can I feel them?" Joona asks in his deep voice.

"Kazakhstan isn't making things easy for us," Corinne tells him. "But I—"

"Jurek's from Russia," Joona says, taking a handful of candy from a bowl.

"Russia," she repeats.

"He speaks perfect Russian."

"Would Dmitry Urgov have lied to me? Sorry, but I know him, and I really don't believe that."

"He probably doesn't know anything," Joona says, putting the candy in his pocket. "Jurek's old enough that it must have been in the days of the KGB."

128

POLLOCK, JOONA, AND CORINNE are leaning over the table, poring over their notes. Not long ago, they didn't have anything. Now, thanks to Saga's infiltration, they have a place to start. Jurek let something slip when he whispered "Leninsk." He grew up in Kazakhstan, but because Susanne Hjälm had heard him speaking educated Russian, it seems highly likely that his family came from Russia.

"But the security police there didn't know anything," Corinne reiterates.

Joona takes out his phone and starts looking for a contact he hasn't spoken to in many years. He can feel himself getting excited as he realizes he might finally be on the trail of the mystery of Jurek Walter.

"What are you doing?" Corinne asks.

"I'm going to talk to an old acquaintance."

"You're calling Nikita Karpin!" Pollock exclaims. "Aren't you?"

Joona moves away, holding the phone to his ear. It rings with a hissing echo, and then there's a crackle.

"Didn't I thank you for your help with Pichushkin?" Karpin asks abruptly.

"Yes, you sent some little bars of soap—"

"Isn't that enough?" he interrupts. "You're the most persistent young man I've ever met. I might have guessed that you'd call out of nowhere and disturb me."

"We're working on a very complex case here, which—"

"I never talk on the phone," Nikita interrupts.

"What if I organize an encrypted line?"

"There's nothing we couldn't crack in twenty seconds," the Russian says, laughing. "But that's beside the point. I'm out of it now. I can't help you."

"But you must have contacts?" Joona tries.

"There's no one left, and they don't know anything about Leninsk. And if they did they wouldn't say so."

"You already knew what I was going to ask," Joona sighs.

"Of course. Russia is a small country."

"Who should I talk to if I need an answer?"

"Try the charming Federal Security Service in a month or so. I'm sorry"—Karpin yawns—"but I have to take Zean out for his walk. We usually go down the Klyazma, on the ice, as far as the bathing jetties."

"I see," Joona says.

He ends the call and smiles at the old man's exaggerated caution. The former KGB agent doesn't seem to trust that Russia has changed. Maybe he has a point.

It wasn't exactly a formal invitation, but, coming from Nikita Karpin, it was almost generous.

Nikita's old Samoyed dog, Zean, died when Joona was visiting eight years ago. Joona had been invited to give three lectures on the work that led to Jurek Walter's capture. At the time, the Moscow police were in the middle of the hunt for the serial killer Alexander Pichushkin.

Joona knows that the dog is dead. And Nikita knows that Joona knows where to find him if he goes for a walk on the ice on the Klyazma River.

129

It's ten to seven in the evening, and Joona Linna is sitting on the last flight to Moscow. By the time the plane lands in Russia, it's nearly midnight. The country is in the grip of a crisp chill, and the low temperatures make the snow quite dry.

Joona is taking a taxi through the vast, monotonous suburbs. At first it feels as if he's been trapped in a loop of sprawling public housing, but when he reaches the city center, the view from his window finally changes. He catches a glimpse of one of Stalin's Seven Sisters—the beautiful skyscrapers—before the taxi turns onto a back street and stops outside the hotel.

His room is very basic and dimly lit. The ceiling is high, and the walls are yellow with cigarette smoke. On the desk is a brown plastic electric samovar. The fire-escape notice on the back of the door has a cigarette burn over the emergency exit.

As Joona stands at the only window, looking down at the alley, he can feel the winter chill through the glass. He lies back on the rough brown bedspread, gazes up at the ceiling, and listens to the muffled voices laughing and talking in the next room. He thinks it's too late to call Disa and say good night.

Thoughts are swirling through his mind, and their images carry him into sleep. A girl waiting for her mother to braid her hair. Saga Bauer looking at him, her head covered with cuts. Disa lying in his bathtub, humming, her eyes half closed.

AT HALF PAST FIVE in the morning, Joona's phone starts to vibrate on the bedside table. He slept in his clothes, with all the blankets and covers on top of him. The tip of his nose is freezing, and he has to blow on his fingers before he can switch off the alarm.

Through the window, the sky is still dark.

Joona goes down to the foyer and asks the young woman in Reception to rent a car for him. He sits at one of the ornately laid tables, drinks tea, and eats warm bread with melted butter and thick slices of cheese.

An hour later, he is driving a brand-new BMW X3 on the M2 highway out of Moscow. Shiny black tarmac rushes under the car. There's heavy traffic through Vidnoye, and it's already eight o'clock by the time he turns off onto winding white roads.

The trunks of the birch trees look like skinny young angels in the snow-covered landscape. Russia is so beautiful, it's almost frightening.

It's cold and clear, and Lyubimova is bathed in wintry sunshine when Joona pulls into the yard in front of the house. He was once told the place used to be the Russian theater legend Stanislavsky's summer residence.

Nikita Karpin comes out onto the veranda.

"You remembered my grubby old dog." He smiles, shaking hands with Joona.

Nikita Karpin is a short, stout man with an attractively aged face, a steely gaze, and a military haircut. When he was an agent, he was a frightening man.

Though Nikita Karpin is no longer formally a member of

the FSB, he's still employed by the Ministry of Justice. Joona knows that if anyone can find out whether Jurek Walter has any connection to Russia, it's Karpin.

"We share an interest in serial killers," Nikita says, showing Joona in. "For my part, they can be thought of as empty wells that can be filled with unsolved crimes—which of course is very practical. But, on the other hand, we have to arrest them so as not to appear incompetent, which makes the whole business much more complicated."

Joona follows Karpin into a large, beautiful room whose interior seems to have remained untouched for a hundred years. The old medallion wallpaper shimmers like thick cream. A framed portrait of Stanislavski hangs above a black grand piano.

The agent pours a drink from a frosted glass jug. On the table is a gray cardboard box.

"Elderflower cordial," he says, patting his stomach.

Joona takes the glass, and they sit down facing each other. Nikita's face changes. His friendly smile vanishes.

"The last time we met, most things were still secret. In those days, I was in charge of a specially trained group that went by the name of the Little Stick, in direct translation," Nikita says in a low voice. "We were fairly heavy-handed, both my men and I."

He leans back in his chair, making it creak.

"Maybe I'll burn in hell for that?" he says pensively. "Unless there's an angel who protects people who defend the motherland."

Nikita's veined hands are lying on the table between the gray box and the jug of cordial.

"I wanted to come down harder on the Chechen terrorists," he continues gravely. "I'm proud of our actions in Beslan, and in my opinion Anna Politkovskaya was a traitor."

He puts down his glass and takes a deep breath.

"I've looked at the material that your Security Police sent to the FSB. You haven't managed to find much, Joona Linna."

"No," Joona admits.

"We used to call the young engineers and workmen who were sent to the cosmodrome in Leninsk 'rocket fuel.'"

"Rocket fuel?"

"Everything surrounding the space program had to be kept secret. All reports were carefully encrypted. The intention was that the engineers would never come back from there. They were the best-educated scientists of their day, but they were treated like cattle."

The KGB agent pauses. Joona raises his glass and drinks.

"My grandmother taught me how to make elderflower cordial."

"It's very good."

"You did the right thing, coming to me, Joona Linna," Karpin says. "I've borrowed a file from the Little Stick's own archives."

130

THE OLD MAN pulls a gray file out of a cardboard box, opens it, and places a photograph on the table in front of Joona. It's a group picture of twenty-two men standing in front of polished stone steps.

"This was taken in Leninsk in 1955," Karpin says.

In the middle of the front row sits the legendary Sergei Korolev, smiling on one of the benches, the chief engineer behind the first man in space and the world's first satellite.

"Look at the men in back."

Joona leans forward and looks along the row of faces. Half hidden behind a man with tousled hair stands a skinny man with a thin face and pale eyes.

Joona jerks his head back, stunned.

He's found Jurek Walter's father.

"I see him," Joona says.

"Stalin's administration picked out the youngest and most talented engineers," Nikita says, tossing an old Soviet passport in front of Joona. "And Vadim Levanov was without a doubt one of the best."

As he opens the passport, Joona feels his pulse quicken.

The black-and-white photograph features a man who resembles Jurek Walter, but with warmer eyes and fewer wrinkles. So—Jurek's father's name was Vadim Levanov.

His journey here has not been in vain. Now they can begin to investigate Jurek's past properly.

Nikita lays out a set of ten fingerprints, a few small personal photographs of Jurek's father's christening and childhood, school yearbooks, and a child's drawing of a car with a chimney on its roof.

"What do you want to know about him?" Karpin smiles. "We've got pretty much everything. Every address he ever lived at, names of girlfriends before his marriage to Elena Mishailova, letters home to his parents in Novosibirsk."

"His son," Joona whispers.

"His wife was also an engineer, but she died in childbirth after they'd been married two years."

"The son," Joona repeats.

Karpin stands up, opens the wooden cupboard, gets out a heavy case, and puts it on the table. When he lifts the lid, Joona sees that it's a sixteen-millimeter film projector.

Nikita Karpin asks Joona to close the curtains, then takes a reel of film from the box.

"This is a private home movie from Leninsk that I think you should see."

The projector starts to click, and the image is projected directly onto the medallion wallpaper. Karpin adjusts the focus, then sits down again.

The saturation of the image varies, but otherwise it's fine. The camera must have been on a stand.

The film was taken by Jurek Walter's father during his time in Leninsk. The image on the wall in front of him shows the back of a house and a verdant garden. Sunlight filters through the leaves. In the background he can make out power lines.

The image shakes a little; then Jurek's father comes into view. He puts a heavy case down in the long grass, opens it, and gets out four camping chairs. A boy with neatly combed hair enters the frame from the left. He looks about seven years old and has chiseled features and big, pale eyes.

There's no doubt that it's Jurek. Joona hardly dares to breathe.

The boy says something, but all that can be heard is the clicking of the projector.

Father and son help each other unfold the metal legs of the case, which transforms into a wooden-topped table when they turn it over.

Young Jurek disappears from view but returns with a jug of water from the opposite side of the frame. It happens so quickly that Joona thinks there must have been some trick.

Jurek bites his lips and clasps his hands tight as his father speaks to him.

He disappears from view again, and his father strides after him.

The water in the jug sparkles in the sunlight.

A short while later, Jurek returns with a white paper bag, and then his father comes back with another child on his shoulders.

The father is shaking his head and trotting like a horse.

Joona can't see the other child's face.

The child's head is out of frame, but Jurek waves up at it.

Feet with small shoes on kick at the father's chest.

Jurek calls out something.

And when his father puts the second child down on the grass in front of the table, Joona sees that it, too, is Jurek.

The identical boy stares into the camera with a serious face. A shadow sweeps across the garden. The father takes the paper bag and disappears out of the picture.

"Identical twins." The agent smiles, stopping the projector.

"Twins," Joona repeats.

"That was why their mother died."

131

JOONA IS STARING at the medallion wallpaper, repeating silently to himself that the Sandman is Jurek Walter's twin brother.

That's who's holding Felicia captive.

That was whom his daughter, Lumi, saw in the garden when she was going to wave at the cat.

And that was why Susanne Hjälm saw Jurek in the parking lot outside the hospital.

The warm projector is making small clicking sounds.

Taking his glass with him, Joona walks to the window and opens the curtains. He looks out at the ice-covered surface of the Klyazma River.

"How were you able to find all this?" he asks when he's confident his voice won't crack. "How many files did you have to go through? I mean, you must have material covering millions of people."

"Yes, but we only had one defector from Leninsk to Sweden," Karpin replies.

"Their father fled to Sweden?"

"The summer of 1957 was a difficult time in Leninsk," Nikita says cryptically, lighting a cigarette.

"What happened?"

"We made two attempts to launch *Semyorka*. The first

time, the auxiliary rocket caught fire and the missile crashed
four hundred kilometers away. The second time—the same
fiasco. I was sent down there to remove the people responsible. Give them a taste of the Little Stick. Don't forget that no
less than five percent of the entire GDP of the Soviet Union
went to the installation at Leninsk. The third launch attempt
succeeded, and the engineers could breathe again, until the
Nedelin disaster three years later."

"I've read about that," Joona says.

"Mitrofan Nedelin rushed the development of an intercontinental rocket," Nikita says, looking at the glowing tip of his
cigarette. "It exploded in the middle of the cosmodrome, and
more than a hundred people burned to death. Vadim Levanov
and the twins were unaccounted for. For months, we thought
they'd been killed along with everyone else."

"But they hadn't," Joona says.

"No," Nikita says. "He fled because he was afraid of reprisals, and he would certainly have ended up in the Gulag. Probably the Siblag work camp. Instead, he turned up in Sweden."

Nikita stubs out his cigarette on a small porcelain saucer.

"We kept Vadim Levanov and the twins under constant
surveillance and were prepared to liquidate him," Karpin continues. "But we didn't need to. Because Sweden treated him
like garbage and arranged a special Gulag for him. The only
work he could get was as a manual laborer in a gravel quarry."

Nikita's eyes flash cruelly.

"If you'd shown any interest in what he knew, Sweden
could have been first into space." He laughs.

"Maybe," Joona says.

"Yes."

"So Jurek and his brother arrived in Sweden at the age of
ten or so?"

"But they only stayed a couple of years," Nikita says.

"Why?"

"You don't become a serial killer for no reason."

"Do you know what happened?" Joona asks.

"Yes."

Nikita turns toward the window and wets his lips. The low winter light shines in through the uneven glass.

132

TODAY SAGA IS FIRST into the dayroom. She runs for four minutes and has just lowered the speed and started to walk when Bernie comes in from his room.

"I'm going to start driving a taxi when I'm free. Shit, like some fucking Fittipaldi. You can ride for free, and I'll get to touch you between—"

She cuts him off. "Just shut up."

He nods, looking wounded, then walks straight over to the palm leaf, turns it over, and points at the microphone with a grin.

"Now you're my slave," he says, laughing.

Saga jabs him hard, making him stumble back and sit on the floor.

"I want to escape as well," he hisses. "I want to drive a taxi and—"

"Shut up," Saga says, checking over her shoulder to see if the guards are on their way in through the security door.

But no one seems to be watching them on the monitor in the surveillance room.

"You're going to take me with you when you escape, do you hear—"

"Shut up," Jurek interrupts behind them.

"Sorry," Bernie whispers at the floor.

Saga didn't hear Jurek come into the dayroom. A shiver runs down her spine when she realizes that he may have seen the microphone under the palm leaf.

Maybe her cover is already blown?

Maybe it's going to happen now, she thinks. The crisis she's been dreading is happening now. She feels adrenaline rushing through her and tries to visualize the plan of the secure unit. In her thoughts, she moves quickly through the marked doors, the different zones, the best places to take temporary shelter.

If Bernie blows her cover, she'll have to barricade herself in her room to start with. Ideally, she would get hold of the microphone and shout for immediate backup.

Jurek stops in front of Bernie, who's lying on the floor, whispering his apologies.

"Pull the power cord off the treadmill, go to your room, and hang yourself from the top of your door," Jurek tells him.

Bernie looks up at Jurek with fear in his eyes.

"What? What the fuck?"

"Tie the cord to the handle on the outside, throw it over the door, and pull your plastic chair over," Jurek instructs.

"I don't want to. I don't want to," Bernie says, his lips trembling.

"We can't have you alive any longer," Jurek says.

"But—what the fuck, I was only joking. I know that I can't come with you. I know it's just your thing . . . just your thing . . ."

133

POLLOCK AND CORINNE both stand up from the table when the situation in the dayroom becomes critical. They realize that Jurek has decided to execute Bernie and are hoping that Saga won't forget that she has no police responsibilities.

"There's nothing we can do," Corinne whispers.

Slow, thunderous rumbling sounds emerge from the speakers. Johan adjusts the sound levels and scratches his head anxiously.

"Give me a punishment instead," Bernie whimpers. "I deserve a punishment."

"I can break both his legs," Saga says.

Corinne wraps her arms around herself and is trying to control her breathing.

"Don't do anything," Pollock whispers to the speaker. "You have to trust the guards. You're only a patient."

"Why hasn't anyone come in?" Johan says. "The guards must have noticed what's going on, for God's sake?"

"If she acts, Jurek will kill her," Corinne whispers.

"Don't do anything," Pollock pleads. "Don't do anything."

134

Saga's heart pounds in her chest. She can't make any sense of her thoughts as she gets off the treadmill. It's not her job to protect other patients. She knows she must not step out of her role.

"I can break his kneecaps," she tries. "I can break his arms and fingers and—"

"It would be better if he just died," Jurek concludes.

"Come on," she says quickly to Bernie. "The camera's hidden here—"

"Snow White, what the fuck?" Bernie snivels, moving closer to her.

She grabs hold of his wrist, pulls him closer, and breaks his little finger. He screams and sinks to his knees, clutching his hand to his stomach.

"Next finger," she says.

"You're both mad," Bernie says through his sobbing. "I'll call for help. My skeleton slaves will come."

"Be quiet," Jurek says.

He walks over to the treadmill and removes the power cord, yanking it out from the baseboard and sending a shower of concrete dust over the floor.

"Next finger," Saga tries.

"Just stand back," Jurek says, looking her in the eye.

Saga remains where she is, with one hand against the wall, as Bernie follows Jurek.

The situation feels absurd to her. She watches Jurek tie the cord around the handle on the side of Bernie's door facing the dayroom and throw it over the top of the door.

She feels like shouting out.

Bernie looks at her beseechingly as he climbs onto the plastic chair and puts the noose around his neck.

He tries to talk to Jurek, smiling and repeating something.

She stands there, immobile, thinking that the staff must surely see them now. But no guards come. Jurek has been in the unit for so long that he's learned their routines by heart. Maybe he knows that this is when they have a coffee break or change shifts.

Saga backs away slowly toward her own room. She doesn't know what she's going to do and can't understand why no one's coming.

Jurek says something to Bernie, waits, and repeats the words, but Bernie is shaking his head as tears spring to his eyes.

Saga keeps moving backward. A sense of unreality is spreading through her body.

Jurek kicks the chair away, then walks through the dayroom and straight into his own room

Bernie is dangling in the air with his feet just off the floor. He tries to pull himself up with the cord, but he isn't strong enough.

Saga goes into her room and walks over to the door with the reinforced glass window. She kicks at it as hard as she can, but all she can hear is a muffled thud from the metal. She pulls back, turns and kicks again, backs up and kicks, then kicks again. The solid door vibrates slightly, but the heavy sound of her kicks carries into the concrete walls. She continues kicking until, finally, she hears agitated voices in the corridor, followed by rapid footsteps and the whirr of the electric lock.

135

THE LIGHTS in the ceiling go out. Saga is lying on her side in bed with her eyes open.

What should I have done?

Her feet and ankles ache from the kicks.

She doesn't know if she should have intervened. Maybe she could have. Maybe Jurek wouldn't have been able to stop her. But there's no doubt that she would have exposed herself to danger and ruined any chance of saving Felicia.

So she went into her room and kicked the door. She kicked the door as hard as she could, hoping that the guards would wonder where the noise was coming from and finally glance at their monitors.

But nothing happened. They didn't hear her for a long time. She should have kicked harder.

It felt like an eternity before the voices and footsteps approached. She's lying on her bed and trying to tell herself that the staff got there in time, that Eernie is now in intensive care, that his condition is stable.

She's thinking that Jurek might have tied a bad noose, even though she knows that wasn't the case.

SAGA LIES IN THE DARKNESS, remembering Bernie's face as he shook his head with a look of total helplessness. Jurek had moved like a shadow. He had conducted the execution dispassionately, simply doing what he had to do. He had kicked the chair away and then walked, without hurrying, into his room.

Saga switches on the lamp by her bed, then sits up and plants her feet on the floor. She turns her face toward the CCTV camera in the ceiling, toward its black eye, and waits.

As usual, Joona was right, she thinks, as she stares at the camera's round lens. He thought there was a chance that Jurek would approach her. Jurek had started talking to her in such a personal way that even Joona would be surprised.

Saga broke the rule about not discussing her parents, her family, but it worked. She just hopes that the officers listening don't assume that she lost control of the situation.

She's never forgotten what Jurek Walter has done, but she hasn't felt threatened by him. She's been more scared of Bernie. Up until the moment when Jurek hanged him with the cord.

Saga rubs her neck with her hand and continues to look into the camera. She sits like this for more than an hour.

136

Anders Rönn has logged in and is sitting in his office trying to summarize the day's events for the medical records.

Why is everything happening now?

The same day every month, the staff clean out the medicine stockroom. It takes no longer than forty minutes.

He, My, and Leif were outside the stockroom when they heard the noise.

Deep rumbling, echoing within the walls. My dropped the inventory list on the floor and ran to the surveillance control room. Anders followed her. My reached the large monitor and cried out when she saw the image from Patient Room 2. Bernie was hanging against the door to the dayroom. Urine was dripping from his toes, forming a puddle beneath him.

Anders's skin is still crawling. As a result of the suicide in the ward, he was summoned to a crisis meeting of the hospital committee. The hospital manager came straight from a children's birthday party, annoyed to have been called away. The manager looked at him and said that perhaps it had been a mistake to allow an inexperienced doctor to assume the role of chief.

Anders blushes when he recalls how he stood up and apologized, stammering and trying to explain that, according to his medical notes, Bernie Larsson had been extremely depressed and that he had found the transfer difficult.

"You're still here?"

He looks up to see My standing in the doorway, smiling wearily at him.

"Hospital management wants the report first thing tomorrow morning, so you're probably going to have to put up with me for a few more hours."

"Tough shit," she says with a yawn.

"You can go and lie down in the staff room if you like," he says.

"Don't worry."

"I mean it. I have to be here anyway."

"Are you sure? That's really sweet of you."

He smiles at her.

"Get a couple hours' sleep. I'll wake you up when I'm ready to leave."

Anders hears her walk down the corridor, past the changing room, and into the staff room.

The glow from the computer screen fills Anders's little office. He clicks to open the calendar, then adds some newly arranged meetings with relatives and care workers.

His fingers pause above the keyboard as he thinks about the new patient. He feels caught in that moment, the seconds when he was in her room, pulling down her pants and underwear. Her white skin had turned red after the two injections. He'd touched her as a doctor, but he had also looked between her thighs at her genitals, her blond hair and closed vagina.

Anders types in a note about a rescheduled meeting. He's unable to concentrate properly.

He works on the report for Social Services, then gets up and goes over to the surveillance control room.

As he sits down in front of the large screen to look at the nine squares, he immediately notices that Saga is awake. Her bedside light is switched on. She is staring into the camera, directly at him.

Feeling a strange weight inside him, Anders looks at the other cameras. Patient Rooms 1 and 2 are dark. The security doors and dayroom are quiet. The camera outside the room in which My is resting shows nothing but a closed door. The security staff are beyond the first security door.

Anders highlights Patient Room 3, and the image fills the second screen. He moves his chair closer. Saga is still sitting there, looking up at him.

He wonders what she wants.

Her pale face is lit up.

She massages the back of her neck with one hand, rises from the bed, and takes a couple of steps forward, all the while looking up at the camera.

Anders clicks away from the image, gets up, and glances at the guards and the closed door of the staff room.

He goes over to the security door, runs his card through the reader, and walks into the corridor. The nocturnal lighting has a flat gray tone. The three doors are glowing dully, like lead. He walks up to her door and looks in through the reinforced glass. Saga is still standing in the middle of the floor, but she turns to look toward the door as he opens the hatch.

The light from the bedside lamp is shining behind her, between her legs.

"I can't sleep," she says with big, imploring eyes.

"Are you scared of the dark?" he says, smiling.

"I need ten milligrams of Stesolid. That's what I always used to get at Karsudden."

He's thinking that she's even more beautiful and slender in reality. She moves with a strange awareness, confident in her body, as if she were an elite gymnast or a ballerina. He can see that her tight, thin vest is damp with sweat. The perfect curve of her shoulders, her nipples beneath the fabric.

He tries to recall if he's read anything about sleeping problems in her notes from Karsudden. Then he remembers that it doesn't really matter. He's in charge of decisions about medication.

"Hold on," he says, then goes and gets a tablet.

When he comes back he can feel sweat between his shoulder blades. She reaches her hand through the hatch to take the plastic cup, but he can't resist teasing her: "Can I have a smile?"

"Give me the tablet," she says simply, still holding out her hand.

He holds the plastic cup in the air, out of reach of her outstretched hand.

"One little smile," he says, tickling the palm of her hand.

197

SAGA SMILES at the doctor and maintains eye contact with him until she has the plastic cup. He closes and locks the hatch but remains outside the door. She retreats into the room, pretends to put the pill in her mouth, gets some water, and swallows, tipping her head back. She's not looking at him, isn't sure if he's still there, but she sits down on the bed for a while and then turns out the light. Under cover of darkness, she slips the pill under the inner sole of one of her shoes.

Before she falls asleep, she sees Bernie's face again, tears filling his eyes as he puts the noose around his neck.

The little thuds as his heels hit the door follow her as she sinks into a deep sleep.

The hourglass turns.

Then, like warm air, she drifts up toward wakefulness and opens her eyes in the dark. She doesn't know what's woken her up. In her dream, it was Bernie's helplessly kicking feet.

A distant rattling sound, perhaps, she thinks.

But all she can hear is her own pulse inside her ears.

She blinks and listens.

The reinforced glass in the door gradually appears as a rectangle of frozen seawater.

She closes her eyes and tries to go back to sleep. Her eyes are stinging with exhaustion, but she can't relax.

The water heaters in the walls are clicking. She opens her eyes again and stares over at the gray window.

Suddenly a black shadow appears against the glass.

She's instantly wide awake, ice-cold.

A man is looking at her through the reinforced glass. It's the young doctor. Has he been standing out there the whole time?

He can't see anything in the darkness.

But he's still standing there in the middle of the night.

His head is nodding slightly.

Now she realizes that the rattling sound that woke her was the key slipping into the lock.

Air rushes in. The sound expands, grows deeper, and fades away.

The heavy door opens. She knows she must lie absolutely still. She should be sleeping soundly because of the pill. The lighting from the corridor shimmers on the young doctor's shoulders.

She wonders if he saw that she only pretended to take the pill, if he's coming to get it from her shoe. But staff aren't allowed in patients' rooms alone, she thinks.

Then it dawns on her: the doctor is here because he thinks she's taken the pill and is fast asleep.

138

THIS IS MADNESS, Anders thinks as he shuts the door behind him. It's the middle of the night. He's gone in to see a patient and is now standing in her darkened room. His heart is pounding so hard in his chest that it actually hurts.

He can just make out her figure in bed.

She'll be sound asleep for hours, practically unconscious.

The door to the staff room where My is sleeping is closed. There are two guards by the most distant security door. Everyone else is asleep.

He doesn't actually know what he's doing in Saga's room. All he knows is that he had to come in and look at her again, had to come up with an excuse to feel her warm skin beneath his fingers.

He can't stop thinking about her perspiring breasts and the look of resignation she gave him when she tried to get away and her bra pulled up.

He repeats to himself that he's only making sure everything's okay with a patient who's just taken a sedative.

If anyone sees him, he can say he detected signs of sleep apnea and decided to go in and check, seeing as she's so heavily medicated.

They'll say it was an error of judgment not to wake My, but the intrusion itself will be regarded as justified.

He just wants to make sure everything's okay.

Anders takes a couple of steps into the room. He suddenly finds himself thinking of trap nets and lobster pots, large openings leading you toward smaller ones, until, eventually, there's no way back.

He swallows hard and tells himself he hasn't done anything wrong. He's exceptionally conscientious about his patients' welfare. That's all.

He walks over slowly and looks at her in the darkness. She's lying on her side.

Carefully, he sits down on the edge of the bed and folds the covers back from her legs and backside. He tries to listen to her breathing, but his own heartbeat is too loud in his ears.

Her body is radiating warmth.

He strokes her thigh softly, a gesture that he tells himself any doctor might make. His fingers reach the waistline of her underwear.

His hands are cold, and he's far too nervous to be sexually excited.

It's too dark for the camera in the ceiling to be able to register what he's doing.

He lets his fingers slip cautiously over the underwear and in between her thighs, feeling the heat of her genitals.

Gently, he presses a finger into the cotton fabric of her underwear, running it along the lips of her vagina.

He'd like to stroke her to orgasm, until her whole body is crying out for penetration, even though she's asleep.

His eyes have gotten used to the darkness, and now he can make out Saga's smooth thighs and the perfect line of her hips.

He reminds himself that she is fast asleep. He knows that. He pulls down her underwear without ceremony. She groans in her sleep but is otherwise completely still.

Her body is glowing in the darkness.

The blond pubic hair, sensitive inner thighs, her flat stomach.

She'll stay asleep, no matter what he does.

It makes no difference to her.

She won't say no. She won't shoot him a look that's pleading with him to stop.

A wave of sexual excitement crashes over him, filling him, making him pant for breath. He can feel his penis swelling, straining against his clothes. He adjusts it with one hand.

He can hear his breathing and the thud of his heartbeat. He has to get inside her. His hands fumble with her knees, trying to part her thighs.

She rolls over, kicking gently in her sleep.

He slows down, leans over her, pushing his hands between her thighs and trying to spread them.

He can't do it—it feels like she's putting up resistance.

He rolls her over onto her stomach, but she slips to the floor, sits up, and looks at him with wide eyes.

Anders hurries out of the room, telling himself that she wasn't properly awake. She won't remember anything. She'll think she was only dreaming.

139

Veils of snow are blowing across the highway outside the roadside café. The vehicles thundering past rattle the windows. The coffee in Joona's cup trembles with the vibrations.

Joona looks at the men at the table. Their faces are calm, if a little tired. After taking his phone, passport, and wallet, they seem to be waiting for instructions. The café smells of buckwheat and fried pork.

Joona looks at his watch and sees that his plane out of Moscow departs in nine minutes.

Felicia's life is ticking away.

One of the men is trying to solve a sudoku puzzle, while the other is reading about a horse race in a broadsheet newspaper.

Joona goes over his conversation with Nikita Karpin.

The old man acted as if they had all the time in the world, until they were interrupted. He smiled to himself and wiped the condensation from the jug of cordial with his thumb. He said that Jurek Walter and his twin brother had stayed in Sweden for only a couple of years.

"Why?" Joona asked.

"You don't become a serial killer for no reason."

"Do you know what happened?"

"Yes."

The old man had run his finger over the gray file. He said that the highly trained engineer had most likely been prepared to sell what he knew.

"But the Swedish Aliens Department was only interested in whether or not Vadim Levanov could work. They didn't understand anything. They sent a world-class missile engineer to work in a gravel pit."

"Maybe he realized you were watching him and had enough sense to keep quiet about what he knew," Joona said.

"It would have been more sensible not to have left Leninsk. He might have gotten ten years in a labor camp, but—"

"But he had his children to think of."

"Then he should have stayed," Nikita said, meeting Joona's gaze. "The boys were extradited from Sweden, and Vadim Levanov was unable to trace them. He contacted everyone he could, but it was impossible. There wasn't a lot he could do. He knew that we'd arrest him if he returned to Russia, and then there was absolutely no way he'd find his boys, so he waited for them instead. That was all he could do. He must have thought that if the boys tried to find him they'd start by looking in the place where they'd last been together."

"And where was that?" Joona asked, as he noticed a black car approaching the house.

"Migrant workers' accommodations, Barrack Number Four," Nikita replied. "That was also where he took his own life, much later."

Before Joona had time to ask the name of the gravel pit where the boys' father had worked, Nikita had more visitors. A shiny black Chrysler turned in and pulled up in front of the house, and there was no doubt that the conversation was over. Without any apparent urgency, the old man replaced all the material on the table concerning Jurek's father with information about Alexander Pichushkin, the so-called Chessboard

Killer—a serial killer in whose capture Joona had played a small part.

The four men came in, walked over to Joona and Nikita, shook their hands politely, and spoke for a while in Russian. Then two of them led Joona out to the black car while the other two stayed with Nikita.

Joona was put in the back seat. One of the men, who had a thick neck and little black eyes, asked to see his passport in a voice that was not unfriendly, then asked for his cell phone. They went through his wallet and called his hotel and the car rental company. They assured him that they would drive him to the airport, but not just yet.

Now they're sitting at a table in a café, waiting.

Joona takes another small sip of his cold coffee.

If only he had his phone, he could call Anja and ask her to do a search for Jurek's father. There has to be something about the children, about where they lived. He suppresses an urge to overturn the table, run out to the car, and drive to the airport. They have his passport, as well as his wallet and phone.

The man with the thick neck is tapping the table gently and humming to himself. The other one, who has close-cropped ice-gray hair, has stopped reading and is sending texts from his phone.

There's a clatter from inside the kitchen.

Suddenly the gray-haired man's phone rings, and he gets up and moves away a few steps before answering.

After a while, he ends the call and tells them that it's time to go.

140

SAGA IS UNEASY after the doctor's nocturnal visit. Her medication is making her feel oddly cut off from reality, but she has a very strong sense that she's in over her head and that her cover is about to be blown.

That doctor would have raped me if I'd really been asleep, she thinks. I can't let him touch me again.

She just needs a little more time to complete her mission. She's so close now.

She's going to save the kidnapped girl.

The rules are simple. Under no circumstances can she let Jurek escape. But she can plan the escape with him. She can show interest and ask questions.

The most common problem with escapes is that people have nowhere to go once they're out. Jurek won't make that mistake. He knows where he's going.

The lock on the door to the dayroom clicks open. Saga gets up from her bed, rolls her shoulders as if preparing for a fight, then walks out.

Jurek Walter is standing by the opposite wall, waiting for her. She can't understand how he could have gotten out into the dayroom so quickly.

There's no reason to stay close to the treadmill now that

the cord is gone. She just hopes the range of the microphone is wide enough.

The television isn't turned on, but she goes and sits on the sofa.

Jurek is standing in front of her.

She feels as if she doesn't have any skin, as if he has a strange ability to see straight into her bare flesh.

He sits down beside her, and she discreetly passes him the tablet.

"We only need four more," he says, looking at her with his pale eyes.

"Yes, but I—"

"And then we can leave this terrible place."

"Maybe I don't want to."

When Jurek Walter reaches out his hand and touches her arm she almost jumps. He notices her fear and looks at her blankly.

"I have a place I think you'd love," he says. "It's not that far away from here. It's just an old house behind an old brick factory, but at night you could go outside and swing."

"A real swing?" she asks, trying to smile.

She needs Jurek to keep talking to her. His words are little pieces that will form a pattern in the puzzle Joona is putting together.

"It's just an ordinary swing," he says. "But you can swing out over the water."

"What, a lake, or—"

"You'll see. It's lovely."

141

SAGA'S HEART is beating so loudly it seems to her that Jurek must be aware of it. If the microphone is working, then her colleagues will be identifying every abandoned brickworks. They might even be on their way already.

"It's a good place to hide until the police give up the hunt," he continues. "And you can stay in the house if you like it there—"

"But you'll be moving on?" she says.

"I have to."

"And I can't come with you?"

"Do you want to?"

"Depends where you're going."

Saga is aware that she might be pushing him too far, but right now he seems keen to involve her in his escape attempt.

"You have to trust me," he says curtly.

"It sounds like you're planning on dumping me at the first house we come to."

"No."

"Sounds like it," she persists, sounding hurt. "I think I'll stay here until I get discharged."

"And when will that be?"

"I don't know."

"Are you sure they're going to let you out?"

"Yes," she replies honestly.

"Because you're a good little girl who helped your sick mother when she—"

"I wasn't good," Saga interrupts, pulling her arm away. "Do you think I wanted to be there? I was only a child. I was just doing what I had to do."

He leans back on the sofa and nods.

"Compulsion is interesting."

"I wasn't forced into it," she protests.

He smiles at her. "You just said you were."

"Not like that. I mean, I was able to do it," she explains. "She was only in pain in the evenings and at night."

Saga thinks of one morning after a particularly difficult night, when her mother made breakfast for her. She fried some eggs, made sandwiches, and poured two glasses of milk. Then they went outside in their pajamas. The grass in the garden was damp with dew, and they took the cushions from the dining chairs with them down to the hammock.

"You gave her codeine," Jurek says, in a strange tone of voice.

"It helped."

"But those pills aren't very strong. How many did she have to take that last night?"

"A lot. She was in terrible pain."

Saga rubs her hand across her forehead and realizes that she's perspiring heavily. She doesn't want to talk about this. She hasn't thought about it for years.

"More than ten, I suppose?" Jurek asks lightly.

"She used to take two every night, but that evening she needed much more. I spilled them on the rug, but . . . I don't know, I must have given her twelve, maybe thirteen pills."

Saga feels the muscles in her face tighten. She's afraid she's going to start crying if she stays, so she gets up quickly to go to her room.

"Your mother didn't die of cancer," Jurek says.

She stops and turns toward him.

"That's enough," she says.

"She didn't have a brain tumor," he says.

"I was with my mom when she died. You know nothing about her. You can't—"

"The headaches," Jurek interrupts. "The headaches don't subside the following morning if you have a tumor."

"That's how it was for her," she says firmly.

"The pain is caused by the pressure on brain tissue and blood vessels as the tumor grows. That doesn't pass. It just gets worse."

She looks into Jurek's eyes and feels a shiver run down her back. "I . . ."

Her voice is no more than a whisper. She feels like shouting and screaming, but she's powerless.

If she's honest with herself, she's always known that there was something odd about her memories. She remembers yelling at her father when she was a teenager, saying he lied about everything, that he was the biggest liar she'd ever met.

He had told her that her mother hadn't had cancer.

She'd always thought he was lying to her in an effort to excuse his betrayal of her mother. Now, standing here, she's no longer sure where the idea that her mother had a brain tumor came from. She can't recall her mom's ever saying she had cancer, and they never went to the hospital.

But why did Mom cry every evening if she wasn't sick? It doesn't make sense. Why did she make me call Dad all the time and tell him he had to come home? Why did Mom take codeine if she wasn't in pain? Why did she let her own daughter give her all those pills?

Jurek's face is a somber, rigid mask. Saga turns away and starts walking toward the door. She wants to run. She doesn't want to hear what he's about to tell her.

"You killed your own mother," he says calmly.

142

SAGA STOPS ABRUPTLY. Her breathing has become shallow, but she forces herself not to show her feelings. She has to remind herself who's in charge of this situation. He may believe that he's deceiving her, but in fact she's the one deceiving him.

Saga adopts a neutral expression, then turns slowly to face him.

"Codeine," Jurek says, smiling joylessly. "Codeine-Meda only comes in the form of twenty-five-milligram tablets. I know precisely how many it takes to kill a human being."

"Mom told me to give her the pills," she says.

"But I think you knew she'd die," he says. "I'm sure your mom thought you knew. She thought you wanted her to die."

"Fuck you," she whispers.

"Maybe you deserve to be locked up here forever."

"No."

He looks at her with terrifying gravity in his eyes, with metallic precision.

"Maybe it'll be enough if you get just one more sleeping pill," he says. "Because yesterday Bernie said he had some Stesolid wrapped in a piece of paper, in a crack under his sink. Unless he only said it to buy time."

Her heart races. Bernie hid sleeping pills in his room?

What's she going to do now? She has to stop this. She can't let Jurek get hold of the sleeping pills. What if there are enough for him to carry out his escape plan?

"Are you going into his room?" she asks.

"The door's open."

"It would be better if I did it," she says quickly.

"Why?"

Jurek is giving her a look that seems almost amused, while she tries desperately to come up with a reasonable answer.

"If they catch me," she says, "they'll just think I'm addicted and—"

"Then we won't get any more pills," he retorts.

"I think I'd be able to get more from the doctor anyway," she says.

Jurek considers this, then nods.

"He looks at you as if he were the captive."

She opens the door to Bernie's room and goes inside.

In the light from the dayroom, she can see that his room is an exact copy of hers. When the door closes behind her, every-thing goes dark. She walks over to the wall, feeling her way around, picking up the smell of stale urine from the toilet. She reaches the sink, the edges of which are wet, as if it's recently been cleaned.

The doors to the dayroom will be closing in a few minutes. She tells herself not to think about her mother, just to con-centrate on the job at hand. Her chin starts to tremble, but she manages to pull herself together, stifling the tears. She kneels down and runs her fingers across the cool underside of the sink. She reaches the wall and feels along the silicone seal but can't find anything. A drop of water falls on her neck. She reaches farther down and touches the floor. Another drip falls between her shoulder blades. She notices that the sink is sloping slightly. That's why the water at the edges is dripping onto her instead of draining back into the bowl.

She feels along the underside of the sink, where it joins the wall. Her fingers find a crack. There it is. A tiny package, tucked inside. The sink creaks as she tries to grab the package. Carefully she manages to pull it out. Jurek was right. Pills. Tightly wrapped in toilet paper. She's breathing hard as she crawls out, tucks the package in her trousers, and stands up.

As she feels her way to the door she dreads having to tell Jurek that she didn't find anything, that Bernie must have been lying about the pills. But she can't let him escape. She reaches the wall and moves along it until she finds the door and emerges into the dayroom.

Blinking hard against the bright light, Saga looks around. Jurek isn't there. He must have returned to his room. The clock behind the reinforced glass tells her the doors to the dayroom will be locked in a few seconds.

143

Anders Rönn taps lightly at the door of the surveillance room. My is sitting there reading a copy of *Expo*, paying no attention to the large monitor.

"Are you coming to say good night?" she asks.

Anders smiles back at her, sits down next to her, and watches Saga leave the dayroom and go into her room. Jurek is already lying on his bed, and of course Bernie's room is dark. My yawns and leans back in the swivel chair.

Leif is standing in the doorway, draining the last drops from a can of Coca-Cola.

"What does male foreplay look like?" he asks.

"Is there such a thing?" My asks.

"An hour of begging, pleading, and persuasion."

Anders chuckles, and My laughs so hard the piercing in her tongue glints.

"They're a bit short on staff up in Ward Thirty tonight," Anders says.

"Funny how we're so short on staff when there's such high unemployment," Leif sighs.

"I said they could borrow you," Anders says.

"There always have to be two of us here," Leif says.

"Yes, but I'm going to have to stay and work until at least one o'clock anyway."

"Okay. I'll come back down at one o'clock."

"Good," Anders says.

Leif tosses the soda can into the trash and leaves the room.

Anders sits beside My for a while. He can't take his eyes off Saga. She's pacing anxiously in her cell, with her thin arms wrapped around her body.

He can feel himself aching with desire. All he can think about is how to get into her room again. He's going to give her twenty milligrams of Stesolid this time.

He makes the decisions. He's the doctor in charge. He can have her put in a straitjacket and tied to her bed. He can do whatever he wants. She's psychotic and paranoid, and there's no one she can talk to.

My stretches and says something Anders doesn't hear.

He looks at the time. Only two hours until the lights go out and he can let My go get some sleep.

144

SAGA IS PACING around the floor of her cell, feeling the little package from Bernie's room moving in her pocket. Behind her back, she hears the electronic lock whirr and click. She should wash her face, but she can't be bothered. She goes over to the door to the corridor and looks through the glass, then leans her forehead against the cool surface and closes her eyes.

If Felicia is in the house behind the brick factory, I'll be free tomorrow. Otherwise, I have a couple more days in me before I have to put a stop to the escape attempt, she thinks.

She's been willing herself not to break down.

She hasn't let the pain in. All she can think about is completing her mission.

She's breathing fast and knocking her head gently against the cold glass.

I'm in charge of this situation, she tells herself. Jurek thinks he's controlling me, but I've gotten him to talk. He needs sleeping pills in order to escape, but I went into Bernie's room and found the package, and I'm going to hide it, say it wasn't there.

The palms of her hands are sweaty.

As long as Jurek believes he's manipulating me, he'll give himself away, piece by piece.

She's sure he's going to tell her his escape plan tomorrow.

I just have to be here a few more days. I need to stay calm and not let him inside my head again.

He said that she had killed her mother on purpose. That she wanted to kill her.

Saga bangs her hands against the door.

Could her mom have thought ... ?

She turns, grabs the back of the plastic chair, and hits the sink with it. She loses her grip and it clatters to the floor, but she grabs it again and bashes it against the wall, then the sink.

She sits down on the bed, panting.

"I'm going to be okay," she whispers to herself.

She's on the brink of losing control of the situation. She can't still her thoughts. Her memory is only showing her the long strands of the rug, the pills, her mom's wet eyes, the tears running down her cheeks, her teeth hitting the edge of the glass as she swallows the pills.

Saga remembers her mom shouting at her when she said that Dad couldn't come. She remembers her mom forcing her to call him, even though she didn't want to.

Maybe I was angry with her, she thinks. Tired of her.

She tries to calm herself down.

She walks over to the sink and splashes water on her face, rubbing her eyes.

She has to regain control.

Maybe the neuroleptic injection is what's stopping her from just breaking down and crying.

Saga lies down on the bed and makes up her mind to hide Bernie's package, tell Jurek she didn't find anything. Then she won't have to ask the doctor for sleeping pills. She can just give Jurek the ones she got from Bernie's room.

One at a time, one per night.

Saga rolls over onto her side and turns her back on the CCTV camera in the ceiling. Covered by her own body, she takes out the package. She carefully unrolls the toilet paper, little by little, until she sees that it contains just three pieces of chewing gum.

Chewing gum.

She takes a deep breath, traces the streaks of dirt on the walls with her eyes, and thinks with vacant clarity that she's done exactly what Joona warned her against.

I've let Jurek inside my head, and everything has changed.

I can't stand myself.

Her stomach is churning with anguish as she thinks about her mom's cold body that morning. A sad, immovable face with an odd froth at the corner of her mouth.

It feels as if she's falling.

I can't lose it now, she thinks. She struggles to regain control of her breathing.

I'm not sick, she reminds herself. I'm here for one reason alone. That's all I have to think about. My task is to find Felicia. This isn't about me. I don't care about myself. I'm undercover, pretending to go along with the plan, and I'll keep Jurek talking about escape routes and hiding places for as long as I can.

145

IT'S BEEN ALMOST twenty-four hours since Joona was picked up from Nikita Karpin's house by the men from the Russian Security Service. They haven't answered any of his questions, and they haven't explained why he's been detained.

After sitting in a café for hours, they took him to a bleak concrete apartment building and led him along one of the exterior walkways into a two-room apartment.

Joona was taken to the farther room, which contained a dirty sofa, a table with two chairs, and a small bathroom. The steel door was locked behind him, and then nothing happened until a couple of hours later, when they gave him a warm paper bag containing soggy food from McDonald's.

Joona has to get in touch with his colleagues and ask them to look up Vadim Levanov and his twin sons, Igor and Roman. Maybe the names would lead to new addresses. Maybe they'd be able to identify the gravel pit where the father worked.

But the metal door remains locked, and the hours are passing. He's heard the men talk on the phone a couple of times, but apart from that it's been silent.

Joona has been dozing off and on, curled up on the sofa, but snaps awake toward morning at the sound of footsteps and voices in the next room.

He turns on the light and waits for them to come in.

Someone coughs, and he hears voices talking irritably. Suddenly the door opens and the two men from the previous day come in. They both have pistols in their shoulder holsters and are absorbed in a rapid-fire conversation in Russian.

The man with gray hair pulls out one of the chairs and puts it in the middle of the room.

"Sit down here," he says.

Joona gets up from the sofa and notices that the man backs away as he walks slowly over to the chair and sits down.

"You're not here on official business," the thick-necked man with black eyes says. "Tell us why you went to see Nikita Karpin."

"We were talking about the serial killer Alexander Pichushkin," Joona replies.

"And what conclusions did you reach?" the man with gray hair asks.

"The first victim was his presumed accomplice," Joona says. "We were talking about him—Mikhail Odichuk."

The man tilts his head, nods, then says amiably: "Naturally, you're lying."

The man with the thick neck and black eyes has turned away and drawn his pistol. It's hard to see, but it might be a high-caliber Glock. He's hiding the gun with his body as he feeds a bullet into the chamber.

"What did Nikita Karpin tell you?" the man with gray hair presses.

"Nikita believes that the accomplice's role was—"

"Don't lie!" the man with black eyes roars, and turns around, holding the pistol behind his back. "Nikita Karpin no longer has any authority. He isn't in the Security Service."

"You knew that, didn't you?" the man with gray hair asks.

Joona might be able to overpower the two men, but without his passport and money, it would be impossible to get out of the country.

The agents exchange a few words in Russian. The man with gray hair says sharply, "You discussed material that has been declared confidential, and we need to know exactly what you were told before we can take you to the airport."

For a long time, no one moves. The gray-haired man looks at his phone, says something to the other one in Russian, and gets a shake of the head in response.

"You have to tell us," he says, putting his phone in his pocket.

"I'll shoot your kneecaps," the other man says.

"So—you drove out to Lyubimova, met Nikita Karpin, and—"

The gray-haired man breaks off as his phone rings. He looks stressed. He answers, exchanges a few short words, then says something to his colleague. They have a brief, heated conversation.

146

THE MAN with the thick neck and black eyes moves aside and takes aim at Joona with the pistol. The floor creaks under his feet. A shadow slips away, and the light from the lamp reaches his hand. Joona can now see that the black pistol is a Strizh.

The gray-haired man rubs one hand over his head and barks an order. He looks at Joona for a few seconds, then leaves the room and locks the door behind him.

The other man walks around Joona and stops somewhere behind him.

"The boss is on his way," he says in a low voice.

There's the sound of angry shouting behind the steel door. The smell of gun grease and sweat is suddenly very noticeable in the small room.

"I need to know. Do you understand?" the man says.

"We were talking about serial ki—"

"Don't lie!" he yells. "Tell me what Karpin said."

Joona can hear the man's impatient movements behind his back. He sees the man's shadow move on the floor and can feel him coming closer.

"I have to go home now," Joona says.

The man with black eyes moves quickly, pressing the barrel of the pistol hard against the back of Joona's neck from a position just to the right of him.

His rapid breathing is loud.

In a single movement, Joona pulls his head out of the way, twists his body, and knocks the gun aside with his right hand. He stands up and throws the man off-balance. He grabs the barrel of the pistol and twists it down before jerking it upward to break the man's fingers.

The man howls, and Joona concludes by ramming a knee into his kidneys and ribs. One of the man's legs is lifted from the floor by the force of the blow, and he tumbles backward, crashing into the chair behind him.

Joona has already moved out of the way and turned the pistol on him when he rolls onto his side, coughing, and opens his eyes. He tries to get up but coughs again, then lies there with his cheek to the ground, inspecting his wounded fingers.

Joona removes the magazine and puts it on the table. He takes the bullet out of the chamber and dismantles the entire pistol.

"Sit down," Joona says.

The man with black eyes groans with pain as he gets up. His brow is beaded with sweat, and he sits down.

Joona puts his hand in his pocket and pulls out a piece of candy.

"This might help a bit," he says as he unwraps the cellophane and pops the candy into the guy's mouth.

The man looks at Joona in astonishment.

The door opens, and two men come in. One is the man with gray hair, and the other an older man with a full beard, wearing a gray suit.

"Sorry for the misunderstanding," the older man says.

"I urgently need to get home," Joona says.

"Of course."

The older man accompanies Joona out of the apartment. They take the elevator down to a waiting car and are driven to the airport together.

The driver carries Joona's bag, and the older man goes with him through check-in and security. He escorts Joona all the way to the gate and onto the plane. Only when boarding is complete does Joona get his phone, passport, and wallet back.

Before the bearded man leaves the plane, he hands Joona a paper bag containing seven small bars of soap and a fridge magnet of Vladimir Putin.

Joona barely has time to send a text to Anja before he is told to switch off his phone. He closes his eyes and considers the bars of soap. There's no doubt that this is a gift from Nikita Karpin. Joona got the same kind of soap the last time he visited him. Nikita is a hard and cautious man. The entire interrogation must have been arranged by him as a test to see if Joona had the sense to protect his source.

147

IT'S EVENING by the time Joona's plane lands in Stockholm. He switches on his phone and reads a message from Carlos, informing him that a big police operation is under way.

Maybe Felicia's already been found?

Joona tries to get ahold of Carlos as he hurries past the duty-free shops, down to the exit by the baggage claim area, and then over the bridge to the garage. Tucked inside the compartment for the spare wheel is the shoulder holster containing his black Colt Combat Target .45 ACP.

He drives south as he waits for Carlos to answer his phone.

Nikita had said that Vadim Levanov expected the boys to make their way to the place where they were last together if they ever tried to find him.

"And where was that?" Joona had asked.

"Migrant workers' accommodations, Barrack Number Four. That was also where he took his own life, much later."

Joona is heading down the highway toward Stockholm at 140 kilometers an hour. The pieces of the puzzle have been coming together thick and fast, and he's confident that he'll soon be able to see the overall picture.

Twin brothers forced to leave the country. The father commits suicide.

Their father was a highly educated engineer but was doing manual labor in one of Sweden's many gravel pits.

Joona puts his foot down as he tries to reach Carlos again. Before he has time to pull up the number, his phone rings.

"You should be grateful I'm here," Anja says. "Every police officer in Stockholm is out at Norra Djurgården."

"Have they found Felicia?"

"They're busy searching the forest beyond the industrial complex in Albano. They have dogs and—"

"Did you get my text?" Joona interrupts, his jaw clenched with stress.

"Yes, and I've been trying to work out what happened," Anja says. "It hasn't been easy, but I think I've managed to track down Vadim Levanov, though the spelling of his name was Westernized. It looks like he arrived in Sweden in 1960, with no passport, from Finland."

"And the children?"

"I'm afraid there's no mention of any children in the records."

"Could he have smuggled them in?"

"During the fifties and sixties, Sweden absorbed a huge number of migrant workers and the welfare state was expanded, but the regulations were still very old-fashioned. Migrant workers were thought incapable of looking after their children, and Social Services often placed them with foster families or in group homes for children."

"But these boys were extradited," Joona says.

"That wasn't unusual, especially if there was suspicion that they were Roma. I'm talking to the National Archive tomorrow. There was no immigration bureau in those days, so the police, the Child Welfare Committee, and the Aliens Department used to make the decisions fairly arbitrarily."

He turns off at Häggvik to fill up on gas.

This can't slip away, he thinks. There has to be something here that will crack the investigation.

"Do you know where the father worked?" he asks.

"I've started investigating all the gravel pits in Sweden, but it may take a while, because we're dealing with such old records," she says, and sighs.

Joona thanks Anja several times and ends the call.

Joona suddenly remembers Mikael's confused words about the Sandman. He talked about the porcelain fingers and said more than once that the Sandman smells like sand. It may just have been something from the old fairy tales. But what if there was some connection to a gravel quarry or a sand pit?

A car horn sounds behind Joona, and he starts to drive again but pulls over to the side of the road shortly afterward and calls Reidar Frost.

"What's going on?" Reidar asks.

"I'd like to talk to Mikael. How is he?"

"He feels bad about not being able to remember more. We've had the police here several hours a day."

"Every little detail could be important."

"I'm not complaining," Reidar says hurriedly. "We'll do anything, you know that. That's what I keep saying—we're here, twenty-four hours a day."

"Is he awake?"

"I can wake him. What did you want to ask?"

"He's said a few times that the Sandman smells like sand. Is it possible that the capsule is near a gravel pit? At some gravel pits they crush stone, and at others—"

"I grew up near a gravel pit, on the Stockholm Ridge, and—"

"You grew up near a gravel pit?"

"In Antuna," Reidar replies, slightly bewildered.

"Which pit?"

"Rotebro. There's a large gravel factory north of the Antuna Road, past Smedby."

Joona pulls onto the opposite on-ramp and heads north again on the highway. He's already fairly close to Rotebro, so the gravel pit can't be far.

Joona listens to Reidar's weary, rasping voice while Mikael's voice plays in his head: *"He smells like sand.... His fingertips are made of porcelain, and when he takes the sand out of the bag they tinkle against each other ... and a moment later you're asleep...."*

148

The traffic thins out as he speeds north.

After all these years, three major pieces of the puzzle are finally fitting together.

Jurek's father worked in a gravel pit and killed himself in his home there.

Mikael says the Sandman smells like sand.

And Reidar grew up near a gravel pit in Rotebro.

What if it's the same gravel pit? This can't be a coincidence. The pieces have to fit together somehow. In which case, this is where Felicia is, not where all his colleagues are searching, he thinks.

The ridges of slush between the lanes make the car swerve. Dirty water sprays up onto the windshield.

He speeds up again, past the Rotebro shopping center and up the narrow Norrviken Road, which runs parallel to the high ridge.

He reaches the top and sees the entrance to the gravel works a moment too late. He turns sharply and brakes in front of two heavy metal barriers. The wheels slide on the snow, Joona wrenches the steering wheel, the car spins, and the rear bumper slams into one of the barriers.

The red glass from the brake light shatters across the snow.

Joona throws the door open, gets out of the car, and runs past the blue shed that houses the office.

He runs down the steep slope toward the vast crater that has been excavated over the years. Floodlights on tall towers illuminate this strange lunar landscape, with its static excavators and vast heaps of sifted sand.

No one could be buried here. It would be impossible to hide any bodies, because everything is constantly being dug up. A gravel quarry is a hole that gets wider and deeper every day.

Heavy snow is falling through the artificial light. He runs past stone crushers with massive caterpillar tracks. He's in the most recent section of the pit. The sand is bare, and it's obvious that work is still being done here every day. Beyond the machinery are several blue shipping containers and three RVs. A floodlight hits him from behind a pile of sand. Half a kilometer away, he can see a snow-laden area in front of a steep drop. That must be the older part of the pit.

He makes his way up a slope where people have dumped old fridges, broken furniture, and trash. His feet slip on the snow, but he keeps going, sending cascades of stones down behind him.

He makes it to the original level of the ridge, more than forty meters above the current ground level, and has a good view of the pitted landscape. Cold air tears at his lungs as he surveys the illuminated landscape of sand with its machines and makeshift roads.

He starts to run along the narrow strip of meadow grass between the slope and Älvsunda Road.

There's a crumpled car wreck by the side of the road in front of the chain-link fence plastered with "No Trespassing" signs. Joona stops and peers into the falling snow. At the far corner of the very oldest section of the gravel pit is an area of tarmac, on top of which is a row of single-story buildings, as long and narrow as military barracks.

149

Joona steps over rusty barbed wire and heads toward the old buildings; the windows are broken, and there are graffiti tags sprayed on the brick walls.

It's dark up here. Joona gets out his flashlight and shines the light at the first building.

There's no door. Snow has blown in over the first few meters of the blackened wooden floor. The beam sweeps quickly across old beer cans, dirty sheets, condoms, and latex gloves.

He goes from door to door, peering through the broken or missing windows. The guest workers' old housing has been abandoned for many years. Nothing but dirt and dereliction. In some places, the roofs have caved in, and whole sections of walls are missing.

He slows down when he sees that the windows in the second-to-last building are intact. An old shopping cart is lying on its side by the wall.

On one side of the building, the ground drops away toward the bottom of the quarry.

Joona switches off the flashlight as he makes his way to the building, where he stops and listens before turning it on again.

All he can hear is the wind sweeping across the rooftops.

In the darkness a short distance away, he can make out

the last building in the row. It seems to be little more than a snow-covered ruin.

He goes over to the window of the second-to-last building and shines the flashlight through the dirty glass. The beam pans across a filthy hot plate connected to a car battery, a narrow bed with rough blankets, a radio with a shiny antenna, several tanks of water, and a dozen cans of food.

When he reaches the door, he can make out an almost eroded number "4" at the top left corner.

This could be the building that Nikita Karpin had mentioned.

Joona carefully pushes the handle down, and the door opens. He slips inside, shutting the door behind him. The space smells like damp old fabric. A Bible lies on a rickety shelf. There's only one room, with one window and one door.

Joona realizes that he is clearly visible from the outside.

The wooden floor creaks under his weight.

He shines the flashlight along the walls and sees piles of water-damaged books. In one corner, the light flashes back at him.

He sees that there are hundreds of tiny glass bottles lined up on the floor.

Dark glass bottles, with rubber membranes.

Sevoflurane, a highly effective sedative.

Joona pulls out his phone and calls the Emergency Control Room. He asks for police backup and an ambulance to be sent to his location.

Then everything is silent again. All he can hear is his own breathing and the floor creaking beneath him.

Suddenly, from the corner of his eye, he sees movement outside the window. He draws his Colt Combat and releases the safety catch in an instant.

There's nothing there, just some loose snow blowing off the roof.

He lowers the pistol again.

On the wall by the bed is a yellowed newspaper clipping about the first man in space—the "Space Russian," as *Expressen*'s headline describes him.

This must be where the father killed himself.

Joona is thinking that he ought to search the other buildings when he catches sight of the outline of something protruding from under the filthy rag-rug. He pulls the rug aside and exposes a large hatch in the wooden floor.

He lies down and puts his ear to the hatch, but he can't hear anything.

He glances at the window, then shoves the rug aside and opens the hatch.

The dusty smell of sand rises from the darkness.

He leans forward and shines the flashlight into the opening, where he sees a steep flight of concrete steps.

150

THE SAND ON THE STAIRS crunches under Joona's shoes as he heads down into the darkness. After nineteen steps, he finds himself in a large concrete room. The flashlight beam flickers across the walls and ceiling. There's a stool in the middle of the room, and on one wall is a foam board with a few pushpins and an empty plastic sleeve.

Joona realizes that he must be in one of the many bomb shelters built in Sweden during the Cold War.

There's an eerie silence down here.

The room tapers slightly, and tucked beneath the staircase is a heavy steel door.

This has to be the place.

Joona puts the safety catch back on his pistol and slips it into its holster to free up his hands. The steel door has large bolts that slide into place when a wheel at the center of the door is turned.

He pulls the wheel counterclockwise. There's a metallic rumble as the heavy bolts slide from their housings.

The door is hard to open, the metal fifteen centimeters thick.

He shines the flashlight into the shelter and sees a dirty mattress on the floor, a sofa, and a tap sticking out of the wall.

There's no one here.

The room stinks of old urine.

He points the light at the sofa again and approaches cautiously. He stops and listens, then moves closer.

She might be hiding.

Suddenly he has a feeling that he's being followed. He could end up trapped in the room. He turns and in that instant sees the heavy door closing. The immense hinges are creaking. He reacts immediately, throwing himself backward and jamming the flashlight into the gap. There's a crunch as it gets squeezed and the glass shatters.

Joona shoves the door open with his shoulder, draws his pistol again, and emerges into the dark room.

There's no one there.

The Sandman has moved remarkably quietly.

Strange light formations are flickering in front of Joona's eyes as he tries to make out shapes in the murky gloom. The flashlight is giving off only a faint glow now, barely enough to illuminate anything.

All he can hear are his own footsteps and his own breathing.

He looks over toward the concrete steps leading up to the main room. The hatch is still open. He shakes the flashlight, but it keeps dimming.

Suddenly Joona hears a tinkling sound and holds his breath as he finds himself thinking about porcelain fingertips. At the same moment, he feels a cold cloth pressed to his mouth and nose.

Joona spins around and lashes out hard but hits nothing and loses his balance.

He turns, holding out his pistol. The barrel scrapes the concrete wall. There's no one there.

Panting, he stands with his back to the wall, extending the flashlight toward the darkness.

The tinkling sound must have come from the little sedative

bottles when the Sandman took them out to pour the liquid onto the cloth.

Joona is feeling dizzy. He desperately wants to get out into the fresh air, but he forces himself to stay where he is.

It's completely silent. There's no one here.

Joona waits a few seconds, then returns to the capsule. His movements feel strangely delayed, and his gaze keeps slipping sideways. Before he goes inside, he turns the wheel of the lock so that the bolts slide out, preventing the door from closing.

In the weak glow of the flashlight, he makes his way forward once more. He reaches the sofa and nudges it carefully away from the wall. A skinny woman is lying on the floor.

"Felicia? I'm a police officer," he whispers. "I'm going to get you out of here."

When he touches her he can feel that she's boiling hot. She has an extremely high fever and is no longer conscious. As he picks her up from the floor she starts to shake with fevered chills.

Joona charges up the stairs with her in his arms. He drops the flashlight and hears it clatter down the steps. She's going to die soon unless he manages to get her fever down. Her body is completely limp. He doesn't know if she's breathing as he climbs through the hatch.

Joona runs across the main room, kicks open the door, lays her down on the snow, and detects that she's still breathing.

"Felicia, you have a really high fever."

He covers her with snow, speaking to her in a soothing voice, all the while keeping his pistol trained on the door of the building.

"The ambulance is on its way," he says. "Everything's going to be fine, Felicia, I promise. Your brother and your dad are going to be so happy. They've missed you so much, you know that?"

151

The ambulance arrives, its blue lights flashing across the snow. Joona stands as the stretcher is wheeled past the old buildings. He explains the situation to the paramedics and keeps his pistol aimed at the entrance to Barrack 4.

"Hurry up," he cries. "She's running a dangerously high fever, and she's unconscious."

Two paramedics lift Felicia out of the snow. Her hair is hanging in black, sweaty locks over her impossibly pale forehead.

He walks toward the open doorway with his weapon raised.

He's about to go back inside when he glances toward the flickering blue light of the ambulance playing over the remains of the last building. There are fresh footprints in the snow, leading away from the building and into the darkness.

Joona runs toward them, thinking that there must be another exit, that the two buildings might share an underground shelter.

He follows the footsteps at a run, through clumps of grass and scrub.

As he rounds an old fuel tank he sees a thin figure limping along the edge of the pit.

Joona is moving as quietly as he can.

The figure is leaning on a crutch. He seems to realize he's being pursued and tries to move faster along the steep cliff.

There are sirens in the distance.

Joona races through the deep snow.

I'm going to get him, he thinks. I'm going to arrest him and drag him back to the cars.

They're approaching a bright section of the gravel pit containing a large concrete factory. A single floodlight illuminates the bottom of the crater.

The figure stops, turns, and looks at Joona. His mouth is open, and his breathing is labored. He's standing right at the edge.

Joona approaches, his pistol pointed at the ground.

The Sandman's face is almost identical to Jurek's, but much thinner.

Far in the distance, Joona can hear the police cars arrive at the old barracks.

"It all went wrong with you, Joona," the Sandman says. "My brother told me to take Summa and Lumi, but they died before I had the chance. Fate sometimes chooses its own path."

Flashlight beams circle the barracks.

"I wrote to my brother and asked him about you, but I never found out if he wanted me to take anything else from you," he says.

Joona feels the weight of the weapon in his tired arm and looks into the Sandman's pale eyes.

"I thought you'd hang yourself after the car accident, but you're still alive," the Sandman says, shaking his head. "I waited, but you just went on living."

He pauses, then smiles suddenly, looks up, and says, "You're still alive because your family isn't really dead."

Joona raises his pistol, aims the barrel at the Sandman's heart, and fires three shots. The bullets go straight through his skinny frame. Black blood sprays from the exit wounds between his shoulder blades. The gunshots echo around the gravel pit.

Jurek's twin brother falls backward. His crutch remains where it is, stuck in the snow.

The Sandman is dead before he hits the ground. His emaciated body rolls down the slope until it hits a discarded stove.

152

Joona sits in the back seat of his car with his eyes closed. His boss, Carlos Eliasson, is driving him back to Stockholm.

"She's going to be okay. I spoke to a doctor at the Karolinska. Felicia's condition is serious but not critical. They're not making any promises, but even so, this is great news. I really think she's going to make it, I—"

"Have you told Reidar?" Joona asks, without opening his eyes.

"The hospital's dealing with that. You just need to go home and get some rest, and—"

"I tried to reach you."

"Yes, I know, I saw I had a bunch of missed calls. You might've heard that Jurek mentioned an old brick factory to Saga. There were never very many, but there used to be one in Albano. When we went into the forest, the dogs identified graves all over the place. We've been busy searching the whole damn area."

"But you haven't found anyone alive?"

"Not yet, but we're still looking."

"I think you're just going to find graves." He pauses. "Is everything okay at the prison?"

"THE NIGHTMARE'S OVER, JOONA," Carlos says. "We're working on getting the Prison Service Committee to pass the decision to transfer Saga again. We'll pick her up as soon as they do and clear her record."

They reach Stockholm. The light around the streetlights looks like fog because of the snow. A bus pulls up beside them, waiting for the lights to change. Exhausted faces look out through the steamed-up windows.

"I talked to Anja," Carlos says. "She found the records for Jurek and his brother in the Child Welfare Committee's files in the council archive, and she tracked down the decision from the Aliens Department in the National Archive in Marieberg."

"Anja's smart," Joona says.

"Jurek's father was allowed to stay in the country on a temporary work permit," Carlos says. "But he didn't have permission to keep the boys with him. After they were discovered, the Child Welfare Committee was notified and the boys were taken into custody. Presumably, the authorities thought they were doing the right thing. The decision was rushed through, but because one of the boys was sick, the cases were dealt with separately."

"They were sent to different places."

"The Aliens Department sent the healthy boy back to Kazakhstan, and then a different caseworker made the decision to send the other boy to Russia—to Children's Home Number Sixty-seven, to be precise."

"I see," Joona whispers.

"Jurek crossed the border into Sweden in January 1994. Maybe his brother was already at the quarry by that time, maybe not. But by then their father was dead."

Carlos pulls up smoothly in an empty parking space on Dala Street, not far from Joona's apartment at 31 Wallin Street.

They both get out of the car, walk down the snow-covered pavement, and stop at Joona's front door.

"As I mentioned, I knew Roseanna Kohler," Carlos says with a sigh. "And when her children disappeared, I did all I could, but it wasn't enough."

"No."

"I told her about Jurek. She wanted me to tell her everything, wanted to see pictures of him, and . . ."

"But Reidar didn't know."

"No. She said it was better that way. I don't know. . . . Roseanna moved to Paris after that. She used to call all the time. She was drinking too much."

Carlos rubs his neck with one hand.

"What?" Joona asks.

"One night, Roseanna called me from Paris, screaming that she'd seen Jurek Walter outside her hotel, but I didn't listen. Later that night, she killed herself."

"You should have told me about her phone call," Joona says.

"I didn't believe her."

"It led to a lot of suffering—you know that?"

Carlos nods and hands Joona the car keys.

"Get some sleep," Carlos says.

153

My looked slightly bemused when Anders told her she could take a nap in the staff room again.

"I just don't see any reason for us both to be awake," he'd said. "I don't have a choice—I have a couple hours of work left to do. After that, you and Leif can divide things up however you like."

Now he's alone. He walks down the corridor, stops outside the staff room, and listens.

Silence.

He continues to the surveillance room and sits down in the operator's seat. At last, it's time to turn out the lights. The large monitor depicts nine different scenes. Jurek seems to have gone to bed early. Anders can see his thin frame outlined beneath the covers. He's lying unnervingly still, almost as if he isn't breathing. Saga is sitting on her bed with her feet on the ground. Her chair is on its side on the floor.

He leans closer to the screen and looks at her. His eyes follow the outline of her shaved head, her slender neck and shoulders, and the muscles in her thin arms.

There's nothing to stop him.

He doesn't know why he got so scared last night when he was in her room. There was no one watching the monitors, and even if there had been, the room was so dark that they wouldn't have been able to see anything.

He could have had sex with her ten times. He could have done whatever he wanted.

Anders takes a deep breath, inserts his ID card into the computer, types the code, and logs in. He opens the unit's administrative program, highlights the patients' zone, and clicks on nocturnal lighting.

Now all of the patients' rooms are black.

Seconds later, Saga turns on her bedside lamp and lifts her face up toward the camera.

It's as if she's looking at him because she knows he's looking at her.

Anders checks on the two guards. They're talking to each other by the entrance. The male guard is saying something that makes the tall female guard laugh. He's smiling as he mimes playing a violin.

Anders stands and looks at Saga again on the screen.

He takes a pill from the stockroom and puts it in a plastic cup, then goes over to the security door and runs his card through the reader. As he approaches her door, his heart starts thumping. He opens the hatch and sees her turn her head in his direction. She gets to her feet and walks toward him.

"Did you sleep well last night?" he asks in a friendly voice, but she doesn't respond.

When she reaches her hand through the hatch, he holds her fingers for a few moments before giving her the plastic cup.

He closes the hatch and watches her walk toward the sink. She fills the cup with water, puts the pill in her mouth, and swallows it. She turns off the lamp by the bed and lies down.

Anders retrieves the straps for the bed, removes the plastic covering, and stands outside the steel door, watching her through the reinforced glass.

154

UNDER COVER OF DARKNESS, Saga hides the pill in her shoe and lies down on the bed. She doesn't know if the young doctor is still standing outside the door, but she's sure he's planning to come into her room as soon as he thinks she's asleep. She could see quite clearly in his eyes that he wasn't finished with her.

Yesterday she was so taken aback by his abuse of power that she let it go way too far. Today she doesn't even know if she cares what happens.

She's here to save Felicia, and she may have to put up with this place for a couple more days.

Tomorrow or the day after, Jurek will reveal everything to her. Then this will be over, and she can go home and forget what she's been through.

Saga rolls onto her other side, glances at the door, and immediately sees the silhouette behind the glass. Her heartbeat begins to speed up in her chest. The young doctor is waiting outside the door until she's knocked out by the medication.

Is she prepared to let herself be raped in order to conceal her mission? Her thoughts are too chaotic for her to be able to prepare herself for what seems to be happening.

She hears the scrape as the key opens the lock.

Cooler air sweeps in through the door.

She watches the doctor walk over to the bed.

She shuts her eyes and listens.

Nothing happens.

Maybe he just wants to look at her.

She tries to breathe out soundlessly, then waits for ten seconds before breathing in again. In her mind, she envisions a square for which each side is a moment.

The doctor puts his hand on her stomach, following the movement of her breathing. She feels it slide to her hip and take hold of her underwear. She lets him pull her pants off, easing them over her feet.

She can feel the warmth of his body.

He strokes her right hand and raises it gently above her head. At first she thinks he's going to measure her pulse, but then she realizes that she can't move. When she tries to pull her hand away, he puts a broad strap over her thighs and tightens it before she has a chance to wriggle off the bed.

"What the hell are you doing?"

She can't kick. He must have tied her ankles while she was trying to free her right hand with her left. He switches on the bedside lamp and looks at her, wide-eyed. The fingers of her free hand are frantically grasping at the thick strap around her right wrist.

He stops her, quickly pulling her free hand away.

She jerks to get loose and tries to twist around, but it's impossible.

She slumps back, and he starts to attach another strap across her shoulders, but when he leans over she punches him in the mouth with her clenched fist. As the blow connects, he stumbles back and sinks down onto one knee. Shaking, she starts to untie her right hand.

He's back at the bed now, shoving her hand away.

There's blood running down his chin as he roars at her to

lie still. He tightens the strap around her right wrist again, then moves behind her.

"I'll kill you," she shouts, trying to follow him with her eyes.

He's quick and seizes her left arm with both hands, but she pulls free, gets hold of his hair, and yanks him toward her. She rams his forehead against the bed frame as hard as she can. She pulls him forward again and tries to bite his face, but he slaps her with such force across the neck that she lets go.

Using all her strength, she claws her free hand toward him and tries to turn her body, but she's completely stuck.

The doctor takes hold of her head and bends it hard to one side, almost dislocating her shoulder. The cartilage in the joint makes a creaking sound, and she howls with pain. She struggles to pull one foot free, but the strap cuts into her skin. She hits him on the cheek with her free hand, but without any real force. He pushes her hand down to the top of the bed, fixes the strap around her wrist and tightens it.

He wipes the blood from his mouth with the back of his hand, panting, then takes a couple of steps back and just looks at her.

155

THE DOCTOR slowly walks up to her and fastens the last strap across her chest. Her left hand is stinging after her desperate blows. He stands there for a while, then goes to the foot of the bed. Blood is trickling from his nose, over his lips. She can hear him taking shallow, excited breaths. Without hurry, he slowly pulls her thighs farther apart with the straps. She looks him in the eye. She can't let this happen.

He strokes her calves with trembling hands and stares up between her thighs.

"Don't do this," she tries to say in a composed voice.

"Just keep quiet," he says, removing his doctor's coat without taking his eyes off her.

Saga turns her face aside. She doesn't want to look at him. She can't believe that this is happening.

She closes her eyes, desperately trying to think of a way out.

Then she hears a strange rattling sound beneath the bed. She opens her eyes and sees a figure mirrored in the stainless-steel sink.

"Get the fuck out of here," she gasps.

The doctor picks her underwear up off the bed and stuffs it roughly in her mouth. She tries to scream as she realizes what the reflection in the shiny metal of the sink is.

It's Jurek.

He must have hidden himself in her room while she was looking for Bernie's sleeping pills.

With growing panic, she struggles to free herself.

She can hear the buttons of Jurek's shirt clicking against the struts under the mattress as he moves.

One button comes loose and slides out across the floor. The doctor looks at it in surprise as it rolls in an arc and spins to a stop.

"Jurek," the doctor mutters at the moment when a hand grabs his leg and pulls him to the ground. Anders hits the back of his head and gasps, but he manages to roll over onto his front and crawl away.

Run, Saga thinks. Lock the door and call the police.

Jurek rolls out onto the floor and gets to his feet at the same time as the doctor. Anders makes for the door, but Jurek gets there first.

Saga is struggling to get the underpants out of her mouth. She coughs, takes a deep breath, and starts to feel sick.

Anders trips over the plastic chair and backs away, staring at the elderly patient.

"Don't hurt me," he pleads.

"No?"

"Please. I'll do anything."

Jurek comes closer, and his wrinkled face is completely expressionless.

"I'm going to kill you, my boy," he says. "But first you're going to experience a great deal of pain."

Saga screams through the gag and strains against the straps.

She can't understand what's happening, why Jurek hid in her room, why he changed their plan.

The doctor is shaking his head, retreating and trying to fend Jurek off with his hands.

Sweat is running down his face.

Jurek follows him slowly, then suddenly grabs his hand and forces the doctor down on the floor. With terrible force, he stomps on the arm, close to the shoulder. There's a crunch, and the young doctor screams. With military precision, Jurek pulls in the opposite direction and twists the arm around. It's completely detached from its socket now, just hanging from muscle and skin.

Jurek yanks the doctor to his feet, holds him up against the wall, and slaps him several times to prevent him from losing consciousness. His loose arm is darkening from internal bleeding. The doctor is weeping like a child.

Saga's having trouble breathing. She manages to shift her position slightly and pulls her left arm so hard that her vision starts to go black before the strap comes loose. She tugs the fabric from her mouth and gasps for breath.

"We can't escape now—there weren't any sleeping pills in Bernie's room," Saga says to Jurek.

The hand she's just pulled free hurts like hell. She can't tell how badly wounded it is. Her fingers are burning like fire.

Jurek starts to go through the doctor's clothes, finds the keys to the cell door, and slips them into his pocket.

"Do you want to watch while I cut his head off?" he asks, glancing at Saga.

"Don't do it, please. There's no need, is there?"

"There's never any need to do anything," Jurek says, grabbing the doctor by the neck.

"Wait."

"Okay. I'll wait. For two minutes, for your sake, little police officer."

"What do you mean?"

"The one mistake you made was when you only broke one of Bernie's fingers," Jurek says, taking the doctor's pass card.

"I was going to kill him slowly," she tries, even though she knows there's no point.

Jurek slaps the doctor again.

"All I need is the two codes," he says.

"Codes," the doctor mumbles. "I can't remember, I—"

Saga tries to loosen the other straps, but the fingers of her left hand are so severely injured that it's impossible.

"How could you tell that I'm a cop?" Saga asks.

"Thanks to him, I got to send a letter."

"No," the doctor whimpers.

"I assumed the police were going to bring someone in here when Mikael Kohler-Frost escaped and was found alive."

Jurek finds the doctor's phone, drops it on the floor, and crushes it beneath his foot.

"But why—"

"I don't have time," he interrupts. "I'm going to destroy Joona Linna."

Saga watches as Jurek Walter leads the doctor out of the cell. She hears their footsteps in the corridor, then the sound of the pass card being pulled through the reader and the tones of the keypad as the code is tapped in, followed by the whirr of the lock.

156

Joona rings his own doorbell and smiles to himself as he hears footsteps approaching. The lock rattles, and the door swings open. He walks into the dimly lit hall and takes off his shoes.

"You look completely wiped out," Disa says.

"I'm okay."

"Do you want something to eat? There are some leftovers I can warm up."

Joona shakes his head and hugs her close. He's too tired to talk now, but later he'll ask her to cancel her trip to Brazil. There's no need for her to go now.

A small flurry of sand is released as she helps him get his clothes off.

"Have you been playing in a sandbox?" she says, laughing.

"Just a little," he replies.

He goes into the bathroom and gets into the shower. His body aches. With the hot water coursing over him, he leans against the tiles and feels his muscles slowly start to relax.

The hand that pulled the trigger and shot an unarmed man is tingling.

As long as I can live with what I did, I can be happy again, he thinks.

Even though Joona knew the Sandman was dead, even

though he saw the bullets go straight through his body, even though he saw him tumble into the quarry like a corpse into a mass grave, he still went down after it. He slid down the slope, digging in his heels to stop himself from going too fast, and made his way to the body. Keeping his pistol aimed at the back of the man's head, he felt his neck with the other hand. The Sandman was dead. His eyes hadn't deceived him. The three bullets had all passed straight through his heart.

The thought that he no longer has to fear Jurek's accomplice is so warm and comforting that he can't help letting out a groan.

Joona dries himself and brushes his teeth, then suddenly stops and listens. It sounds as if Disa's talking on the phone.

When he walks into the bedroom, he sees Disa getting dressed.

"What are you doing?" he asks, lying down on the fresh sheets.

"My boss called," she says with a weary smile. "Some company is excavating at the old oil harbor at Loudden. They're working day and night to decontaminate the ground. And it sounds like they've found an artifact, some kind of ancient board-game set. I have to get out there and stop the digging, because if it really is—"

"Don't go," Joona begs, feeling his eyes prick with exhaustion.

Disa hums to herself as she takes a folded sweater from the top dresser drawer.

"You've taken over my dresser now?" he jokes, closing his eyes.

Disa walks back and forth in the room. He hears her brushing her hair and lifting her coat off the hanger.

He rolls onto his side and feels memories and dreams begin to join up like snowflakes.

The Sandman's body tumbles down the steep slope and stops when it hits an old stove.

Samuel Mendel scratches his head and says: "There's nothing at all to suggest that Jurek Walter has an accomplice. But you have to stick a finger in the air and say: Perhaps the opposite is the case."

157

SAGA MAKES ANOTHER ATTEMPT to loosen the strap around her right wrist, but she fails and slumps back again.

Jurek Walter is escaping, she thinks.

Panic is rising in her chest.

She has to warn Joona.

Even if she screams, the door to the dayroom is too thick for the microphone to register the sound.

Saga twists her body to the right but has to give up.

In the distance, she can hear a noise.

She holds her breath and listens.

There's a squeaking sound, then several heavy thuds, before everything is silent once more.

It dawns on Saga that Jurek never needed the pills. All he wanted was for her to lure the doctor into her room. Jurek had seen through the doctor's intentions and had realized that he wouldn't be able to resist the temptation to sneak into her room if she asked for sleeping pills.

That had been the plan all along.

That was why he had allowed himself to be punished for her actions, because the fact that she was dangerous had to be concealed.

She was a siren, just as he had said on the first day.

She whimpers with pain as she stretches to the side and

picks at the catch of the strap across her shoulders. Now she can move her shoulder and raise her head.

We all walked into his trap, she thinks. We thought we were deceiving him, but he effectively put in an order for me. He knew someone would be sent, and today he found out for certain that I was his Trojan horse.

She gathers her strength and cranes her head to the side, trying to grab the strap around her right wrist with her mouth.

She slumps back, panting. She has to alert the staff and call the police.

Saga takes a deep breath and tries again. Straining hard to hold her position, she manages to sink her teeth into the thick strap, loosen the catch, and release another half-inch or so of the strap. She falls back, feeling nauseated, then twists and pulls her hand until she frees it.

It doesn't take long for her to remove the remaining straps. Her inner thighs are aching, and her muscles shiver as she pulls on her pants.

She leaves her cell and runs out into the corridor barefoot. One of the doctor's shoes is wedged in the security door to prevent it from closing.

She opens the door cautiously and listens. The secure unit is ghostly quiet. She can hear the sound of her feet sticking to the vinyl flooring as she creeps into the room to her right and over to the operator's desk. The screens are dark, and the lights on the alarm unit are all out. The electricity supply to the surveillance room has been cut.

Somewhere there has to be a phone or a functioning alarm. Saga hurries past a number of closed doors until she reaches the staff kitchen. The cutlery drawers are open, and there's a toppled chair on the floor.

In the sink there's a vegetable knife and some browning

apple peel. Saga snatches up the little knife, checks that the blade is sharp, and moves on.

She hears a strange, faint buzzing sound.

Her right hand is squeezing the knife too hard.

There should be security staff here, but she doesn't dare call out. She's scared that Jurek will hear her.

The buzzing is getting closer as she makes her way down the corridor. It sounds like a fly caught on a piece of flypaper. She creeps past the inspection room, feeling increasingly apprehensive.

The door to the staff room is ajar. There's a light on. She reaches out her hand and opens the door wider.

She sees the end of a cot. Someone's lying on it. Two feet in white socks.

"Hello?" she says tentatively.

Saga tells herself that somebody is lying there listening to music and has missed everything that's been going on.

She steps forward. The bed is completely drenched in blood.

The girl with pierced cheeks is lying on her back, her body quivering. Her eyes stare up at the ceiling.

Her face is twitching. From her pursed lips a mixture of blood and air is bubbling out with a hissing sound.

"Oh God."

The girl has a dozen knife wounds to her chest, deep cuts into her lungs and heart. There's nothing Saga can do. She needs to call for help as soon as she can.

Blood is dripping onto the floor, next to the remnants of the girl's smashed phone.

"I'll get help," Saga says.

The girl's lips hiss as a bubble of blood inflates.

158

SAGA RUNS out of the room with a horrible vacant feeling inside.

"Please, God, please, God . . ."

She is numb with shock as she approaches another set of security doors. The guard is sitting on the other side of the far door. The thick glass makes him look muted and indistinct.

Hiding the little vegetable knife in her hand so as not to frighten him, Saga knocks on the glass.

"Help! We need help in here!"

She knocks louder, but he doesn't react. She moves to the side, toward the door, and sees that it's open.

All the doors are open, she thinks as she walks through.

Saga is about to say something when she sees that the guard is dead. His throat has been cut so brutally that it's sliced right through to the vertebrae. His head looks as if it's hanging limply from a broom handle. The blood is running down his body and gathering in a pool around his chair.

She skids across the wet floor with the knife in her hand, then runs up the stairs and through the open gate.

She tugs at the door leading to secure forensic psychiatric Ward 30. It's locked. It's the middle of the night. She bangs on it a few times, then continues along the corridor toward the main entrance.

"Hello," she calls out. "Is anyone here?"

The doctor's other shoe is on the floor in the harsh glare of the fluorescent ceiling light.

Saga sees movement up ahead, through several panes of glass. It's a man, standing and smoking. He flicks the cigarette away and disappears off to the left. Saga runs as fast as she can, toward the glassed-in exit and the passageway leading to the main hospital building. She turns the corner and notices that the floor beneath her feet is wet.

At first it looks as if the floor is black. Then the smell of blood becomes so tangible that it's all she can do not to throw up.

There's a large puddle. Footsteps lead away from it toward the exit.

She sees the young doctor's head. It's lying on its side on the floor, next to the trash can against the wall to her right.

Jurek aimed and missed, she thinks absently. She breathes rapidly and feels light-headed.

She keeps moving while her thoughts drift, unable to make sense of things.

It's impossible to accept that this is happening.

Why has he taken the time to do all this?

Because he didn't just want to get out, she tells herself. He wanted revenge.

She hears heavy steps from the passage leading to the main building. Two guards run toward her with bulletproof vests, guns, and black uniforms.

"We need doctors in the secure unit," Saga calls.

"Get down on the floor," the younger one says.

"It's only a little girl," the other one says.

"I'm a police officer," she says, throwing away the knife.

It bounces across the vinyl floor and stops in front of them. They look at it, open their holsters, and draw their service pistols.

"Down on the floor!"

"I'm getting down on the floor," she says. "But you have to warn—"

"Fuck," the younger one exclaims when he sees the head. "Fuck, fuck . . ."

"I'll shoot," the other one says in a shaky voice.

Saga gets down on her knees, and the guard hurries over, pulling the handcuffs from his belt. The other guard moves aside. Saga holds out her hands and stands up.

"Nice and fucking slow, now," the guard says in a jagged voice.

She shuts her eyes, hears boots on the floor, feels his movements, and takes a small step backward. The guard leans forward to cuff her hands, and Saga opens her eyes at the same time that she throws a right hook. There's a crunch as she hits him hard above his ear. She swings around and meets the jolt of his head with her left elbow.

The only sound is a brief thump.

Saliva sprays from his open mouth.

His legs give way, and Saga snatches his pistol from him. She releases the safety catch and fires at him before he hits the floor.

Saga shoots the other guard twice, right in his bulletproof vest. The shots echo in the narrow passageway, and the guard staggers back. Saga rushes over and knocks the pistol out of his hand with the butt of hers. The gun clatters across the floor toward the bloody footprints.

Saga kicks both his legs out from under him, and he falls flat on his back with a groan. The other guard rolls over onto his side, clutching his face with one hand. Saga grabs one of their radios and takes a few steps away.

159

Joona is awakened by the sound of the phone ringing. He hadn't even realized he was dozing off. He'd plunged straight into a deep sleep while Disa was changing into her work clothes. The bedroom is dark, but the glow of his phone is casting a pale elliptical shape on the wall.

"Joona Linna," he answers with a sleepy sigh.

"Jurek's escaped. He's managed to get out of—"

"Saga?" Joona asks, leaping out of bed.

"He's killed a lot of people," she says, a note of hysteria in her voice.

"Are you hurt?"

Joona walks through the apartment, adrenaline coursing through him as Saga's words sink in.

"I don't know where he is. He just said he was going to hurt you. He said—"

"Disa?" Joona calls.

Her boots are gone. He opens the front door and calls her name down the stairwell, his voice echoing in the darkness. He tries to remember what she said before he fell asleep.

"Disa went to Loudden," he says

"I'm so sorry for—"

Joona hangs up, pulls on his clothes, grabs his pistol and holster, and leaves the apartment.

He runs down the stairs and out onto the pavement, then off toward Dala Street, where Carlos parked his car. It's snowing heavily. As he runs, he pulls up Disa's name in his contacts and calls her. No answer.

Joona rushes over to the car, gets in, and drives straight through a bank of snow, scraping the side against a parked car.

As he accelerates past Tegnérlunden and down toward Svea Boulevard, the loose snow flies off the car in soft clouds.

Joona is aware that everything he's afraid of could flare up like a firestorm tonight.

Disa is alone in her car, on her way out to Frihamnen.

Joona's heart is pounding against his holster.

He's driving fast, remembering that Disa's boss called and asked her to take a look at something that had been found. Samuel's wife, Rebecka, had gotten a call from a carpenter, asking her to go out to their summerhouse earlier than arranged.

The Sandman must have mentioned Disa in the letter that Susanne Hjälm gave Jurek. His hands are shaking as he calls Disa again. He listens to the phone ringing and feels sweat trickling down his back.

She doesn't answer.

It's probably nothing, he tries to convince himself. He just has to reach Disa and tell her to turn around and drive home. He'll hide her away somewhere until Jurek has been recaptured.

The car slides on the brown slush on the tarmac, and a semi swerves violently out of his way. He calls again. Still no answer.

He speeds past Humlegården. The road is lined with grubby banks of snow, and the streetlights reflect off the wet tarmac.

He calls Disa again.

The traffic lights have turned red, but Joona turns right onto Valhalla Boulevard. A cement mixer swerves out of his way, and a red car pulls up sharply with a shriek of brakes. The driver blows his horn as Disa finally answers.

160

DISA DRIVES CAREFULLY over the rusty railroad tracks and up to the huge harbor of Frihamnen, with its ferry-and-container traffic.

The yellow glow of a hanging streetlight sways across a hangarlike building.

People are walking with their heads bowed to prevent the snow from getting in their eyes. Far off, through the snow, she can just make out the large Tallinn ferry, lit up but as hazy as a dream.

Disa turns right, away from the illuminated premises of one of the big fruit importers, and drives past a succession of low industrial units as she peers into the gloom.

Trucks start to drive on board the ferry to Saint Petersburg. A group of dockworkers are smoking in an empty parking lot. Darkness and snow make the world around the little gathering seem muffled and isolated.

Disa drives past Warehouse 5 and in through the gates of the container terminal. Each shipping container is the size of a small cottage and can weigh more than thirty tons. They stand there stacked on top of one another, fifteen meters high.

The stacks of containers form a network of passageways

wide enough for the huge semis. Disa heads down one of the alleys; it feels oddly narrow because its sides are so high. She can see from the tracks in the snow that another car has driven this way quite recently. Some fifty meters ahead, the passageway opens up onto the dockside. The vast bulk of Loudden's oil tank is just visible through the snow, beyond the cranes that are loading containers onto a ship. The men with the ancient board-game set are probably waiting for her up ahead.

In the distance, a large piece of machinery resembling a scorpion moves sideways but stops in the middle of its arc. A red container is swinging from its claw, just above the ground.

She drives closer.

The container door is ajar.

And there's no one in the driver's seat. The wheels are quickly being obscured by snow.

She startles when her phone rings and smiles to herself as she answers: "You're supposed to be asleep," she says brightly.

"Tell me where you are right now," Joona says, his voice intense.

"I'm in the car, on my way to—"

"I want you to skip the meeting and go straight home."

"What happened?"

"Jurek Walter has escaped."

"What did you say?"

"I want you to go home right away."

The headlights form an aquarium of swirling snow in front of the car.

"You have to listen to me," Joona says. "Turn the car around and drive home."

"Okay, then."

He waits and listens to her over the phone.

"Have you turned around?"

"I can't right now. There seems to be some kind of problem here. There's an open Hamburg Süd container blocking me in front, and I don't have enough room to turn around," she says as she catches sight of something odd in the rearview mirror.

"Disa, I know I might sound a little—"

"Hang on," she interrupts.

"What are you doing?"

In her rearview mirror, she looks at the large bundle lying on the ground in the middle of the passageway. It wasn't there a minute ago, she thinks. It looks like a gray blanket tied with duct tape.

"What's going on, Disa?" Joona asks, sounding agitated. "Have you turned around yet?"

"The container is still in the way," she says as she stops. "I can't get past."

"You need to reverse."

"Just give me a second. There's a bundle or something on the ground behind me," she says, and puts the phone down on the seat.

"Disa!" he shouts. "Do not get out of the car! Reverse over the bundle and get away from there! Disa!"

She can't hear him. She's already out of the car and walking toward the bundle. It's quiet, and the light from the tall cranes doesn't reach into the deep gully between the stacks of containers.

The wind forces its way between the containers and makes high whistling noises.

In the distance, she can see the warning lights of a huge forklift.

She'll drag the bundle to the side so she can reverse past and head home.

The forklift disappears around a corner, leaving just the car's ice-cold taillights to guide her.

Disa blinks and tries to focus her gaze. It looks as if there's something moving under the gray blanket. Everything in this moment is astonishingly silent.

She hesitates, then walks forward.

161

Joona is driving too fast when he turns left at the rotary, and the front bumper thuds into the snowbank. The tires rumble over the packed ice. He wrestles with the steering wheel as the car slides sideways. He straightens it out and drives on along Lindarängs Road without losing much speed.

The vast expanse of Gärdet stretches like a white sea up toward Norra Djurgården.

He overtakes a bus, hits 160 kilometers an hour, and flies past yellow-brick housing complexes. The car skids through the snow as he brakes to turn left toward the harbor. Through the tall wire fence surrounding the port he can see a long, narrow ferry being loaded with containers in the blurred light of a crane.

A rust-brown freight train is on its way into Frihamnen.

Joona peers into the murky shadows surrounding the deserted warehouses. He bounces across a median as slush flies around the car and the tires spin.

He comes to a railroad crossing. The barriers are already starting to close, but Joona accelerates across the tracks and just makes it through; the final barrier scrapes the roof of the car.

He drives as fast as he can through Frihamnen. There are

people leaving the Tallinn ferry terminal, a scant line of black figures vanishing into the night.

She can't be far. She stopped the car and got out. Someone forced her to come out here. Got her to leave the car.

He sounds his horn, and people leap out of his way. One woman drops her suitcase, and Joona drives straight over it.

A semi is moving slowly down the ramp and onto the ferry to Saint Petersburg.

Joona drives past an empty parking lot between Warehouses 5 and 6 and in through the gates of the container terminal.

The dockyard, with narrow alleys and tall, windowless buildings, is like its own city. He sees something from the corner of his eye and brakes immediately.

Disa's car sits in the passageway ahead of him. A thin layer of snow has settled on top of it. The driver's door is open. Joona runs over to it and looks inside. There's no sign of violence or struggle. The engine is still warm.

He breathes ice-cold air into his lungs.

Disa got out of the car and walked toward something behind it. He sees her footprints now. Snow is filling them softly.

"No," he whispers.

There's a patch of compacted snow ten meters behind her car and a broad track that leads a meter or so between the containers before it stops. It looks like something's been dragged off to the side.

Drops of blood are just visible under the powdery snow.

Beyond that, the snow is smooth and untouched.

Joona stops himself from calling Disa's name.

He takes a few steps back and sees five containers hanging in the air above. The one at the bottom has white writing on a red background: "Hamburg Süd."

Just like the one that was blocking Disa's way.

An open Hamburg Süd container.

That must be where Jurek has taken her.

Joona starts to run toward the crane holding the container.

He emerges onto Dock 5. His heart is hammering in his chest.

A dockworker in a helmet is speaking into a walkie-talkie. A vast crane on rails is loading a container ship.

Joona catches sight of the red container and sprints toward it.

Hundreds of containers, all different colors, bearing different shipping companies' names, have already been loaded.

Two dockworkers are walking briskly along the shore in bright-yellow vests. One of them is pointing up at the lofty bridge of the ship.

162

Joona hops over a concrete barrier to the edge of the quay. Sludgy ice is floating in the black water. The smell of the sea mixes with the diesel fumes from four caterpillar trucks.

Joona clambers up the gangway onto the ship. He hurries along the railing, shoving a box of shackles out of the way and finding a shovel.

"You there!" a man behind him calls.

Joona rushes forward and sees that there's a sledgehammer next to the railing, among wrenches, lifting hooks, and a rusty chain. He drops the shovel, grabs the sledgehammer instead, and runs over to the red container. He hits it with his hand, and the metal echoes back dully.

"Disa," he shouts, as he hurries around it.

A heavy lock is fastened to the double doors. He holds the hammer in both hands and swings it across the lock with incredible force. There's a crash as the lock shatters. He drops the hammer and flings open the doors.

Disa isn't there.

All he can see in the gloom are two BMW sports cars.

Joona doesn't know what to do. He looks back toward the dock at the vast stacks of containers.

Far in the distance, he spots Loudden's oil tank through the heavy snowfall.

He picks up the hammer and starts to run back.

At the end of the harbor, a truck covered in a filthy tarp is driving on board a car ferry to Saint Petersburg.

On the ramp, behind the first truck, is a second one, pulling a red container behind it.

On the side of the container are, again, the words "Hamburg Süd."

Joona tries to work out the quickest way to get there.

"You're not allowed up here," a man shouts behind him.

Joona turns and sees a thickset dockworker in a helmet, bright-yellow vest, and heavy gloves.

"National Crime," Joona explains. "I'm looking for—"

"I don't care who you are," the man interrupts. "You can't just climb on board a—"

"Call your boss and tell him that."

"You're going to wait right here and explain everything to the security guards, who are—"

"I don't have time for this," Joona says, turning away.

The dockworker grabs his shoulder. Through reflex, Joona jerks around, wraps his arm over the man's, and twists his elbow up.

It all happens very fast.

The pain in his shoulder makes the dockworker lean back, and Joona kicks his feet out from under him.

Instead of breaking the dockworker's arm, Joona releases him and lets him collapse onto the deck.

The large crane rumbles, and everything suddenly goes dark when the glare of the floodlights is obscured by the cargo dangling from the crane, directly above him.

Joona quickly walks away, but a younger dockworker in high-visibility clothing is standing in his way, holding a large wrench in his hand.

"Be very careful," Joona warns.

"You need to wait until the security guards get here," the dockworker tells him. He looks nervous.

Joona shoves him in the chest with one hand to force his way past. The dockworker takes a step back, then strikes out with the wrench. Joona blocks the blow with his arm, but it hits him on the shoulder. He groans with pain and lets go of the hammer. It falls to the deck with a clang. Joona yanks off the man's helmet and hits him hard over the ear, making him sink to his knees and howl in pain.

163

JOONA PICKS UP the hammer and hops off the ship. He runs along the edge of the seawall. He can hear shouting behind him. Large blocks of ice are rolling in the sludgy water. The water sprays up when it hits the dock.

Joona sprints up the ramp onto the ferry. Behind a gray container, toward the stern, he sees a red one.

Joona is getting tired. His arms are trembling from the exertion. The ferry is full now, and the bow is being lowered into place. The deck rumbles as the ferry pulls away from the shore. Ice knocks against its hull. He's heading toward the stern to a red container with the words "Hamburg Süd" on the side.

"Disa," he calls.

He runs around the cab and stops when he sees the blue lock on the container. He wipes the sweat from his face and continues toward it but fails to notice the person approaching from behind.

Joona raises the hammer and is about to strike when pain explodes across his back. His lungs roar, and he almost blacks out. He falls forward, hitting his forehead against the container and landing in a heap on the deck. He rolls to the side and gets to his feet. Blood is running into one eye, and he stumbles and reaches out to a nearby car for support.

In front of him is a tall woman with a baseball bat over her shoulder. Her padded jacket is pulled tight across her chest. She blows a lock of blond hair from her face and takes aim again.

"Leave my cargo the fuck alone!" she yells.

She swings again, but Joona moves quickly, grabbing her throat with one hand and kicking the back of her knee so that her leg buckles. He throws her to the deck and points his pistol at her.

"National Crime," he says.

She whimpers and looks at him as he picks up the hammer again and shatters the lock. A piece of metal casing lands with a clatter in front of her face.

This container is packed with large boxes of televisions. He pulls out a few, but Disa isn't there. He wipes the blood from his face and hurries up some steps to the open deck.

The ferry is now twenty meters from the shore. In front of the ship he can see the channel through the ice to the open sea.

A feeling of anguish washes over him when he looks back at the dockyard and catches sight of a train with similar red containers on three of the cars.

He takes out his phone and calls Emergency Control. He asks for all traffic from Frihamnen in Stockholm to be stopped. The duty officer knows who Joona is and puts his call through to the regional police commissioner.

"All rail traffic from Frihamnen has to be stopped," he repeats breathlessly.

"That's impossible," she replies.

"We have to stop all traffic," Joona insists.

"That can't be done," the commissioner says. "The best we can do is—"

"I'll do it myself," Joona says abruptly, and jumps off the ferry.

Hitting the freezing water feels like being struck by icy lightning, like getting an adrenaline injection straight into the heart. His ears are roaring. He sinks through the black water and loses consciousness for a few seconds, dreaming of a bridal crown of woven birch root. Though he can't feel his hands and feet, he wills himself to kick out with his legs and finally manages to stop himself from sinking deeper.

164

JOONA BREAKS THE SURFACE, emerging through the icy slush.

The subzero temperature is making his head pound, but he's conscious.

His time as a paratrooper saved him—he managed to resist the impulse to gasp and breathe in when he sank through the water.

With numb arms and heavy clothes, he swims through the black water. It's not far to the dock but his body temperature is dropping alarmingly quickly. Lumps of ice are tumbling over all around him.

He coughs, feeling his strength drain away. His vision is fading, but he forces himself to take more strokes and finally reaches the pilings along the shore. He grabs on to the narrow gaps between the metal plates of the seawall. On the verge of fainting, he clambers sideways until he reaches a ladder.

The water splashes beneath him as he starts to climb. His hands freeze to the metal, and he has to keep tearing them off.

He rolls onto the dock with a groan, gets to his feet, and walks toward the train.

He looks down to check that he hasn't lost his pistol.

He emerges into the glare of the headlights of a truck. He sees that it also carries a red Hamburg Süd container.

The driver is behind the vehicle, checking that the brake lights are working, when he notices Joona approaching.

"Have you been in the water?" he asks, taking a step back. "Christ, you'll freeze to death if you don't get indoors."

"Open the red container," Joona slurs. "I'm a police officer. I need to—"

"That's down to Customs. I can't just open it."

"National Crime Unit," Joona says, his voice weak.

He's having trouble keeping his eyes focused and is aware how incoherent he sounds when he tries to explain what powers he has.

"I don't even have the keys," the driver says, regarding him kindly. "Just a pair of bolt cutters, and—"

"Hurry up," Joona says.

The driver runs around the truck, climbs up, and leans into the cabin. An umbrella tumbles onto the ground as he pulls out a set of long-handled bolt cutters.

Joona bangs on the container, shouting Disa's name.

The driver runs back, and his cheeks turn red as he presses the handles together.

The lock breaks with a crunch.

The door of the container swings open on creaking hinges. It's packed full of boxes on wooden pallets, strapped into place, right up to the roof.

Without saying a word to the driver, Joona takes the bolt cutters and walks away. His hands hurt terribly.

"You need to go to the hospital," the man calls after him.

165

THE TRAIN by the warehouse has just started to move, its wheels squealing as it rolls forward. Joona tries to run, but his chest is burning. He scrambles up the snow-covered railroad embankment, slips, and hits his knee on the gravel. He drops the bolt cutters but gets to his feet and stumbles onto the railroad track. He can no longer feel his hands or feet. The shaking is now uncontrollable, and he is experiencing a frightening sense of confusion because he's so cold.

His thoughts are strange, slow and disintegrating. All he knows is that he has to stop the train.

Joona stands in the middle of the track, raises his eyes toward the light, and holds up his hand. The train blows its whistle, and he can just make out the engineer's silhouette inside. The track is vibrating under his feet. Joona draws his pistol, raises it, and shoots into the air.

The shot echoes harshly between the containers.

There's a thunderous squeal as the train brakes and stops with a hiss just three meters away from him.

Joona almost falls as he steps off the track. He picks up the bolt cutters and turns to the train engineer.

"Open the red containers," Joona says.

"I don't have the authority to—"

"Just do it," Joona shouts, throwing the bolt cutters on the ground.

The engineer climbs down and picks up the bolt cutters. Joona follows him along the train and points at the first red container. Without a word, the engineer jumps up onto the rust-brown coupling and clips the lock.

Joona staggers forward and shoves the catch up, and the big metal door swings open.

Disa is lying on the rusty floor of the container. Her face is pale, and her eyes are open wide with a look of bewilderment. One of her boots is missing, and her hair is frozen stiff.

THERE'S A DEEP CUT on the right side of her long, slender neck. The pool of blood beneath her throat is already covered with a film of ice.

Gently, Joona carries her off the container and takes a few steps away from the tracks.

"I know you're alive," he says, falling to his knees with her in his arms.

Blood is trickling over his hand, but her heart has stopped. It's over. There's no way back.

"Not this," Joona whispers against her cheek. "Not you."

He rocks her slowly as the snow falls. He doesn't notice the car stopping near them and is unaware of Saga running toward him. She's barefoot, wearing just pants and a T-shirt.

"There are people on the way," she cries as she gets closer. "God, what happened? You need help."

Saga shouts into her radio and swears. As if in a dream, Joona hears her force the train engineer to take off his jacket and feels her wrapping it around his shoulders. She puts her arms around him as the sound of sirens fills the harbor area.

A large circle of snow flies up as a yellow EMS helicopter lands, settling onto its runners. The sound is deafening, and the train engineer backs away from the man sitting there with the dead woman in his arms.

The rotors are still turning as the paramedics leap out and run over. The draft from the helicopter is blowing trash against the high fence. It feels as if all the air is being sucked away from them.

Joona's vision is starting to blur when the paramedics force him to let go of Disa's body. He mutters incoherently and resists when they try to coax him to lie down.

Saga is crying as she watches the paramedics carry him into the helicopter on a stretcher. She has no idea if he'll survive.

The noise of the rotors changes as the helicopter rises off the ground, swaying in a side wind that has picked up. The angle of the rotors shifts. The helicopter leans forward and disappears across the city.

As they cut off his clothes, Joona starts to sink into a death-like torpor. He has reached a state of severe hypothermia. His body temperature has fallen below thirty-two degrees centigrade as they land on the helicopter pad on Building P8 at Karolinska Hospital.

166

THE POLICE arrive quickly on the scene at Frihamnen and put out an alert for a silver-gray Citroën Evasion that was captured by several surveillance cameras as it drove up to the harbor fifteen minutes before Disa's car arrived. The same cameras recorded the car leaving the area seven minutes after Joona Linna got there.

Every police car in Stockholm is involved in the search, as well as two Eurocopter 135s. It's a massive deployment, and just fifteen minutes after the alarm is sounded, the vehicle is observed on Central Bridge before it disappears into Söderleden Tunnel.

Police cars are on their way, with sirens and flashing lights, and roadblocks are being set up at the exits when a huge explosion blasts out of the entrance to the tunnel.

The helicopter hovering above lurches, and the pilot only just manages to escape the force of the shock wave. Dust and debris are scattered across the highway and the adjacent railroad tracks, all the way down to Riddarfjärden.

IT'S HALF PAST FOUR in the morning, and Saga Bauer is sitting on an exam table as a doctor sews up her wounds.

"I have to go," she says, staring at the news on the dusty flat-screen television.

The doctor is bandaging her left wrist when the item about the big traffic accident comes on. A reporter explains that a police chase in the center of Stockholm has ended. A single car crashed with fatal consequences inside the Söderleden Tunnel.

"The accident happened at half past two this morning," the reporter says, "which may explain why no other vehicles were involved. The police have given assurances that the road will be reopened in time for the morning rush hour but have otherwise declined to comment on the incident."

The screen shows a cloud of black smoke billowing out of the tunnel entrance. The cloud envelops the Hilton Hotel in rolling veils, then slowly disperses over Södermalm.

Saga refused to go to the hospital until she received confirmation that Jurek Walter was dead. Two of Joona's colleagues from National Crime told her. To save time, their forensics experts had accompanied the fire crews into the tunnel. The violent explosion had torn Jurek Walter's arms and head from his body.

On the screen, a politician is sitting in the studio with a female presenter. Their faces heavy with sleep, they discuss the dangers of police pursuits.

"I have to go," Saga repeats, slipping down onto the floor.

"The wounds on your legs need—"

"Don't bother," she says, and leaves the room.

167

JOONA WAKES UP in the hospital. His arms are itching where a drip of warm liquid is slowly being fed into him. A male nurse stands by his bed and smiles at him when he opens his eyes.

"How are you feeling?" the nurse asks, leaning forward. Joona tries to read the ID badge but can't get the letters to stay still long enough.

"I'm freezing," he says.

"In two hours, your body temperature should be back to normal. I'll give you some warm soup."

Joona tries to sit up to drink but feels a sharp pain in his bladder. He lifts the insulating blanket and sees that two thick needles are sticking out of his abdomen.

"What's this?" he asks.

"A peritoneal lavage," the nurse says. "We're warming your body up from the inside. You have two liters of warm liquid in your abdomen right now."

Joona closes his eyes and tries to remember. Red containers, icy slush. The shock as he jumped from the ship straight into the incredibly cold water.

"Disa," Joona whispers, and feels goose bumps rising on his arms.

He leans back on the pillows and looks up at the heater above him. He can't feel anything but cold.

After a while, the door opens and a tall woman wearing a silk sweater under her doctor's coat comes in. It's Dr. Daniella Richards. He's met her many times before.

"Joona Linna," she says. "I'm so sorry—"

"Daniella," Joona interrupts. "What's going on?"

"You were at the point of freezing to death, in case you hadn't noticed. We thought you were dead when you were brought in."

She sits down on the edge of the bed.

"You have no idea how incredibly lucky you were," she says slowly. "No serious damage, from the looks of it. We're warming up your internal organs."

"Where's Disa? I have to—"

His voice cracks. There's something about his thoughts, his brain. He can't put the words together properly. All his memories are like crushed ice in black water.

The doctor lowers her gaze and shakes her head. Her hair is pulled up neatly, and she wears a delicate diamond necklace.

"I'm so sorry," Daniella repeats slowly.

As she tells him about Disa, her face starts to quiver. Joona looks at the veins in her hand and watches her rib cage rise and fall. He tries to understand what she's saying, and suddenly it comes back to him. Disa's white face, the cut on her neck, the frightened twist of her mouth. Her slender foot in her nylon stocking.

"Leave me alone," he says in a hoarse voice.

168

JOONA LINNA is lying still, feeling the glucose running through his veins and the warm air from the heater above his bed, but he's not feeling any warmer. Waves of cold are rolling through his body, and every so often his vision goes black.

An impulse to grab his gun, put the barrel in his mouth, and shoot himself flickers through his thoughts.

Jurek Walter has escaped.

Joona knows he'll never be able to see his daughter or wife again. They've been taken from him for good, in the same way that Disa was torn from his hands. Jurek's twin brother worked out that Summa and Lumi were still alive. Joona knows it's only a matter of time before Jurek realizes as well.

Joona tries to sit up but doesn't have the energy.

It's impossible.

He can't escape the feeling that he's sinking deeper and deeper into the mosaic of icy water.

The door opens, and Saga Bauer walks in. She's wearing a black jacket and dark jeans.

"Jurek Walter is dead," she says. "It's over. We found his body in Söderleden Tunnel."

She stands at the foot of the bed and looks at Joona. His eyes are closed again. She feels as if her heart's about to stop. He looks terribly ill. His face is almost white, his lips pale gray.

"I'm heading over to see Reidar Frost now," Saga tells him. "He needs to know that Felicia's alive. The doctors say that Felicia's going to make it. You saved her life."

He listens to what she says and turns his face aside, keeping his eyes closed to hold back the tears. Suddenly he understands the pattern.

Jurek is closing a circle of revenge and blood.

Joona repeats the thought to himself, moistens his mouth, takes several deep breaths, then says, "Jurek's on his way to Reidar."

"Jurek's dead," Saga says. "It's finally over—"

"Jurek's going to take Mikael again. He doesn't know that Felicia is free. We can't let him find out that she—"

Saga looks perplexed. "I'm about to see Reidar, to tell him you saved his daughter."

"Jurek only let Mikael out on loan. He's going to take him again."

"What are you talking about?"

Joona looks at her, and the expression in his gray eyes is so cold it makes her shiver.

"The real victims aren't the ones who were locked up or killed," he says. "The victims are the ones who were left behind, the ones who were waiting until they couldn't bear to wait anymore."

She places her hand on his. "I have to go now. Reidar needs to know about Felicia. The hospital hasn't been able to reach him."

"Make sure you're armed," he says.

"I'm just going to tell Reidar and—"

"Do as I say," he commands.

169

IT'S NOT YET DAWN when Saga reaches the manor. There's only one light visible, in a window on the ground floor.

Saga walks up the driveway, shivering. The snow is untouched, and the darkness stretches across the fields. There aren't any stars visible in the night sky. The only sounds are from a river nearby.

As she approaches the house, she sees a man sitting at the kitchen table with his back to the window. There's a book on the table next to him. He's drinking slowly from a cup.

Saga continues up the stone steps to the big front door and rings the bell. The man who had been sitting in the kitchen opens the door.

It's Reidar Frost. He's wearing striped pajama pants and a white T-shirt. White stubble covers his chin.

"Hello. My name's Saga Bauer. I work for the Security Police."

"Come in," he says.

She takes a couple of steps into the dimly lit hall with its broad staircase. Reidar backs away with a fearful expression.

"No, not Felicia, not—"

"We've found her," Saga reassures him. "She's alive, and she's going to be all right."

"I . . . I have to . . ."

"She's seriously ill," Saga explains. "Your daughter has advanced Legionnaires' disease. But she's going to be okay."

"She's going to be okay," Reidar repeats. "I have to go. I have to see her."

"She's being moved from intensive care to the infectious-diseases unit at seven o'clock."

He looks at her with tears trickling down his cheeks.

"Then I have time to get dressed and wake Mikael."

Saga follows him to the kitchen. The ceiling light casts a pleasant glow over the table.

The radio is on, playing gentle piano music.

"We've been trying to call," she says. "But your phone—"

"That's my fault," Reidar says, wiping the tears from his cheeks. "I've had to start turning off the phone at night. I don't know, so many crazy people keep calling with tip-offs, people who—"

"I understand."

"Felicia's alive," Reidar says tentatively.

"Yes," Saga says.

His face cracks, and he looks at her with bloodshot eyes. It seems as if he's going to ask her again, but he just shakes his head and takes a deep breath. He picks up a large pot of coffee from the black stove and pours a cup for Saga.

"Some warm milk?"

"No, thanks," she says, taking the cup.

"I need to wake Mikael and tell him."

He starts to head for the hall but stops and turns back toward her.

"I have to know. Did you catch him? The Sandman?" he asks. "The man Mikael calls the—"

"He and Jurek Walter are both dead," Saga says. "They were twin brothers."

"Twin brothers?"

"Yes, they were working togeth—"

The light in the ceiling goes out, and the music on the radio stops. It's pitch-black and silent.

"Power outage," Reidar mutters, testing the light switch. "I have candles in the cupboard."

"Felicia was locked up in an old bomb shelter," Saga explains.

As their eyes adjust, the glow of the snow outside seems to penetrate the darkness of the kitchen, and Saga can see Reidar feeling his way toward a large cupboard.

"Where was the shelter?" he asks.

Saga hears a rattling sound as Reidar rummages through a drawer.

"In the old quarry out in Rotebro," she replies.

Saga sees him pause thoughtfully and take a step back.

"That's where I'm from," he says slowly. "And I remember that there were twins. I used to play with them when I was little. Could it—could it have been Jurek Walter and his brother? I don't remember their names. But why, why would . . ."

"I'm not sure there are any answers," she says.

Reidar finds some matches and lights a candle.

"I lived fairly close to the quarry as a child," he says. "The twins were a year or so older than me. They were just sitting in the grass behind me one day when I was fishing in the river that runs into the small lake nearby."

Reidar takes an empty wine bottle from under the sink, pushes the lit candle into it, and sets it on the table.

"They were a bit odd. But we started to play, and I went to their house once. I remember it was spring, and I was given an apple."

The light from the candle makes the windows opaque.

"They took me to the quarry," Reidar continues. "It was off-limits, but they'd found a hole in the fence, and we'd meet to play there every evening. It was exciting. We would run up the mounds and roll down in the sand, and—"

Reidar falls silent.

"What were you about to say?"

"I haven't thought about this for a long time, but one evening I heard them whispering to each other, and then they just vanished. I rolled down myself and was about to go looking for them when the foreman showed up. He grabbed me and started shouting . . . you know, saying he'd tell my parents and all that. And I was terrified. I told him that I didn't know it was off-limits, that the boys had said we could play there. He asked who the boys were, and I pointed to their house."

Reidar lights another candle from the first. The light bounces off the walls and ceiling. A smell of wax spreads through the kitchen.

"I never saw the twins again after that," he says, then leaves the kitchen to go wake Mikael.

170

Saga stands at the kitchen table, drinking the strong coffee and gazing absently at the reflections of the two candles in the double layer of glass in the window.

Joona's so badly hurt, she thinks. He didn't even understand her when she told him Jurek was dead. He just kept saying that Jurek was on his way to get Mikael.

Saga feels the weight of her Glock 17 against her side, then moves away from the window and listens to the sounds of the large house.

Something makes her suddenly alert.

She takes a few steps toward the door, stops, and imagines she can hear a faint metallic scraping sound.

It could be anything. A loose shutter moving in the wind. A branch against a window.

She takes a sip of coffee. She looks at the time, takes out her phone, and calls The Needle.

"Nils Åhlén, Forensics Lab," he answers after a few rings.

"It's Saga Bauer," she says.

"Good morning, good morning."

A gust of cold air sweeps across the floor around Saga's legs. She goes and stands with her back against the wall.

"Have you seen the body from Söderleden Tunnel?" she asks. The candlelight flickers.

"Yes, I'm here now. They dragged me out of bed to deal with it."

She sees the candle flicker again and hears The Needle's nasal voice echo off the walls of the postmortem room.

"The body suffered severe burns. It's all cracked, pretty much charcoal. The heat shriveled it up badly. The head's missing, as well as both—"

"But have you been able to identify him?"

"I've only been here a quarter of an hour, and it's going to be several days before I can come up with any sort of reliable identification."

"Of course, but I was wondering—"

"All I can say right now," the Needle goes on, "is that this man was approximately twenty-five years old, and he's—"

"So it isn't Jurek Walter?"

"Jurek Walter? No, this . . . Did you think it was Jurek?"

Saga hears rapid footsteps upstairs. She looks up and sees the kitchen lamp quivering. Caught in the candlelight, it casts a wavering shadow over the ceiling. She pulls her pistol from her holster and says in a low voice: "I'm at Reidar Frost's house. You have to help me get an ambulance and police backup out here, as soon as possible."

171

REIDAR IS WALKING through the silent rooms upstairs. His left hand shields the candle flame. The light flickers over walls and furniture, its reflection multiplied over rows of black windows.

He imagines he can hear steps behind him, but when he turns around, all he can see is the shiny leather furniture and the big bookcase with glass doors.

The entrance to the living room is a gaping dark rectangle. It's impossible to tell if anyone's in there. Something glints in the shadows, then disappears.

Hot wax is running over his fingers.

The floor creaks beneath him. Unease spreads through his body as he stops outside Mikael's room.

Reidar looks back down the long corridor with its rows of old portraits.

He knocks lightly on Mikael's door, then opens it.

"Mikael?" he calls.

He holds up the candle toward the bed. The walls seem to sway in the yellow light. The covers are bunched up and hanging over the edge of the bed, down onto the rug.

He looks around, but Mikael has vanished. Beads of sweat break out on his forehead as he bends over to look under the bed.

He hears rustling behind him and spins around so fast that the candle almost goes out. The flame shrinks into a tremulous blue before growing again.

His heartbeat accelerates, and his chest starts to ache.

Something creaks inside the closet. Reidar slowly edges over and hesitates before opening one of the doors.

Mikael is huddled among the clothes.

"The Sandman's here," he whispers, shrinking farther into the closet.

"It's just a power outage," Reidar says. "We're going—"

"He's here," Mikael insists. "He's here."

"The Sandman's dead," Reidar says, holding out his hand. "Felicia's safe. She's going to be fine. She's getting the same treatment as you. We're going to go and see her now—"

A scream rips through the walls. It's muffled but sounds bestial, like the cry of a man in terrible pain.

Reidar's heart seizes as a chill shoots down his spine. He urges his son out of the closet. Wax drips to the floor.

"Dad . . ."

"It's going to be okay, Mikael," Reidar says, trying to keep his voice calm. "I'm right here. We'll be okay, but we need to leave the house."

"No, no, no . . . I can't. . . ."

Mikael tries to curl up on the floor, but Reidar drags him to his feet.

Sweat is running down Reidar's back. He can feel his son trembling with fear as he leads him out of the bedroom and along the corridor.

"Wait," Reidar whispers as he hears a creak in the sitting room ahead of them.

A slender figure emerges from the doorway at the far end of the corridor. It's Jurek Walter. His eyes are shining in his butcher's face, and the knife hanging in his right hand glints heavily. Reidar backs away and loses his slippers. Mikael is paralyzed. Reidar throws the candle at Jurek. The flame is extinguished in midair, and the candle clatters to the floor.

"Follow me," Reidar says, grabbing Mikael's hand.

They run down the corridor without looking back. It's dark, and Mikael stumbles over a chair, his hand flailing over the wallpaper.

A picture frame crashes to the floor, and the glass shatters, splintering across the hall.

They push open a heavy door and stumble into the old dining room.

Reidar has to stop. He's coughing and fumbling for something to lean on. Rapid steps approach along the corridor.

"Dad!"

"Close the door, close the door!" he pants.

Mikael slams the heavy door shut and turns the key in the lock three times. A moment later, the handle is pushed down and the door creaks.

Mikael backs away across the parquet floor, eyes fixed on the door.

"Don't let him take me, Dad," he says, sobbing.

Pain spreads through Reidar's chest and down his left arm.

"I need a moment," he says weakly. His legs feel unsteady.

Jurek thuds against the door with his shoulder, but it doesn't give way.

Mikael is cowering against his father's body.

"He can't get in," Reidar whispers. "I promise. I just need a few seconds."

The pressure in his chest is so strong he can hardly speak.

172

Saga sweeps the corridor with her pistol as she creeps toward the staircase in the hall.

She has to reach Mikael and Reidar and get them out to the car.

The sky has brightened slightly, and it's now possible to detect the pictures on the walls and the shapes of the furniture. The sound of her footsteps vanishes as she walks over a rug and past the black grand piano. Something flashes in the corner of her eye. She turns and sees a cello balanced on its stand.

Saga creeps along with her pistol aimed down at the floor. Gradually, she moves her finger to the trigger, squeezing it carefully, just past the first notch.

She hears a rushing sound behind her and spins around to see snow slipping off the roof past the bay window.

Her heart is thudding in her chest.

When she turns back toward the hall, she sees a hand at one of the doors. Someone's skinny fingers are reaching around the edge.

Saga aims her pistol at the door, ready to shoot through it, but suddenly there's a terrible scream. The hand slides down and disappears. There's a thump as something hits the ground.

Saga rushes in and sees a man lying on the floor, one leg

twitching spasmodically. She recognizes him as the actor Wille Strandberg. He's gasping and clutching his stomach.

Blood bubbles out between his fingers.

He stares at Saga in confusion, then blinks rapidly.

"I'm a police officer," she says as she hears the stairs creak. "The ambulance is on its way."

"He wants Mikael," the actor groans.

173

Mikael is whispering to himself and staring at the locked door when the key is suddenly pushed out and falls onto the parquet floor with a muffled clunk.

Reidar is standing with his hand pressed against his chest. He's in agony now. He's tried several times to tell Mikael to run, but the boy won't move.

"Save me," Mikael whispers.

"Mikael, can you come here and help me walk?"

There's a scraping sound from the lock as Mikael puts his father's arm over his shoulder and tries to pull him toward the library.

Behind them, the scraping sound from the lock continues.

They carry on slowly past a tall cupboard, along a wall lined with large tapestries stretched over wooden frames.

Reidar stops, coughing.

"Hold on," he says.

He slips his fingers along the edge of the third tapestry. It's a concealed door leading to a servants' staircase down to the kitchen. They creep into the narrow passageway and let the tapestry fall into place softly behind them.

Reidar leans against the wall. He coughs as quietly as he can, feeling the pain radiating down his arm.

"Keep going down the stairs," he whispers.

Mikael is about to say something when the door in the other room crashes open.

Jurek's broken in.

They stand there paralyzed and watch him through the fabric covering the hidden door.

He's creeping forward, crouched down, with the long knife in his hand, scanning the room around him like a predator. His soft breathing is audible.

Jurek is so close now that a cloying smell of sweat hits them through the tapestry.

They hold their breath as Jurek passes the tapestry door, heading toward the library.

With tears running down his face, Mikael looks at his father as Reidar points down the narrow staircase, waving at him to go before Jurek realizes he's been deceived.

Reidar stifles a cough, tries to take a step toward Mikael, then stumbles. A floorboard creaks under his right foot. Mikael looks at him in anguish.

Jurek turns and looks straight at the hidden door. His pale eyes become strangely calm when he realizes what he's looking at.

There's a loud bang in the corridor, and splinters from the edge of the tall cupboard fly through the air.

Jurek slips to the side like a shadow and takes cover.

Mikael pulls Reidar with him down the narrow staircase toward the kitchen.

Behind them, Berzelius bursts into the passageway leading to the library. He's holding Reidar's old Colt in his hand. The little man's cheeks are red as he pushes his glasses up his nose and moves forward.

"Leave Micke alone!" he shouts, walking past the tall cupboard.

Death comes so quickly that Berzelius's main reaction is

surprise. He feels a tight grip on the wrist holding the revolver, then a burning pain in his side as the knife blade penetrates his ribs and hits his heart.

There isn't much pain after that.

It's more like a protracted cramp, although a profuse quantity of warm blood runs down his hip as the blade slides out again.

Berzelius slumps onto his side, thinking that he should try to crawl and hide somewhere, but an overwhelming tiredness sweeps over him.

He doesn't even notice when Jurek sticks the knife into his body a second time. The blade goes in at a different angle, straight through his ribs, and stays there.

174

SAGA REACHES THE TOP of the staircase and hurries through the rooms on the upper floor. Tactically, she tries to check off every dangerous angle and secure each zone as she passes through, but she has to take risks so she can move quickly.

She aims the pistol at a shiny leather sofa as she passes it, then points it toward the doorway, then to the left, then in.

There's a wax candle on the floor of the long, portrait-lined corridor.

The door to one of the bedrooms is wide-open, and the sheets are on the floor. Saga hurries past, catching a glimpse of herself as a fleeting shadow in the window to her left.

There's a loud bang from a firearm in one of the rooms up ahead. Keeping close to the right-hand wall, Saga starts to run toward the noise with her pistol raised.

"Leave Micke alone!" a man cries.

Saga leaps over an upturned chair, covers the last stretch, and stops in front of a closed door.

She pushes the handle down and lets the door swing open on its hinges.

The smell of a recently fired gun is heavy in the air.

The room is dark and still.

Saga moves more cautiously now.

She's starting to feel the weight of the pistol in her shoulder. Her finger is trembling on the trigger. She tries to breathe evenly as she leans to her right to get a better view.

There's a damp thud with a metallic echo.

Something's moving—a shadow vanishing.

She sees a pool of blood gleaming on the floor next to a tall cupboard.

Stepping forward, she sees a man on the floor with a knife sticking out of him. He's lying on his side, completely still, with a fixed stare. Her first impulse is to rush over to the man, but something stops her.

The room is too hard to read.

She lowers her pistol and rests her arm for a few seconds before raising it again and moving farther to the right.

One section of the wall with tapestries is open. Through it Saga sees a short landing leading to a narrow staircase. She can hear steps and dragging sounds from below and raises her Glock toward the opening before moving closer.

The door at the other end of the room opens on a dark library.

There's a faint sound, as if someone were moistening their mouth.

She can't see anything.

The pistol is shaking in her hand.

She takes a step forward, holds her breath, then hears someone breathing behind her.

Saga reacts instantly and swings around. It's still too late. A strong hand wraps around her throat and drags her toward the cupboard in the corner with great force.

Jurek's grip on her neck is so tight that the blood supply to her brain has been cut off. He looks at her without expression, holding her still. Her vision starts to go black, and the Glock drops from her hand.

Impotent, Saga tries to twist free. Just before she loses consciousness she hears Jurek whisper, "Little siren . . ."

He slams her head against the corner of the cupboard, then smashes her temple against the stone wall. She collapses, her eyes flickering. She sees Jurek bend over the dead man and pull the knife out of his body. A moment later, everything goes black again.

175

THEY'RE NO LONGER TRYING to keep quiet. Mikael grips
Reidar as they stumble down the staircase to the narrow servants' passageway. They turn left and walk slowly along it, past
the old cupboard with the Christmas dinner set, and into the
kitchen.

Reidar has to stop. He can't go any farther. The cramps in
his chest are unbearable. He needs to lie down.

"You have to get out of here," he gasps. "Run. Run out to
the main road."

"Not on my own," Mikael says. "I can't, Daddy, please. . . ."

Reidar takes a deep breath. He has to do this. He takes a
step, then another. His eyes flare as he leans against the wall,
knocking a big painting askew.

They make their way through the music room. Reidar can
hardly feel the floor under his bare feet.

There's blood on the parquet. The front door is open, and
snow is blowing in across the Persian rug.

They pass the closet, and Reidar fumbles for the pink nitroglycerin spray in his coat. He sprays some under his tongue,
takes a few steps, and sprays again.

The dish containing the car keys is on the other side of the
room.

They hear heavy footsteps nearby. There's no time. They rush out into the winter morning.

The cold burns Reidar's naked feet. But the pain in his chest has eased up slightly, and they can move faster now. Together they run over to Saga Bauer's car.

Reidar pulls at the door, looks in, and sees that the keys are missing.

Jurek Walter steps out the front door and catches sight of them in the gloom. He shakes the blood from his knife and heads straight for them.

They run through the snow up toward the stables, but Jurek is faster. Reidar glances across the fields. The dark ice of the river is a ribbon through the snow, curling in the direction of the roaring rapids.

176

SAGA WAKES to find blood running into her eyes. She blinks and rolls onto her side. Her temple is throbbing. She has a splitting headache, her throat feels swollen, and she's having trouble breathing.

She touches the wound on her temple and groans. With her cheek to the floor, she can see that her Glock is lying in the dust under the large chest of drawers by the window.

She closes her eyes again and tries to work out what's happened. Joona was right, she thinks: Jurek wants Mikael back.

She has no idea how long she's been unconscious. It's still dark in the room.

She rolls over onto her stomach and whimpers.

"Oh God."

With a great effort, she gets up on all fours. Her arms shake as she crawls through the pool of blood from the dead man toward the chest of drawers.

She stretches for the gun but can't reach it.

Saga lies down on the floor, reaches in as far as she can, but only manages to nudge the Glock with her fingertips. It's impossible. She's so dizzy that the room is lurching violently, and she has to close her eyes again.

Light seeps in through her closed eyelids. She looks up and notices a strange white glow. It's bouncing across the ceiling.

Saga forces herself to stand up, gasping as she leans against the chest of drawers for support. A string of bloody saliva is dripping from her mouth. She looks out the window and sees a man running, holding a burning flare in his hand. The bright light spreads in a blazing circle around him.

Everything else out there is black.

The glow of the flare reaches all the way to the stable in the distance.

That's when Saga catches sight of Jurek's back.

She bangs on the window and tries to open the latches, but they've rusted in place and are impossible to move.

177

With stiff fingers, Reidar tries to open the combination lock on the stable door. His fingertips are sticking to the frozen metal. Mikael whispers to him to hurry.

Jurek is pushing through the snow with the knife in his hand. Reidar blows on his fingers and manages to get the last digit. He undoes the lock, slides the catch back, and tries to open the door.

There's too much snow on the ground.

As he tugs at it, he can hear the horses moving in their stalls. They're snorting quietly and stamping in the darkness.

"Come on, Dad," Mikael shouts, pulling at him.

Reidar pushes the door harder, turns around, and sees Jurek Walter right behind them.

With a practiced gesture, Jurek wipes the knife blade against his trousers.

It's too late to run.

Reidar holds up his hands in self-defense, but Jurek grabs his neck and forces him back, against the wall of the stable.

"Sorry," Reidar manages to say. "I'm sorry that—"

With immense force, Jurek thrusts the knife straight through Reidar's shoulder and pins him to the wall. Reidar screams with pain. The horses whinny, their heavy bodies rubbing against the dividing walls of their stalls.

Reidar is stuck. His shoulder is burning. Every second is unbearable. He can feel hot blood running down his arm and hand.

Mikael is trying to squeeze into the stable, but Jurek catches up with him. He grabs the young man's hair from behind, pulls him out, and slaps him so hard across the face that he collapses in the snow.

"Please," Reidar begs as he sees a bright light approaching from the manor.

It's David Sylwan, running toward them with an emergency flare in his hand. It's crackling with white light.

"The ambulance is on its way," he yells, but stops when he sees Jurek turn.

178

SAGA TUGS at the chest of drawers and manages to pull it a few inches away from the wall. She spits blood, then takes hold of the bottom of the chest with both hands and overturns it with a grunt. She snatches up her pistol and smashes the windowpane with the butt. Glass rains down onto the floor and skims off the window ledge outside.

She sees the bright light shimmering across the snow. Jurek is heading toward the man with the flare. The man backs away and tries to hit him with the burning flare, but Jurek grabs the man's arm and breaks it.

Saga knocks pieces of glass from the bottom of the window.

Jurek is standing over his prey like a lion, moving quickly and efficiently, hitting the man in the neck and kidneys.

Saga holds out her pistol and blinks the blood away from her eyes so she can see.

The man is lying on his back in the snow, his body jerking. The flare beside him is still casting a bright glow.

Jurek slips out of the way just as Saga fires her pistol. He moves away from the light and into the shadows.

The flare illuminates a circle of white snow. The man stops moving and lies completely still. The red stable is visible only in brief bursts. Otherwise, there is nothing but darkness.

179

REIDAR IS PINNED TO THE WALL. The pain from the knife is excruciating. It feels as if that one burning point is all that exists. The warm blood steams as it runs down his body.

He sees Jurek vanish right after the shot. David is motionless in the snow. There's no way of telling how badly wounded he is.

To the east, the sky has brightened slightly, and Reidar can see Saga Bauer in a window on the first floor.

It was she who fired and missed.

Reidar is breathing too quickly. He's losing a lot of blood. He realizes that he's going into shock.

Mikael gets unsteadily to his feet but has no time to escape before Jurek is back. He knocks the boy down again, then grabs him by one leg and starts to drag him off into the darkness.

"Mikael," Reidar screams.

Jurek drags Reidar's son off through the snow. Mikael is flailing with his arms, trying to find something to grab hold of. They disappear toward the rapids. Reidar can only see them as pale shadows now.

Jurek came here for Mikael, he thinks in confusion.

It's still too dark for Saga to be able to tell the figures apart from her vantage point in the window.

Reidar howls as he grabs the handle of the knife and pulls. It's stuck. He pulls again, shifting the angle down slightly to get a better grip, and it cuts into his flesh.

He screams and pulls again, and finally the point comes free from the wall behind him. The knife slips out, and Reidar falls forward onto the snow. The pain is so intense that he's sobbing as he crawls forward.

"Mikael!"

He crawls to the flare in the snow, picks it up, and feels the sparks prick his hand. He looks toward the open water of the rapids and can just make out Jurek's figure against the snow. Reidar starts to follow them but has no energy left. He knows that Jurek is planning to drag Mikael into the forest and vanish with him for good.

180

SAGA POINTS HER PISTOL through the window and sees Reidar holding the flare. He's picked it up, and blood is pouring down his body; he stumbles and looks as if he's going to fall, and then he throws it.

Saga follows the light with her eyes as it spins through the darkness in a wide arc and lands in the snow. Now she can clearly locate Jurek Walter. He's dragging Mikael behind him. They're more than a hundred meters away, but Saga rests her arm against the window frame and takes aim.

The pistol's sights keep shaking. The black figure keeps moving out of the line of fire.

Taking slow breaths, she squeezes the trigger, past the first notch, and sees Jurek's head slide away.

She keeps losing focus and blinks quickly.

A moment later, the angle of fire is better, and she squeezes the trigger three times as the sights gradually slip lower.

The blasts echo between the manor and the stables.

Saga sees that at least one of the bullets hits Jurek in the neck. Blood is squirting out, hanging like a red haze in front of him in the bright white light.

She fires off several more shots and sees him let go of Mikael and fall into the shadows.

Saga backs away from the window and runs through the hidden doorway.

She rushes down the stairs, through the large hall, and out into the snow. Panting, she approaches the glowing light with her pistol raised. Farther away, she sees the black water of the rapids glint like a metallic fracture in the white landscape.

She pushes through the deep snow.

The light of the flare is weakening and will soon go out. Mikael is curled up in the fetal position. There's blood spattered at the very edge of the trembling circle of light, but the body isn't there.

"Jurek," she whispers, spotting his tracks through the snow.

Saga's head aches as she picks up the flare and holds it aloft. Shadows and light play across the snow. Suddenly she sees movement off to the side.

Jurek stands up and moves away through the snow.

Saga fires before she has time to aim properly. The bullet goes through the top of his arm and he lurches to one side, then takes a few steps down the steep slope leading to the rapids.

Saga follows, with the flare held high. She spots him again, takes aim, and hits him in the chest with three shots.

Jurek falls backward, over the icy fringe and straight into the black water of the rapids. Saga fires as he's falling and hits him in the cheek and ear.

He gets sucked down into the water. She runs over and shoots him again, in the foot, before he disappears. Saga replaces the cartridge and skids down the steep slope. She falls and hits her back on the ground, sliding under the snow, but scrambles back up to her feet and fires into the black water. The light of the flare penetrates the surface of the rapids, past the spinning bubbles and all the way to the dark-brown bottom. Something large is tumbling down there. She catches a glimpse of a wrinkled face among the stones and twisting weeds.

Saga fires again, and a cloud of blood billows out into the dark water. She walks along the shore, following the current, and keeps shooting until she has no more ammunition left and Jurek Walter's body vanishes beneath the ice where the rapids spread out.

Panting, Saga stands at the edge of the water as the flare dies away to a shimmering red glow.

She just stares down at the water as tears run down her face.

The first rays of sunlight are starting to reach over the treetops, and the warm light of dawn is spreading out across the sparkling landscape. She hears the sound of helicopters approaching. It's over at last.

181

Saga was taken by ambulance to Danderyd Hospital, where she was examined and given a bed. She lay down for a while in her room but left the hospital by taxi before she received any treatment.

Now she's limping along a corridor at Karolinska Hospital, where Reidar and Mikael were taken by helicopter. Her clothes are dirty and wet, her face is streaked with blood, and all she can hear in her right ear is a loud buzzing.

Reidar and his son are in Emergency Room 12. She opens the door and sees the author lying on a hospital bed.

Mikael is standing beside him. He won't let go of his father's hand.

Reidar is telling the male nurse over and over that he has to see his daughter.

The moment he sees Saga, he falls silent.

The nurse takes clean compresses from the trolley and gives them to Saga. He points at her forehead, where blood has once again started to trickle from the blackened wound on her eyebrow.

"I'm a police officer," Saga says, feeling for her ID.

"You need help," the nurse tries to say, but Saga interrupts him and asks to have the three of them taken to Felicia Kohler-Frost's room in the infectious-diseases unit.

"We have to see her," she says gravely.

The nurse makes a call, gets the go-ahead, and wheels Reidar's bed toward the elevator.

The bed's wheels squeak on the vinyl floor.

Saga follows, feeling an overwhelming urge to cry.

Reidar is lying with his eyes closed, and Mikael is walking alongside, still holding his father by the hand.

A young nurse meets them and shows them into an intensive-care room with subdued lighting. The only sound is the slow wheezing and ticking of the monitors.

In the bed lies an extremely slight woman. Her long black hair is spread out over her pillow. Her eyes are closed, and her small hands rest by her sides.

Her breath is shallow, and her face is covered with beads of sweat.

"Felicia," Reidar whispers, trying to reach her with his hand.

Mikael leans his cheek toward his sister and whispers something to her with a smile.

Saga stands behind them, staring at Felicia, the captive girl who has now been rescued from the darkness.

EPILOGUE

TWO DAYS LATER, Saga is walking through the park toward the headquarters of the Security Police. There are birds singing in the bushes and snow-covered trees.

Her hair has started to grow out again. She has twelve neat stitches on her temple and five across her left eyebrow.

Yesterday her boss, Verner Zandén, called and told her to report to his office at eight o'clock this morning to receive the Security Police Medal of Honor.

The ceremony strikes her as rather odd. Three men died at Råcksta Manor, and Jurek Walter's body was washed away, deep under the ice covering the river.

Before she was discharged, she managed to visit Joona in the hospital. He patiently answered her questions about why Jurek and his brother had done what they did.

Vadim Levanov fled from Leninsk with his two sons, Igor and Roman, after the disastrous accident in 1960, when an intercontinental missile exploded on the launch pad. He eventually reached Sweden, was granted a work permit and given a job at the quarry in Rotebro, with accommodations in the migrant workers' barracks. His children lived with him in secret. He would homeschool them in the evenings and keep them hidden during the day, hoping that he would eventually be granted Swedish citizenship and the opportunity for a new life for him and his sons.

Joona had asked for a glass of water, and when Saga leaned forward to help him drink, she could feel him shaking as if he were freezing, even though his body was radiating heat.

Saga recalls Reidar's account of how he met the twins by Rotebro. The twins had taken Reidar back to the quarry, where they played in the great mounds of sifted sand. One evening, Reidar was caught by one of the foremen. He was so scared of reprisals that he blamed everything on the older boys and pointed out where they lived.

The twins were taken into the custody of the Child Welfare Committee, and because they weren't listed in any Swedish registries, the case was passed to the Aliens Department.

Joona explained to Saga that Jurek's brother had pneumonia and was being treated at a hospital when Jurek was extradited to Kazakhstan. Because Jurek didn't have any family there, he ended up in a children's home in Pavlodar.

From the age of thirteen, he worked on the barges trafficking the Irtysh River, and during the troubles in the years after Stalin's death, he was forcibly recruited by a Chechen militia group. They took the fifteen-year-old Jurek to a suburb of Grozny and turned him into a soldier.

"The brothers were sent to different countries," Joona said in a low voice.

"That's crazy," Saga whispered.

Sweden had little experience with immigrants in those days and had no effective way of dealing with them. Mistakes were made, and Jurek's twin brother was sent to Russia as soon as he was well enough. He ended up at Children's Home 67, in the Kuzminki district of southeastern Moscow, and was written off as mentally handicapped as an aftereffect of his illness. When Jurek, after many years as a soldier, left Chechnya and managed to track down his brother, the brother had been transferred to a mental hospital, the Serbsky Institute, and was a complete wreck.

Saga is so absorbed in her thoughts about the twin brothers that she doesn't notice Corinne Meilleroux walking toward the security doors. They come close to colliding. Corinne's hair is tied up and she's wearing a black trench coat and high-heeled boots. For once, Saga is conscious of the way she's dressed. Maybe she should have chosen something different from her usual jeans and thick parka.

"Very impressive," Corinne says, smiling, and gives her a hug.

SAGA AND CORINNE get out of the elevator and walk side by side down the corridor leading to their boss's office. Nathan Pollock, Carlos Eliasson, and Verner Zandén are already waiting for them. On the table is a bottle of Taittinger and five champagne glasses.

The door closes, and Saga shakes hands with the three men.

"Let's start with a moment of silence in memory of our colleague Samuel Mendel and his family, and all the other victims," Carlos says.

Saga lowers her head and has trouble maintaining a steady gaze. In front of her, she can see the first pictures of the police operation in the industrial complex where the old brick factory used to be. Toward morning, it had become clear that no victims would be found alive. In the muddy snow, the forensics officers had begun placing numbered signs by the fourteen graves. Samuel Mendel's two sons had been found tied together in a shaft, covered by a sheet of corrugated metal. Rebecka's remains were found buried ten meters away, in a drum fitted with a plastic air tube.

The voices are drowned out by Saga's tinnitus. She squeezes her eyes closed and tries to understand.

The traumatized twins made their way to Poland, where Roman killed a man, took his passport, and became Jurek Walter. Together they caught a ferry from Swinoujscie to Ystad, in Sweden, and then traveled up through the country.

Middle-aged by that point, the brothers returned to the place where they had been separated from their father, to Barrack 4 in the migrant workers' accommodations at a quarry in Rotebro.

Their father had spent decades trying to trace the boys but couldn't travel to Russia himself because he would've been sent to the Gulag. He had written hundreds of letters in an effort to find his children and had waited for them to return, but just one year before the brothers arrived in Sweden, the old man had given up and hanged himself.

Learning of his father's suicide had wrecked what little was left of Jurek's soul.

"He started to draw up a circle of blood and revenge," Joona said.

Everyone who had contributed to the breakup of his family would experience the same fate. Jurek would take their children from them, their grandchildren and wives, sisters and brothers. The guilty parties would be left alone, just as their father had been in the quarry. They would have to wait, year after year. Only after they had killed themselves would those of their relatives who had survived be allowed to return.

That was why the twins didn't kill their victims. It wasn't the people who were buried whom Jurek wanted to punish, but those left behind. The captives were placed in coffins or drums with air tubes. Most of them died after a few days, but some lived for years.

The bodies that were discovered in Lill-Jan's Forest and in the vicinity of the industrial complex in Albano cast a cruel light on Jurek's terrible revenge. He was following a ruthless logic, which was why his actions and his choice of victims didn't seem to fit the pattern set by other serial killers.

It was going to take the police a while to fill in all the details, but it was becoming apparent how the victims were connected. Apart from Reidar Frost, who revealed the existence of the boys to the foreman in the quarry, they included those responsible for the family's fate at the Child Welfare Committee and the case officers at the Aliens Department.

Saga thinks of Jeremy Magnusson, who was a young man when he dealt with the twins' case at the Aliens Department. Jurek took his wife, son, and grandson, and then finally his daughter, Agneta. When Jeremy hanged himself in his hunting cabin, Jurek went to the grave where Agneta was being kept alive to let her out.

It dawns on Saga that Jurek actually had been in the process of disinterring her, just as he'd claimed to Joona. He had opened the coffin, sat by the graveside, and watched her blind fumbling. In Jurek's mind, she was a version of him, a child doomed to return to nothing.

Joona explained that Jurek's brother was so psychologically damaged that he lived among their father's old possessions in the abandoned barracks. He did everything that Jurek told him to do, learned to handle sedatives, and helped his brother seize people and watch over the graves. The shelter that their father had built in anticipation of a nuclear war acted as a sort of holding cell before the victims could be placed in graves.

Saga is torn from her thoughts when her boss breaks the silence and taps a glass. With great solemnity, he fetches a blue box from the safe, snaps it open, and takes out a gold medal. A wreathed star on a blue-and-yellow ribbon.

Saga feels her heart clench unexpectedly when she hears Verner say that she has demonstrated remarkable courage, bravery, and intelligence. Carlos's eyes are moist, and Nathan smiles at her with a serious look in his eyes.

Saga takes a step forward, and Verner affixes the medal to her chest.

Corinne claps her hands and grins. Carlos pops the champagne, firing the cork at the ceiling. Someone makes a toast, and Saga receives their congratulations.

"What are you going to do now?" Pollock asks.

"I'm on sick leave, but after this . . . I don't know."

She knows there's no way she can sit around in her dusty apartment with its withered plants, with her guilt and memories.

"Saga Bauer, you have done a great deed for your country," Verner says, then goes on to explain that, unfortunately, he's going to have to keep her medal locked in the safe, seeing as the whole case is confidential and already erased from all public records.

He carefully removes the medal from Saga, puts it back in its box, and closes the safe door.

THE SUN IS SHINING in a hazy sky when Saga emerges from the subway station.

After they arrested Jurek, Samuel Mendel and Joona Linna ended up on his revenge list. His twin brother seized Samuel's family and was closing in on Summa and Lumi when they were killed in a car crash.

Mikael and Felicia were kept in the capsule. Maybe Jurek never had a chance to give his brother orders about where to bury them. It's not exactly clear why Mikael and Felicia were held captive for all the years that Jurek was in solitary confinement in the secure psychiatric unit. His brother gave them scraps of food and made sure they couldn't escape. Perhaps he was waiting for orders from Jurek, as usual.

Presumably, Jurek hadn't foreseen how restrictive the verdict from the Court of Appeal would be: a life sentence and no contact with the outside world.

Jurek bided his time and formulated a plan as the years passed. The brothers had probably each been trying to work out a solution when Susanne Hjälm chose to give Jurek the letter from a lawyer. It's impossible to know now what the encrypted letter said, but the evidence suggests that Jurek's brother was telling him how to get in touch with him and giving him a status report about Joona Linna and the two surviving captives.

Jurek needed to get out, and he realized that he could create an opportunity if he could only smuggle a letter out to the PO box address given in his brother's letter.

Jurek managed to make his letter look like a plea for legal help. In fact, it was an order to release Mikael. Jurek knew that the news would reach Joona and that the police would engage him to find Felicia. He didn't know at that point what form this mission would take, but he was convinced it would give him the opening he had been waiting for.

Because no one had attempted to negotiate with him about finding the girl, he suspected that one of the unit's new patients might be an undercover police officer. When Saga tried to save Bernie Larsson, he knew for certain that she was a cop.

Jurek had been watching the young doctor, Anders Rönn, as he overstepped his authority and enjoyed the power he wielded in the secure unit. When Jurek understood that the young doctor was fascinated with Saga, he knew how his escape could be accomplished. All he had to do was lure the young doctor—with his keys and pass card—into Saga's cell. There was no way the doctor would be able to resist this sleeping beauty. Jurek spent several nights wetting toilet paper, drying it against his face, and creating a head that would make it look as if he was asleep in his bed.

SAGA STOPS OUTSIDE the bakery in the cold wind. She recalls what Joona had said about Jurek's lying to everyone. Jurek listened and pieced together everything he found out, using it to his own advantage and mixing lies with truth to make his lies stronger.

Saga turns and makes her way across Maria Square.

She didn't want to kill her mom. She knows that. It wasn't intentional.

Saga walks slowly, thinking about her dad. Lars-Erik Bauer. A cardiologist at Sankt Göran Hospital. She hasn't spoken to him since she was thirteen years old. Yet Jurek made her remember how he used to push her on the swing at her grandparents' when she was little, before Mom got sick.

A shiver runs down her neck and through her arms.

A man walks past, pulling a little girl on a sled.

Jurek lied to everyone.

Why does she think he was telling her the truth?

SAGA SITS DOWN on a snow-dusted park bench, takes her phone out of her pocket, and calls The Needle.

"Nils Åhlén, Forensic Medicine Department."

"Hello, Saga Bauer here," she says. "I'd like—"

"The body from the car crash has been identified now," the Needle interrupts. "His name's Anders Rönn."

A short silence follows. "That wasn't what I wanted to ask."

"What is it, then?"

Saga watches the snow blowing off the statue of Thor raising his hammer against the Midgard Serpent. She hears herself ask, "How many Codeine-Meda pills would it take to kill someone?"

"Child or adult?" The Needle asks, without seeming remotely surprised.

"Adult," Saga replies, swallowing hard.

She hears The Needle breathe through his nose as he taps at his keyboard.

"It would depend on size and tolerance, but between thirty-five and forty-five pills would probably be a fatal dose."

"Forty-five?" Saga asks. "But if she was only given thirteen, could that kill her? Could she die from thirteen pills?"

"Not likely. She'd fall asleep and wake up with—"

"So she took the rest herself," Saga says under her breath.

She can feel tears of relief in her eyes. Jurek was a liar. That was all he did. He destroyed people with his lies.

All her life, she's hated her father for leaving them. For never coming home. For letting her mom die.

She has to find out the truth. There's no other way.

She calls the operator and asks to be put through to Lars-Erik Bauer in Enskede.

Saga walks slowly across the square as the phone rings.

"This is Pellerina," a child's voice says.

Saga is rendered speechless and ends the call without saying anything. She looks up at the white sky above Sankt Pauls Church.

"Christ," she mutters, and dials the number again.

She waits in the snow until the child's voice answers a second time.

"Hello, Pellerina," she says. "I'd like to talk to Lars-Erik, please."

"Who may I say is calling?" the girl asks.

"My name's Saga," she whispers.

"Oh! I have a big sister named Saga," Pellerina says. "But I've never met her."

Saga can't speak. There's a lump in her throat. She hears Pellerina pass the phone to someone and say that Saga wants to speak to him.

"This is Lars-Erik," a familiar voice says.

Saga takes a deep breath. It's too late for anything but the truth.

"Dad—it's me. I have to ask ... when Mom died ... were the two of you married?"

"No," he replies instantly. "We'd gotten divorced two years earlier, when you were five. She never let me see you. I had a lawyer who was going to help me to ..."

He falls silent. Saga closes her eyes and tries to stop shaking.

"Mom said you'd abandoned us," she says. "She said you couldn't deal with her illness and that you didn't want me."

"Maj was ill. She was mentally ill, bipolar and ... I'm so sorry you had to go through that"

"I called you that night," she says.

"Yes," her dad sighs. "Your mom used to force you to call. She would call, too, all night long, thirty times, maybe more."

"I didn't know that."

"Where are you? Just tell me where you are. Let me come and get you."

"Thanks, Dad, but . . . I can't right now."

"Please," he says. "When—when you're ready."

"I'll call."

"Please, Saga. Please do," he says.

She hangs up, then walks to Horns Street and hails a taxi.

SAGA IS IN THE LOBBY at Karolinska Hospital. Joona is no longer in intensive care and has been moved to a smaller room. As she walks toward the elevators, she thinks of the look on Joona's face after Disa's death.

The only thing he asked of her when she last visited him was to find Jurek Walter's dead body and let him see it.

She knows she killed Jurek, but she still has to tell Joona that Carlos sent police divers under the ice for several days without finding the body.

The door to his room on the eighth floor is half open. Saga stops in the corridor when she hears a woman say she's going to fetch a thermal blanket. A moment later, a smiling nurse steps out but turns back toward the room again.

"You have very unusual eyes, Joona," she says, then walks off.

Saga closes her burning eyelids for a moment before walking over.

She knocks on the open door, walks into the room, and stops in a patch of sunlight shining through the dirty window.

Saga stares at the empty bed. The drip is dangling from its support with blood on the needle. The tube is still swaying in the air. There's a broken wristwatch on the floor, but the room is empty.

FIVE DAYS LATER, the police put out an alert. Joona Linna has vanished. After six months, the search is called off. The only person who doesn't stop looking is Saga Bauer, because she knows he isn't dead.